# KING OF ALWAYS

## JUNO HEART

King of Always: A Fae Romance - Black Blood Fae Book 2

Copyright © Juno Heart 2020

All rights reserved.

Cover and chapter header design by: saintjupit3rgr4phic

Map: Isle Brookes Design

Editor: Cissell Ink

Ebook  978-0-6487442-1-4

Paperback 978-0-6487442-2-1

Hardcover 978-0-6487442-7-6


Contact: juno@junoheartfaeromance.com

*Set your life on fire. Seek those who fan your flames*

RUMI

# Prologue

## Rafael

Once upon a time, I smiled. Once, I laughed as sunshine warmed my skin, and I took joy in the glow. And once, I looked down upon my brother, Ever, the Black Blood heir with sorrow storming through his mind and black poison icing his veins. Once, I thought him weak.

But, no longer. Because now I know.

Now I understand.

Savage darkness creeps and crawls like cold iron through my being. Blackness digs and bites, always pulsing, pounding through my heart. Thrashing to the end until I'm no more.

Who will the curse fall to should I die before any sons are born? Back to Ever's line?

Who knows? Salamander does. Salamander, the mage with her hair afire, who will not answer my pleas for help.

Ever is gone. Aer, for now, is tethered. Salamander hides. Therefore, the poison wins.

The poison will always win.

Unless I find her first.

Time. How much of it do I have?

I do not know.

And so, I wait.

I wait for a girl marked with a phoenix consumed by flames. My cure. My queen. And perhaps more than that—the cure for the land of Talamh Cúig? The Black Blood will one day be annihilated. Aer, the Sorceress of the Seven Winds, has said it is so. The end has been written. The end is certain.

But when?

I drop my head against the wooden throne, carved scorpions, sunflowers, and thorns digging into my skull. Such bright symbols for one now solemn and bleak. The absurdity astounds me.

I close my eyes and fire rises around me, flames licking at my core. A girl stands in the middle of the pyre, her pale skin charred and burning. Her hair is richest buttermilk, her eyes a blistering blue, and her smile—her smile is a flame in itself—fierce and taunting. For she is not afraid as the flames leap higher and take her over, pull her down, drag her under. Consume her.

My black heart pulses in time with her screams of agony.

Every time I close my eyes, this is what I see. The girl with the orange and purple tattoo. The girl with laughing eyes.

I will find her.

I will.

For I am not my brother, and I am determined to win.

I want my queen.

I will live and rule and end this darkness.

These words are written:

*Black will fade to gray, gray to white, and white to never. Never was the darkest taint and never will it ever be.*

But these are the words I dream of:

*Take the chosen for a bride, and the poison ceases deep inside.*

The poison ceases deep inside...

So it is written.

And so it shall be.

# 1

## *Faery Vacation*

### Isla

Life is crazy and so am I.

Okay, that's not entirely true. I'm sane enough, just bored, that's all. Crazy bored and feeling about as content as a caged lion in a circus.

It sucks to be waiting tables in boring old Blackbrook while my cousin traipses around Faery with her hot, fae prince husband and their bouncing baby girl. It's not fair. Why should Lara and Ever have all the fun while I serve greasy hash browns and double cheeseburgers to frowning, grumpy customers?

Instead of working tables, I'd prefer to be in the kitchen, surrounded by sizzling flames and tendrils of curling smoke. Not that I want to fry burgers for a living—that's Lara's gig. Or *was* her gig before she became fae royalty and high-tailed it out of the human realm for who knows how long.

Nope, I'll never be fully satisfied operating the grill at Max's Vinyl City diner. I'd rather be the boss of my very own French bakery and create sweet delights that make people laugh and smile and, okay, if I'm being honest, I should mention that one time when my pastries made a family of three cry—a mom, dad, and a cute little curly haired toddler. They sobbed and bawled, but still swore they loved the taste of my chocolate eclairs—go figure! So weird.

So yeah, triple-layer mousse cakes and cinnamon and ginger madeleines—that's my kind of alchemy. I don't need my own magical, pointy-eared fae prince. Nor do I want one, no matter how good looking they are.

Anyway, it's Friday night, and here I am, plopping two plates of soggy waffles in front of a father and son duo seated at a red vinyl booth, an Elvis Presley tune blaring through the house speakers making my hips rock ever so slightly beneath my purple uniform.

"That'll be all, Miss. We don't need your help with the eating of it," says the dad. Shoulders slumped, faces pinched, he and his son look like they're at the end of a long, exhausting day.

I smile instead of poking my tongue out like I want to. "Mister, you'd have to pay me to eat that stuff."

The skinny kid, his face hidden beneath a baseball cap, reaches for the syrup and snorts like a gorilla.

"Hey, don't add any of that until after you taste them," I tell him. "The cook's already drowned them in syrup."

The kid gives me a grim, sharp-toothed sneer that matches the shark's on his hat, warning me to mind my own business.

With a sigh, I shrug as he drizzles about a gallon of gunk over his plate. "Okay, then. Hope you enjoy your meals." And the dental cavities.

Father and son grunt as I spin on my heels and head over to clear the table opposite.

Four plates of half-eaten mashed-up burgers and gravy-soaked napkins stack neatly in my arms. Bang. Bang. Bang. I'm a whiz at this. Normally, I'd pile the coffee cups on top as well, but I'm too tired and don't want to risk the lot crashing down and getting my paycheck docked for the breakage. Guess I'll have to make a second trip.

The four jocks who'd been sitting here ten minutes ago, whispering about me and guffawing into their hands as they stuffed fries in their faces, left a heck of a mess. Thanks, guys, the two-dollar tip was worth it.

Feeling decades older than my eighteen years, I stifle a groan, massaging my lower back before picking up the pile of plates. As I move toward the kitchen, an image of my boyfriend's look of total surprise when I politely dumped his ass over homemade crème brûlée in my kitchen three days ago floats across my mind. Since I broke up with him, I guess that means I should be calling him my *ex*-boyfriend.

Sam and I had been together nearly two years and mostly got along fine, but the guy loved studying accounting a lot more than he did me. And, honestly, he was about as romantic as a Christmas ham and almost as boring.

"Hey, Isla, looking cute tonight," says Jaxon at table three as I pass by.

I wink. "Oh, thanks. You too." Not really. My gaze skims his bloodshot hazel eyes and the dirty, button-down shirt covering his paunch. Another drunk businessman. Sweet enough, but he doesn't look like the outdoor type who loves camping trips and making out fireside under a sea of twinkling stars. Just like my ex, in a word—he's dreary.

Sighing, I tuck a loose strand of blonde hair behind my ear and smile at Kate, the other waitress working tonight.

Wish I wasn't hung up on wanting a passionate guy who's prepared to do something dramatic to prove his love for me—like Ever did for Lara. Someone interesting and maybe a little dangerous.

It'd be much easier to get a date because, let's face it, there aren't too many fae princes hanging around Blackbrook hoping to hook up with a human girl. I think of Ever expressing his undying love for Lara by battling evil air mages and then giving up his crown for her. Unfortunately, he's set the boyfriend bar pretty high.

"Isla," yells, Max from his serving hutch, his chef's hat falling over his heavy brow. "Table seven's order is up. If it's not too much to ask, can you come and get it ASAP? The guy looks kinda hungry."

I grin at his sweat-beaded face and push through the swing door into the kitchen. "On my way, Boss." I dump the leaning tower of plates next to the sink. "But then I'm out of here. I swapped with Mandy tonight. She's doing the late shift, and I'm leaving at ten because I'm going on vacation, remember?"

"Yeah, yeah. Go ahead and desert me the same as Lara did. But before you go have fun for a month, you can give the ladies' bathroom a quick once over."

"But, Max..." I give him my best sad-puppy face.

He sighs. "Fine. Just refill the paper towels, then get outta my sight."

"Sure thing. You're the best." I hide my grimace as I take fried chicken wings and a rainbow-colored smoothie to another businessman at table seven. All three look gross.

If there's one thing I hate, it's cleaning restrooms. The stench is unbearable. Even though Max let me off the hook for a full clean, my annoying sense of duty has me pulling out cloths and spritzing down the mirrors.

As I polish my reflection, scowling at the piles of hair escaping from my ponytail, my tired blue eyes rimmed with dark circles, I count my blessings because the drudgery of part-time waitressing and full-time studying is about to come to an end in the most thrilling of ways, well, for a while at least.

Tonight!

Lara and Ever have been gone a whole two weeks, and I think I've finally found a way to follow them into Faery.

I would never have dreamed that a late-night internet search would lead me to an online spirit conjurer who does business with the local supernatural community, but that's what happened. Three days ago, I had no idea groups of magical beings lived here in the human realm, let alone that one of them resided a few suburbs away from mine.

The spirit companion dealer put me in touch with a fae in hiding who goes by the ridiculous name of Sally Salamande. Apparently she has a thing for lizards, so maybe it's not such a crazy nickname after all. And, tonight, as soon as I leave work, that's where I'm heading—to Sally's place.

Pastry school has wrapped up for the year, and Mom thinks I'm going to stay with Lara and Ever in Brazil for the summer. It's completely bizarre how she still believes that Ever runs a charity helping street kids in Sao Paulo. If she'd known what he did to Lara when he first met her in Faery, she would have kicked his butt into the next century instead of welcoming him into our home.

Thankfully, he's reformed his wicked-prince ways somewhat since Lara freed him from the Black Blood poison, and now the curse has passed on to his younger brother, Rafael. I've never met the guy, but by all accounts, he sounds like a typical faery prince—in other words, a self-entitled jerk. Not worth thinking about, really. But I wish him all the best because living with the curse sounds awful—as does a lot of what I've heard about Faery, to be honest. It's a dangerous, frightening place. But still, I'm determined to go there at the earliest opportunity.

Why? Because I want adventure. When I was a child, just like Lara, I was fascinated by her mom's freaky paintings of the Land of Five. I know what it looks like—a bizarre and beautiful dream that I plan to witness with my own eyes.

I mean, *newsflash*, faeries and elves and emerald castles are real. Who wouldn't want to check it all out and drink goblets of mulberry wine at a fae feast? Or run through a magical meadow alongside blue bunny rabbits with butterflies the size of dinner plates trailing behind us? And let's not forget all the beautiful fae men I could stare at. All things considered, it sounds like a whole lot of fun to me.

After I freshen the towels and wipe down the bathroom counters, I swap my uniform for travel clothes—chunky boots, jeans, a black sweater, and a hooded down jacket, then swing my backpack over my shoulder. I bid my co-workers farewell for the next month, or if I manage to get myself eaten by a mythical creature, possibly forever. Then I ride the subway three stops to the old Gothic quarter where, at ten past eleven, the main street's restaurants and dive bars are still pumping.

A bright crescent moon winks down at me as I weave through folk coming in and out of the neon-lit joints, then stride past closed dollar stores and a vinyl record cafe. A pizza-delivery guy on a bike whistles at me, and I give him the finger and cross over at the stop lights.

I round a corner into a quiet tree-lined avenue, my attention flicking from my phone to the branch shadows tangling over the pavement. I follow map directions two blocks past the main drag until I reach a sorry-looking brownstone squashed between its taller, tidier neighbors, the number seventy-seven glowing in the harsh light of the entrance lamp.

Dogs howl in the distance, the mournful sound prickling over my skin. I shove my phone in my pocket, push open a low iron gate, and then head up the stoop.

I knock on the wooden door, and it swings open, a blast of heat whooshing out of it that nearly knocks me off my feet.

The middle-aged lady standing in the arched doorway and peering down at me is tall and so thin I could blow on her and she'd snap in half like a pretzel. She's dressed in a navy pantsuit with massive shoulder pads that, a couple of decades ago, would have been a perfect power outfit for a businesswoman. With her brown hair drawn into a tight ponytail, she looks like a retired lawyer rather than the fae creature she's alleged to be. So, unless she's Sally's housekeeper, I'm beginning to think I paid the spirit conjurer fifty bucks for nothing. She conned me, damn it.

I think of Lara's faery prince—his fae beauty always peeking through his hot-jock glamor—and inspect the woman more closely, just like she's doing to me. I'm looking for pointy ears, and she's wondering who the hell the skinny blonde chick on her doorstep is.

Something dark flickers across her gray eyes, her thin brows arching. "By the Eternal Elements, here you are at last! What took you so long to come visit me?"

Huh? Maybe I resemble a long-lost relative. Or maybe she's half blind. Or totally crazy. If I have a choice, I'll take the half-blind option. Sounds safer.

"Hello," I say, offering her my hand. "I'm Isla." I give her a polite smile. "I don't think we've met before, so I don't get how I've supposedly kept you waiting. But, anyway, I'm looking for Sally Salamande. I hear she has a thing for lizards."

Her eyes sparkle as she pushes my hand away like it's a limp, smelly rag. "Yes, child, you are correct. I do enjoy lizards. Very much so." She licks her lips. "Well, don't just stand there. Come inside and sit by the fire with an old herpetologist. I believe we may be of use to each other."

"What does a herpetologist do, study diseases?"

She chuckles and waves me forward. "No, dear. Reptiles are my specialty."

"Oh." A shiver crawls down my spine as I step over the threshold. "I see."

She leans close and takes a big sniff of my neck, making me thankful for the switchblade in my pack. I'm not sure how to use it, but it's certainly good to know it's there.

While I follow her down a long, dark hallway, she whistles a strange tune. It's sad and mournful and more than a little spooky and makes me think she's trying to mess with my head and unnerve me. If that's her plan, it's working just fine.

In case I'm about to die, I start running through all my past sins, asking for forgiveness and absolution from whichever god or gods are keen to give it to me. I'm not fussy about which one will have me, I'd just prefer not to go to hell or be reincarnated as a snail to be squashed beneath someone's careless shoe if I can avoid it.

When we come to a bright red door, she gives me a sly grin over her high shoulder pad, then pushes through into a red-glowing room. I suck in a quick breath and blink around, squinting against brightness and a confusing mix of shadow and flame. Am I in hell already?

The air is hot and dry enough to cook a perfect sponge cake in, and I wonder if, like me, she's a baker of... Hmm...probably not cakes. More likely toads and lizards.

Even the room's decor is Nouveau Gothic Furnace—dark crimson walls, heavy red-velvet drapes and furnishings, an intense groovy-vampire-mansion vibe. On the far wall of the open plan lounge and kitchen area, a fire roars inside a massive fireplace, gargoyle heads peering between vines and leaves carved into its wooden mantle.

Forget what I said before about it being hot as an oven in here. This is more like a dinner date in a steel mill. Or maybe she's about to bring out her welding equipment and work on some lovely garden sculptures. Luckily for me, I'm a fan of the flames.

I smile at her and wipe sweat from my brow. The heat is wonderful. I could live here.

"Please," she says, pointing at two armchairs on either side of the fire. "Take a seat. How did you finally manage to locate me?"

Finally? I step around a fur rug before sinking into a deeply padded chair. "Through Sylvia's Supernatural Megastore."

Throwing back her head, she laughs loudly. "Oh, Sylvia—that old windbag. Did you meet with her?"

"Nope. I sent her an email, paid a PayPal invoice, and then—bingo—she handed over your address."

The rug has a bear's head attached to it—and gross, it totally looks real! "You're a hunter?" I ask, nodding at the beast's glassy gaze fixed on my combat boots. "Or just a collector of... curiosities?"

With a loud huff, she plops inelegantly opposite me.

"Perhaps the latter, but most definitely the former. I do so love a good chase and a fight." Tapered fingers with the nails painted bright orange fling out and stroke the bear's fur, and I swear her arm grew three feet just to reach it. The heat must be making me hallucinate. Blinking rapidly, I shake my head to clear it.

She grins. "This one you see here had the heart of a great warrior. His death was exquisite. It happened over a thousand human years ago, but I will never forget it."

Exquisite for *her* maybe. The bear? Not so much. I swallow hard, wondering how she killed it. Probably *bear*-handed.

"So…" I say, stalling for time as I gawk at the room. A large cauldron-like pot hangs over the flames on a metal rod. I don't like the look of it. What does she cook in it? Past conquests? Human girls who stupidly drop in unannounced? I force my gaze back on her flame-bright nails still tapping the chair's armrest.

"What can I do for you, Isla of Blackbrook?"

"How did you know where I live—"

She silences me with a flick of her hand. "I know many things about you, girl, so don't mince words and waste my time. Tell me what you want."

Wiping a sheen of sweat from above my lip, I shuffle to the chair's edge. "I've been told you can get me into Faery, to a city called Talamh Cúig. Is that true?"

"Why, yes, it is. What reason do you wish to go there? Faery is not a nice place for a young mortal girl. How old are you, dear thing?"

"Eighteen."

"Wonderful. You are of age, then."

"Really? For what exactly?"

Her lips thin into a sly smile. "For everything, my dear, absolutely everything. I can do what you ask, but the price will not be cheap."

I'd prefer not to hand over my hard-earned savings, but if that's what it takes, I will.

"I need to arrive as close to the Emerald Castle as possible, near where my cousin, Lara, and her husband will be. No funny business like dropping me in the middle of a raging sea or a deserted forest to be eaten by one of those wretched othrius things. Can you promise to get me where I need to go?"

The fae's brow rises. "I'm surprised you mentioned your connection with the Prince of Air, brother to the current Black Blood Prince, and his lady."

"Why wouldn't I mention it?"

"Why indeed? Being known to fae kind is more often a curse than a blessing."

As if Ever would hurt me. "Fine. Well, what do you want from me? Money? A little bird told me you're into sunflowers and creepy lizards. I know people who could firm up your supply chain if it's weird stuff you're interested in." It's true; I have a couple of friends with awesome jobs—a zookeeper and a flower grower.

A cunning smile slides over her face. "No, mortal. I do not want tributes and trinkets or even your worthless Earth-realm money. Instead, I would extract a promise from you in payment, a vow, if you will."

"A promise? It better not be for my firstborn child." I don't want kids, and even if I do have them some day, she won't be getting her bear-killing claws on them.

The flames crackle beside us then leap higher as if she's stoked the coals. But she hasn't moved, not even flickered an eyelash. "Listen closely—the forever-cure to the Black Blood curse will show itself to you, and you will know him—"

"*Him?* The cure is a person, a guy? What does that mean?"

"Do not interrupt me, child. Simply listen, for your survival may depend upon how well you heed my next words. You will come to know the cure. But you must promise never ever to share this knowledge. Not with your cousin. Not with her husband, the Prince of Air. And certainly not with the cursed Prince of Fire himself."

"You're telling me I'll have the answer to the riddle that the Elemental Court has been seeking for nearly a thousand fae years, and I won't be able to help them?"

"That's correct. If you do, the life of the current Black Blood heir will be forfeit." She issues a dry cackle, and leans toward the fire, spreading her hands in front of it in the shape of an explosion. "Instant death for the Master of Fire. Kaboom!" Sparks explode accordingly.

"Prince Rafael? I've never met the guy. Maybe I won't care too much if he's barbecued alive for all eternity. And I'm not the least bit afraid of fire."

"Clever girl. You are right to have no fear of the flames. Creation. Destruction. Transformation. This is the way of fire. You understand its principles well. Now, why is that I wonder?"

Who knows? I've always loved the alchemy of fire. It's why I'm studying to be a chef, a legitimate way to make money from dabbling in the chaos of heat and sparks and flames.

"But how can you ask that of me? It's wrong to promise not to help the princes. After all, they're Lara's family, so by extension mine too. It's cruel."

"Does it help if I tell you it is not your job to end the curse? That particular honor will fall to someone else. Remember this. It is important. No matter what you do, Isla, you cannot end it. Even if you were to tell them when you learn of the cure, it will do no good. In fact, it would most likely prevent the curse from ending.

The outcome is beyond your control. This I promise you. And fae cannot lie."

"Okay." I take a slow breath. "Then I promise you that if I happen to learn the cure to the curse, I won't tell a soul."

"Nor will you write it down."

"Fine. I won't write it down, either. Or burn it into the bark of a tree trunk. Or sing it from a rooftop. I'll guard the secret with my life. I vow it. Wait...but what do you get out of this bargain?"

"You wish to know how I will benefit?"

"I do."

"It is simple. I serve the princes of Talamh Cúig." Otherwise known as the Land of Five. "And your presence will give them great pleasure. Your presence is *required*. Therefore, by taking you there, I am *helping* the kingdom."

Right. That seems unlikely. But, apparently, she can't lie. So she must at least believe what she said to be true, which means she isn't planning to harm me. "Great. Count me in then."

"Very well." She gives a sharp nod. "But if you wish to go, you must go now."

"Sylvia warned me you might say that." With my boot, I jostle the bulging backpack on the bear rug. "As you can see, I've come prepared for a trip. She also said she wasn't sure if you could open a portal yourself, thought you might need your sister to help—the High Mage who got Lara in and out of Faery."

Sally's eyes narrow, and she breathes an indignant puff of air through flared nostrils. "I assure you I can manage this one on my own." She thrusts her hand out. "Shake on it and seal our deal."

As I extend my hand, the air around her body shimmers, and the plain-faced woman sitting opposite me disappears, replaced by an incredible sight—a freaky, supernatural creature.

Dressed in a flowing river of orange and red silk that streams over a longer, lithe form, a slow smile spreads over her newly angular face. Red eyes burn, the pupils slitted and emerald green. Her hair is a riot of orange, yellow, and scarlet waves—flames of blue and purple licking over the tips. This lady's hair is literally on fire.

She spits into her hand and nods at mine. Hiding my grimace, I spit too, then shake her hand, the skin of my palm sizzling like I've made a deal with a red-hot fire poker.

A snicker slithers from her lips. "Good. Now put your ugly little pack on and follow me."

I stand and shrug my backpack over my shoulders. "Where are we going?"

"Below," she says, and then slinks over to a large painting on the far wall. As she lifts and sets the heavy, gilt-framed artwork on the floorboards as though it's as light as feathers, I study the hunting scene rendered in rich colors, like an old-fashioned masterpiece.

A pack of giant wolfhounds attacks a creature with the body of a horse and the head of a wild boar, and beside them stands a fiercely handsome blond warrior wearing gold and silver armor and a bloodthirsty smile, about to launch a shining spear into the fray.

"That's Ever!"

"Yes, your cousin's husband at his worst. Of course, most fae would consider it his best."

My heart quickens at seeing him in his natural element, no trace of the glamor that hides his true nature, more than a glint of cruelty sharpening his features. This had to have been before he met Lara. Back when the curse had him in its full grip.

A flash of bright color in the top corner of the canvas catches my attention. Another fae warrior, this one with his back to the viewer. Black and gold armor. A burnished-copper mane of hair. The hint of a strong chin visible as he looks toward the sun setting behind a dark mountain range. Something about his posture makes him appear carefree and easy going. Especially compared to Ever.

"And that other fae is Prince Rafael, the current cursed heir to the Throne of Five," says Sally, breathing down my neck and making me shudder.

"He looks fun," I state, not sure why I say it. Both those dudes look scary. To think my cousin married one of them. A shiver rolls down my back.

"He *was* fun once upon a time. But those days are long past. Come, girl. Let's not waste any more of my precious time." She creaks open a long black door that was hidden behind the painting, and I follow a trail of red silk down concrete stairs into a basement. As she walks, she lights ancient-looking wall torches with a snap of her fingers, not once breaking her stride.

"Why do you live in an old place like this?" I ask, just to fill the death-march silence with some noise. "Being a faery, I'm sure you could magic up a stunning, light-filled mansion in the swanky part of town."

She laughs. "Yes, but it is more convenient to reside directly over a portal with direct access to my realm."

"This place is a portal?"

"Beneath this basement, yes. And this one is all mine." She drops off the last step onto a dirt floor, and flames suddenly burst out of the darkness and lick up the stone walls.

"Awesome," I say, entranced by her fire magic. Despite the low, concrete ceiling, the hexagonal-shaped room seems a lot bigger than the house above, but I guess that's magic too. Who knows what's real and what's illusion? A metallic, coppery scent fills the air as I step down into the room next to Sally.

She fixes those strange red and green eyes on me. "For a magical being to use this portal, they must pass by me. You were correct that out of all my sisters, it is Ether, the High Mage who has a talent for opening portals. But during my time in the mortal world, I have given many valuable sacrifices and worked many spells into the fabric of this portal, so I can open it at will. Step into the center of the circle."

Heart pounding in my ears, I do as she bids and walk over a line of glittering red dust.

A high-pitched hum vibrates through the air, its intensity making me grit my teeth.

"Look at the floor, if you don't want to blind yourself, silly girl."

I drop my gaze as smoke fills the room.

"One more thing," she says, her palms manipulating the smoky gray clouds, shaping them into bizarre patterns. "When you are in Faery, you must meet and speak with my associate."

"That wasn't part of our deal!"

"And now it is. I do not ask much, only that you listen to his words. I will arrange the meeting when the time comes. Do you agree to do this?"

If I want to crash the party in Faery, what freaking choice do I have? "As long as this friend of yours isn't going to hurt me in any way, then sure. Can you promise me they won't?"

She cackles like a witch. Seems appropriate, I guess. "Yes, child. I promise I will not hurt you nor will physical harm come to you as a result of meeting my associate. By pain of fire, I swear this."

Coughing, I close my eyes against the sting, and Sally begins to chant. It's a horrible echoing noise that sounds like one hundred people reciting a black mass rather than one, the only distinguishable words being, "*as above, so are flames below. As below, so are flames above.*"

Her voice rises, growing louder and louder, her whole body shuddering and shaking like she's in the middle of a terrible fit.

"Sally? Holy shit! Are you okay?"

"I suggest you improve your language when in Faery. The fae are unimpressed by profanity. They will think badly of you and, take my word, you should never wish for that."

Huh. Ever seemed to think swearing was pretty funny.

The chanting grows louder, the heat of the room unbearable, even for *me*. I feel sick. I might lose my dinner right here, right now, all over a portal into Faery. "Wait, stop. I think I'm gonna pass out... I think I've changed my—"

The flames disappear, and I'm swallowed by a vortex of stars, my limbs flung wide as I spin in total darkness. Black; it's so black and barren and as cold as the grave.

The droning sound is violent, and I wish I would just lose consciousness so I don't have to hear it, a horrible pressure building inside my skull, undulating through my blood. My veins feel like bike tires pumped to maximum capacity, the air inside still building and building.

*Lara, why didn't you tell me it was like this?*

This is it, the end—I'm dying.

I drift on my back like a helpless lump of flesh and bone, endless galaxies rushing past me, a neon whirl of purple and orange lights shooting across the edges of my vision as I float through space and, *heck*, possibly even time.

If I survive this portal, with my luck, I'll probably land back in the Jurassic Period and have to use my switchblade against a dinosaur—then I'll most definitely die. I just hope it'll be over quickly.

Suddenly, the colors fold in on themselves, dropping me back into the sea of blackness—no stars, no white light, no sound, nothing—and I float onward in an endless void, a forever-night so deep and empty that icy terror fills me.

I feel every molecule of my body begin to shift and swirl and dissolve until, finally, I can't see myself, or feel myself. I'm nothing—I no longer exist.

Then, like a sack of flour dropped from a great height, I crash into something hard.

The universe stops moving.

I'm still alive, but everything *hurts*! Where the hell am I?

First my eyes fly open, then my mouth. And I scream as loud as I can.

Then I'm swallowed by the void again.

And I'm gone. Gone. Gone.

# 2

# Forget Me Not

## Isla

I jolt awake to find a pair of bright blue lights beaming down on me. Nope, not lights, they're narrowed, angry-looking eyes.

Strands of poppy-red hair tickle my cheeks and nose, making me sneeze loudly. Someone grunts—the owner of the ticklish hair whose pale face hovers above me like a nightmarish wraith. He sounds male.

My gaze focuses, and I scan him quickly, relieved to find that he has a nose, a mouth, two arms and two legs. It's a man who's found me, not a ghost or a dinosaur. And that's good news. I think.

Pleased to note I haven't broken every bone in my body and can actually move, I push onto an elbow and bump noses with the frowning red-haired guy. A fae, I presume, going by his fancy peacock-blue leather armor. I peer around his steel-capped shoulders and check out my surroundings. I seem to be in a damp musty cave, not a luxurious castle chamber.

Damn that Sally Salamande.

"Ow, shit, that really hurts." I rub my nose. "How about you back off and give me some space?"

"Of course," he says politely as he stands and draws a long blade from an ornate belt at his waist. "Why do you say *shit*? I understand the meaning, but what has it got to do with anything? Have you landed in gnome dung?"

Oh, yeah, he's most definitely a fae. And with that lethal-looking sword, possibly a violent one.

"Easy," I say, ignoring his question. "You won't be needing that weapon. I'm not sure about you yet, but I certainly don't bite."

His red brows rise, and he studies me more closely.

Hopefully, this dude is an Elemental fae and can direct me to the Emerald Castle where I'll find Lara and her family, and they'll be shocked and surprised but ultimately overjoyed by my arrival, enfolding me in warm hugs as they break out the mulberry wine.

I give him a friendly smile. "Are you going to tell me who are you?" I wriggle until I'm sitting cross-legged on the dusty floor. "Damn. My clothes are wet! How did that happen?"

Golden light flickers on the trees outside the cave's entrance. It's daytime, then. Water gushes behind me. I look around and see a waterfall. A huge one! Have I been for an accidental swim?

"My name is Kian." His nostrils flare like he smells something bad. "And *you* are a human."

Tall and thin and sporting far too many shiny straps and buckles on his extravagant armor, he inspects me while wearing a malicious expression that I'd most definitely find worrying if I didn't already know who he is.

Kian Leondearg—a childhood friend of Ever and Raff's and, according to Lara, a first-class jerk. A massive pain in the ass who, rumor has it, is fortunately more talk than action. The shiny-blue cape he wears matches his forget-me-not eyes and is an interesting addition to his fae warrior's armor. It screams try-hard attempting to mask an inferiority complex with extravagant clothes. It fits the profile Lara gave me—a bully, with a giant chip on his shoulder.

"The portal you entered through is behind the waterfall. That is why you're wet. I was nearby tormenting a wandering sea witch and heard the portal open. It makes an unholy racket. And now, thanks to you, I've lost her. Do you have a name, mortal?"

"I do. It's Isla."

An unpleasant smirk slides over his face—in the way of all fae, he's strikingly handsome, but a nasty energy rolls off him, spoiling the effect of his beauty. He frowns. "Why is your name familiar to me?"

"I have no idea," I lie. He must have heard Lara or Ever mention me. "Where am I? I'm telling you now; it had better be near the Emerald Castle or I'm going to scream again."

He goes unnaturally still. "What do you know of it?"

"I have friends there." I'd be wise to pretend I've never heard of Kian the Painful, but to ensure he doesn't chop my head off with that sword, I probably should mention my royal connections pretty damn quick. "Do you know Ever?"

A mix of shock and amusement infuses his face. "That would be Prince Everend to you."

"If you say so. He's my cousin's husband."

"Oh, is he now?" Sly interest sparks in his gaze. "And what is your cousin's name?"

"Lara. She must have mentioned me."

"Oh, yes. Lara has most definitely spoken of her cousin who is currently living in safety in the human city of Blackbrook. If you are this alleged cousin, there has been no mention of your visit. And, besides, with your mortal talent for telling untruths, I cannot be sure that you are who you say you are. You could be a Merit, glamored with an unpleasant human scent and countenance."

"I promise I'm Lara's cousin. Why would I lie to you?"

"Now that is a stupid question. To say one thing and mean something entirely different is a great power. It is a freedom I can only dream of possessing. Rise, girl. And I will bring you fairly close to where Lara dwells."

"Only close to?" I stand and brush mud and tiny glittering stones off my wet clothes. "Sorry, but that won't do. I want you to take me straight to her."

"Then I must apologize. It is the best offer I can make to a prisoner."

"What? No way. I'm definitely not your prisoner. Take me to Ever if you don't believe me. He'll confirm who I am."

He snarls and starts toward me, polished boots kicking up clouds of silvery dust.

I push my palms out, a measly barrier. "Kian, wait...try asking me some questions. Lara's told me many things about the city and—"

"Silence," he commands.

I zip my lips and shuffle backward, closer and closer to the pond and the waterfall. I'm too cold to get wet again, but if I have to, I'm prepared to jump in.

Laughing, he stalks forward, dips a shoulder into my stomach, and throws me over his back. Then he strides out of the cave, bouncing me through the upside-down ruins of a black stone castle.

Holy cow. This wasn't part of my plan. Here in the Land of Five, I'm related to royalty, so Kian must be committing some kind of treason by treating me this way.

The wild sound of waves crashing somewhere far below almost drowns out my shouts as I kick and punch Kian's body. *Calm down, Isla, think.* We're near the sea, and I believe we've just walked through the ruins of the Black Castle, which means I most likely landed in the Moonstone Cave, kind of right on target. Thank God I listened carefully to all those stories Lara told.

A blazing neon sunset behind us, we enter a thick covering of trees—a forest with deep shadows, chirping birds, and screeching who-the-hell-knows-what. Could be monkeys for all I know, which is fine. As long as they don't have terribly long fangs and an insatiable taste for human flesh.

Okay. I'm pretty sure this isn't the infamous Ithalah Forest where Ever found Lara after Ether dumped her in Faery. I'm on the coast and within walking distance to the Emerald Castle. Miraculously, it seems Sally has kept to our bargain and transported me to the correct place. All is well. Except for the berry-haired fiend whose butt my bouncing head is currently massaging.

"Stop thrashing about," says the fiend. "And be quiet or I shall cease your mewling permanently."

That doesn't sound like fun, so I stop moving and pay attention to my surroundings, upside down and confusing as they are.

The fresh smell of pine needles clears my blood-filled head a little as we travel downhill, weaving through scrub and around giant boulders that block the wooded trail. A few creatures scratch and hoot as dusk falls, but I remain quiet.

I wasn't afraid when I woke in the cave, but my sense of unease is growing. I don't trust this guy at all. His vibe is similar to my dad's, who Mom divorced when I was seven. A frustrated guy itching for a fight, his longing to cause pain is almost tangible, floating in the air around us, setting off alarm bells inside me.

When the sky is black, he steps out of the forest into a large, flat area, sliding me down his front until my feet nearly touch the ground but, before they do, he spins me quickly so we're both looking in the same direction.

I grunt in surprise, not from his rough handling but because, even in the dark, I recognize the Emerald Castle's spires. The iridescent needles pierce the star-studded sky in exactly the way Lara described them. Breathtaking and surreal. And just how Lara's mom painted them.

Dangling like a puppet, I can only gape and imagine the many splendors of the town—the green tourmaline pathway that winds up to the castle, gushing waterfalls, emerald towers, black-jet walls, the vast columns of the Great Hall, and the beautiful, horrible creatures within. So many wonders. And magic everywhere!

I wriggle in his grasp. "That's the city of Talamh Cúig...so you decided to bring me here after all."

"Yes, to Stone Hill and the back of the city at least." With a sharp wrench, he turns me to face him, then shifts his grip to my jacket collar, leaving me hanging nose-to-nose with him. "I hope you've looked your fill, human, because that may very well be the most you'll ever see of the Emerald Castle."

"What? Aren't we going there now?"

"No, *we* most certainly aren't." His voice drops to a rumbling whisper. "You're bound for the dungeons below that pretty castle. And I am bound for a romp in my chambers with three delightfully wicked trooping sylphs."

I have no idea what a trooping sylph is, but I certainly don't plan on visiting the dungeons. I kick him hard, pleasure spiking when he winces. "Put me down you shit-for-brains douchebag jerkwad! Prick!"

His thin lips stretch into a cruel smile that sends chills skittering down my spine.

I may be scared, but fury blazes through me. "You know what, you smug, pointy-beaked, red-headed stepchild?"

Scarlet eyebrows twist in confusion. I totally get that—because I don't even know what I'm talking about. "You're going to catch hell when Ever hears what a complete dick you've been to me."

He snorts. "Fortunately, angering the Prince of Air is one of my favorite pastimes. I've missed him while he's been wasting time in the Earth realm. Now shut your vulgar mouth before I do it for you."

He waves his long fingers, and a spray of toxic-smelling dirt hits my face.

*Earth magic*, I think as I spit and cough, choking on the vile stuff.

And then I don't think at all.

I can't—because I'm dead.

# 3

# The Sun King

## Raff

"**Y**ou have been gone far too long," I tell the scowling fae pacing across my chamber—Everend Fionbharr, my older brother who, not long ago, was the Crown of Five's thirteenth Black Blood heir. Presently, I am the fourteenth.

Lucky me.

"Much has changed since you left. And do stop prowling back and forth or you'll wear a channel in my floor."

He halts and indicates the massive carved chair I sit upon with a furious wave of his hand. "*Indeed*. And it seems that *you* are what has changed the most since I have been gone. By the Elements, Brother, at what point did you decide it was a good idea to have a throne moved in here so you could sit upon it like an ancient dryad and sulk your days away in private?"

Silently, I stare him down, but far from being dissuaded, he continues his boring tirade.

"You are a creature of the sun, yet you mope here in the dark. I cannot believe my eyes."

I tip my head toward the bay windows where burnt-orange drapes hang wide open, revealing a glowing sun sinking behind the Dún Mountains. "It is hardly dark in here. Clearly, you have forgotten the way the poison corrupted your soul. Look at me closely and you will see a past version of yourself. Ponder the sight, and then be kinder in your judgment."

Ever rakes a hand through his long hair—gold tangled with silver. So different than mine, threaded with fire and coal. "But look at Spark!" he declares. "Even she looks depressed."

I gaze at the mire fox sleeping in my lap and stroke her white ears and her matted, soft red pelt. Not long ago, she spent her days wreaking havoc throughout the castle. Now she hardly bothers to squeak. I look at Balor, Ever's monster wolfhound, his tongue lolling in adoration as he watches my brother's every move, most likely terrified he's going to disappear back to the human realm and desert him once again.

"And let us consider your hound. Don't forget you left him and your órga falcons to pine for you whilst you cavorted in the human cities. And what of Jinn? Kian rode your horse into a dripping lather whenever he managed to trick his way onto his saddle. Don't dare speak to me of cruelty. Your heart was once the coldest in the kingdom. At least mine brings eternal summer to our lands. Your time as heir brought only dark clouds and storms."

Ever sighs. "What you say is true, Raff. Let us not argue. Lara and I are here to introduce our daughter to the court, to decide if we can keep her here in Faery safely. And now that my mind is clear of the poison, I have a renewed desire to help you find a cure for the curse, and I believe—"

I interrupt his meddling rant with a harsh laugh. "A cure? You are too amusing."

"Aer is hiding the most important part of this riddle. I am sure of it. And perhaps her sisters do the same. All we need do is—"

"Ridiculous. If Ether knew the cure, she would tell us. As the High Mage, she always has the kingdom's best interests in mind."

Shoulders slumping in defeat, Ever says, "Fine. Do not trouble yourself with these ideas then. Leave them to others to riddle. At least come to the feast tonight. You could do with a happy distraction."

"I prefer to remain here and indulge in other entertainments."

Ever's silver eyes bore through me, and I feel his anger, no, his disappointment like a barbed arrow through my flesh.

"Do not look at me thusly," I say. "You were once as I am now—bored and heartless, facing a long and painful death by poison. Can you really fault my actions?"

"Before I left Talamh Cúig, you told me you wanted to be king. You welcomed the idea! I had hoped when I returned, that I would find you content, but you look far from happy, Brother."

"How can I be content without a queen? My mage prophesied no Crystalline Oak for me to wait by every month. I have had to search the land high and low and still I have no mate to show for it."

"Lara wasn't found beneath the tree. The foretold symbol was tattooed on her back, the oak's branches worked into the design engraved on her skin, along with the dragonfly. But you already know all this."

"Yes, yes. But I thought I would have found my mate by now, and I have no clear direction on how to do so, and therefore no hope."

"Raff." He gives me a wide smile replete with dimples. It casts me back to our boyhood, my mind awash with carefree memories—fishing with our eldest brother, Rain, long before his death. Rambling through forests, hunting and chasing nymphs together.

Ever leans close, his hand resting on my shoulder. "Relax, Brother. You'll meet your queen when it is time. The prophecy always unfolds."

"It is you who has changed, Ever. You've become more like the boy I remember. Calm and certain you can fix all the wrongs in the seven realms. Life as a husband and father suit you well, that much is clear to me."

Impossibly, his smile grows wider.

"Oh, I see you are besotted still." I shake my head at the sight of him—a prince of Faery, a warrior encased in leather and gold armor beneath a cloak of darkest silver, grinning like a court jester. Deciding to indulge him, I say, "So tell me of your plans. Will you be performing a second wedding ceremony now that you are back?"

"Yes, of course. You know I must. If we are not wedded under the Laws of Five, she will be fair game for the Merits and they will try to steal her. You know they value nothing higher than a human pet to toy with."

I take my circlet from my brow and rest it in my lap over the snoring Spark. Sighing, my thumbs rub over the metal sunflower petals. "And you want to hold this ceremony at Merrin Creek?"

"Yes. You will come?"

I would prefer not to.

"I will attend the marriage, but I refuse to travel almost three tediously long days in your wedding procession just to see you reenact the first days of your relationship. I hope you realize that by doing this, you are glorifying the time Lara spent as your captive. That is hardly very romantic, Brother."

He grins as if I have said something amusing. It is shocking to see him smile so frequently. Jarring and unnatural. I can only conclude he must be blissfully happy with his human bride and dimpled halfling baby. I recall that once upon a time, I liked Lara very much, enjoyed laughing with the cheeky red-haired mortal. But I was a different person, then. Before the curse took hold.

Stretched on the marble floor, Balor groans and Ever squats down to pat him. "So, you plan to shift and fly to meet us at the creek in time for the ceremony?"

"Yes. And, of course, our mother will not lower herself to ride in a carriage or sit upon a horse, so she will use her water magic to travel through the rivers."

Ever takes a breath to speak just as the doors burst open. Kian enters taking great strides, his hair streaming behind him like a river of blood.

"Last night I caught a human trespasser," he announces in a breathless jumble of words, coming to a halt beside Ever.

"What?" Ever and I say, both jolting upright.

"And by the law of finders keepers, I claim her as my property to torment according to my whims. Just like you did, Ever, when you found the one you called the wasp."

Fury flares in Ever's silver eyes. "Do you mean the wasp who is now my *wife*, Lara? I warn you to take care how you speak of her. After my time living in the mortal world, my nature may seem tempered, but I assure you, I have not lost my taste for spilling blood. And I did *not* torment Lara when I found her."

"Perhaps not physically," I remind him. "But you must admit you were far from kind."

Ever's cheeks darken.

Kian sneers down at Balor—he has always been jealous of the hound's bond with Ever. "Wait until you see this girl," he tells us proudly. "She's a fearless, brainless fool if ever I saw one, but pretty enough for a human."

"What is her name?" Ever asks.

Kian struts about the chamber, flapping his cape like a peacock in heat. "She says it is Isla and that she is connected by blood to Lara, but I do not believe her. And, Ever, you of all fae know how easily humans can lie."

"*Isla?*" In two steps Ever has Kian in his grip, shaking him hard. "Tell me what this girl looks like."

"Yellow hair. Eyes bluer than a summer sky. A nature as fierce and bold as a little lioness. A mouth as rude and coarse as a mountain troll. In fact, that's exactly how she smelled, like a—"

"That's definitely Isla, and it's her sweat you scented, you imbecile. Humans they have..." Ever's words trail away, his fists clenching, skin paling as the truth sinks in. "You are telling me you took Isla captive?" he thunders.

A bank of gray clouds race past the window, and the sky rumbles, rattling the window glass so hard I fear it may break. Interesting. Since I have become the Black Blood heir, Ever's magic no longer controls the weather. For it to be affected by him now means his emotions are running wild.

"If you've hurt her, I shall crush your lungs, wring them dry, and feed them to the draygonets. Where is she?"

"In the dungeons," Kian crows, not sensible enough to be afraid. But he should be. Very afraid.

"You moron," Ever hisses. "Is she alive?"

"Yes. At least she was when I left her."

The room darkens, and I lean forward, elbows on my knees, to watch Ever shake with fury.

"You should have brought her to me immediately!" In a rush of wind, Kian's hair flies out and wraps around his throat, strangling him. When he begins to turn blue, Ever flicks his hand, and Kian crumples to the floor.

Balor stalks to loom over him, red eyes glowing as he snarls like an enraged troll. I smirk when I notice his long tail, thumping steadily. The hound despises Kian and is always pleased to see him punished.

"Go now, Kian," I say. "You have harmed a member of my family. That was badly done. To ensure your safety, I suggest you stay out of Ever's sight for some time."

"She's a human!" Kian croaks. "And only family by marriage."

Knuckles cracking, I stretch my fingers and sparks dance around our tiresome friend's body. "If you are wise, Kian," which I am well aware that he isn't, "you will leave now. While you are still able to walk."

"This is far from over," growls Ever. "In fact, I'm working on a fitting punishment as I speak. One that is sure to make you miserable." Frowning, my brother watches Kian scramble through the door, then smiles so widely those dimples slash his cheeks again. "I must also take my leave and see to Isla. She has taken a great risk in coming here." When he reaches the doors, he turns to flash the charming smile again.

"Stop smiling at me," I command, biting on my own grin. "It is unpleasant and discomforting."

"I advise you to attend the feast tonight, Brother. And dress in all the finery befitting our land's future Sun King. I promise you will want to meet this human intruder, for I predict that if you like her, every single one of your troubles may soon be over. And please...don't be as idiotic as I was when I met Lara. Come, Balor, we have a human to find, which should please you no end. I know how much you like them."

"Wait...before you go... What do you mean when you say my troubles may soon be over?"

"Tonight, you shall see." He gives me the foolish smile again and then disappears, the doors groaning shut behind Balor.

"Ever! Get back here!"

As his footsteps fade away, I sink back against russet cushions and rub the ache from my chest, willing the constant drip drip drip of the poison though my blood to still its progress.

*Flaming fires.* A feast.

It seems, tonight, I must endure hours of my mother's nagging at the queen's table in the Great Hall. Are all mothers as irritating as she, or is it only royal ones who sink their barbs with such deadly precision?

I hardly feel like fae company, let alone having to meet a mortal brat, but curiosity has long been my downfall. It's the one trait that the curse has not yet destroyed.

For better or worse.

# 4

## Dungeon

### Isla

"**I**sla, you'd better wake up before I strangle you in your sleep, and then you'll never get to eat another triple chocolate eclair again!"

"What? Where are the eclairs?" My eyes shoot open, and I squint at the scowling faery princess crouched beside me who's jostling my shoulder roughly. My gaze focuses, trailing over the braided red hair that glints with green and gold jewels, her incredible gown of sewn-together petals, bright green eyes, and freckled skin. She smells of roses with the barest hint of sweat. So, not a faery then—just my cousin, Lara.

A very angry Lara.

"Hi, Cuz! Do you have to yell at me like that?" I fumble to sit up, rubbing my temple. "I've got a shocking headache." Mouth gaping, I look around the room. It's small. Damp. Flames from two sconces flicker over black-stone walls. Opposite where we sit is a wooden door with a barred window across the top. This place is creepy and stinky like an actual gross dungeon or prison. "Am I in a cell—"

"Yep," says Lara. "You're in the old dungeons beneath the Emerald Castle. And since it was Kian who put you here, you should count yourself extremely lucky a headache is *all* you've got."

I quickly look down to make sure I'm still wearing clothes—yep, I am, thank goodness—and Lara folds me in her arms, kissing my cheeks. "What are you doing here, you stupid, stupid girl? You have no idea what you've done, what you've set in motion!" She pats my body, checking for injuries. "Are you alright?"

I nod. "How did you find me?"

She pulls back and inspects me further, her palms framing my face, squeezing too tightly. "Kian couldn't help but gloat to Ever and Raff the first chance he got." Her frown turns into a grin. "You've probably just made the dumbest mistake of your life coming here. But I'm so glad to see you!"

"You too. By the way, you make a spectacular fae princess in that freaking strange dress."

"This old thing? It's probably a thousand years old. Where does Aunt Clare think you are?"

"I told Mom you're a super-amazing cousin who invited me to visit you in Brazil. But you and I both know you didn't invite me anywhere—hence you are neither super *or* amazing. Hey! Where's Merri?"

Lara picks at the embroidered falcons on her dress. "Hanging with her grandmother, Queen Varenus. If you think I look cool in Faery get up—wait until you meet *her* tonight. She looks like a goddess. So, how did you get into Faery? It's no easy feat."

"Through a portal that popped me into the Moonstone Cave. That's the same cave you departed faery from, right? Did you know spirit conjurers are for real? They even have websites and answer emails these days. I had no idea."

Her eyes narrow. "I don't believe for a moment that one of these phony operators opened a portal for you, Isla."

"They didn't. A fae called Sally Salamande did. The conjurer just hooked me up with her."

Lara's jaw drops. "Sally Salamande! What'd she look like?"

"Oh you know, hair on fire, red eyes, demonic slitted pupils—basically, pretty terrifying."

"Wow. That has to be Salamander, Raff's fugitive fire mage. She's been MIA for a while now, which basically sucks for Raff. His power is connected to hers, and with the way the curse is trashing him mind and body, he needs her ass back here like...*yesterday.* Did you get any intel on what the conniving old lizard breath is up to?"

Guilt scorches my skin as I remember the deal I made with Sally about the curse and the cure I've sworn to keep secret if I ever do come to learn it. I hope I don't. Who wants to hide such things from people they love? Not me.

*It doesn't matter—the outcome is beyond my control.*

*Sally promised.*

I can't quite meet Lara's eyes when I say, "Nope, not really. The only thing worth mentioning is she seemed very keen to keep guarding that portal she lives on top of."

"Oh, boy, wait until Raff hears about this." She shoots to her feet, seizing my wrists and dragging me along with her. "From personal experience, I remember exactly how bad you're feeling right now—human bodies aren't optimized for crossing dimensions, so I'm sorry to rush you, but we need to get you settled in the castle and then cleaned and primped in time for tonight's banquet."

She pulls open the door and beckons me down a narrow hallway to a decrepit-looking spiral staircase lit by blue-flamed torches. Blue? I've never seen their like before, but they're pretty awesome.

"Oh, and you need to try hard not to cuss like a chef while you're here."

"Why? I'm sure the fae can handle the odd expletive—"

"They don't like it. Think of alternatives."

I laugh. "Really? Like *what*? Oh, my furry fudge nuts that really hurt?"

She shakes her head. "Nope, too close to the hairy ball sack truth."

"How about just plain old fudge nuggets, then?"

"Perfect."

"Yeah, as long as I don't mind sounding like a deranged clown, it's a great alternative."

"Listen, Gordon Ramsay, just promise me you'll try."

I blow a chunk of dirty hair off my face. "Fine. Anything for you, Cuz."

Linking her arm through mine, Lara says, "I can't wait to see your jaw hit the floor when you check out your room."

"And I can't wait to lie on an actual bed, so bring it on. Wait... Fae sleep on beds, right?"

She laughs and pulls me onto the first step. "Wait and see."

"No. Scratch the bed. What I can't wait for is a bath and something to eat besides strange fruit muffins and cheese. And, of course, to see all of those gorgeous, freaky faeries."

"And don't forget about all the hideously terrifying ones. You'll see plenty of them, too."

"Speaking of faeries, what happened to Kian?"

She giggles. "Ever has magicked him up a pair of bat wings, and he has to wear them for a whole moon turn. Kian's not a happy boy right now. All he cares about is appearing superior to everyone else, and at the moment he looks like a dime-store Halloween costume."

"Bit like Dracula?"

"Yeah. Half blood-sucking vampire and, with that gorgeous hair of his, half Ariel the Little Mermaid."

"Sounds awesome." Our laughter echoes off the walls as we climb the stairs.

Lara wraps an arm around my shoulders, pulling me close. "I'm really mad at you for following us here. It's not safe, Isla. But I have to admit I'm kind of glad I can finally share it with you—Faery in all its wondrous and terrifying glory. And I can't wait for you to meet Raff."

"The fire prince? *Why*?"

She laughs, her eyes sparkling in the dim light. "Oh, you'll see. Believe me, Isla. You will definitely see."

"What? Tell me! What will I see exactly?"

"A magnificent cursed faery prince, among other things."

"Well, that sounds interesting. And ominous. But what about these *other* things? Spit it out, Lara!"

"Only two hours until the moon rises."

"What's going to happen when the—"

"Quick. We'd better hurry," she says. "You need a fair bit of scrubbing and polishing before you'll be presentable for court. It could take hours." Then she dashes ahead of me, sprinting around a bend in the stairwell and leaving me to chase an effervescent ribbon of light trailing in her wake.

"Wait. Lara," I yell. "Something weird is following you!"

"I know." Her voice echoes from the darkness above. "It's called Isla."

"Very funny."

"Hurry, before the dungeon troll gets you."

"What dungeon troll?"

"The one I released before I opened your cell."

"*Shit.* I mean shivers."

It's a good thing I'm an experienced up-hill jogger. Being a committed foodie, I exercise a lot to stay healthy. I'm sure Lara's lying about the troll, but even so, I race up the stairs faster than I've ever moved in my life.

I don't plan on getting eaten before I get to attend my first-ever Faery feast.

# 5

## The Feast

## Isla

"**S**o what do you think? Are you regretting your reckless decision to follow us here yet?" asks Lara, bouncing cute baby Merri in her arms as we enter the Great Hall via one of the castle's maze-like internal staircases.

To be clear, Merri isn't a proper baby. Being half-fae, appearances are deceiving, and she looks more like a two-year-old human child than her actual age, which is only nine months. As Ever would have me believe, Fae don't spend very long as helpless babes. It's a survival thing because Faery can be such a dangerous place—as he and Lara keep reminding me. Over and over and over.

Of course, the bizarre creatures gathered in the spectacular Great Hall make me feel a little nervous, but I force a relaxed grin as I turn to Lara. "I followed you into a supernatural realm, that's all. Stop going on about it as if I murdered someone."

She sighs and adjusts the delicate shoulder strap of another petal-soft faery gown. This one is a dreamy mix of mint green and rosy pink colors that offsets her crimson locks to perfection. My dress is made up of layered strips of different hues of silky red fabric—the rust of dried blood, juice from a blood orange, and bright slashes that resemble freshly cut wounds—a gruesome yet beautiful blend of colors.

"It's not *you* murdering anyone that I'm worried about," Lara says. "It's the other way around. Open your eyes and look closely at these people, Isla. This is not a safe place for humans with no magic."

"*Isn't it?* Oh, gosh, if only someone had thought to mention that to me about five trillion times, I might have stayed home cowering in my room. Oh, wait...you already did."

She whacks my shoulder. "Be serious. Elemental fae are Seelie; they're kind of like the good guys or the lesser of two evils. Just make sure you never cross paths with the Folk of the Unseelie court. If you meet one, run fast. Very. Fast. Okay?"

My gaze sweeps over soaring emerald columns that support the vaulted-glass ceiling before landing on the shining throne set upon a lavishly decorated dais. All around me, hundreds of fae—strange and beautiful creatures every one—whisper and cackle, presided over by the pale white queen on her throne of translucent crystal wands.

Earlier, during the set-up of the feast, Lara led me around the hall, introducing me to a few faeries, most of them servants, as a way to acclimatize me to the grandeur of the hall and the strangeness of the castle's people. I'm glad she did, but nothing could have prepared me for the sight of the queen and her attendants.

A row of stony-eyed advisers hover behind Queen Varenus, and on her left sits Prince Ever, looking awesome dressed in black and silver, smiling as he talks to her. The queen's face is a barely moving mask of frigid, ethereal beauty, framed by sheets of white hair that fall like rippling water to her sparkling slippers.

The wooden throne on her right is empty, and my gaze fixes on the carved sunflowers, scorpions, and thorns adorning its surface. Fire symbols—just like the type I usually decorate my favorite cakes with—in bright red and orange frosting.

Lara takes my arm, and we walk down a long central aisle of green marble, edged by tables filled with cavorting fae who turn to watch us as we move slowly toward the dais. And the beautiful, creepy queen.

"The fae can't be all that bad," I whisper out of the side of my mouth. "You married one. And then named your baby after the creek where he first stumbled upon you."

A smile on her lips, her green eyes glaze over as she loses herself in, no doubt, disgustingly romantic memories—which I decide to ruin. "The creek where Ever, on first sight, mistook you for a troll and then a goblin, before finally deciding you reminded him of a freckled wasp. Charming creature, your husband."

Pursing her lips, she says, "What can I say? Our love isn't a shallow thing based on looks alone."

Merri gurgles and reaches out to grab a chunk of my hair in her chubby little fist.

"Hey, give that back," I say untangling my blonde locks. "Lucky you're so cute, you little imp."

And she is adorable—with blood red hair and eyes so silver that gazing into them is like falling into those mesmerizing mirrors at a fun park. Her ears are already pointier than her dad's, and she sports the cheekiest grin. That unbridled, sassy smile of Merri's is a gift from her mom, and it turns Ever, once the cruel prince of Talamh Cúig, into a besotted fool.

It's sweet. And, yeah, I'm a little jealous of their happy family unit, even if two of them aren't the same species as me.

The queen drags pale fingers, the tips sharp like blue-tapered talons, through the air, beckoning us forward.

"Oh, shit." I nod toward the dais. "I think your scary mother-in-law wants us to walk faster."

"No matter what she says or does, do not show fear," Lara whispers, stopping in front of the lineup of regally dressed fae. "And, for the love of pizza, no swearing! Think of them as evil little children. Use words appropriate for Merri."

I pull an ugly face at her. "Yes, Mom. I'll do my best."

The faeries' eyes glow like torchlights, offsetting their fantastical outfits made of cobweb-thin materials—barks and leaves and flowers—their heads crowned with metal circlets studded with gemstones. Their look is a potent mix of power and whimsy combined with an unnerving, unnatural beauty.

Silence settles over the room as Lara bows her head and makes a deep curtsy. A second too late, I do the same, wobbling a little despite the meeting-royalty practice drill Lara and her best fae-friend, Magret, subjected me to earlier in her rooms.

Magret has the most incredible velvety antlers that, much like a dog's tail, quiver with emotion. They're fascinating, and it's a trial not to stare at them when I'm with her. I hope I get to sit next to her tonight. If I ask politely, she might let me touch them.

"Good evening, Queen Varenus," Lara says at the exact moment a commotion ripples through the crowd.

"Ah, finally, my Rafael arrives." The queen's voice is crisp and resonates with power. The pale-blue gown she wears ripples like a river with each slow movement of her elegant arms.

A tall fae dressed in black, highlighted by rich, fiery reds similar to the ones on my dress, steps onto the dais and bows before kissing her jeweled fingers. It's the famous Raff, the cursed fire prince of Talamh Cúig.

My heart pounding, I watch his warrior's frame fold with surprising grace into the sunflower-emblazoned throne on his mother's right. His brother, Ever, is a vision of silver and gold. Raff is golden too, but darker, his hair lit with every shade of tawny summer. Dark coal. Flickering flames. Hot—in every sense of the word.

Instead of checking out the room, he's looking down at his goblet of wine. I wonder what color his eyes are. Silent, his dark head lolls indolently against his chair, a silver circlet embedded with a golden sunstone slipping down his brow.

"Lara's cousin has honored our court with a surprise visit," the queen tells him as Lara pulls me forward. Closer to the fire prince.

He stifles a yawn. "Yes, just what our court needs—another human," he says in a deep voice. "Kian has already apprised me of the fascinating news."

So similar to Ever, this prince is arrogant and sarcastic, but humorless and dour, which makes him much worse than his brother.

Finally, his gaze tracks over the sea of twitching, tittering fae, and then...and then he looks at me.

*Amber.*

His eyes are wild and intense—sparks of yellow and gold swirling through a background of burning amber.

*Wolf's eyes.*

His lips part, and he takes a breath as if to speak but says nothing. His gaze flicks over my body, head to toe and back up again. He blinks twice, for some reason, speechless.

"Raff, Queen Varenus," says Ever, offering me a dimpled smile. "This is Isla Delaney of Blackbrook, my wife's cousin."

The queen inclines her head slowly. Raff keeps staring.

Ever clears his throat, frowning at his brother. "Isla, this is my brother, Prince Rafael Leon Fionbharr, the fourteenth Black Blood heir to the Throne of Five. And my mother, Queen Varenus, Empress of the Land of Five, Sovereign of the Five Elements and Ruler of the Seas of All Time."

The queen nods. "Welcome to our city of Talamh Cúig. May the time you spend here with us be of value to all."

That's an unnervingly strange greeting. "Thank you," I say, dipping another ridiculous curtsy.

"Despite your first chamber being a cell, your visit is off to a far more auspicious start than Lara's. Her initial audience with the crown was in the guise of my son's bedraggled captive." She smiles, silver eyes burning right through to the back of my skull. "And now look at your cousin—married to fae royalty. I wonder what will become of you?"

That sounds vaguely like a threat.

My gaze flicks to the Prince of Fire. I'm interested to hear what he has to say on the matter. But he doesn't greet me. And he doesn't even smile.

"Raff?" Ever growls. "Since when have basic civilities been a chore for you? Please pay your regards to my wife's cousin."

The tawny prince lets three beats pass in silence, defying his older brother's wishes. As the heir, I guess he feels comfortable doing that. Most people immediately do whatever Ever suggests—even my boss, Max.

Then with Raff's strange eyes locked on mine, he says, "Welcome to our kingdom, Isla of Blackbrook, cousin of Lara, now mortal-wedded to my brother, the Prince of Air." Amber jewels flash on his fingers as he taps them on the carved-lion armrest. "My mother has said it is your first time in our land, but I do not believe this is the case. I cannot name the time or the place, but I am certain we have met before."

What the...? What is this guy playing at?

"You lying *dii*..." Gasps hiss through the air. Quick, think of Merri-appropriate words. "...dung bucket. I've never been to Faery before! Why would you say that I have?"

Snickers erupt in the crowd, and the fire prince narrows his eyes, cracking his knuckles loudly. I'm not brave enough to look at the queen and see what she's doing. Or Lara. Damn my fiery temper. It's always getting me into trouble. I hope one day I can learn to control it.

"You know he cannot lie, Isla," says Ever, looking disappointed in me. "So it follows that if my brother says he has met you before, then he speaks the truth. Or at the very least must believe whole-heartedly in the veracity of his own words. Have you infiltrated our lands on another occasion?"

Lara laughs. "Ever, you make her sound like some kind of covert spy up to no good. Before I returned from Faery, she had no idea it even existed, or that beings like *you* existed. And you lived with us in the mortal world for a year and a half. You ate Cheerios for breakfast with her nearly every day. She hasn't a devious bone in her body. Plenty of reckless ones though."

"Of course Isla is good. I wasn't meaning to suggest she came here intentionally. On occasion, humans have been known to fall into our lands by accident." His mercurial gaze drifts off to the side, a dreamy expression on his face. "I do miss the human breakfasts made of sugar. They were very enjoyable."

"And I find myself bored by human prattle," states the queen. "Isla, do join us at our table for the meal. Sit next to your cousin." She points to the farthest seat on her right. "And, Lara, bring my granddaughter to my lap. She will eat with me."

Lara says, "In a minute. Merri wants a cuddle from her father first."

While Merri bounces in Ever's lap, servants carry out a long gold-lacquered table and place it in front of the royal family. Dishes appear, served by creatures with rainbow-colored skin, their hair long twisted spikes of green that remind me of punk-style shield maidens.

The queen claps her hands and silver moths explode between them, tumbling onto her plate. "To the Elements Five that have returned my son and his family from the human realm, bless us with food, nurture our magic, and sharpen our wits and pleasures, we pay our debts in kind. Tonight, we do so with power."

Her white head swivels my way, a mocking smile fixed on her face. She holds her wrist high, purple veins on display as the sleeve of her gown falls away. With a slash of her blue nail across translucent skin, dark blood flows down her arm, dripping onto her plate of delicacies, drowning the flailing moths.

Gross.

"Eat," she says, before tucking into her disgusting meal.

In some countries back home, blood pudding is a popular meal, but seasoning food from your own veins is taking culinary daring a little too far. Still, everyone obeys her command and starts eating their non-blood drenched meals, including me—even though I feel pretty queasy.

Laughing at my pinched expression, Ever transfers Merri to the queen's lap—the poor kid—and I try to hold a reasonably sane conversation with him and Lara. Despite my best efforts, I regularly lose track of my thoughts as I gape at the squealing, screeching, raucous Fair Folk feasting below the dais.

Varenus entertains her granddaughter, iridescent green and blue butterflies bursting into the air every time she claps, making Merri giggle as she tries to capture them.

I turn and watch the queen's green-skinned consort, Lord Stavros, play with his waist-length plait, then lean and taste her blood sauce with his bony finger, black eyes gleaming in a thin angular face. He looks like a ghoul.

I also glance frequently at the sullen fire prince picking at his food. I don't know why I'm so fascinated. I hate to judge so soon, but I'm already fairly sure I don't like him. Maybe the curse gives him a special magnetism. A compelling charisma. That might explain why my attention flicks his way so often.

Or it could be the heat in his horrible, beautiful eyes, the sizzling current of banked power that calls to my pyromaniac's obsession with all things fire. He burns with it.

I've always loved the danger of flames, the thrill of being burnt. I'm not an idiot, though. I'm talking about a tiny lick. A hiss, a little kiss of fire. Nothing demented. Nothing like me getting close to Raff to test the caliber of his heat; that would be dangerous. That would be insanity.

When the main course, a richly flavored stew, is cleared away, the queen calls for dancing, and the musicians in the far corner pick up their instruments.

Prince Rafael stands and squares his broad shoulders, gaze intent on the stairs off to the side of the dais.

"Fleeing so soon, Rafael?" asks his mother.

His shoulders drop a fraction, then he turns to her. "Ever and I plan to hunt draygonets tomorrow at dawn. I have bowstrings to wax and blades to sharpen."

"Leave that lowly task to the armorers and please your mother instead. I wish to see you dance."

"*Dance?*" he barks. "I am afraid no one would find that pleasing, Mother, least of all you."

"You do it well enough when you set your mind to it," she insists. "You used to love to dance, and it would amuse me to see you open the set with the little human."

"It is Ever's duty to dance with Lara—she's *his* wedded wife, not mine."

"Ever and Lara's vows made in the mortal realm count for naught here in Faery, but that is a discussion for another day. I meant the *new* human visitor, Isla."

"*Isla?*" he growls at the same moment I splutter, "*Me?*"

"Yes. I wish the both of you to open the dancing. *Together*. Now hurry along. The court grows impatient for entertainment, and you know how unpleasant it can be for humans when we get bored."

Lara clutches her goblet, biting at her lip as she stares at her plate and ignores me. Ever wears an amused smirk, reminding me that even though I'm used to seeing him at home, glamored to look more human as he scoffs burgers at Max's or shoots hoops with our friends on the weekend, he's still very much one of *them*.

A *fae*.

*Volatile.*

*Other.*

I'm not sure how Lara deals with the notion that his true feral nature is always simmering away beneath his golden skin and charming set of dimples.

Whole body rigid, Raff stalks over and takes my hand. "Come, human. Let us be dutiful and do as her Majesty bids."

"My name's Isla. If you're gonna keep calling me *human*, then it only seems fair I call you *fae*," I snipe as we sweep down the steps together.

"To speak thusly to one of my kind on your first night in our land, you're either brave or very stupid."

Planting a hand on my hip, I pretend to consider his words. "Actually, Prince *Fae*, I think I'm a mixture of both. Mostly brave and only occasionally stupid."

In a surprising move, he laughs.

The tables have been rearranged around the edges of the hall, creating a large dance floor edged by green columns dripping with the kind of vines and flowers that have never appeared in any garden in Blackbrook.

Faeries stare at us in anticipation, and I goggle at the tattoo covering Raff's throat and upper chest, a spooky fire demon's skull-like face with glowing red eyes. Then my gaze lifts, fixing on the lush shape of his mouth.

Ever has a pouty upper lip, whereas Raff's mouth is sumptuous all over, the corners curving upward in adorable little arcs that are entrancingly kissable.

Ugh. What am I thinking?

Arms outstretched, he steps closer. "Come here, human, and we shall dance."

"You'll regret this. Believe me; it's pointless. The only dancing I can pull off is solo stuff...weird booty-shaking in front of the bedroom mirror kind of dancing."

Those sensual lips quirk. "After we have satisfied the Queen of Five, you may indulge in this *solo stuff*, as you call it, to your heart's content. I admit I wish to observe it."

Oh, yeah. I can picture myself busting my best funky bedroom moves for the entire Seelie court's amusement. Unless I drink a barrel-full of mulberry wine, that's so not going to happen.

The first notes from the fiddles lilt through the air, and Raff cuts me a quick bow. "You do not need to know the steps. Simply take off your shoes and hold on tightly. Before long, we will be flying."

Yikes! I hope he doesn't mean that literally.

This tall Prince of Fire is an arrogant ass, and his presence sucks all the oxygen from my lungs as I slip my heeled faery shoes off and then step into his arms. It's not difficult to move closer because I'm drawn to him like a moth to a flame. Stupid moths. Do they realize their mistake as the heat licks over their wings, catching fire as it consumes them?

A shiver runs down my spine as his palm presses into my back, radiating heat, and we begin to move. Raff was right about me not needing dancing skills; he has plenty enough for both of us. He guides me so smoothly I begin to think I've been doing this all my life. I can dance! Wheeeeeeeee!

My skirt whirls, wrapping around our legs while our gazes lock hard. We spin faster and faster as stars rush past the edges of my vision like we're whirling through the night sky. The music and chatter disappear, the rhythm of our breathing carrying us onward—faster, then faster still.

Sufficiently entertained, the queen applauds, and the court follows suit. Couples flow onto the floor, surrounding us, and within seconds it's a crush, my hair catching on rough horns and fragile wings as we twirl through a maze of bodies that somehow miraculously get out of our way a second before collision—a magical choreography.

I smile at Lara as she and Ever dance close by. Merri is perched on Ever's shoulders, giggling as she tries to catch the flowers produced by his air magic that float around them. It warms my heart to see them so happy. Lara waves back. Ever raises a silver eyebrow at his brother.

After some time—minutes, hours, I don't know which—Raff slows to a gentle rocking pace, allowing me to catch my breath again.

"Where's Spark, the mire fox I've heard so much about?"

"Thankfully, she's being cared for elsewhere. The little demon has wreaked havoc at past banquets, leaping on the Folk, licking their plates clean, then slapping their faces when there is no more food left. She has been banished from such occasions for three moon turns."

"Spark sounds like a true fiend. I look forward to meeting her and Ever's monstrous-sized dog too. Lara's told me lots of funny tales about them."

Lips curving into an almost-smile, he says, "You dance well, human."

"Don't you know that sarcasm is the lowest form of wit, *fae*?"

"Even so, we fae cannot lie, but bending the truth amuses us."

"So it seems."

"But just now, I vow I wasn't employing sarcasm. By the Elements, I swear you are as warm and bright as a candle flame in my arms—a pleasure to partner in any kind of dance."

"A compliment! How unexpected."

His grip tightens as we sway even more slowly, our feet barely moving while other couples continue to twirl like showers of glitter. We're the couple in the center of a snow globe, still and calm as the turbulent world shudders and shakes around us.

Closing his eyes, which is a welcome relief from their intensity, he lifts his face toward the glass ceiling. His hand squeezes mine until my bones ache, then suddenly, his scent changes from fresh pine to warm and smoky. He smells like a campfire!

Then he makes a long sighing sound and tiny sparks tumble from above, spiraling like fireflies. As they land on my skin, each sharp sting only makes me laugh. Raff watches my reaction to the fire shower he's made with great interest.

This feels dangerous, the way he's looking at me, the burning embers eddying around us like a tornado. It's madness. I know I should be frightened of him, but I'm not. I'm completely entranced by his magic.

*Fire magic*, my heart whispers. *He's using fire magic.* And it totally intoxicates me.

When a large ember starts smoking in my hair, he extinguishes it with a tiny flick of his hand. "Apologies. I nearly set you ablaze."

"Your powers don't scare me. I can handle fire no problem."

His pupils flare, a border of bright gold rimming them. "Say that again," he commands.

"You don't scare—"

"No. The part about fire."

"I said I know how to handle fire, so don't think you can intimidate me with your magic tricks."

He stares for an age into my eyes, then tosses his head back and laughs like a maniac. "At last I have realized who you are, little firefly."

"Sure you have. Do I remind you of a long-lost relative? Someone you slaughtered in a long-ago battle?"

Smiling, he ignores my jibe. "I would wager half the kingdom that you have an impressive tattoo somewhere on your body. Am I correct?"

"So what? In the human world, everyone is covered in tattoos. But I've only got one, and I love it so much. It's of a—"

"Firebird," he interrupts. "Rendered in shades of orange and purple, a rare phoenix rising from the ashes."

My mouth gapes open. "How did you... Did Lara tell you about it?"

"Ha! I knew it was so!" His golden gaze burns through me. "It *is* you! I can hardly believe I have you in my arms. 'Tis a miracle."

"What are you—"

"The reason I thought we'd met before is because you, little firefly, have long featured in my dreams, a girl covered in smoke and fire and ash. Your eyes as blue as the Lake of Spirits. Your smile more joyous than even the sun's rays."

What the freaking freak?

This prince guy is insane. He may be regal and imposing and beautiful, but he's a total nutjob.

"You, human, are my queen. My fated mate. The girl destined to halt the black poison crawling through my blood."

I laugh as the music quickens, and the couples whirl around us like spinning tops. This is one of those dreams when something beautiful, something magical wavers at the edges before dissolving into a nightmare, dark horror taking over.

"When we first began to dance," he says, his voice light, his face animated, "I felt peace, the ache of the poison settling into a steady, bearable hum. Since Ever left our land, I have been pleading with the Elements to hurry up and send you to me, but my appeals had gone unheard. Until now. And here you are in my arms—finally—the answer to every question, every problem."

Shaking my head, I drop his hand and step backward. "Can you hear yourself? You sound like a madman. I'm not your fated mate. I'm Lara's cousin. How could both of us, two girls from the same family, be the ones to still the poison of two fae princes. And brothers at that. It's dumb. You're only seeing what you want to be true, chasing shadows, that's all."

We're standing perfectly still at the center of a bad dream. I give myself a mental slap and look around the Great Hall, searching for an escape route. Musicians play faster than seems possible. The dancers' feet stomp so hard I fear the marble might crack beneath us, and the earth will open up and swallow us whole. Singers warble nonsensical lyrics—screeches, hoots, and howls.

This place is a madhouse. I'm insane for ever wanting to come here—to the Seelie Court. What was I thinking?

"You *are* the right girl." Raff's deep voice pulls me from my panic. "I've dreamed about you, and you bear the mark of my queen. Tomorrow, I shall speak to the High Mage and she will confirm it."

"Isn't your fated mate meant to wait for you under some kind of crystal oak tree?"

He shakes his head. "No. That was the direction Ever's air mage gave to find his mate. And it was interpreted incorrectly anyway. The branches of the Crystalline Oak were etched into Lara's back. The tattoo is the key. And you bear the correct one."

"What direction did the fire mage give you?"

"None. Wait and she will come was all Salamander would say. Lara told me you found my fire mage hiding in the human world—she refuses to come home—and she helped you through a portal. This is not a coincidence. Salamander sent you to me."

"Let's say for argument's sake that I am this fated mate you've been waiting for. What would you want from me?"

"As I said...*everything*. We must marry without delay and then—"

"Marry you? That's hilarious." I laugh while he stares solemnly, as though his words are reasonable and perfectly normal instead of demented. "You're serious? No way!" I point at my chest. "This girl here is waiting for true love. I'm gonna open a French bakery when I finish college, not marry some fae dude I don't even know just because you mistakenly believe it'll save you from a curse. That's not fair! What's in it for me?"

He gives me a charming smile. "It is no surprise that the future Queen of Fire is passionate and strong willed. This pleases me a great deal. I will change your mind, and you will marry me, Isla Delaney of Blackbrook. It is written. And so it shall be."

As outrage boils in my blood, he grips my fingers, bends at the waist, and presses his lips to the back of my hand, searing my skin with his kiss. He straightens and looms above me, his heated gaze sizzling into mine. "I thank the Elements for this day. It is a pleasure to finally meet you, human."

"Isla. My name is Isla."

"Yes, of course. Isla. I look forward to spending more time with you." Wearing a self-satisfied smirk, he bows and turns away.

"Cool your jets. I doubt that'll be happening." As the crowd parts for him, anger rolls through my gut. I clear my throat and yell, "And for your information, acting like an entitled ass and demanding marriage is a major turn off. I'm not interested in hanging out with you."

A few fae whip their heads my way, their expressions startled.

Prince Rafael stops walking, and I wait, watching his broad shoulders heave as I count.

One. Two. Three. Four.

Without turning, he flicks his hand behind him, and a scarlet cloud appears above me. Sparks burst from it, blue and soft as petals, falling down like rain. Fire masquerading as water. My skin buzzes with that dark thrill again, the one caused by *him*—Rafael, the Prince of Fire.

"He wasn't always like that," says Lara, tugging on my sleeve and scaring the crap out of me. "So intense and grumpy."

"Can you please not sneak up on me in your cute, quiet little faery slippers? It's been a heck of a night. My nerves are shot."

"Sorry. When I arrived in this city as Ever's prisoner, Raff was my first real friend. He was a certified hell raiser, but warm and funny and completely adorable. He was actually a lot of fun."

That's hard to believe. "And now he's the Black Blood heir; he's rude, conceited, and he's—"

"Incredibly good looking..."

"An incredibly good-looking jerk. And don't try and change my mind about him. I don't trust your motives because you obviously knew all about this loony stuff with my tattoo before you left home, didn't you?"

"Uh, yep. During our time here, Ever and I were planning to work out what to do about the crazy fact you're Raff's mate. It's been messing with our heads. Should we bring you here to meet him? Hide you away forever? You landing here out of the blue has solved the dilemma for us. You've set the wheels of fate in motion and there's no stopping them now."

"Oh, great. Glad to be helpful." I take her by the shoulders and draw her close so she can hear me over the noise. "Listen closely. You need to know that I'm not the least bit interested in any weird marriage of convenience. Remember, your situation with Ever was very different. You'd already fallen hard for him before you found out you were his chosen mate. Well, I want the chance to fall in love too. And I want to be loved. I won't settle for anything less. Rafael Fionbharr can shove his precious fated mate up his butt."

Lara smirks. "Better be careful what you wish for here in Faery, Isla. You wouldn't want that to actually come true now, would you?"

"Shut up," I say, biting back a laugh as I watch Raff bid his mother goodnight with a dramatic sweeping bow.

But she's right, I really, *really* wouldn't want that to happen. Because *I'm* that fated mate.

Apparently.

# 6

## A Proposal

### Raff

The human is avoiding me.

For three days, I've followed the court's whispered gossip throughout the castle and city grounds in the hopes of finding her, but to no avail. One morning I hear she's breakfasting with Lara on the iolite balcony—by the time I arrive, she is gone. Visiting the moss elves with Lara? The red willow is deserted when I arrive. Pruning fruit trees with Magret in the orchard on a sunny afternoon? Not when I reach the gardens.

It's beyond frustrating. I only wish to speak with her. To come to know her. How will I ever convince her she is to be my queen if she will not stop running from me?

At present, I stride alongside my brother through a sunlit glade, returning from a patrol in the Emerald Forest, uncomfortable and hot in my leather armor. Still, I laugh as my squealing mire fox scampers through the grass and pulls on Balor's shaggy, gray tail. Poor Balor. Spark can be an insufferable pest when the mood strikes her. Which is often.

Seven silver and gold birds swoop from the dark-green treetops to skim over our heads, Ever's órga falcons, screeching as they go. With a flick of my wrist, I cast a ring of fire into the sky which they fly through three times before disappearing behind clouds.

"I suppose Lara's cousin greatly admires the Emerald Castle," I say, careful to keep my gaze on a mass of golden birch leaves to my left.

I feel Ever study me. In the silence, I count four heartbeats, but still, he doesn't speak.

"Did you hear me?" I ask.

"Yes."

"I wonder which are her favorite places in the city?" I clear my throat. "It is fascinating to me how a mortal sees our world."

"Really?" Ever raises his brow.

Dana damn him. He simply cannot be baited. I suppose I must be more direct. "I also wonder which courtiers are working in the pear orchard this morning. They have a new design for—"

"And I wonder about your idiotic questions of late."

"What is wrong with what I asked? I take great interest in the gardens," I say, rubbing the throbbing pain beneath my chest plate.

Black blood crawls, hisses and snarls. Foulest of toxins always invading, corrupting, corrupting. What I would give to silence its whispers.

"Rubbish." Ever scoffs. "In the past, your main involvement in the gardens has been to roll about them with pretty fae while drinking copious amounts of wine made from their vines. But, of course, now that you are the heir, it's only natural each blade of grass in the kingdom is of the highest importance to you. That makes perfect sense." He shoves my shoulder, pushing me into a holly bush.

"I grow weary of your vague and ridiculous questions, Raff. Speak plainly. If you wish to know where Isla is, I am only too happy to tell you."

"*Isla?*" I say, paying great attention to tightening a buckle on my bracer as I prepare for the lashing of pain my next words will bring me. "I'm not troubled by *her* movements. It is of absolutely no interest to me where she—"

"—might search for opals?" Ever interrupts, grinning far too widely. "If you move with haste, Brother, you may still find her in the grotto looking for gemstones. *Alone* and perhaps even wishing for company."

I take a second to grin back before I begin to run, swinging Spark onto my shoulders without slowing my pace as Balor nips at my heels, and I sprint in the direction of Firestone Creek.

"Balor!" Ever's sharp whistle rings through the forest, frightening birds from their nests. "I wasn't speaking to *you*. You're certainly not needed in the grotto. Let us go find Lara and Merri instead—they will appreciate your gamboling and drooling considerably more than Isla will."

Before slipping into the trees, I turn back around. "You are wrong, Ever. I believe the human would much prefer Balor's company over mine."

I salute them, and then smash through the forest, leaping over giant logs, bounding over rocks and boulders, my sheathed sword battering the foliage. I'm desperate to shift into my phoenix. If I did so, I could be at the girl's side in moments.

I grit my teeth and tense every muscle, fighting the urge to change. The girl already distrusts me, and a light scent of fear perfumed her silky skin the night we danced, the night I realized, like a broad arrow shot between my ribs, exactly who she is. My foretold mate. A cure to the bleakness, the dark pain that lives inside me.

*She is mine.*

But given her reaction to me at our first meeting, I suspect seeing my wild, fiery creature today would hardly endear me to her.

Only several moons ago, I lived for tricks and laughs, the thrill of playing with fire and burning an entire chamber to ash simply because I could. But as the poison progresses through my blood, my love of fun deserts me. I was once a wholly frivolous creature. And now? Now I'm more monster than a Seelie prince of Faery.

Detached.

Capable of immense cruelty.

A true Black Blood heir.

Spark squawks as a branch knocks her off my shoulders onto the forest floor. White-hot rage flashes inside me. I run back and collect Spark from the ground, blasting the offending branch with a beam of fire. It explodes, ash showering the tree's scarred trunk and mossy roots—the dryad living inside it screeching in pain. Cursing, I keep moving, ignoring the hot wave of nausea that burns inside my gut.

These days, a wild and constant anger simmers beneath the surface of my skin, ready at the slightest provocation to break out and attack, whether violence is warranted or not. Most of the time, it's not. Lately, I disgust myself.

Before Ever left Faery and followed Lara to the human realm, he gave me a choice—if I didn't wish to become the heir, he'd stay and continue to bear the curse. At the time, I laughed and told him to hurry up and leave because, fool that I was, I thought it would be amusing to one day become king. I thought I was stronger than Ever, *brighter*, and that my light would defeat the evil of the curse, counteract the foul nature of the poison.

But alas, here I am—a prince who smites harmless tree spirits for the misfortune of being in my mire fox's way. Is this the action of a good and just future king? I think not. My fists clench as I pick up speed, reminding myself that my queen can reverse the effects of the poison. My mate is the key.

The land snakes slowly downward, and, finally, a pool of emerald is visible through the trees. Surrounded by vine-covered cliffs, the creek's surface is deceptively calm and mirror-still. Of all the terrible creatures that lurk beneath the water, kelpies are the worst, but thankfully this section is too shallow, and they cannot harm the girl who is sitting on the grassy banks. Undoubtedly, she'd make them a tasty treat. But they can only watch and yearn from a distance. Just as I am doing now.

There she is—Isla. My fiery future queen. Now, how to win her favor?

Dappled light casts curious patterns over her amber tunic and dark-colored leggings. They look wet, so she must have been fishing for stones, but why didn't she remove her clothes first? Perhaps humans always bathe covered in cloth and only show their skin to lovers or mates.

Fire sears my veins as I imagine being wedded to her. She's human, frail and plain compared to my own kind, therefore, my pulse should not be racing at the idea. But it has been a while since I've bothered to bed anyone. And there, right in front of my eyes, sits my mate. The girl whom the original curse bringer—Ever's air mage—chose to join me with forever. Given the situation, perhaps experiencing a small thrill is reasonable.

My heart pounding faster, I watch her profile as she uncrosses her legs and trails tanned fingers through the water, her expression peaceful. Spark sits forward on my shoulders, chirruping in my ear and strangling my neck in her impatience to be introduced. No doubt she wishes to leap upon the girl and shower her with kisses. Not a completely unappealing idea, I must admit.

"Alright," I tell Spark. "Wish me luck." I step forward, twigs and branches cracking underfoot, echoing off the walls of the grotto, the only other sound the constant drip of water.

"Human!" I call loudly.

She flinches and turns, a hard scowl twisting her features.

My heart booms harder.

Humans are nothing special, I remind myself. High fae possess staggering beauty, but mortals are merely pretty. Sweet, in the manner of kittens or baby goslings.

I stop beside her, my thoughts a muddle as I stare at her frowning blue eyes, brighter even than the sun-kissed water. What should I say?

If I could manage to do it without her noticing, I would roll my eyes at myself. There is no reason to second guess my every word when speaking to such an ordinary creature. I must simply part my lips and begin.

Taking a deep breath, I point at the stones in her lap. "You've found the fire opals you sought. You must have ventured deep into the creek to gather so many of—"

"Hey, my name is *Isla*. Or are you too thick to remember it? Calling me *human* all the time is insulting."

I take another quick breath, but she speaks before I can reply. "What do you want, Raff? I thought I made it quite clear the other night that fae princes aren't high on my list of people I want to hang with."

"How does one *hang* together? Do you mean the way draygonets roost upside down from tree branches?"

"Don't be ridiculous. You're such a... oh! You've got a thing on your... Is that Spark?"

Her crystal-blue eyes flare in excitement as she spies my mire fox peering around my head. Spark chatters and points at the mortal as if she's never seen one before. The girl smiles, and my bones melt like wildflower honey on hot bread.

*I am under your spell.*

I watch the way she studies Spark and hope fills my chest. My presence may not please the mortal, but she does seem to like pets. It has been my experience that people who love animals are usually kindhearted and treat all beings with fairness.

I crouch beside her, swiping hair from my eyes "I've brought Spark to meet you. Lara has said you enjoyed the tales of her escapades, and my mire fox loves nothing more than making new friends, especially human ones for some strange reason."

I drop my gaze to the ground, shaking my head. Why does everything I say to her sound like I wish to start an argument? Here is the girl who will change my life, and all I can do when in her presence is trip over my tongue like a boneheaded youth.

Discomfort rising, I cast around for a neutral topic. "Similar to a Dún mountain troll who hides in underground caverns, you are very difficult to find."

Daggers shoot from her eyes, and I sigh loudly. Once again, my words sounded like an insult.

"And I don't suppose it occurred to your conceited royal brain that the reason for that is because I actually don't want to be found?"

"But I have heard tales of your adventures these past days. You've enjoyed picnics with Lara and the moss elves, river frolics with Balor and Magret and other ladies of the court, you even attended a formal dinner with the tedious queen's council. You are not hiding from anyone."

"Yes, I am. I'm hiding from *you*."

"But, for what possible reason? I've told you; you are my mate and future queen. You've seen evidence of the curse in the story of

Lara and Ever, so why would you doubt it? And now your cousin is mortal-wed to my brother. When Mother dies, you and I will rule over this land together, then our children after us."

"Our cursed children?" She turns away, plucking grass from the banks in angry snatches. "You're crazy, Raff. Leave me alone."

Moving just a little closer, I say, "I have never been saner. Your presence brings a flame's clarity, hope of a brighter future."

She laughs, but it is not a happy sound.

"What is funny?"

"You are," she replies, her hair glinting like spun gold.

Folding my legs, I sit next to her so I can better admire its shine, my smile faltering as she inches away from me.

I lower my voice to beguile her, to charm but without magic. "We could marry alongside Ever and Lara when they take their fae vows at Merrin Creek. Or immediately after, if you'd prefer it. You only need say what you desire, and you shall have it; your wishes are my own."

"Well, then I wish for you to go away."

Spark flinches at the human's tone, then swings off my back into her lap and begins to inspect her gold locks. Isla giggles as they play a child's game, clapping their palms together in a complicated pattern, both of them pretending I do not exist.

In this moment, I am an outsider, and this is a new and unpleasant feeling. As their prince, everyone at court notices and welcomes me. No matter what I do. Scuffing my boot heel through tufts of grass, I consider my next move.

This human is stubborn and difficult. Never in my wildest imaginings did I guess that when I found my chosen mate, she would not want me. Doesn't everyone, human or fae, wish to rule over a kingdom? Perhaps Aer and Salamander were wrong about the phoenix tattoo she bears? Perhaps she is not the one.

She squeals in delight as Spark tickles her, and warmth spreads through my being. No—she's the one.

The proof is in my diminished pain, the gentler flow of blood through my veins, the burgeoning power of my fire magic, kindling once again.

For *her*.

I wait for her to look at me. When her eyes meet mine, shock ripples through my stomach. It's not their bright color that astonishes me, but the spirit shining through them. The banked power bubbling in their depths.

Closing my eyes, I quickly turn my head away, relaxing my senses, feeling the subtle shifts of energy emanating from her. Yes—this human has magic; I am sure of it.

*Isla is my queen.*

With renewed determination, I say, "Tomorrow, the entire court will begin a journey of nearly three days to reach the place of Ever and Lara's Faery wedding. I wager that some time before the ceremony, you will have changed your mind about me."

Eyes narrowing to slits of blue, her chest rises faster. "I won't."

I stand abruptly, pulling Spark into my arms. The mire fox screeches as though I tore her ear off. "Listen to me, Isla. The air mage saw your tattoo. I have been dreaming of you since Ever left Faery and the curse shifted to my blood. You are destined to be my queen. This has been foretold, and our mages are never wrong. I tell you it will come to pass."

"Right. So, is that an actual proposal? If so, it must be the worst one in history—fae or human. Who wants to marry a guy just because of a stupid prophecy?"

"But you would be queen of this land. Ruler of the Court of Five and all the Elemental Fae."

"So what? When and *if* I marry, it'll be for love and for no other reason. And as you feel compelled to keep reminding me, I'm human. So how could a mortal be queen of the Seelie fae anyway?"

"The first Black Blood prince's queen was mortal. Aer often chooses mortals as mates to punish the heirs. Gadriel and then Ever rejected her twisted affections; they are the reason she seeks to humiliate us by selecting mates who are beneath faekind."

She leaps to her feet, tucking the opals into her tunic's shallow pocket. "Is that how you see Lara and me? As embarrassments to your *royal* family?"

"No, I... Here, Isla, take this." I unhook a leather pouch from my sword belt. "You can keep your stones safe inside it."

"No thanks." She swipes my hand away, pushing past me.

My most treasured possession, the pouch my brother Rain made me before he died, crumples to the ground where she blindly stomps over it.

"Nice to meet you Spark. You're a real cutie. And, Raff—you're a total asshat."

My heart drops to my stomach. I whirl on my heels, tripping on my sword blade, and watch her stalk toward the trees. "Isla? What is an asshat?"

"Exactly what it sounds like."

I collapse back onto the grass and bury my face in my palms, shaking my hands out in front of me when flames lick my skin, singing my eyelashes once again.

When will I learn to control my temper?

Probably the day the poison ceases to move through my blood. And given how much Isla dislikes me, that means possibly never.

Dana be damned—curses are no fun at all.

# 7

## The Procession

### Isla

The night of the grotto encounter with the Prince of Fire, I skip dinner in the Great Hall, choosing instead to take my anger out on the glowing coals in my hearth by smashing them repeatedly with a fire poker. Juvenile, I know, but I'd rather sulk by myself than listen to anymore of Raff's unflattering demands that I agree to a stupid marriage of convenience.

The only person the marriage would be convenient for is him.

I give the coals another whack and sit back on the rug to stare at the flames. Shadows from the corners of the room creep toward me, and I hug my knees and suppress a shudder.

The opulent chamber is decorated with blue and gold murals of lithe-limbed fae dancing around red flames and skeletal tree branches. It sounds a little gruesome, but the effect is whimsical and uplifting, like paintings in old children's books about myths and fables.

Dark drapes hang over massive curved windows, currently hiding a majestic view of the sparkling black and green city. The floor is glittery-veined black marble. Ruby chandeliers drip like glowing flames from the ceiling. My bed, which could easily sleep six, is covered in lush fabrics and huge velvet cushions fit for a queen or three.

A few days ago, when Lara first threw open the carved doors to reveal my chambers, I squealed with joy. I'd never seen anything so magical and palatial. When I'm hanging out here, I feel like a princess in a fairy tale instead of a permanently exhausted student who waits tables to make ends meet, which is the point, I suppose, of her accommodating me here. To get me used to the idea of excessive beauty and luxury.

A log explodes, showering me with sparks, and I scoot backward, the hair on my arms standing on end as I wait to see what will happen next. This is magic—I smell it in the air, a bitter flavor on my tongue.

The crackling of the fire becomes a long hissing sound which somehow turns into words. "Silly girl," the flames say. "What reason have you to shiver and shake while you lie in luxury's bosom, a cosseted pet of the Elemental fae?"

About to spring onto my feet and race around the room in a panic, not a helpful activity, I force my muscles to relax, sucking in a long breath at the sight of Sally Salamande's red and green eyes peering at me from between the flames.

"What are you doing in the fire, Sally? Are you trying to scare me to death?"

She cackles like an evil witch. "There are untold ways to kill you, dear Isla, every one of them significantly more enjoyable than through fear alone. I came to ask how you are enjoying Faery. Is it as you expected it would be?"

"Much worse. Listen, you're freaking me out, your head floating without your body in the flames like that. What do you really want?"

"I would like to arrange the meeting with the man we spoke of when we made our bargain. The one you must listen to."

I grimace. "Yuck. I'm so over arrogant men right now. Can't I meet with a nice faery girl instead?"

A scarlet eyebrow rises, her lips pursing. "No, you cannot. When the wedding procession nears Merrin Creek, you must listen carefully. A bronze bird will call to you from the treetops: three pips and a long caw, sung three times over. You will follow it and meet the green-haired male as you promised."

*Did* I promise? I agreed to hear someone out, but I can't remember if it was part of the actual vow I made. She can't lie, so I must have, and I keep my promises. So I guess that means I'll be rendezvousing with mister green hair, whoever he is. "Fine. Is this guy the curse-breaker I'm not meant to tell anyone about?"

Blue and orange flames whip out from the hearth, flickering against my face. They warm my skin but don't cause any pain.

"This man is not important, but he will lead you to one who knows words, long hidden, that are of utmost significance. Prick your ears when you hear them, human, for they will foretell of a future in which the curse is no more."

What. The. Living. Hell?

"Okay, great tip," I say, my voice laced with sarcasm. Why can't fae just speak plainly? "Lara advised me to arrange an audience with Ether, the High Mage, but whenever I knock on her door, there's no answer. I'm starting to believe she doesn't exist."

Sally spits into the flames. "Pfft. Do not trouble yourself with my sister. She's too grand to bother with your troubles."

"Lara paints a different picture of her, and she helped Ever—"

"*Rafael* is the fire prince. His magic is connected to mine, which makes him *my* problem. Do not speak to Ether or you will put the entire kingdom, including your cousin's charming young daughter, at risk. You must sleep now. You will need your strength for tomorrow's journey. Fae wedding processions are akin to a Wild Hunt and often a trial for humans to endure."

Her scarlet locks twist and writhe as her palm shoots out, fingers snapping in front of my nose. Instantly, my eyes shut, muscles melting as I crumple over the black furs piled in front of the fireplace.

I fall into a restless sleep, plagued by dreams of smoldering gold eyes and a red-furred mire fox who screeches and points at me while pulling my hair.

When my maid, a sweet-faced fae called Fairwyn, wakes me at dawn, I've got a pounding headache, and I shrink from the light streaming through the open curtains like a vampire dumped in the desert.

Grumbling, I untangle myself from the hearth's furs and stumble up to prepare for three days' travel with the Emerald Court, still thinking about Sally's comment about processions and Wild Hunts.

Did that actually happen last night? Was she even real or am I going mad?

I wash quickly in an ornate copper bathtub and then dress in soft leggings and a finely embroidered gold tunic with capped sleeves made of long red and orange feathers that dance like flames every time I move. The outfit would look great on a Babylonian priestess, but Fairwyn refers to it as *plain travel clothes*, massively undermining its appeal.

With graceful movements, she packs a leather satchel, side-eying me as I inch toward the door, preparing to escape.

"Whatever you're thinking, it's okay to say it," I tell her.

"And wherever you're going, Miss Isla, please do not be long. Remember, you cannot speak with Princess Lara this morning because she and the prince are meeting Queen Varenus in her chambers."

I laugh, and she gives me the evil eye. "Sorry. I'm still getting used to Lara and the princess thing."

Hiding a grin, she busies herself making the bed. "The court will gather outside the main gates at noon. As soon as you arrive there you must find Princess Lara's guard, Orlinda, and she will show you to your carriage. Your belongings will be waiting for you."

"Thank you." I give her a friendly salute before following the intricate web of servants' staircases all the way down to the enormous kitchen, a mixture of excitement and unease churning in my belly.

I bustle past the staff busy assembling travel baskets of food and sweet talk the head cook, a very hairy hobgoblin, into letting me bake a couple of batches of pistachio nut cookies. When life gets weird, bake. That's my motto. And I know the delicious treats will lift my spirits no matter what happens out on the road today.

Trouble is, when I start creaming the butter and sugar, sifting in flour, and mixing and shaping, I'm not feeling my usual baking bliss. Instead, a terrible homesickness overtakes me. I'm filled with longing to see my mom, our bright apartment, and the kitchen that houses my one prized possession—a beautiful commercial-grade oven. Just picturing its shiny beveled edges and sleek surfaces makes me cry. Oh, Beryl, I miss you so much.

And, yes, my oven has a name. Nothing wrong with that.

After I wrap the buttery, cardamom-scented cookies in waxed cloth, I make my way through mostly deserted streets under the shadows of the castle's green turrets, the buzz of a chattering crowd and the intermittent scrape of cart wheels against paving stones growing louder as I approach the city's main entrance.

Out front of the carved jade gates sits a platform woven from brambles and decorated with roses, and on it stand Lara and Ever, both looking regal in gold and silver finery, the Elemental court surrounding them. The air smells of cinnamon and freshly baked bread, making my mouth water.

Standing on my tiptoes, I peer around wings and horns and the elaborate, multi-colored hairstyles that are all the rage at court toward a golden bridge at the end of the plaza. It stretches from the city's black-cliffed mountaintop rising in a high arc over gushing waterfalls to the other side of Terra River where it leads onto wide green plains, a dark mountain range shining in the distance.

According to Lara, beyond the mountain range lies the famous Lowlands through which we'll travel before following Fire River to our destiny—Merrin Creek, the place where Balor found her unconscious and Ever thought he'd caught a troll. What a romantic meeting! A great story to bore the grandchildren with, that's for sure.

I have no idea why they want to suffer nearly three days on the road to legitimize their Faery marriage at the very place Ever took her captive. To me, it seems weird.

But as I picture him back at Max's diner, broad shoulders straining his band t-shirt as he helped Lara fry burgers, I remind myself that he's not a typical fae prince. He's unpredictable and irrational and a complete fool for love—I shouldn't be surprised by anything he does, really.

For me, the trip will be an adventure, a chance to explore the wonderful land of Faery. Living with the fae these past few days has been a mind-blowing experience, but on the whole, instead of being monstrous, they've been reasonably civil, no extreme revelries or gruesome cruelties to mention.

And maybe that's because this is the Seelie court, not the dark one, and I'm related by marriage to one of their precious princes. I feel safe with them, but I hope they don't change into heinous beasts with a taste for murder and mayhem and the flesh of human girls while they're roaming about the wild forests.

Back on the dais, Jinn stands patiently beside Ever, his black mane braided with flowers and gemstones, shining coat draped in silver chains strung with bells and charms that tinkle when he moves. Merri is off to the side, snuggled in Magret's arms, playing with the fae's impressive antlers.

All around the grand courtyard people bustle, loading supplies into the horses' packs, fine carriages, and carts. Amid shouts and laughter, baskets and parcels materialize above our heads, rotating through the air from one side of the assembly to the other. Wow. That's cool. Magic makes packing a breeze.

After a time, the crowd stills and Ever raises his hand, silencing the chatter. "Many moons ago a black-hearted hunter sought his prey in the silent forest. Expecting to find only tedium and boredom, he stumbled upon the brightest, most precious gift the Elements could bestow—a kindred heart, the truest companion, a love mightier than storms and fiercer than lightning. With every beat of my free heart, I thank Dana for giving me Lara Delaney and my daughter, Merrin Airgetlám Fionbharr. Today my human bride and I will walk the path of our courtship in reverse. When we take our first step back in the direction of the Emerald Keep, she will be a true princess of the fae, honored and protected in the Land of Five and the seven realms beyond."

The crowd applauds.

Ever takes Lara's hand and presses his lips against her tear-bright cheeks.

She smiles, entwining their fingers together, then faces the court. "My deepest thanks to the Elemental Court for walking alongside us on our wedding procession. I wish each one of you equal joy to ours—for there is no greater magic than love. Blessed be the Five Elements that unite our land in peace and the mages who connect our people's power to the source." She sweeps her arms wide, gesturing toward the mages who stand by the bridge. All three incline their heads.

The High Mage, Ether, wears silver robes that shine bright as a winter sun, a halo of white cotton-candy hair framing her angular face. Beside her, the earth mage, Terra, grins widely, the black and purple crystals on her dark gown glinting in the light. Opposite them, Undine stands solemn-faced, her blue hair rippling with her iridescent robes.

Raff's fire mage, Salamander, is suspiciously absent. According to Lara, she hasn't been seen in Faery for at least a moon's turn, which means roughly a month. So what exactly is she up to, appearing in my hearth last night while she's hiding from everyone else?

Thankfully, Aer, the most dangerous of the mages and the cause of Ever and Lara's recent trouble, isn't here either. She's imprisoned in the forest and safely guarded by the moss elves, which is comforting to know. I have no desire to meet the original Black Blood curse-maker in the flesh. By all accounts, she's as sour as unsweetened lemonade mixed with strychnine and about as pleasant as a shark attack. I don't think anyone's missing her terribly.

"Dear Prince and Princess," says Ether, raising her palms skyward, "may each step you take together be as light as the eastern breeze and may your sorrows be mere shadows that fade swiftly in the light of love. Blessed be the Five that weaves through the realms and binds all matter together." She bows toward the dais. "Prince of Air, Everend Calidore Fionbharr and the mortal Lara Delaney, with the blessing of feathers, let your wedding procession begin."

The High Mage blows a kiss in their direction, and a flock of starlings appears and circles around Ever and Lara's crowns of twisted silver and garnet gemstones, the birds' glossy black feathers shot with iridescent purple and green, tumbling over them.

High above the proceedings, silver and gold órga falcons eddy through blue skies, their screeches long and shrill. Holding hands, Lara and Ever laugh as they watch the falcons play.

A raucous cheer rises over the roar of the waterfalls as the colorful parade of fae pours past the mages onto the bridge—some on foot, some astride prancing ponies or leaning out open carriages to share jokes and tease each other, the supply carts rolling through last. It's incredibly noisy and chaotic, and I can't help being swept up in the festive atmosphere.

Stepping deeper into the moving cavalcade, I glance around. I need to find my ride before I get left behind. But instead of looking for Orlinda, I search the strange and beautiful fae faces for the white queen and a certain tall prince who's usually dressed in red and black with a golden sunstone glinting at his brow. Surprisingly, neither the queen nor her heir apparent appear to be present.

My stomach twists, and I sigh in relief. It's a good thing Raff isn't here. If I had a choice, I'd rather not endure his arrogance for three whole days of travel. It's great he's not coming.

Although, he would definitely improve the scenery. I wouldn't mind ogling him from a safe distance whenever I get bored along the way. I groan. I should slap myself. *No gawking at Prince Rafael, Isla.* He's unsafe and nothing like the guys from home. In fact, he's not even a *guy.* He's a supernatural *faery.* Best not to forget that. Ever.

Finally, I notice a slate-blue arm directing traffic near a fancy horse-drawn carriage. The arm is attached to the body of Lara's personal guard and friend, Orlinda. As if sensing my gaze on her, she glances up and waves me over. I push through the ever-flowing stream of fae until I reach her.

"Good morning, Lady Isla of Blackbrook," she says, smiling as she bows. "Are you ready to begin the journey?"

I squint up at her broad face, the rows of silver piercings flowing from her lobes to the sharp tips of her ears. "Please don't call me that. My name's Isla," I say, grinning back at her.

She tosses a blonde braid over her armored shoulder then adjusts the strap and sheath that secures the huge sword across her back. "If you insist, *Isla.* You seem very much like your cousin, Princess Lara, which means, before long, we shall be friends."

"I bet there's no flipping way she lets you call her *princess.*"

"True. She does not." Orlinda nods at a beautiful horse-drawn carriage. "Your transport awaits, *Isla.*"

The vehicle's bronze-colored roof is folded back, open to the clear blue sky. Delicately painted sunflowers with bright-green stems and petals swirl over deep-red side panels, the effect striking and whimsical. Well, this is a little different than the grimy, uncomfortable, beige-colored trains and buses I'm used to traveling on between school, Max's diner, and my apartment.

Things are looking up.

"Not too shabby," I say, as Orlinda swings opens the scarlet door, beckoning me up the steps.

The plush cushions sigh as I drop my head back and gaze at the glowing orb in the sky, its soothing rays warming my skin. In Faery the sun is different, its light more silvery as if it's shining through a veil of water. It's softer, more magical, and makes me feel sleepy. My eyelids grow heavy, and I struggle to keep them from closing.

This isn't right. It's only midday. Sure, I slept badly last night—thanks to Sally—but I'm a student and I'm used to operating on minimum shuteye. Shaking my head, I lurch up and grab Orlinda's leather bracer. "Hey, did you just use magic to try to make me fall asleep?"

Orlinda's lips quirk. "No. It is the sun in this realm. If you stop staring at it, your alertness will soon return."

With an amused snort, she shuts the door and braces her hands on the sides of the carriage. "The horses leading your wagon, Bran and Brindle, are intelligent creatures. If you need to stop, simply ask and they will obey. Be warned that while on procession, we fae love to socialize and frequently swap horses and carriages. You will no doubt have many visitors, some more pleasant than others. Should you wish the freedom of riding in the saddle, simply ask anyone, and your request will be granted."

"You won't be riding with me?" I ask. She's a fearsome looking gal, handy to have around in case the faeries flip out and decide to eat me for dinner one night.

She flicks her head toward the dais where Magret is mounting a dappled gray horse, baby Merrin already seated in a special carrier at the front of the saddle. "I shall stay close to your family. High fae have powerful magic, especially the princes, as long as the curse does not hold them too tightly in its grip. Still, there are many creatures in the lands we will travel through who aren't fond of human princesses and may have plans to harm your cousin and her child. I must protect them. And you must take care as well. Trust no one."

"So, I don't get a guard?" I'd prefer not to have one—it leaves me freer to explore—but I'm interested in why I don't.

"Do not worry, every single Elemental fae is watching you."

That's not exactly comforting news.

In the square below the dais, Ever lifts Lara, placing her on Jinn's saddle before mounting behind her. They whisper and laugh like a couple on their first date heading out on a picnic. Magret and Merri's horse trots past me, and Jinn, with Balor at his heels, follows close behind.

Ever pulls Jinn up beside my carriage, his silver gaze sparkling with mischief. "Cousin Isla," he says, "You're looking well, dressed in proper clothes, and for once not covered in flour. I hardly dare say it, but you almost look fae. How did you manage to hold your tongue long enough to submit to grooming?"

"Oh, be quiet. Just because you're a big deal here doesn't mean I've forgotten how you looked cleaning toilets at Max's joint. Want me to tell that story to Lord Ephron? I suspect your army's supreme commander would find that tale rather difficult to believe, given how pompous I've heard he is."

Mercury swirls in his silver eyes, and he laughs with genuine pleasure. "Enjoy your ride, and please don't lean too far out of the carriage. If you fall out, you are on your own. We never turn back to collect stragglers while on procession."

Lara swivels in the saddle and smacks his head. He laughs.

"Don't frighten her, Ever. You're a beast sometimes."

He laughs louder.

"It's okay, Lara," I say. "He can't help it. It's hard for people who only pretend to be civilized to be nice all the time, isn't it, Ever?"

"As they say, Isla, it takes one to know one." He flicks his fingers toward me, and a gust of wind blows my hair straight up in the air, then it tumbles down, wrapping around my face.

Lara rolls her eyes as I attempt to bring order to my hair. "I've forgotten how intolerable you and Ever are together."

"We love each other really," I say. "But we also enjoy pretending we don't."

She sighs. "Arggh. You are both so similar. But seriously, Isla, take a good look at the members of the court." She gestures to the parade of fae streaming past us. "Please be careful these next few days. I won't be able to keep an eye on you like I can at the castle. The one thing, *the* single most important thing I want you to remember is to not strike a bargain with anyone, even if they promise to make you the most famous baker who'll ever live in the entire seven realms."

It's my turn to roll my eyes skyward. "Jeez—for the love of butter! I'm aware already. You've told me this like a trillion times."

Her green eyes narrow. "Promise me."

"Okay." Crossing my fingers beneath the hem of my tunic, I meet her stony gaze. "I promise I won't make any bargains with creepy fae dudes," I lie.

She pinches my wrist. "Or fae ladies. Or pookas. Or anyone."

"Yes. All of those. I promise." I don't even know what a pooka is—nor do I care. "Do I look like I'm an idiot?"

"Yes. Sometimes. I'll see you at camp tonight. Be good." She bends and drops a kiss on my cheek, then Ever pinches it.

Jinn saunters onto the bridge, his tail swishing in time to Lara's singing. Somehow, her clear, high voice makes The Gypsy Rover sound both jaunty and sinister. A warning, instead of a ballad about star-crossed lovers.

"Since it's their wedding procession, shouldn't they be leading the parade?" I ask Orlinda.

The muscular fae bobs down to test the attachment of the long shaft that connects the horses to the carriage. "They'll slowly make their way from the rear of the parade to the head, spending time with all members of the court as they travel."

She leaps with ease onto her huge gray warhorse. "If you need me, Isla, just call my name. I have air magic and hear every whisper."

God, she sounds like Ever.

*I hear you. Every whisper is mine*—he was fond of telling Lara and me whenever we gossiped about him in the human world, which with his near constant faery shenanigans, was frequently.

For example, his favorite trick was to tangle Mom's hair into elflocks so she'd wake and find it fashioned into shapes of various animals, similar to topiary bushes. The giraffe was the most hilarious.

And one week he created an Armani business suit glamor that only Mom could see and walked around the apartment talking about business meetings with the Brazilian government while he was actually bare-chested and dressed only in jeans, making Lara and me choke on our laughter. Poor Mom.

Once a faery always a faery, I guess. Turns out they're really hard to house train.

"Enjoy your trip, Lady Isla," Orlinda says, wheeling her horse around. "When the road rises to meet you, may it always be the path you deserve."

"Pardon?"

Grinning wickedly, she whistles sharply and trots away, her wheat-colored braid whipping the air behind her.

My horses burst into action, and the carriage rolls along the golden bridge, leaving behind the castle's glittering emerald spires and the jagged black mountain it's sprawled upon.

In a loose formation, the strange procession bumps over the wide green plain that stretches east to west as far as the eye can see. When we reach the Dún Mountain range, we follow a narrow pathway through the Valley of Light, which flows between the mountains' spectacular jet cliffs.

Ever's falcons soar high above, and music from pan pipes and weird-shaped stringed instruments travel on the light, warm breeze. It's quite heavenly lying back on my luxurious cushions as I absorb the beauty of the land.

The day goes on at a gentle, rambling pace, and other than engaging me in a few friendly chats, most of the fae leave me alone, free to enjoy the scenery. The deep-blue skies and startlingly green grasses of the Lowlands are beautiful, but when we leave the banks of the muddy River Terra and enter the lush forest of the northern side of Mount Cúig, my mouth gapes in wonder.

As we climb uphill, the tall pines groan, a magical path appearing between their branches. Unimaginable beings peek through the silvery foliage, some hovering in the air above us and showering the procession with rainbow-colored petals, their translucent wings a whirring hum as they flutter past.

I let my horses dawdle, preferring to linger at the back of the parade so I can enjoy the spectacle of the magically parting trees for longer.

Out of nowhere, hoofbeats drum the earth in a steady rhythm, the sound coming from behind me and growing closer every second. I'm about to turn around and see who's in such a hurry to catch up with us when three purple-winged sylphs with luminous bodies swoop down and hang off the side of my carriage.

Instantly, my horses stop.

"Isla. Isla," they chant, their heads nodding solemnly and cold voices echoing through the forest. "Take the chosen for a bride, and the poison ceases deep inside."

Ugh. That's part of the curse they're chanting, trying to freak me out, I suppose. "What are you talking about?" I ask, forcing steel into my voice, refusing to let them know their efforts to scare me are working. "You're not making any sense."

Three sets of obsidian eyes narrow as they lean closer and drone on and on in dry, papery whispers. "If by another's hand the chosen dies, then before their blood fully weeps and dries, black will fade to gray, gray to—"

"*Téigh anois*," growls a voice at my side, prickling the hairs on the back of my neck. "Be gone."

I whip my head up and see Raff seated on Flame. Spark rides his shoulders looking proud of herself in fancy red and black mini-armor, pretty amber earrings hanging from her ears.

The sylphs disperse into the air, screeching like bats as they go.

"Hello, Raff," I say, running my gaze over his armor-clad body. "What are you doing here?"

"Protecting you." His golden gaze meets mine, a half-smile on his lips. "In this land, sylphs bite humans and suck away their life force, especially pretty ones. They'd love a tasty morsel like you."

Did he just call me pretty? If so, I'm officially shocked.

"And take care not to listen to a word they say. They're ill-informed, spiteful beings."

"So they can lie, then?"

"Well...no. But they adore causing trouble for almost everyone except Ever. They are creatures of air, and they delight in meddling where they don't belong."

"Well, we were only having a chat. You know, you surprise me. Lara always said you were the fun brother. Funny even. But you come across as nothing but an arrogant grump."

Anger flashes over his handsome features as he flicks Flame into a walk, my horses following suit. He rides close beside me. "I was different before the curse took hold. Since then, I have changed."

"It's a shame. The way you were before...we might have gotten along. I thought you weren't coming on the procession. Rumor has it that you were planning to fly in for the ceremony at the last moment in the form a giant squirrel."

Dark eyebrows dive low. "My creature is not a *squirrel*. It's a phoenix—an elegant firebird."

"Really?" I say, quashing a flicker of admiration. I'd really love to see his phoenix. Huh. Why does that sound crude somehow? "I was sure you'd turn into some kind of magical rodent."

"Very funny."

I have no clue why he's decided to ride alongside me. Wearing a sulky expression, he doesn't look very happy. Long, tawny hair flows over the black and red armor, molding lovingly to his well-formed warrior's body. Spark pats his shoulder as though consoling him, and his white horse, Flame, prances along gaily enough. I'm glad to see at least one of his party is pleased to be joining the procession.

Gaze scanning the nearby trees, his frown deepens, and I begin to feel a little sorry for him. It can't be easy being a cursed prince. "Well, to be honest, the rumor I heard was that you'd be flying in on some great bird thing, not a squirrel. I didn't realize it was a phoenix."

"I won't be riding one; I *am* the phoenix." He smirks and leans closer, the saddle creaking as he shifts his weight. "So you've been inquiring about me?"

"Nope. For some reason, the courtiers seem to enjoy talking about their Prince of Fire and divulge all sorts of unwanted information to me, like you riding the bird thingy."

"You lie. I see it clearly. Each time you do so, your eyes give you away. Did you not hear me properly? I do not ride an impressive bird. I *become* one."

"So what?"

"So what? I am an Elemental fae and can shift into a magnificent creature. What can you do, foolish girl, that I cannot?"

"As you said—I can *lie*."

The lovely angles of his face sharpen with anger. "Then, since it is so hard for you to tell the truth, I challenge you to do so now. Say one thing that is true. Can you do it?"

"What will you give me if I do?"

Dark eyebrows lift, then he laughs, a warm and comforting sound. "So, you wish to *sell* me your truth?"

"It wouldn't be a sale. More like a present—for which I'll receive something in return."

"Once you put a price on something, small or large, or expect anything in return, it is no longer a gift."

"Maybe, but a person's truth is precious, and if you want mine, you'll have to take a risk. You'll owe me a favor, which could turn out to be anything because I'm not setting a time limit on it. It could be weeks until I call the favor in. In the meantime, you'll just have to wait and wonder."

He twists the garnet ring on his finger. "And what might you want from me?"

"Perhaps that ring you're always fiddling with."

He frowns down at the band glowing brightly in the green-tinged light.

"Or I might like to take Spark out for a day of fun, and we'll ramble around the forest together."

Spark shrieks in excitement, bouncing on her master's broad shoulders, making Flame whinny in protest.

"Or maybe I'll ask you to fetch me wine from the kitchen in the middle of the night and treat you like a servant."

His pillowy lips part as my gaze lifts to them.

"Or I might request a kiss...just one, so I can die knowing what it's like to make a fae prince squirm."

"Alright," he says abruptly. "It is a bargain. Tell me one truth, and I shall give you whatever you want, at whatever time you wish to receive it."

A surprised laugh bursts out of me, and Raff smiles broadly—a glimpse of the warm young man Lara spoke so fondly of. My heart stutters, responding to his happy expression. I wish he wouldn't look at me like that.

I give him my hand to shake, and he clasps it, heat rushing up my arm.

"The bargain is set. Now pay me what you promised," he orders.

"Okay, one single truth is yours. Or maybe two if you're lucky. Are you ready to hear it?"

The muscles of his throat ripple. "Yes."

I steady my breathing. My next words will no doubt reinstate his permanent scowl. "Okay. Here goes... I will never marry you, Rafael. Not for promised riches or glories, not for the sake of any curse, and not even if it would save five freaking fae kingdoms. I don't want you to mention this fated-mate-thing in my presence ever again. Do you understand?"

His eyes burn fiercely, like he'd love nothing more than to reach out and strangle me. But he says not a word.

Growing uncomfortable with the silence, I say, "That's the truth you wanted. And now you've heard it."

I've witnessed Ever's anger many times—the darkening light, the sky shaking and trembling, a prelude to the crash of thunder which always follows. But *this*... Raff's fury is different, hot and wild, it rushes through the air scorching my skin. I smell burning embers. Destruction. Devastation. And a tiny part of me regrets mocking him. But only a little.

"Be careful what you wish for, human. One day you may find yourself begging for that kiss—"

"Which I'll be sure to receive if I ever happen to decide I want it. You struck a bargain and *promised* to give it to me."

"So now you're arguing to secure it? Interesting. One moment you're vowing you will never ever have me. The next you're demanding I surrender my lips the moment you desire them. Make up your mind, fickle human, my time need not be squandered on insignificant prattle."

"Fine. What are you doing hanging around, then? Go!"

"I will. When I'm good and ready."

I snort loudly. "You're ridiculous."

"No, you are the one who is—"

"Just *leave*."

"Yah!" he yells, dark hair flying out behind him as Flame rears onto his hind legs and then gallops away.

Three beautiful fae girls ride past on a green and gold striped horse, their limbs tangling together as they whisper and point at me. I fling them a middle-finger salute and stretch back in the carriage, folding my hands behind my head, hoping I appear unruffled by them.

I glance over my shoulder and watch the trees close their branches over the path behind me and begin to wish I wasn't at the very end of the procession.

"Do not worry, tiny yellow-haired relation of Prince Everend," calls one of the three snickering fae on the horse ahead of me. "We are nearly at the top of Mount Cúig where we shall camp for the night. If you remain quiet, you won't attract the deevs attention, and you should make it there in one piece."

Laughter cackles from their gaping mouths, making anger sizzle down to my fingertips.

I blow the fae kisses, and sparks sail through the air, starkly visible against the purple dusk. Wow, that's pretty. What were they—fireflies maybe? I blow on my palm again and, this time, nothing happens. Weird.

Shrugging to myself, I say, "Giddy-up, Bran and Bramble. Let's move to the front."

They neigh softly, and the trees separate, the path broadening as my carriage bounces past pretty wagons and horses, and even prettier fae.

If this was a race, I'd be winning it. Because there's no way I'm going to let the deevs get me.

# 8

## Fire

### Raff

"Prince Raff, what in Dana's name are you up to?"

Damn. The rough voice behind me is nauseatingly familiar. I let go of the gooseberry bush and it springs back, a thorny branch lashing my face. "Son of a draygonet!"

Rubbing my smarting eye, I glance up, wishing it were anyone other than Kian who had discovered me.

A tiny pair of bat wings—a recent edition to his pompous appearance—rasp loudly as they unfurl above his shoulders, looking more than a little ridiculous.

His bright-blue eyes glare at me as I fight a grin, laughter bubbling in my chest. He stares down his pompous nose as though *he* is the one with royal fae blood, the shriveled wings fluttering like a young pixie's. If Kian Leondearg could see himself at this moment, he would be appalled. For him, appearance is everything.

"Nothing terribly exciting. I am searching for berries for Spark," I say, omitting key details concerning this morning's quest as I point at my mire fox on my shoulders.

He sniffs and elbows me aside, his bejeweled fingers parting the gooseberry branches. Then he peers through the gap into the clearing, just as he found me doing only moments before. "I see. That is quite an interesting view."

My anger burns, a fierce, almost uncontrollable urge to set his hair alight. But alas, I cannot hurt him because this is Kian—my oldest, most despicable friend. The friend who my brother Rain begged me to take care of as he died in my arms. So, in honor of Rain's memory, I must suffer the insufferable—Kian's constant jealousy and petty meddling.

"Move over. Let me see," I say, hustling in the space beside him.

In the clearing, the mortal girl sits cross-legged inside a circle of blue-capped mushrooms. Does she not realize that elf rings are dangerous in Faery too?

"How did you manage to pass a lie through your lips?" snarls Kian. "You were most definitely *not* seeking gooseberries for Spark. You were seeking a human for *yourself*."

I mold my expression into one of great offense and pull a pitiful collection of berries from my pocket, passing them to my mire fox. With one hand, Spark stuffs them in her mouth, and with the other, she slaps Kian's head.

Cornflower eyes simmering with rage, his cheeks turn the same color as his hair.

"Control your wicked little ape or I will do it for you."

Spark screeches, the sound nearly bursting my eardrums. "You will do no such thing. If you touch her, I shall consider it a declaration of war. Is that what you wish, to be at war with your prince?"

Expression contrite, he laughs and pats my shoulder. "Of course not, old friend. I merely jest with you." Wisely, he draws me around to peer through the shrubs again, distracting me with locks of gold tumbling around the lithe shoulders of a perplexing girl. "Look, Raff. What do you think the little human is doing?"

A tiny fire kindles on the ground in front of her, wisps of smoke curling through her fingers. "I believe she's playing with fire."

His gaze shoots to mine. "Oh, ho! How appealing you must find this remarkable vision. But you must calm yourself, for that girl is not the fated mate you seek."

"And when did you become an expert in such matters?"

"Every Elemental in the kingdom knows it would be preposterous to have a human queen. We would be the laughingstock of all the lands."

"You forget that the first Black Blood heir's mate was human, and Queen Holly was much admired throughout the realms. Their reign was one of long-lasting peace."

He shakes his head. "It seems you are as foolish as your brother, Everend, is."

No. Kian is the foolish one. Does he want me to fry him alive? For that is what he is risking with his insolence. I compress my lips to seal in the rage. "If you are as fond of your well-coiffured locks as I think you are, I suggest you leave me in peace."

"As you wish." He shrugs and begins to turn away, but because he must always try for the last word, he glances back over his shoulder to give a parting jibe. "I shall leave you to spy on the girl to your heart's content, but be quick about it, or you may find yourself left behind. The procession departs after breakfast."

"I am not *spying* on her. I need to speak with her, that is all."

"Call it what you will. At last night's revel, your spellbound gaze did not leave the human once. She sat frozen, desperate to close her eyes and cover her ears. And I watched your face, read your thoughts, your longing to soothe her. I saw you. Can you deny this?"

Each slow breath I take is painful, hot as a desert wind. I want to deny the accusation. I *need* to deny it. Shaking my head, I open my mouth. Words will not form because what Kian says is the truth. I watched the girl all night. I longed to go to her.

Bitter triumph alights in his eyes. "Then it is precisely as I thought. Please try to remember that humans are stupid animals. They respond best to a firm hand rather than being cosseted and coddled."

"As do you," I reply, lifting my chin in challenge.

Nostrils flaring, he bows, which causes his wings to spread out behind him like angled sails.

Delivering my own parting blow, I say, "I am much amused by your new appendages and note they suit you perfectly."

"Then pay your compliments to your brother, for they are his design." With a sneer, he spins on his heels and hurries through the forest, heading in the direction of the main camp.

*Humans respond best to a firm hand*, I think, grimly. Kian obviously hasn't spent much time with this particular girl. *She* responds best to nothing and to no one! But, still, it is inconceivable that anyone would wish to harm her or attempt to subdue her magnificent, spirited nature. Wild and beautiful, fire cannot be tamed.

As obnoxious as Kian is, it irks me no end that he witnessed my behavior last night, the way I watched as she sat on her hands and tried not to run screaming from the rituals taking place at the Lake of Spirits.

Fae and all manner of unnatural creatures writhed together. Gods took human shape to join with whoever or whatever would have them. Beings in their animal forms, coupled with abandon. Bonfire flames and sparks leapt for the stars as the entire court replenished their magic at the source—naked in the moonlight, bathing in the glowing waters of the Lake of Spirits.

But I sat white-knuckled, rebuffing each invitation to join the debauchery, while telling myself not to go to Isla. To leave her be, to not browbeat and cajole, and repeat the fated-mate story until I wore her down and she accepted her role in it.

Last night the poison begged me to approach her, to take what is mine. To claim. To own. *It is your right*, it chanted. But I did not listen, for I am not a monster.

Not yet. Not yet.

As I watch her now in clearing, the same dark feeling tugs at my chest, an invisible cord running from my heart to hers, pulling me forward. Under a spell, I push through brush and foliage and move into the clearing, my boots crunching twigs and Spark chirruping excitedly in my ear.

With each step, my black heart pounds harder.

*Move close,* whispers the poison.

*Closer.*

*Yes, and closer still.*

Be quiet, I tell it. You are not my master yet.

Sunlight shines through the emerald tree canopy, tiny insects floating in the golden beams. My favorite smell of burning pine perfumes the air. I draw the fresh scent into my lungs, stopping in my tracks when the scene ahead of me crystallizes, the girl's actions clear and distinct.

A tiny fire made from twigs and leaves burns at Isla's feet. She blows once and the flames rise higher, then her fingers play through them one by one as if she caresses a delicate instrument. To my astonishment, her expression, tight with concentration, shows no sign of pain. Why do the flames not scorch her?

I tug Spark around to face me. "Quickly, you must go now. Balor is waiting for you to terrorize him."

Disappointed, she scolds me with loud chirrups and then scurries through the long grass toward the wagons and silk pavilions positioned on the edge of the lake.

Isla's head snaps up as I arrive beside her.

"You should move out of the circle of blue caps before you are spirited away to an even more dangerous realm than this one."

She curses under her breath as I blast the mushrooms with fire, destroying them. I wait for her to greet me, but she says nothing, her gaze fixed on the flames in front of her.

I walk around the fire and crouch opposite, watching her in silence for a few moments. I take a stick and rearrange the burning twigs. "Don't you know it is dangerous to play with fire?"

She laughs. "Everyone knows that."

"Perhaps. But do humans understand how perilous fire's true nature is? The most ruthless of elements—it will reveal all secrets before taking everything, purifying and regenerating without mercy. And when the flames are done, there will be nothing left."

The quick smile she flashes is sorcery in its purest form, drawing me closer. "Not all humans know this, but I certainly do. I understand that it brings destruction, followed by renewal, and sometimes...eternal damnation. It's terrifying really."

"And even so, you are not afraid of it." I turn my palm up and tiny flames, only a finger-tip high, burst into life, spiraling over my skin.

Sky-blue eyes widen as she leans close, entranced by the fire magic. She brings her hand up and moves her fingers through the tips of the flames. "Does it hurt?" she asks, her breathing shallow and rapid.

Staring at my palm, I whisper, "No. It doesn't hurt." Our heads lift, gazes locking. "I feel the heat," I tell her. "It tingles, but that is all."

She nods. "Yes. It feels good, doesn't it?" Her tone is certain, as though she has experienced it herself.

"Raff, what did the sylphs mean yesterday about the chosen one dying?" Her fingers lift higher, and my flames stretch toward them as if drawn by a strong breeze. Or magic.

My pulse quickens. I can hardly believe what I see. She is beckoning the flames, controlling my elemental power. But by conscious act or by accident? Chest tightening, I scrutinize her face, searching for her secrets.

*Fire Queen. The Queen of Fire. The very thing you have long dreamed of, cursed one, is now before your eyes—within reach. Take it.*

Take *her.*

The beating pulse at her neck taunts, dark savagery clouding my vision. And red, the color red washes through my being, blinding me. I imagine biting her open like she's a ripe peach, spilling dark juice over my chin. Licking blood from my lips.

*Take what you want,* snarls the poison.

*Take it now.*

*She is yours. It cannot be denied.*

*Protect or destroy—decide as you will. Decide now.*

My muscles tremble, jaw clenching so hard it cracks.

"Raff? What's wrong?"

Shaking my head, I blow out a harsh breath and wake from the poison's grip. "It was nothing. What question did you ask? Oh, yes, the sylphs. They were reciting part of the Black Blood curse. Most likely the nonsensical section. Do not worry about it."

"Sure, if you say so," she says, her voice full of suspicion and doubt. Slowly, her palm passes through the center of the fire on my palm, the flames vanishing in her wake.

Shocked, I blink at her then study my palm again to be certain I'm not hallucinating. There is no fire. No flame. How in the seven realms is that possible? My magic—extinguished by a human girl.

I flick my wrist and fire ignites once more. This time the flames dance even higher.

She gives me a cheeky smirk and moves her palm above mine, lifting it slowly, her brow creased in concentration. At once, the flames leap to follow her hand. Incredible. This girl is controlling the fire and is well aware that she is doing so.

Then, hard and fast, she presses her hand down, and my magic vanishes. Boom. Gone.

I reel backward on my heels. "You vanquished my fire magic!"

Hands covering her mouth, she laughs. "Yeah. I did, didn't I?"

"Have you done such a thing before?"

"Never."

I leap to my feet and pace in a tight circle. "Seven hells, human, let us try again."

With a slow breath, I expand my chest and set the wildness inside me free, conjuring flames at my feet. Blue flames. Crimson flames. They roar, sparks flying, as I draw them to chest height, my fingers spread wide. "Can you put this out?"

She rises and stands opposite, planting her bare feet wide. The fire writhes and crackles between us. She points at my neck. "Whoa. That's wicked, Raff! The tattoo on your throat is glowing like lava."

"Yes, that happens when my elemental forces are released." And for other reasons I'd best not mention. "Stop distracting me and try to destroy the flames."

"Sure thing, Fire King." She thrusts both palms forward, and the shell of my magic tears like it's made of silk instead of a tough, flexible field of elemental energy.

A hot shiver rushes down my spine as I work to keep the fire intact. If fae could sweat, right now my brow would be sheened in it. Despite using all my strength, the flames surge toward me, caressing my jaw. She is winning this battle, and the notion exhilarates me.

"I'm a prince, not a *king*," I remind her, laughing at our game.

"Eh. Whatever. Pretty soon you'll be the big boss of the Emerald Court. And I wonder, will it make you happy, Raff, to be king?"

Moving the flames away from my body, I speak through gritted teeth. "I dare say I'll be happy enough. At the very least I'll be extremely glad to be rid of the poison. But you're forgetting something."

"What's that?"

"To become king, I'll need a queen."

As she registers my meaning, her face tightens. She grunts, flicks her fingers at me, and my fire vanishes again.

Arms folded, she grins smugly while I scowl in disbelief.

Shaking magic residue from my hands, I step closer. "Well that proves it then. There is no doubt you have the power to extinguish fire. But I wonder if it can burn you?"

"It probably would eventually. I'm human, and we're as flammable as hair spray."

"Is that a magical formula from your realm?"

She laughs. "Kind of. It makes people's hairstyles look better...or in many cases, worse."

Sounds interesting. "Then we shall find the ingredients for you to make some, and I will try this spray myself. In the meantime, let us test if the flames can harm you."

The black blood drips through my veins. My heart beats slowly. I step close and cuff her throat with the fingers of one hand. With my other hand, I cradle the side of her face and raise tiny flickering flames against her skin. "Do these hurt?"

Lips parting, her ragged breaths mix with mine. Blue eyes drop to my mouth. "No. There's no pain."

"And curiously the fire doesn't spread either," I say, my voice a low rumble.

"It never spreads. Even at home when I cook, I can play a little with fire."

"What would happen if I made the fire grow?"

"Try it," she whispers, leaning into my touch. "Let's see."

I blow sparks into her hair. At once, flames grow and twine around her loose waves. They caress and stroke, but they don't catch alight. Her hair isn't *burning*, it's merging, becoming one with the fire.

"Isla, you have fire magic," I murmur, my lips so close they almost graze hers. "Just as my queen should."

"No!" She shoves me away, and the flames draw back inside me, the black heart caged in my ribs absorbing them.

She sighs and crumples to her knees on the grass, then crawls to her travel pack and rifles through it. "That was amazing. And now I'm ravenous. Playing with fire is hungry work!"

Fascinated, I watch her closely. For a human, what she can do is near miraculous, but she doesn't seem shocked or even particularly pleased with herself. What a strange being she is.

"Do you want a cookie?" she asks, withdrawing a cloth-wrapped parcel. "I baked these yesterday morning. I wasn't sure what kind of nuts they'd have in the castle larders, so I couldn't believe my luck when I found pistachios. They're my favorite and I—"

"You baked them yourself? Why not leave such menial chores to the cooks? It is their job, and you are a guest in this land."

"Because I love cooking—especially baking stuff. It's my passion, and it fills me with joy; that's why. Do you understand what I mean when I say that?" A smile that rivals the beauty of sunshine glows on her face.

"Yes. I think so. We fae have our obsessions too." I don't offer to tell her what mine are. Gazing at her now, skin shimmering in the dappled light, I wonder if I might be developing a new one.

The scent of wild bluebells permeates the air as she flops backward on the grass and smiles dreamily at the sky. "There's nothing better than watching someone's face when they first bite into something I've cooked, seeing how happy it makes them. Here, Raff, try one."

Leaning on an elbow, she holds out a large biscuit. It's specked with green lumps; the favored nuts she mentioned, I suppose. Or perhaps they're something even more vile.

"Go on, try one," she coaxes. "They're much better hot and gooey straight out of the oven, but still pretty damn good like this."

I wish to please her, but green things are a terrible trial for me to eat, a torture in fact. I've long frustrated the castle's cooks by refusing dishes that contain wild sorrel, fennel, and spinach, and I can't imagine green nuts will be palatable. Even so, I take the cookie and lift it to my lips. She stares at my mouth as I bite into it.

It tastes delicious. Crunchy on the outside, the moist inside dissolving on my tongue. I drop to my haunches next to her and smile, preparing to compliment her baking skills, but without warning, a sickening memory slams into my mind, shuddering through my flesh and bones.

Blood. Thick and black, bubbling from my brother's mouth, the liquid creeping and spreading until I'm certain it will drown me. Rain's death—I see it as if it is happening this very moment. I feel it as intensely as the day I witnessed it.

This vision cleaves my chest in half, scrapes it hollow, refilling it with blinding grief and the sharpest, deepest longing I have ever felt. The pain is so visceral I scramble to my feet.

My arms wrapping my stomach, I frown at Isla, shaking my head as she reaches for me, worry lining her face. "Raff? What's wrong with you?"

I have no idea. But whatever the hell this is, I am certain she is causing it. Magic—hot, bright, and elemental. It emanates from the cookies in rippling waves, fire magic, only perceivable to those who can weave it themselves.

"I'll be fine," I say, which is the truth. Eventually this feeling will pass. "It's naught but a wave of nausea, a residue of magic." *Her magic*, not mine.

Unappeased, her gaze flits over my body, inspecting me.

I fight an urge to drag her close. I would do almost anything to drown this feeling in her warmth and light. I would beg at her feet. Promise her my crown, my city. Anything but my devotion.

Before she can question me further and draw out the truth, I stammer the first words that pop into my muddled brain. "I must go now. Ever waits for me. May I take some sweet treats for later?"

"Of course. So, you liked them? If you did, you can take the rest." She holds out the parcel, and I bend to collect it.

I bite back the words: No, *the truth is, I hated them.* Or at least what they did to me.

"I have never tasted anything like your cookies before, Isla." That's certainly not a lie. "They were incredible."

I want to leave here now. I have a theory, and I cannot wait to test it. But I dare not raise her suspicions. Not yet anyway.

"Are you sure you're okay? You look...weird."

"My thoughts are preoccupied, that is all." I hope she does not ask by what. Gazing down at her as she sits with her travel bag in her lap, I sift through several subjects that might distract her from my peculiar episode, finally deciding on what must be the most boring question in the seven realms. "So, how did you sleep last night?" I ask, admiring her look of rumpled ruin—twigs and leaves crushed into her shining yellow hair.

"Not great. After the revel, there were a lot of weird noises in the dark, odd singing, screaming, and crying. It felt more like a war camp than a traveling wedding party."

"Yes, fae processions are similar to a Wild Hunt. They begin tranquilly enough but quickly devolve. As you witnessed last night, all manner of unspeakable things happen under moon shadow. But do not worry. You and I should form an alliance. A truce, if you like. Then when you are under my protection, no creature, wild or tame, would dare harm you." As soon as the words leave my mouth, I know I could not have chosen them more poorly.

Her eyes narrow, peachy cheeks darkening to scarlet.

Employing my latest talent—I've offended her again.

When will I learn to keep my mouth shut?

"I know you'll find this idea shocking," she says, her eyes flashing fire, "but I'm quite capable of looking after myself, and I certainly don't need your assistance to stay safe."

That cannot be true. She looks young, fragile compared to the creatures of the wild woods who will have her in their sights. "How many human years have you attained?"

"Is that your extremely odd way of asking how old I am?"

She is the one who speaks oddly, not me. Refusing to be baited, I nod.

"I'm eighteen."

"Only *eighteen*? Then you have hardly any experience to speak of! You are a mere babe."

"And how old are you, Mister wizened-old owl? Three thousand and seven?"

"In human years, I am twenty-two. But were I to count by fae time, well, the answer would be considerably more complicated."

"Whatever." She waves her hand in my direction as if she's brushing away an insect. "Run along now, Prince Raff. I've had enough of your smugness for today."

The nerve of this small human! "You ought to be careful how you—"

"Yes, fine, whatever you say. Time for you to go."

She drops her head, foraging through her bag again, ignoring me.

In awe of her boldness, I stare for far too long before I gather my wits and head for the edge of the lake where Ever and Lara are camped.

"Good morning, Raff. What's the hurry?" Lara asks, looking up from her teacup as I crash through the trees toward their breakfast party.

The group of three—Lara, Ever, and Magret—stare up at me from their picnic blanket while Merri leaps around them, trying to catch the dragonflies that flit above her head. Like a typical fae babe, she is sturdy and able-bodied beyond her young age.

"What excites you so, Brother?" asks Ever, shifting his dimpled smile my way. "Is it the thrill of living with the creatures of the woods again? Or does the memory of last night's fire dance still run hot through your veins?"

"Hardly. You of all people know how the curse turns every occasion into a bore." I thrust the cloth-wrapped sweets forward. "But let us not focus on such tedious things. Look—I've brought treats to tempt you with."

"In case you're wondering," Ever says, the flash of his armor nearly blinding me. "Spark is with Balor. They're fishing in the Lake of Spirits, even though they know it is forbidden."

Everyone laughs fondly.

"I blame your mire fox, of course, Brother."

"Rightly so," I reply. "Thank the Elements your hound will bear her company. She's been an insufferable nuisance since sunrise." A nuisance I would gladly lay down my life for.

In the late-morning light, Magret looks like a woodland sprite, ethereal and pale against the picnic cloth's richly embroidered falcons and owls. "We've eaten enough cheese and fruit to last us until tomorrow's breakfast, Prince Rafael," she says, her laughter tinkling like bells. "I could not eat another bite."

And lo and behold—my experiment's first subject has revealed herself—Magret who is always happy and never overcome with sadness.

"But, Magret," I say as I crouch next to her. "Life can be short. My motto is to eat sweets whenever they are offered." Summoning my most charming smile, I withdraw a cookie from its wrapping and offer it to her. "You say you have no appetite, but you will want to sample these. I'm certain of it. They were made by Lara's cousin in our kitchens only yesterday morning. She is a very talented baker."

"Oh, in that case, I would love a sample. Thank you." She plucks one from the pile and takes a delicate bite. "Indeed they are delicious," she says, crumbs sticking to her wide grin as she chews. She takes another bite, and another.

Suddenly, she gasps, her eyes filling with tears.

"Magret, what ails you?" I ask just as Ever reaches over and grabs a cookie, placing it in his mouth. This will be interesting.

"Nothing. It is nothing really," she says. "It's just..." Gut-wrenching sobs spill from her mouth. "I feel such terrible sadness. All I can think of is that one day my brother, Alorus, will die, and there is naught I can do to stop it."

Alorus, with his mischievous yellow eyes and curling ram's horns, is a great favorite of the ladies of the court, a charming troublemaker, and nowhere near close to his death age. "But your brother is young and hale," I remind her, a chill prickling the flesh of my arms. "He will surely live for many thousand more moon turns."

I glance at Ever who is staring at Merri with horror, his silver eyes glistening suspiciously. "Brother," I say, "You look upset. What in the seven realms has come over you and Magret? I have never seen you both so stricken."

Dark clouds sweep overhead, thunder rumbling. Grimacing, Ever rubs his eyes. "I don't know. I can see Lara and Merri as they sit here smiling, but beneath their skin lies rotting flesh and desiccated bones. I see ghosts. Corpses. They will both pass from life one day, and I cannot bear the idea of losing them. I simply cannot."

Lara's arms wrap around his shoulders. "Yes, Ever, one day we will be dead and gone. It is the one thing all beings can be sure of. But as with Magret's brother, our deaths shouldn't mean a thing to you at this moment. We're safe. I have power. Merri has power. We can't be harmed easily. We're not leaving you, my love. Not ever, if we can help it."

Nodding as he scowls, he reaches absently for another cookie, and Lara slaps his hand aside. "No more of those. Isla's sweets are delicious, but they can affect people strangely. These are weird, though, because usually her food makes them happy. I think she somehow unknowingly enchants it."

I move to sit in front of Lara. "You knew about this? You should have warned us."

"I was kind of joking."

"This is no joke. These sweets draw forth a person's greatest fear and drown them in the terror of it."

Ever nods. "It's true. That's precisely how it feels."

"I'll speak with her." Worry darkens Lara's green eyes. "She must have some form of power here in Faery. Her natural talents are exaggerated, like my singing became the weapon that saved me from the draygonets. I'd bet anything she was thinking of something horrible when she baked these cookies. Until we work out what's going on, don't eat anything she makes."

Yes. It is as I suspected. Isla's magic is powerful. And quite possibly very useful.

I wrap up the sweets and stash them under my armor's breastplate. "I shall save these for when the queen arrives."

Ever and Lara freeze, staring at me in horror.

"What's wrong? I cannot wait to see Mother's cruel eyes spilling tears. No matter how hard I tried, never once as I child did I manage to make her cry."

The sky rumbles again as Ever scowls. "Are you mad, Raff? Do you not realize the hell you wish upon us by desiring *her* tears? Her grief for Father and Rain fueled by the vast powers of her water magic could end us all, dispatching us to watery graves, her shrieks and howls tormenting us for all eternity."

"Hm. Perhaps you are correct. I will bury these cookies in the ground." I turn to rush off and do just that when a pertinent thought occurs to me. "Lara, why have you not told your cousin who she is to me? She needs to know her place in our story—what she must do to save our kingdom. Every time I speak of it, she acts as if I ask the impossible and gazes at me as though I am a madman."

"Oh, Raff. It would be a bad move for me to bring that up with her. If you tell Isla she must do something, she's the kind of person who'll do the exact opposite. You need to forget the curse. Forget that she's your queen and *woo* her. It's the only way, believe me. She's as stubborn as Ever is, possibly worse."

In a mocking gesture, my brother raises his silver brow at me, his wide grin evil.

It seems that I am faced with difficult times ahead. Impossible times even. How does a prince who has never been rejected court a human who possesses her own fire magic and is not the least bit interested in him?

Realizing I am doomed, I lean my elbows on my leather-clad knees, hands raking through my hair in despair.

Lara pats my back. "Don't worry, Raff. Isla's not that bad."

"She doesn't even like me."

"She will eventually. I'm sure of it. She won't be able to resist the fire thing. And you're just her type. You're *every* girl's type."

Yes. I'm a cursed fae prince—a brilliant matrimonial prize. Who wouldn't want me?

# 9

## The Bronze Bird

### Isla

So, it's official, I'm nuttier than a fruitcake, a couple of ants short of a picnic. Doesn't matter which way I describe it—what I'm getting at is this: I'm stupid. Why? Because all I seem to think about lately is Raff, the Prince of Flipping Fire and his dark-honey gaze, his distracting warrior's physique wrapped in shiny fae armor. The mocking twist of his lips, his deep laugh, and intolerable earnestness.

And let's not forget the way he looked at me when we played with fire together in the clearing on Mount Cúig yesterday morning. *Ugh.* It was intense and hotter than eating a bowl of Carolina Reapers in more ways than one.

And, lastly, there's his unshakable arrogance that drives me to distraction and makes me want to smack the smirk off his stupidly beautiful supernatural face. I hate him. I really do.

But if that's true, then why can't I stop reliving his freak out after he ate one of my cookies? The shock waves of pain that rippled from him froze me solid, and I couldn't raise a finger to help him.

One thing is certain, though, whatever the hell happened was my doing. My fault and mine alone. But how? Was it magic? And if so, I'd pay good money to know how to do it again—death by crippling sorrow could be quite an effective weapon.

Sighing, I lay back in my pretty red carriage as Ithalah Forest rustles past me, tilting my face toward the sun's warm rays.

It's the third day of travel, and this afternoon we arrive at Merrin Creek where the wedding ceremony will take place under the light of the full moon, and the court will celebrate with an even wilder revel than last night's disturbing bacchanal.

Drunken faeries are unsafe to be around, and I'm considering asking Magret if I can sleep in her tent tonight rather than in my carriage all by myself.

In comparison to the crazy nights, the days have been chilled out, and it's actually been a lot of fun visiting landmarks from Lara and Ever's original journey together.

Yesterday, we enjoyed a lavish lunch on the banks of Fire River, and they reenacted their first kiss to great applause and with far too much enthusiasm if you ask me. I'd bet my pricey Le Creuset cookware set that the original kiss wasn't quite *that* passionate back when Lara was Ever's brand-new prisoner and she hated his Stockholm-Syndrome-inspiring guts.

I'm looking forward to seeing them get hitched again tonight. Their human-realm wedding was basically just a blowout party at Max's diner. It was fun, but the fae version will no doubt be spectacular. Plus, witnessing their misty-eyed bliss as they speak their Faery vows will be super cute, if not a teeny tiny bit sickening.

But in the meantime, I've got a bargain to keep—a meeting with Sally Salamande's mystery friend. Am I worried about rendezvousing with an unknown fae who may glamor me and make me dance naked for seven years in a patch of poison ivy? Or, worse, rape me and beat me and leave my body behind a log in a lonely forest ditch? Oh, yeah, I'm worried.

I remind myself that Sally swore I'd be safe, and faeries can't lie. Right? Man, I really hope I don't miss the wedding tonight because I'm dead. That would be a major bummer.

Stretching my aching neck muscles, I sit taller in the carriage, my gaze landing on the gigantic curling horns of Magret's brother, Alorus.

Since we left Fire River and started following the creek through Ithalah Forest, he's been ambling along directly ahead of me, flirting his ass off with a cart full of questionably dressed pixies. As if he feels my eyes on him, he turns and stops walking, waiting for my horses to catch up.

When he's alongside my carriage, he bows, flashing a devilish grin. "How did you enjoy last night's revels, Lady Isla?"

*Lady* Isla! If he could see me on any given Saturday morning, sweating in my kitchen as I make chocolate eclairs, he wouldn't call me that. He'd call me a freaking wizard!

Smiling back at him, I pretend I'm talking to a normal guy instead of a creature out of Narnia. After nearly three days of his company, I'm still acclimatizing to the wonder of his curling horns and the fawn's legs dusted with caramel-colored fur.

"The revel was great," I say, trying to look like I mean it. "You were all having so much fun. Makes me wish I could—"

"Stop lying?" he quips.

My shoulders drop as I sigh heavily. "Was it that obvious I was freaked out?"

"Well, even if a fae had the Black Blood Prince staring at them all night long, they would feel a little uneasy. I understand why you looked anxious."

Yeah. I never thought I'd have a fae prince for a stalker, but I think he's mostly harmless. So far anyway.

In a swift change of subject, I lean over the side of the carriage and point at Alorus's legs. "Is that fur as soft as it looks?"

He opens his mouth to answer, but I put a finger to my lips as a strange noise draws my attention. "Shhh. Stop, please, Bran and Bramble. Quickly!"

The carriage rolls to a halt, and above the rustle of leaves, I hear the sound again coming from the treetops—three pips and a long caw. It's loud and shrill and exactly how Sally described it would be.

I look around the trees until I spot a bronze bird on a birch branch, its long beak opening and closing in a mechanical fashion as it chirps the song three times.

Alorus's gaze darts over the trees, searching for trouble. "What is wrong, Isla?"

I force a hollow-sounding laugh. "Nothing at all. I just need to pay a visit to the bathroom."

"Bathing facilities will not be available until we reach Merrin Creek."

Why must faeries take everything so literally? I try hard not to roll my eyes. "You misunderstand me. I need to...how shall I put it? Um...take care of personal needs."

He stares blankly.

"I have to...water the pinecones."

Frowning, he cocks his head.

"I have to, you know, take a leak?" I blow out a rough breath. "Don't worry, can you move back, please? I'm getting out."

Fidgeting, he stands blinking at me as I climb out of the carriage.

"Oh, for goodness sakes. I need a pee, okay? And I'm going to find a private bush to squat behind."

"I see. I apologize for not taking your meaning sooner. I will accompany—"

"No, you won't. If you follow me, I'll complain to Ever. Is that what you'd like, a dose of his scary air magic?"

"Indeed I would not." Alorus bows low. "You will be quick then, My Lady?"

"Of course." I lift the hem of my long tunic and run toward the trees.

As soon as the bird spies me, it flies off and flits from branch to branch, leading me deeper into the forest.

After about ten minutes of huffing and puffing through Ithalah Forest, branches scratching my face and tearing my tunic, the bird lands on a log that lies beside a pond of purple water. As I creep carefully toward it, I realize it's not a real bird but a mechanical one made of whirring clockwork parts and gleaming hinges of gold and copper.

"You're not even real!" I tell it, immediately wishing I'd kept my mouth shut. Fae creatures can be quite sensitive to criticism. I don't want it to peck my eyeballs out.

Jumping up and down on the log, it chirps angrily at me.

"Stop that racket," I scold. "I don't have any treats for you."

"But, I do, Olwydd," comes a voice from the shadows of the forest. "Good work, my friend. You found her."

My head snaps up. A lanky, green-haired fae leers at me from the other side of the pond. Holy cow, he's a little terrifying. Crow-like and pale, a cold, dark energy flows from him that makes even the forest creatures hyper aware. Like me, they've gone still. Listening. Waiting for him to reveal his hand.

With a metallic clicking sound, the bird flies and lands on the fae's shoulder, screeching when it receives a wriggly leech-like thing as its reward.

Heart thudding, I walk to the edge of the water, staying safely on my side of the pond. "Hi there," I say in a shaky but cheery voice. "You must be Sally's friend. I'm Isla."

"Is that what the fire mage calls herself these days? Sally. Well, it is hilariously befitting. And I already know who *you* are. My name is Temnen, and I am very pleased to make your acquaintance, human girl."

Temnen.

The name echoes through my mind, warning bells softly chiming. I've heard that name before, but for the life of me, I can't think where.

Long, green hair tangled like seaweed trails over his crimson travel cloak. His orange eyes are shrewd, their coldness lit with a predatory glint, but it's the quivering, slimy bristles sprouting from his forehead like anteaters' tongues that unnerve me the most.

A stray fact from seventh-grade springs to mind and blurts out of my mouth before I can stop it. "Giant anteaters are great swimmers."

A chuckle rumbles from his chest as he checks me out, peering down the thin blade of his nose. "I do not know these *ant reaper* creatures you speak of. Have you brought a specimen from your realm?"

Fighting the urge to run, I say, "Uh, no. I have no anteaters with me. It's just a little fact I remembered from biology class. Thought you might be interested in it."

"Aren't you a strange one?" he muses.

Right back at you, sir. Times one hundred.

With a flick of his cloak, he reveals an unusual pendant hanging over his chest. Set in an ornate frame, its mirror-like surface flashes images and a scrolling series of numbers. When he notices me staring at it, his thin nostrils flare and quiver. "Would you like to view my statistics?" he asks eagerly, petting the screen like it's a precious object.

"What is that thing?"

"It collates and analyzes all my data," he states proudly. "It also shows the current total of my Merit points, which are of course exceedingly high."

"You're a Merit!" My heart somersaults, then beats hard and fast.

Smiling, he sweeps a regal bow. "Prince Temnen of the Court of Merits at your service. You are, of course, honored to meet me."

Definitely not.

"Why would Sally want me to meet you? You're the enemy!" I splutter. "What do you want from me?"

"Although I admit you will be an infinite source of amusement for my court, in truth, I personally do not want much from you at all. It is the fae connected to you who concern me greatly. The Elemental nature worshipers, those Court of Five savages." Sneering, he hisses in a long breath. "In particular, I am interested in the fire-breathing heathen, the Black Blood heir, the great hope of the Seelie court, Prince Rafael Leon Fionbharr himself."

I blink once in shock, and when I open my eyes, Temnen is beside me, eyes flashing with fury. "Do not think too highly of yourself, yellow-haired girl. You are only the tasty bait in this trap."

Okay. This is bad. Catastrophically bad. I've got to get out of here right now! My head whips around wildly. Should I climb a tree? Jump in the pond and hope it's a portal to a better world where evil faeries don't exist? No, stupid, just run. Run now!

I lunge sideways, and Temnen snatches me by the shoulders and drags me close, the bird flapping and squawking on top of his head as though it's the one being attacked. "Not so fast, little pale head," snarls the Merit.

Pale head? With those sickening green tresses of his, I don't think he's a very good judge of hair color. As a fae, he could have glamored up any hue of green—striking emerald, cool mint, or even bright lime locks, but instead he's chosen a gross shade of rotting kelp. A major fashion blunder if ever I've seen one.

"Can you let me go?" I try wriggling out of his grip, further ripping my tunic. "This is all wrong! Sally swore I wouldn't be hurt."

"Be still. It is as she promised. I'm not hurting you, mortal girl. I'm *kidnapping* you. Did Sally swear to you *that* would not occur?"

"No, she didn't," I growl, dire reality settling like stones in my gut. "Well guess what, Bug Face? Someone from the Seelie court saw me duck into the trees. So, if I don't rejoin the procession in a few minutes, he'll tell Ever and Raff and then you'll be screwed. Are you prepared to start a war with the Elementals?"

His snickering laugh makes me shudder. "You are very naive for a relative of Everend's. Has he told you nothing about we Merits?"

"Nope. I guess you're not important enough to talk about."

He struts around me snarling like a rabid dog. "You lie. I've been watching you since you entered Ithalah Forest. As soon as you left the satyr fae's side, I presented myself as a maiden fair and stole his entire memory of your little chat. By now, he's most likely forgotten you exist."

Well then, I'm done for. Nausea rolls through me. "Where are you taking me?"

"South to the Land of Merits where we will wait for Prince Rafael to come to your rescue. If you travel meekly, you may survive the journey."

"Wait…"

Temnen's eyes roll back into his head, and still clutching me by the shoulders, he shakes and shudders, morphing right in front of my eyes into a tar-black stallion with wings. Hot steam curls from the bleached-white maw at the end of his skull, bones and mechanical parts pushing through leathery skin. A grotesque vision, the hot stench and sound of its wretched breathing unbearable.

"Shit shit shit," I say, forgetting my vow to Lara not to swear while in Faery, as the creature grips my clothes by its teeth and tosses me onto its back.

I land with a grunt of pain, wrapping my arms around its sinewy neck, and before I have a chance to scream, we're in the air, soaring toward an amber moon that's rising in a dusky purple sky.

A voice like death itself comes from the creature's mouth. "Merit bound by metal fast wound. Coil to darkening sky, thrice around. Little human, cannot be found, by Seelie sight, touch, and sound."

My cheek pressed against the horrible beast who was Temnen, I squeeze my eyes shut as he darts into a bank of smoky clouds that swallow us whole.

To stop my brain from exploding in terror, I run through the recipe for double chocolate profiteroles with salted caramel cream, picturing my kitchen, my scales, and me measuring out each item with care and precision. All things considered, this distraction works well enough until the skeleton horse roars, the sound vibrating my spine.

Then everything goes black, and I dissolve into nothing, becoming one with the night sky and the planets whizzing by. Just like when I traveled through the portal. This time, I'm pretty sure I'm dying, but if that's true, why am I still conscious, spinning nauseously, and *awake* through every terrifying moment?

Life often seems unfair. But if this is death—it sucks big time.

# 10

## The Wedding

### Raff

For the thousandth time tonight since the moon rose and illuminated the shadows of Merrin Creek, I scan the gathering in search of Isla. And once again, she is nowhere to be found.

The black poison rolls like red-hot lava inside my chest—a dark warning—something is very wrong.

In a few moments, Ever and Lara's wedding ceremony will commence, and I know Isla would not miss this event for all the pistachio cookies in the seven realms. So, where is she?

Perched on my shoulders, Spark tugs the tips of my ears, chirping loudly. She is worried about the human too.

"Yes, I know. Calm yourself. We will find her."

The entire court, including my mother and her advisers are assembled underneath the star-strung purple sky, anticipation humming in the air.

A representative of nearly all of the kingdom's creatures is in attendance. Water sprites. Merrows. Nixies. Even a group of deadly white ladies—the infamous bean fionn, who I hope won't attempt to drown any guests tonight—are seated on the creek's mossy banks.

Gnomes and trolls peek from between long blades of grass and foliage. Dryads wearing crowns of twisted branches, vines wrapping their thick, tree-like bodies, sway at the edges of the forest. There are fauns, brownies, and moss elves milling about. And the seven órga falcons drift through the currents of the night air, calling softly to their master and his lady.

Surely one of these beings noticed where Isla went. In the short time I've been acquainted with her, I've seen enough of her disposition and behavior to realize she will, no doubt, be up to mischief.

Pipers' music floats on the warm breeze, along with the scent of honeysuckle and wisteria that drip from the wedding arches where Ever and Lara stand, their hands clasped together, their smiles as lustrous as their silver and gold attire.

Lara whispers something to Ever, then with a slight frown marring her serene countenance, her gaze scans the faeries gathered nearest the altar. Then she glances toward the queen who presides over all on her elaborate throne of tree roots, moonstones and diamonds sparkling brightly between the woven branches. Lara looks worried. No doubt she is wondering where Isla is, too.

I will find her cousin and return her safely. And if any creature present has tricked or misused her, they will be regretting the day they were born for all eternity.

Moving quickly, I inspect the edges of the assembly and find no golden-haired human. Working my way inward, I weave through the crowd toward Orlinda who's stationed in full battle armor below the wedding arbor. "Where is Isla?" I ask, my voice rough and urgent.

With a jolt, her spine straightens. "When I inquired a few moments ago, Alorus said she was busy helping Magret. But I do not remember seeing her once with Magret and the maids. In fact, I do not recall seeing her since this afternoon. But every time I inquired after Isla's wellbeing, Alorus said she was nearby."

"Dana be damned! Find Alorus. *Now.*" The fire in my veins burns like ice. "Ask every creature you pass if they've seen the human. Do not alert Prince Ever until we have thoroughly checked the area."

"I shall find folk with strong air magic. They may be able to locate her." She salutes and rushes into the fray, taking three more guards with her.

I will search along the creek bank. I pray to Dana that she has not fallen in. If she entered the water, the bean fionn could not resist such a tasty morsel.

"Raff, wait," calls Lara as I spin on my heels, ready to begin searching. "Has anyone seen Isla lately? I haven't. Not for ages, and I'm getting worried."

Me too.

"Be at ease. Orlinda and I will find her."

Lara nods. "Look! She's on her way back now."

Isla is? My head whips around, hope pounding in my chest, dread filling my gut when I see Orlinda striding toward us, dragging only a muttering Alorus behind her. But no Isla. No Isla.

"As I've told you many times over, I haven't seen the girl since last eve," he says to the guard.

"That cannot be possible." Orlinda pushes him and he stumbles, falling at my feet. "And it is not what you told me several times this afternoon and this evening."

I drag Alorus up, and Ever appears beside me, his silver gaze quickly assessing the faun. "Isla is gone?" he asks, immediately closing his eyes, his head dropping back as he expands his senses along air currents searching for disturbances, searching for Isla. His head lifts, a terrible expression on his face. "Nothing. There is no trace of her."

Lara gasps, fingers covering her mouth.

"We saw Alorus with Isla today," squeal a band of pixie girls as they fall over each other, drunk on cherry wine. "He spoke with her this afternoon beside her carriage. Alorus lies. Yes! Alorus is a liar."

My blood burns, flames licking my fingertips, and I fix a death-glare on the faun, wondering how long it will take him to die as my flames eat his flesh and his heart continues to beat, his mind conscious through every gruesome moment. My palm outstretched, I step forward ready to find out.

"Wait, Brother." Ever slams his hand into my shoulder. "Before you flay him, recall that, like us, he is fae and cannot lie." He gives me a hard shake. "Look! Look at his silver pupils. Alorus has been glamored."

Flanked by her consort, green-skinned Lord Stavros, and her war commander, Lord Ephron, the queen glides from her forest throne to join us on the banks of the creek. The diamond encrusted needles of black obsidian in her crown spray glittering light over courtiers' gaping grins and the treetops overhead. As light as sea foam, white hair floats around her body, and she reaches pale fingers out to stroke Alorus's arm.

"Dear Alorus," she says. "How can we trust your words when you have a vile glamor muddling your mind?" She cups his trembling jaw, long blue nails piercing his skin. "Let your queen help you, dear heart."

She closes her eyes and releases a moist sigh. Condensation drips from the forest as her water magic surges, sheets of rain pouring down and washing Alorus clean. They touch no one else and roll back into themselves, disappearing as if they had never been.

Rubbing his face, Alorus shudders and whimpers like a child. "I remember now. I am so sorry. Prince Temnen he—"

"*Temnen?*" Ever, Mother, and I bellow, our combined shouts shaking birds from their nests.

"The Merit prince took Isla?" I ask.

Spark falls from my shoulders as I wrench Alorus by the collar of his leather vest and drag him until our noses touch. His hooves swing in the air, kicking my shins. I release him, and he tumbles to the ground. "Tell me!" I command.

Ever paces. Lara wrings her hands together. Mother stares into space as if she's flying through it. And I cannot take my eyes off the stupid, stupid fae who let my mate be stolen away. "I said, tell me!" Spot fires ignite in the surrounding bushes, thick black smoke curling toward Alorus.

"Isla went to complete the task humans are much preoccupied with—*peeing*, she called it. She refused to let me accompany her. The moment she went through the trees, Temnen appeared declaring that Isla belonged to the Court of Merits. I drew my sword, but then he was gone. A girl stood in his place. She spoke strange words and a spell was cast. Next thing I know, I am here standing before you. I am sorry, Queen Varenus. I'm sorry Prince Everend. I've failed you all."

Lightning flashes, turning the creek silver as Ever approaches him. "It is my brother, your future king, who you should apologize to. You have allowed his queen to be taken by our enemy."

As one, the court gasps and titters. Kian's laughter floats over the din. I can even hear his ugly little wings grating together as they flap in excitement.

Mother clutches my arm, her terrible gaze narrowing on me. "Is this true, Rafael? The human is your mate and you have told no one but Everend? If this is so, you are foolish indeed. How can you expect our court to honor and protect something if we do not realize it is precious?"

"She's a person not a *thing*, but regardless you are right. I should have informed you. Isla has refused me. She doesn't believe the prophecy or at least doesn't care about it, and my pride was wounded. I wanted to win her over before I told you. Can you forgive my prideful disrespect, Mother?"

"There is no time for forgiveness. We must leave at once," says Ever.

"If you're going, I'm coming too," Lara tells him as she takes Merri from Magret's arms and hugs her close, kissing the little halfling's red curls.

"Absolutely not. You must stay, Ever," I say. "Complete the Five Bonds ceremony. Stay with your wife and keep your babe safe. Do not worry, Lara. I will bring Isla back to you." I turn to the Supreme Commander. "Lord Ephron, gather your men. We will raze the Merit city to ashes. Come, follow me."

At my back, the queen's voice crawls down my spine like the deepest winter chill. "I will not sacrifice two of my land's sons to the scrapheap of the Merit court." Her body shakes, her hair dancing like furious snakes around her shoulders. "I refuse to allow it, and my will is law until Rafael weds his queen and takes the crown. On this matter, I will not be defied."

"Indeed, your wishes are law," agrees Ever, his shoulders slumping in defeat. "And I will not defy them."

"Lord Ephron," the queen continues. "You will take no men. Rafael will go alone."

My chest tightens. She is giving me permission to go after Isla? And by myself.

"What?" Ever's jaw snaps shut with an audible click. "Well, then, it seems you are determined to sacrifice at least one of your sons. Have you lost your mind? What will become of the kingdom if Raff cannot retrieve her? You have already watched one son die. Do you want to lose another? Let at least the guards accompany him."

Mother's features elongate, her eyes flashing murder. "How dare you speak of your brother's passing. No pain is equal to that of a mother's who has lost her child—Rain's death destroyed my light, crushed my soul. I will bear the insufferable horror of his death until my last breath."

Her chin lifts and she stabs a blue talon at Ever's chest. "But I am your queen and must do what is best for Talamh Cúig. Rafael is the heir and only he can bring the girl back without starting a full-scale war."

"The queen is right," I tell Ever. "Temnen wants war. He always has. Stealing Isla is his attempt at starting one. I can slip into their kingdom undetected, find her, and bring her back safely."

"If you do not return in a sennight, we will follow and..." Ever's words melt away as Mother's cold eyes skewer him.

"You will *not* follow, Everend. What you *will* do should Raff fail to return, is become the kingdom's heir once more."

Wild wind and silver hair swirl around my brother, the sky above rumbling. He is angry. So very, very angry. "If Raff dies, it will undoubtedly be *your* hand that will have killed him, Mother. How will you reconcile yourself with *that* pain?"

"That is quite enough!" With a single clap, giant black moths burst from between her hands. They whirl in a dark cloud toward the forest canopy before crumbling to glittery dust, death by Queen Varenus's infamous temper.

"Your time in the human realm has changed you greatly, Everend. You have grown even more insolent. Happiness has softened your heart, dulled your understanding of the ways of our people. But hear my words and comprehend their full meaning—your brother must find his mate. War must be prevented. Your involvement is forbidden. Vow it now or I will henceforth withdraw all protection for your human family in the realm of Faery."

The sky shudders with Ever's fury, but he yields to her wishes as he must. "So be it, Your Majesty. I swear to obey your commands, at least regarding Isla and Rafael and their rescue from the Merit court."

"Only that and no more?" she asks, silver brow arching. "We shall see about that."

"Yes, we shall," I agree loudly, thumping Ever's back to startle him from his anger. "As much as I dislike breaking up fascinating family discussions, I must depart. I have some shifting to do."

Lord Ephron steps forward, battle armor clanking. "What are your plans? We must call the war council and meet at the Five Ways Table as soon as we return to the city."

"You may call as many councils as you like, Lord Commander, but I won't be here to attend them." I peel my heavy cloak off. I prefer to make the change hindered by as few clothes as possible. I can always magic up a passable outfit when back in my fae form.

"And here is my excellent plan. I believe I'll shift. Find the girl. And return promptly. A flawless scheme if ever there was one. Do you agree?"

The commander's face tightens. "Please, Prince Rafael, you must—"

I push him gently aside just as Spark tries to clamber up my legs. I shove her down. "You're staying here, Imp."

She squeals like I've set her on fire and clings to my boots.

Throwing Ever and Lara a quick grin, I say, "Felicitations on your wedding. Do not let this ruin it. It is the last thing Isla would want. And please take care of Spark for me. I'm sure I will see you all again soon."

"Raff, wait!" Ever reaches for my shoulder plate, but I rip it off, quickly stripping down to my leggings.

Ignoring my brother, Lara, and even the queen, I mutter the words that will begin the painful shift as I remove my boots. "*By flesh, bone, wing, and fire—the Five gives life. The Five changes all. Lig é a dhéanamh.*"

Fire rushes through my blood as my entire being explodes, sinews stretching, bones shifting and crunching, feathers piercing through skin like so many burning needles. I curse. I moan and roar, my final howl transforming into the phoenix's terrible shriek as I take to the sky. The firebird brings destruction; he is my dark heart set free.

I am the phoenix. At last. At last.

Orange flames rippling behind me, I turn on a wing and head southward toward the Obsidian Sea, toward the Land of Merits and a small human girl who I beg the Elements Five is still alive and unharmed.

# 11

## Captured

### Isla

D rops of water spray my face. My eyelids flicker open, then
close again. Awesome—guess this means I'm not dead after
all.

"Are you alive, human?" asks the obnoxious fae, prodding my
cheeks with his slimy forehead antennae as he shakes me roughly.

"Yes. Unfortunately." I crack my eyes open, and my stomach
groans like a bear. How can I have an appetite after I've spent
hours riding through the night on the back of a skeleton horse?
My stomach has no shame.

He nods. "Good. We have arrived at my kingdom and must now
enter the city. I only stopped to check if you had survived the
journey."

Okay, so I've made it to the Land of Merits. Time to check it out. I shake my head and focus my gaze, quickly scanning the scene.

A dark, velvety sky flecked with glittering stars ranges above Temnen's head, his long cloak glowing crimson against it. So, it's night time then. We're standing on a barren mountain ridge. One side of the flat area falls away into a black abyss and the other slants gently upward until it merges with near-vertical cliffs. We seem to be in the middle of nowhere.

"Speak, girl. Are you well?"

More drops splatter my face, not refreshing ocean spray as I'd hoped, but Merit spittle. Yuck.

"I'm fine. As if you care." I wipe my face with my sleeve. "Can you stop touching me with those tentacle things? You're creeping me out. You've kidnapped me and flown me across the sky on your mechanical horse thing, and now that we've arrived, you're probably going to torture me or kill me. So forgive me for freaking out a little here."

"Well, if you did not enjoy riding on my back, you must prepare yourself for something much worse. The final leg of our journey is quite steep, and I have no desire to fatigue my muscles on your behalf. We will complete a particle transfer—dematerialize and reform at our destination. With your weak constitution, I imagine it will be challenging for you."

The bronze bird from the forest plunges through a bank of crystalline, night-shining clouds, swooping through the sky and squawking as it lands on Temnen's shoulder.

"Shut up, Hollywood," I tell it, focusing my gaze on the cliff face.

"My familiar is called Olwydd, not *Holy Wood* as you say."

"Okay. Sorry, Olwydd."

The bird ignores me, its beak combing through the Merit prince's hair, looking for dinner perhaps. Good luck with that, Olwydd. I'd sooner starve.

Temnen waves a hand behind him. "How do you like the City of Merits?"

City? All I see around me is an endless black sky and a craggy wall of rock. I crane my neck, my gaze scanning the sheer cliff face up, up, and up until I reach the peak.

On the mountain top sits a city of shadows, the many towers and spires forming a serrated silhouette against the moon. Above it floats a dark, formless mass, like a cloud of pollution or a black hole trying to suck the castle into space. I stifle a shudder.

"It looks like a friendly place," I say sarcastically.

He blinks then licks his lips, thick tongue slobbering as he ogles me. "My courtiers will be extremely happy to meet you, Change Bringer."

Change bringer. Now where have I heard that before?

For no reason at all, Olwydd dips his shiny head and pecks my cheek hard.

"Ow! What did it do that for?"

"He's hungry." Looking proud, Temnen pets his bird affectionately. "Olwydd is a tracker, and that is how he serves me best, by locating pesky creatures who wander through dangerous forests like witless fools. If I asked him to, he would peck your tender brain out through your ears and gobble it up as fast as he does moss elves' entrails."

The bird's black-pebble eyes click and whir as they spin in deep sockets. I'll say one thing in Temnen's favor, scary jerk that he is, he manages to make the Prince of Fire seem like a sweet, adorable puppy.

Never show fear to a bully—it only feeds their megalomania and thirst for power. That's what Mom always told me, and she's nearly always right.

Smoothing my tunic, I square my shoulders and poke my thumb in the direction of the city. "Going by the look of that joint, I'm not expecting a welcome buffet, but you'd better have something nice for me to eat when we arrive. I don't behave well if I'm not fed."

"And you will soon find that I do not behave well *all* of the time. Take care with your words, Buttercup. Pretty flowers crush easily." Cruel fingers grip my jaw tightly and squeeze. "Now prepare to transfer, and try not to—"

A deafening roar thunders from above as a wild, hot wind lashes our bodies, and a creature made of fire lands on the plateau in front of us, spraying dirt and stones everywhere.

It's a giant phoenix, a kickass firebird, my favorite fabled creature who, as it turns out, isn't so mythological after all. My jaw hits the ground, the heat frizzing my hair as the beast roars again. Wonder and fear shudder through me.

Part eagle, part dragon, its massive wings of orange and gold stretch wide, fanning furnace-hot air toward us and nearly knocking me off my feet.

The phoenix's hooked beak looks lethal enough to sever a horse's head from its body in a single snap. My heart pounds as I picture my imminent, agonizing death.

I stare into its rage-filled eyes and nearly have a heart attack—they're Raff's eyes! I'd bet my secret stash of Valrhona chocolate on it. I'd know those molten-amber peepers anywhere. Just don't ask me how because I'm not ready to admit it to myself yet.

For a few moments, Temnen stands frozen, still gripping my shoulders. Then he shakes his green head and gathers his senses—what little he has. "Ah, the birdman cometh. What delayed you, Rafael? Too busy preening your pretty feathers?"

The firebird shrieks, a god-awful noise. I cover my ears and squeeze my eyes shut. When I open them again, Raff is standing before us in his fae form, facing off against the Merit prince with a heaving bare chest and...*holy guacamole*...a bare everything else too!

My mouth gapes wide as my gaze trails over his gleaming body, every muscle chiseled and defined, the fire demon tattoo etched over his throat glowing like a river of lava, and his—nope, not gonna mention that particular body part.

Before I can speak, his image wavers and clothes appear, black leather pants and a matching vest that perfectly molds to his hard warrior's body. In typical fae style, his fighting clothes are over-embellished, this particular outfit with metal spikes and black feathers. He looks regal. Terrible. A true Prince of Fire.

At my side, Temnen breathes slowly, deeply. "Well? What brings you here, Rafael? If I recall correctly, the last time you deigned to visit us for the Social Sanctions Festival, you declared our palace the dreariest in the entire seven kingdoms. So, pray tell, do not keep us in suspense. What is your purpose this evening?"

Fists clenched, Raff strides forward. "You do not know it?"

The Merit prince chuckles. "Oh, he has me there, young human, for I cannot lie. Of course I know your purpose. It is so apparent that the rocks beneath my feet know it. But I wish to hear you say it. Your words will delight me."

"I have no desire to play children's games." Raff's voice is gravel-rough, his breathing labored and skin pale. He's weak, struggling, but trying hard to hide it. "*Give me my human.*"

"I'm not *your* human," I blurt, then do a mental face palm. This is not the time to argue with him.

Temnen snickers, his beady gaze darting between me and Raff.

"*Be quiet.*" Raff says to me. "Hand her over, Merit, or I'll grind your bones to ash."

"And what consequences will Mommy Dearest inflict upon you if you maim me without consulting her first?" Temnen makes a show of peering around Raff's shoulders. "I note you come unaided. No guards. No war council. No arrogantly self-righteous Everend—"

"Enough!" Raff thunders, closing the distance between us.

Temnen draws his sword. "And how do you expect to slay me? Did you forget you are unarmed, Rafael? My creature, fashioned from metal and bone, retains a weapon when I change back, while your lesser beast of the natural world does not. *You*, my bitter foe, are at a disadvantage."

Raff merely smirks. Then his hand shoots out and grips my arm like a vice, pulling me to his side as he leans forward and growls in Temnen's face. Fire shoots from Raff's mouth, engulfing the Merit's head in flames. Temnen drops to the ground and rolls around howling.

The stench of barbecuing fae fills my nose, the smell gross, the scene horrifying. I cling to Raff. "Get us out of here. Please! What are you waiting for? Let's go!"

"Shh!" Raff says, closing his eyes.

"What are you doing?" I hiss. "Look at Temnen! He's smothering the flames out."

Eyes still closed and brow furrowed, Raff is silent.

I elbow his ribs. "Come on! He's getting up!"

Sitting sprawled in the dirt, Temnen cradles his Merit pendant, whispering to it fervently.

With his fists clenched at his thighs, Raff shudders and finally speaks. "By *flesh, bone, wing, and fire—*"

"Raff!" I yell, pointing at Temnen who reaches through a tear in the firmament and drags a cloth sack from out of nowhere. I know whatever is inside that bag won't be good for Raff and me. Damn fae and their magic tricks.

"Raff! This isn't the time to recite poetry. Look what Temnen's doing!"

Ignoring me, Raff tips his face to the sky, his neck tendons straining. "Trying to shift...but...so weak from flying. Don't distract me. *The Five gives life. The Five changes all. Lig é—*"

"Do it faster! Hurry, while Temnen's busy grappling with that rope."

No, it's not a rope...it's a chain. I blink twice and Temnen tosses it into the air. The silver mass coils toward us then wraps around Raff's body, neck to toe, with a loud whirring rattle.

The chain must be enchanted or made of some kind of repellent, like cold iron or a fae version of kryptonite because it immediately renders him powerless. All his fight turns to smoke, and he literally wilts before my eyes.

Emanating fury, his chest heaves. "*Temnen.*" His low growl promises violence and the never-ending pain of seven hells. "You will live to regret this moment. I vow it by fire and ash and the Elements Five."

Stepping forward, the Merit bends and snatches up the end of the chain, reeling Raff in like a fish on the end of a line. When they're a foot apart, Raff lurches forward, head butting the Unseelie and sending him stumbling backward. Temnen recovers quickly, his fingers tracing a rapid pattern through the air. The chains flash white. Blue. Then purple. Damn magic again.

Raff drops to his knees, gritting his teeth in agony. Stalking forward, a wicked smile curls Temnen's thin lips. He drags a listless Raff to his feet, wrenches me close, then wraps the chain around my crossed wrists, binding Raff and me together.

"The Black Blood poison makes you an easy conquest, Seelie Prince. And now you are bound for my dungeons. What do you think of that?"

Chin dipped, Raff's hate-filled eyes skewer Temnen. With a dark chuckle, Raff shrugs. "I'm curious to see them. But I won't be dallying there long, I assure you."

Temnen's burnt blackened face twists into a grimace. Roughly, he drags me around until I'm back-to-back with Raff and then wraps the chain around our bodies. The Merit's acrid, charcoal stench sickens my stomach. Maybe I'll be happy to forgo dinner after all.

"Oh, we shall see about that, Rafael. You may find your new chambers difficult to leave. *Ever.*"

"If you hurt the girl, Temnen, I will spear you from ass to gaping mouth and roast you like a boar on an eternal spit."

"Tsk tsk. Idle threats. It will be a long time before you're able to touch a weapon. The girl is no longer your concern." Temnen steps around Raff to stand in front of me. "Prepare yourself, little human, I cannot complete a transfer and take two of you, so we are about to fly again. Are you ready?"

"Not really," I say.

Temnen's bright orange eyes roll back in his skull, and he starts the freaky shaking and shuddering that heralds his change into the black-winged stallion. I don't want to see the revolting creature again, so I close my eyes, shrieking when its hot steamy breath scalds my face.

Against my back, I feel Raff's muscles tense, then his ribcage contracts like bellows in a heavy sigh. "Dana curse you, Merit."

Temnen's creature laughs in reply.

Wings unfurl and flap vigorously, buffeting our bodies around, and then we're ripped off the rocky plateau into the air, this time not on the beast's back, but left to dangle like rodents on the end of the chain.

While we travel, Raff is silent, but I pant and moan as the beast soars to the top of the black cliffs and over the city walls.

We glide over the sprawling castle's black spires and then the town. Far below I see buildings, some low and rambling and others tall and elegant like the apartment towers back home, massive steam-pumping factories, and gardens laid out in geometrical patterns. Peering down through wild eyes, I'm struck by the lack of people. The Merit city is deserted.

Where is the Unseelie beast taking us?

My heart pounds, and I wish my arms were free so I could cling tightly to Raff. If this flight goes on much longer, my heart might stop permanently, and maybe that would be better than suffering through whatever Temnen has planned for us.

Yep, a quick death might be preferable.

"Just drop me already! Please!" I yell to the stars.

My heart answers: Boom. Boom. Boom. But there's nothing but silence from the planets above.

Finally, Temnen circles low over fortress walls at the rear of the city before descending toward another rocky plateau. He lands in a shower of dust and, instead of exploding into a mess of bone shards and bloody pulp, Raff and I bounce against an invisible cushion of magic. We roll along the ground like a tasty human-fae sausage, wrapped in metal and garnished with dirt and sweat—that'd be *my* sweat since fae aren't blessed with such base bodily functions.

Raff somehow scrambles into a crouch, dragging me with him. I scan my limbs for injuries, amazed to find myself in one piece. I guess since Temnen's cushion of magic saved our lives, he must want to prolong his fun, which will no doubt involve copious amounts of pain and torture for me and the fire prince. I can only hope it doesn't go on too long.

Why didn't I listen to Lara and Ever? And every single stranger-danger warning my mom gave me throughout my life.

Temnen's body, a blurry bubble of dark matter, expands and contracts as he begins the change back into his usual creepy-fae form.

The largest moon I've ever seen casts an eerie light over everything. A warm wind ripples through my hair as I scan the surroundings, searching for hope, a sign that this moment, right now, won't be the end of my rather unremarkable life.

Sharp cliffs drop away on every side, the rhythmic pound of waves crashing into them the only sound.

"Raff?" I whisper, while Temnen is still completing his change. A muffled grunt. "Are you okay?"

"No. The chains..."

"What about them?"

"Cold iron... Whatever happens to me, you must watch his pendant. Popularity votes are the court's lifeblood, they mean everything to them. The Merit pendants hold their statistics...you..." He breaks off, panting hard.

"I don't care about his stupid necklace! Why are you telling me this?"

"Just remember...it might be useful when..."

"When what?" I nudge him roughly. "Raff?"

Other than panting harder, he stays silent, immobile.

Shift complete, Temnen smooths his green locks and marches forward. Out of nowhere, three guards materialize at his side, two of them tall, well-formed, and encased in high-tech armor, the third hobbled and grotesque, a mix between a hairy goblin and a moldy mushroom. It curdles my stomach to watch the creature wobble in my direction shedding flaky scabs of puce-colored skin with each step.

"Human," Temnen says, "This is Draírdon our esteemed High Mage, Master of the Dark Arts and Conjurer of Infinite Numbers." The Merit's beady eyes flit away from me. "Didn't I tell you I'd capture her with ease? And the prince too!"

I glance at the grim, black-haired warrior to Temnen's left, gasping in shock when I realize he's tugging on the mushroom goblin's long sleeve like a praise-seeking child.

"You're the High Mage?" I blurt.

The strange being's dirt-brown eyes travel over me once. Dismissing me, he turns to the prince. "Yes, indeed Merits' greatest son, you have done as you promised." He releases a rough chuckle. "And as you predicted, the Seelie fire prince wasted no time in coming for her."

I blink, and the mage disappears, manifesting a moment later directly in front of Raff.

"The chains worked very well," the mushroom-mage muses proudly. "He is barely able to stand."

A dazzling flash of green blinds me, and I squeeze my eyes shut. I'm chained to Raff's back and can't see what's happening behind me, but his sharp hiss and deep groan tells me Draírdon has hurt him badly.

"Pretty pretty, Prince of Fire," the mage coos. "Tell us who this girl is to you. A Black Blood fated mate come to save you from the nasty curse?"

Raff's ragged breathing saws through the air.

"Well?" the mage thunders. "Is she your foretold queen?"

Raff snorts. "Her? She is no match for a Seelie prince," he replies, neither denying nor confirming the mage's guess. "You mistake me for my brother who is very fond of humans. *She*, however, is cousin to his mate and thereby valued in our land. I would not hurt her if I were you."

Brown eyes glint. "If you say so, wretched prince. Separate them," the mage commands.

The warriors step forward, hurrying to obey. Roughly, they remove the chains binding Raff and me together. "Go easy! Can't you magic them off? You're hurting us," I complain.

Raff grunts a quick warning, and I zip my lips, rubbing the ache from my newly freed wrists. The guards tug Raff several feet away to where the cliffs slide down into a wild black sea. Oh, God. I hope they're not chucking him over.

"What...what are you doing to him?"

Raff isn't my friend, but he's the only ally I've got, and I'm quite prepared to beg for his life. "Wait! Temnen, please. Please don't throw him over the cliffs!"

While the Merits laugh at my pleading, a thin footbridge appears through the mist. Hovering high above the churning waves, it's flanked by walls of metal spikes and spans the distance between the cliffs we stand on and a tower that rises from the middle of the ocean like a lonely ebony needle. This must be our prison.

My knees go weak as the guards pull Raff onto the bridge, pressing him forward with two swords at his back and heading in the direction of the tower.

Raff looks over his shoulder. "Tame your tongue and do whatever they tell you to. Please, human. You must survive."

The flash of agony I see in his eyes breaks my heart and makes me dread what's coming next—for both of us. I turn and face Temnen and Draírdon. "Are you going to kill him?"

"Not yet," the mage replies, coming to my side and stroking my arm from shoulder to fingertips. "His poisoned blood will do it slowly. Much more entertaining, don't you agree?"

Temnen and Draírdon walking ahead, two more black-clad fae guards appear and take hold of my arms. We march toward a set of massive, copper-colored gates that must be the rear entrance to the town. "And what's going to happen to me? Imprisonment as well? Torture followed by a gruesome death?"

"Of course not, dear girl. You are much too important for that," Draírdon replies. "You are a change bringer. You must meet the Merit king."

Son of a biii—biscuit!

I'd rather spend time in prison.

# 12

## The Merits

### Isla

Enormous golden doors open wide, and I step into the Great Hall flanked by Temnen and Draírdon, their arms linked tightly with mine. My gaze flicks left, then right, taking in the spectacular sci-fi setting.

The hall is an awesome, cavernous space lined with gold, silver, and bronze, and a myriad of shiny, angular surfaces soaring into infinity. At the end of the vast room is a jaw-dropping sight. A magnificent throne that stops my heart and makes me stumble.

From a central disk, metallic beams span the entire surface of a massive rear wall. Shaped like the rays of a mighty sun, the throne appears magical and industrial, and more like a spaceship than an extravagant seat that serves only to make the king look impressive while he sits on his butt presiding over the Court of Merits.

Every few feet, as the Merits tow me along the center aisle toward the throne, our bodies light up in beams of moonlight that shine through domed windows set high in the ceiling, revealing a glittering night sky.

It's like passing through spotlights on a stage and going by the low hum of chatter filling the air, we have a rather large audience of Merit courtiers. I'm dying, hopefully not literally, to see what they look like, but I can't take my eyes off the king's throne long enough to take a peek.

Impatient with my dawdling, Draírdon tugs me forward, and I pick up the pace, my panting breaths as loud as a firestorm in my ears.

We parade past columns of black, red, and gold that rise like monoliths into the darkness above, lush tropical palms swaying at the edges of my vision, mechanical birds flitting through their broad purple leaves. The birds' high-pitched calls make an eerie but beautiful song as they float along the smoke-scented air.

Fire burns in copper braziers positioned on either side of the walkway, the flames casting flickering green light all around.

The sun throne grows in grandeur and stature as we move closer, finally stopping in front of a set of broad, alternating red and black stairs that climb steeply toward the dais.

In a seat carved into the sun disk's granite center sits the Merit king, his dark head bent over a clockwork cat that's purring and meowing in his lap.

Behind the incredible throne, stars sparkle through the most humongous window ever imagined. Floor to ceiling, it covers the whole rear wall of the building and must be taller than two cathedrals stacked on top of each other.

Positioned around the throne are three smaller but still elaborate chairs, one of them occupied by a girl holding a glowing scepter, the others empty.

A hush falls over the hall, and I feel the weight of every gaze in the room heavy on my body, all except one.

Even though the king would have heard our footsteps approach on the marble floor, he is too busy playing with his pet to greet his son, so Temnen clears his throat twice in an attempt to garner his attention. The king doesn't even glance up.

I shuffle my sore feet, shifting my weight side to side. *Hurry up Merit King. Let's get this over with.*

"Father," calls Temnen loudly, shoving me forward. "Greetings, my King. I have brought you a very special present. Don't you wish to see it?"

At last, Temnen's father lifts his head. His long hair resembles a seventeenth century powdered wig, ridiculously shaped with dark ringlets falling to his waist. His shrewd black eyes widen as they finally settle on me. "Temnen, what have you returned with? If my eyes do not deceive me, I believe it is a *human!*"

With his metallic garments tinkling, the king pushes the cat off his lap, then sweeps down the stairs onto the black marble floor. As he minces forward, he clasps his hands reverently at his chest as if in prayer. "Blessings to the Blood Sun! Temnen, favored child, you have brought me the most meritorious of gifts—a rare *ceann a thugann athrú* for our kingdom at last. Oh, how I wish you were heir to my kingdom instead of your wretched brother."

And I wish I knew what the flaming heck a *shone-doogan athroo* is.

Temnen's pendant lights up as his popularity statistics update, flashing brightly in the dimly lit hall. Amazing! The court seems to like this creep.

"Human," Temnen says with his hand on my back. "You stand before King El Fannon, Highest Ruler of the Merits. Father, this is Isla, cousin of Lara, the Prince of Air's wife. And prepare yourself for further astounding news—I have the Elemental heir, Rafael, in the Black Tower."

The king hugs Temnen, then kisses his brow. "Extraordinary! I can hardly believe you have taken the Fire Prince captive!"

His smile eager and cruel, El Fannon stalks close, grips my chin, and turns my face this way and that as he inspects me. "This is truly wondrous. You, my second son, have gifted me with the greatest prize—a change bringer, something which my heir, your self-absorbed and ungrateful brother, has never achieved."

"Be fair, Father," says the girl sitting in one of the smaller thrones. Her gown is covered in fine silver scales that shimmer like snakeskin. "Riven has never even *tried* to find a change bringer."

This must be Temnen's sister—a delicate-featured fae with green hair of a much brighter shade than his. Her hair, instead of being long and elaborately styled like most female fae, is all chunky layers and spikes, giving her a quirkier, college student look. She has the same orange eyes as her brother but, I'm glad to note, no freaky antennae sprouting from her forehead.

Other than the swirling purple patterns covering her skin that might be tattoos or natural markings, she's rather normal looking for an Unseelie fae.

And then she speaks.

When her mouth opens, a thin forked tongue darts between her lips, reminding me of a strip of split licorice. It's a little gross, and I do my best not to stare like a fool.

"Yes, Daughter," says El Fannon. "Perhaps you are correct. Too fixed of late has Riven been on developing his unpleasantly base earth magic that he's barely left the castle." Looking distraught, the king shakes his head. "Nay, I will not think upon Riven's dedication to the old ways. It will only hinder the digestion of my delicious roasted goat dinner."

El Fannon bends close to me and runs his flared nostrils along my neck and cheek. Taking a big sniff, his long finger follows his nose in a sharp-nailed caress. He steps away and paces back and forth, possibly pondering what to do with me. Temnen and the mage watch him silently.

While I wait for my fate to be decided, I slow my breathing to calm my rising terror and distract myself by wondering what herbs and spices the Merit cooks used to flavor the goat the king had for dinner. Lots of garlic, rosemary, and thyme if they happen to grow well in this land.

The king halts, absently playing with one of the black spires, shaped like glittery cell towers, that decorate his crown. He points at Temnen. "Since we have the Land of Five's heir as our prisoner, I am not certain whether to call for a celebration feast or hunker in our war chambers to prepare for Queen Varenus's impending assault."

Smiling, he rubs his hands together. "Varenus will be livid! I wish I could see her now, tearing her white hair from her skull until it is bloody. And Everend too, blowing tempests and storm clouds. Perhaps I should make your useless brother assist with a bout of scrying in the druid's well so we can enjoy the spectacle of their fury. After all, it is Riven's only talent of worth. I may as well benefit from it."

"Oh, leave Riven be," the snake-tongued daughter says, gliding down the stairs to stop beside the king and link her arm through his. "You know you'll only upset him, and then he will hurt you, and you'll bear the scars of Riven's wrath a full moon's turn. I beg you not to inflict these tedious theatrics upon your court. We all grow weary of it. As our monarch, do you really wish to see your statistics fall again?"

The king pouts like a child, and while the royal family parries back and forth, arguing about the absent prince called Riven, I inspect the hall, searching for the queen. No one else sits on the dais. No woman stands beside El Fannon. Not only is Temnen's brother missing, but it seems his mother is as well.

The courtiers' feral eyes glitter, wide grins flickering in the torchlight, their expressions sinister rather than welcoming. With their wings and horns and gruesome fangs, they're not too dissimilar to the Seelie fae, just a little more savage. When they notice me examining them, they let loose bestial hoots and howls, subsiding into raucous chatter.

I quickly flick my gaze away, then upward until I find the highest point of the vaulted ceiling—it seems another galaxy away.

Something dances to the left of my vision, catching my attention. Water glistening on the floor—or actually *in* the floor. A great triangle is carved into the marble, encompassing the room. The point is on the dais and the base forms a moat or a watery welcome mat near the entrance to the hall.

When we arrived, I was too busy gawking at the throne to notice it, but I do recall Draírdon lifting me over the water and the hem of my tunic getting soaked. Its quietly lapping beauty adds to the menacing atmosphere of the hall.

The channel on my left is quite close, so I bend and peer into it. In this light, the water looks red—*blood* red. I think of the king's recent words about blood sun blessings, and a shiver skitters down my spine as images of Mayan sacrifices and rivulets of blood flowing over ancient stones run wild through my mind.

Temnen clears his throat, then silences the noise of the court by clapping his hands together, the sound like clashing cymbals. "Let us speak no more of Riven." He inserts himself between the king and his daughter. "Sister, meet my new acquisition, the mortal girl, Isla."

"Hello, Isla," she says, the black tongue slithering out with her smile. "You look very tired and weak, but you have a most pleasant face. We may yet be friends. I am called Lidwinia and out of all my siblings, I have the highest Merit statistics."

Interesting. To be so popular, she's either incredibly likable or a manipulative little witch. To discover the answer, I'll try prodding her to see if she bites.

My fist planted on my hip, I lift my chin and say, "It's good to meet you, but as you can see, I'm bruised and battered, hungry, and in shock. Today, I saw not one, but two different people, if I can call fae *people*, turn themselves into bizarre creatures. I've been kidnapped and flown across land and sea while dangling through the air like a rat, then dragged before your court without even being given a sip of water, let alone a bath. So, I hope you can forgive me for appearing tired."

Lidwinia rubs my arm. "Poor Isla." Her snake-tongued smile seems genuine but still a little gross. "Father, you must let her bathe and rest. Human constitutions are not as strong as ours, and you will have ample opportunity to enjoy her company on the morrow."

I hate to think what hanging out with El Fannon might entail, but his daughter seems okay for a Merit.

Olwydd, Temnen's bird, who's been watching the proceedings from his perch on a giant beam above the throne, spreads his bronze wings, swooping down to land on the prince's shoulder. With a rattle of metal, it fluffs its plumage, then squeaks and chirps like a hungry chick. Temnen shoves something in its beak, and it settles to preen its filigree feathers.

"Of course, my dear. Of course," says the king. "Yes. She must take sustenance and then rest immediately after." He snatches my hand and kisses my dirty fingers, leaving a damp spot on my skin that I have to grit my teeth to stop from rubbing on my tunic. "I have decided that you will work with our innovators in the advancement of Merit technology. If you execute your duties well, you will be given the same opportunities to progress through the ranks of Merit society as any other member of our court. Today a prisoner, in several moons, who knows what you will become, dear Change-Bringer?"

What the fruit? How am I meant to help them invent stuff? If they're in the market for a food stylist to take drool-worthy photos for a cooking blog, then, sure, I'm their girl. New and unusual takes on sweets and desserts? Yep, I'm good for that, too. Anything else, they can forget about.

But I think I'll wait until I've had a meal and a full night's sleep before I confess I have no clue about technology. Change-Bringer! I've never been called anything more ridiculous in my life.

The king's eyebrows are raised, his hands clasped at his chest again like he's waiting for me to declare how happy I am to be a prisoner of the Merit Court. With wild emotions swinging between outrage and fear, I'm far from thrilled. Call me a control freak, but I hate not knowing what will happen to me when the next day's sun comes up.

I give the king a serene smile. "Am I going to the dungeons?"

As if I've cracked a wonderful joke, the whole court bursts into laughter, even the sour-faced mushroom mage.

"No, no," El Fannon replies, shaking his head and chuckling. I'm glad he finds me so amusing. "You shall live in the White Tower. It is a special place, very beautiful, and I am most certain you'll be pleased with your fine quarters. Very pleased indeed."

The smug grin Temnen wears makes me doubt the king's assessment of my new quarters. *Pleased* is the last thing he'd want me to be. "But will I be free to move around the castle and the city or am I to be locked in?"

"Free?" The king scoffs. "That is a difficult word, open to many interpretations. Tell me, Change-Bringer, what does freedom mean to you?"

"It means being allowed to come and go from the wheat tower whenever I want—"

Temnen flicks his green locks over his shoulder, rolling his eyes. "It's called the *White* Tower, human, not *wheat*. As a species, mortals have a reputation for being somewhat thick-headed, but I did not realize you were hard of hearing as well."

"Pardon my mistake, Prince Temnen." I dip him a sarcastic curtsy and turn back to his father. "To me, freedom means walking in the fresh air. Moving about without guards following my every move. Cooking whenever I want." At the mention of cooking, the king's eyebrows nearly disappear under his outrageously shaped hairline. "I love wandering around markets and searching for the best produce to make dinner with, and—"

"Yes. Yes. I see. Well, as our guest, I'm sure you can do all of those things." He nods to himself and lifts his pendant, then taps on it with his pointy black nail, entering something on the screen. "Yes, that won't be a problem. You will wear a Merit pendant which will record your statistics and also track your movements at all times."

Given I was expecting to be dumped in a dank cell with wall shackles and torture instruments for company, wearing a tracking device doesn't sound ideal, but the alternative could be much worse.

"But if you take off the pendant, know that you will be put to death within the hour."

Shock surges through my blood. Really? They'd kill me so quickly just for taking off the stupid pendant? Fff—fruit, that's bad news. Good save! I give myself a mental pat on the back. For Lara's sake, I really *am* making an effort to clean up my language. And due to that, nearly every time I speak, I sound like an idiot—even in my head.

"Elas," El Fannon calls, gesturing to a pale-skinned fae hovering by the dais. Elas gives a regal nod and glides over. "Isla, this is our technomancer and Supreme Advancer of the Merits, Lord Elas. Beginning tomorrow, you will work together in the Meritorium."

I will? These Merits are flipping crazy. Even Raff's mire fox would make a better scientist than me! If they're short for staff in their lab, they could at least start me at the bottom on filing duties or record keeping, not working with their top technodancer—or *mancer* or whatever the *bleeping-bleep* he's called.

And they already have their amazing Merit pendants, which are basically wearable tablet computers. What more do they want? Truth be told, the only thing I could help them advance is their sourdough bread starter. If I'm stuck here for a while, can't I work in the kitchen as a baker? Once the courtiers tasted my strawberry macarons, I'm sure my Merit points would soar through the stratosphere. Then they'd have good reason to keep me alive.

Taking a breath, I prepare to inform them of my lack of science and innovation skills but, fortunately, my brain kicks into gear before I fess up. I'm not keen on becoming a sacrifice to their precious blood sun—whatever that is—before I've had my dinner. That thought makes my stomach rumble loudly, which turns my mind to tonight's menu. Besides the king's roasted goat, I wonder what else is available?

Trying to hide my awe, I watch Elas fuss with a Merit pendant, his finger stabbing the screen in a blur. He looks disturbingly like a vampire, dressed in silver and black fitted robes that sweep to the floor from a ridiculously high neck collar. Tiny steel disks cover the material and chink musically when he moves.

Long midnight hair, eyes as dark as bottomless pits in hell, translucent ivory skin, he's quite something to look at. But it's the awesome black metal wings tucked neatly behind his back that really catch my attention. I'd love to see him fly.

He smiles as he leans close to me, white fangs peeking between his lips. I hope he's not planning to feast on my blood! His angular features are pleasant and not at all unkind, and as he drops the pendant around my neck, he surprises me with a wink. "There you are, Lady Isla. It is now calibrated to your personal biorhythms."

Brilliant—a gift I'd never in my wildest dreams think to wish for. Or want.

"Thank you," I say, gritting my teeth.

The pendant is quite big, but very light. What could it be made of? Metal and magic is my best guess.

Elas inclines his head toward the king. "Your Majesty, will you give me leave to escort Lady Isla to her chambers? We have much to speak about together."

"Yes, you may do so, Elas. See that she settles in well."

Elas bows and takes my arm. The other Merits stare at me with shining eyes and quivering grins like I'm a new toy they can't wait to play with.

"Wait." I smooth the wrinkles from my tunic. "Before we go, what's the tower called where the guards took Prince Rafael? If you hurt him, you'll find I won't be inclined to be of much help in the Meritorium." Which, of course, I won't be anyway. "Can you promise to keep the prince alive? I'm not very fond of him, but he is family after all."

"Do not threaten us, mortal!" Temnen yells, his pendant lighting up with fast-changing statistics. Are they going up or down?

"Son, calm yourself. I am certain the change-bringer understands that while she is valuable to us, she is not indispensable. Our technomancer's skills have served us well thus far and, if we must, we will make do without her input. And she will make do without her life."

I fold my trembling hands behind my back.

Draírdon steeples his gnarled fingers under his chin. In the flickering light, his peeling features are ghastly. "You have many questions, young human. Tomorrow, you will be satisfied when some of them are answered."

What does that mean? Are they planning to kill Raff tonight?

After the creepy mage and the royal family bid us goodnight, Elas turns me toward the exit. "Come, Lady Isla. You must be tired."

I give him a weak smile. "That's an understatement."

As we walk up the aisle, my pendant flashes constantly. The Court of Merits are casting their judgment. I lift my chin and steel my spine. *Don't trip. Don't stumble. And, most importantly, do not fall flat on your face.*

When we reach the arched doors that are emblazoned with blood-red suns, the guards stationed on either side crash enormous sets of cymbals, shocking a stupid-sounding gasp from me.

Elas pats my arm. "Not much longer now. The exit is before us." He hoists me into the air, planting me on the other side of the entrance moat.

The golden doors close behind us as soon as we step through them, cutting off the spine-chilling cackles and howls of the Merit courtiers.

Finally, I can breathe again.

An orange moon hangs above the city, so big it nearly swallows up the indigo sky. The air is warm and thickly scented with a mix of jasmine, chimney smoke, and a grimace-inducing dash of rotten eggs.

Trudging through the empty streets, I lean on Elas and take in the sights. Raff's home, Talamh Cúig, is wrapped in black and emerald, the jewel-tone effect beautiful and mystical. The Merit city is black, too, but slashed and bordered with silver and copper, dark and burnished, industrial rather than pretty.

The city streets wind up and down until, finally, we break through the maze and come out onto a flat expanse of ordered gardens. Tree-lined walking paths spread in geometrical designs, and Elas points out the impressive Meritorium at the center, its architectural slopes lit up like a museum.

"Wow." I tug Elas to a stop so I can better admire it. "It's amazing."

He gestures past the gardens. "Look, there is the Obsidian Sea where Temnen would have landed earlier."

Two thin towers are visible in the distance—one black and the other white, set a fair distance apart. "They're both in the sea?"

"Yes. Both towers are set on tiny islands."

"I can't believe I didn't notice the white one when we arrived."

"It shows itself when necessary."

Okay then. "So Raff's locked up in the black one? He's a prisoner, right?"

Elas nods. "Yes. His accommodations are vastly different to the ones you will inhabit."

"Can I visit him?"

"If the journey is not too arduous for you, of course you may." At my shocked expression, he laughs. "It will be impossible for you to free the Elemental prince. In fact, the more often you visit, the more it will please El Fannon. He knows your presence will bring Rafael great pain."

My stomach growls, and the fae steps forward. "Come. You must recover and gather strength. I will expect you in the Meritorium after breakfast tomorrow, which will be served in your chambers."

Right now, I'm more concerned about dinner, which had better be waiting for me or there'll be big trouble. Hell hath no fury like a hungry baker.

I eye the shining tower. It seems so far away. "Do we have to walk? You've got wings. Don't you change into a beast that can fly? Like a giant bat or a pterodactyl?"

"What is a terrodack—"

"It's a type of dinosaur."

His dark brows twist.

"An ancient creature from Earth—long extinct. Don't worry about it."

"I shan't," he says, clearly thinking me a fool. He takes several running steps away from me, then leaps suddenly into the air and changes smoothly into a creature that looks uncannily similar to the flying reptile I'd just described, except it has Elas's black-metal wings and intelligent dark eyes.

He circles above, screeching like a prehistoric monster before landing gently in front of me. The beast opens its gigantic beak, sending me skittering backward when Elas's crisp, cultured voice echoes out of it.

Wow. The creature talks.

"Climb aboard," he says, plucking me off the pavement and flinging me onto his back.

"Home, Elas, and don't spare the horses," I say, slurring my words deliriously. My eyes close and my fingers find bony grooves near his shoulders to cling to. If I fall asleep, I'll probably plummet to my death. Oh well, so be it. I'm too tired to care.

A few minutes later, I jolt awake as we skid to a rough landing in the precise spot Temnen dumped me and Raff earlier this evening.

A warm sea breeze plays through my hair, tangling it over my face. I swipe it away, and the metal-spiked foot bridge comes into focus. My gaze follows its arch over the churning waves, and I notice how it splits into two forks in the middle, one leading to the ivory tower and the other to the black.

"You sure the White Tower isn't a prison?" I ask Elas, who has shifted back into his elegant but still spooky fae form.

"I assure you it isn't. But come and see for yourself."

As we cross the bridge, I search for signs of life from Raff's tower—a guard asleep outside, a light burning in one of the high windows—but find none. He's probably dead already, the idea a dull ache in my gut.

The entrance to the White Tower is unbarred, and I only have to drag myself up two levels of a winding staircase to reach a golden door bordered by a charming pattern of copper and silver suns.

Elas bows. "Here are your apartments."

"You're not coming in?" I ask, immediately realizing it sounds like an invitation to a romp.

"No." He looks slightly offended. "Most definitely not."

"I only thought you might like to eat with me, tell me more about what to expect tomorrow at the Meritorium." A terrible thought occurs to me. "There is food in there, right?"

"Of course. Go inside. Eat. Bathe. Sleep. Someone will come for you in the morning."

"Are there guards or other residents in the tower?"

"No. You are quite alone but watched constantly. If you require help, we will come."

Crap. Watched by who? And how?

I paste a smile on my face. "Thank you." For not killing me yet. "Tell me...is Raff's room located in roughly the same place in the Black Tower as mine?"

"No, he is situated at the top of the tower. You will need your strength to reach him—his cell is a thousand steps high. You won't have time to pay a visit to the fire prince tomorrow morning. Perhaps after our work is complete you may do so."

My smile freezes on my face. Raff's cell being situated halfway to the moon will make escape difficult in his weakened state. "You should see me jogging up Thigh-Cracker's Hill on Sunday mornings after two strong coffees and a poached egg breakfast. Steps don't scare me. Goodnight, Elas."

"I cannot imagine what this jogging activity might be or how you manage to do it with cracked thighs, but I admit it sounds amusing."

"You have no idea."

With a rustle of wings, he disappears from sight, footsteps growing fainter on the stone steps. Then I'm all alone.

If these Merits think a thousand steps are going to stop me from visiting Raff, they're sorely mistaken. I wasn't joking about the jogging. Second to baking, it's my favorite pastime. City streets, winding park tracks, woodland paths, and especially steep hills—I love it all. My thigh muscles are rock-hard.

A turn of a latch, a push of my shoulder, then I stumble into my new temporary home. And cheese and crickets—it's absolutely incredible!

An enormous circular room divided into sections by soft veils and swathed in jewel-tone tapestries and velvets greets my hanging jaw. Five illuminated glass balls of different sizes float about the room, warming the space with their golden light.

I look farther up expecting to see the usual ornate vaulted ceiling of fae castles, but all I find above me is never-ending blackness. It feels immense and ominous, like a portal, as if I might be sucked up any moment by the stars into another world or dimension. A shiver tingles down to my toes. I shake off the feeling. I don't have time to be afraid, I've got to inspect my room and find the food before I faint from exhaustion.

First, I wander over to a bed that sits on a frame of angled gold and silver beams, similar to the sculpture behind the king's throne. I touch the white fur covers and wonder how many poor creatures died to create such luxury.

Behind a carved partition is a wood-fired stove set into the wall of a small kitchen. Yippee! I can cook in this place. Then the smell hits me. Food. Glorious Food.

Tears of joy filling my eyes, I rush over to a round table positioned in front of a white-marble fireplace, on it rests a covered tray. I lift the lid and steam rises from a bowl of stew, making my mouth water. There's even crispy white bread to soak the meal up with.

Without further ado, I take a seat and begin stuffing my face, moaning in ecstasy as the richly flavored juice drips down my chin. Thankfully, there's no one else here to witness this...except for the creepers who are apparently always watching. At the moment, I'm too hungry to care about them. Let the perverts gawk all they like.

As I eat, lilting string music plays, lightening the atmosphere. Where it comes from doesn't bear thinking about.

When I've gorged myself silly, I waddle around inspecting the chamber, thrilled to find a copper bathtub full of rose petal-strewn water behind another lavish partition. It's the perfect temperature to dive right into, so other than the *remove-this-and-you-die* pendant, I peel my filthy clothes off and soak away the horrors of the day.

Was it really only this afternoon when I was lying back in my pretty red carriage chatting with Alorus? It seems another lifetime ago when I was a different person. A safer one.

My muscles melt as I dry off in front of the fire that somehow lit itself the moment I stood in front of its hearth. Then, lulled sleepy by the flames, I put on the soft ivory-colored pajamas laid out for me and climb into bed.

As I settle beneath the covers, the glass balls dim, the firelight still dancing with the shadows on the walls, and I'm glad my eyelids are too heavy to look up into that dark void above. I don't want to know what might be up there looking down at me.

I recall the strip of bare windows circling the tower walls. They're way too high to provide a view, but if the lower arched windows open, I'll be able to hang my hair out tomorrow like Rapunzel. No idea why I'd want to do that. Who do I expect would climb up and rescue me? Certainly not Raff.

Anyway, the Merits said I'm free to leave the tower whenever I want. I don't need rescuing.

Snuggled under the furs and bone weary, I begin to drift off. My last thoughts are of the Prince of Fire and what I can do to ensure the Merits keep him alive—if he's not already dead.

Tomorrow, I'll explore the castle and eavesdrop on courtiers' conversations. If there's a way to break the prince out, I'll find it. I have to.

Hang in there, Raff. You may drive me crazy, but I'm not going to abandon you. I'll come for you as soon as I can.

I promise.

Just hold on.

# 13

## Meritorium

### Isla

My promises are next to worthless because three days later, my rock-solid thighs still haven't propelled me up to the top of the Black Tower to visit the Prince of Fire.

Elas swears that Raff is most definitely alive, which means the fire prince probably thinks I've abandoned him. But in reality, the Merits have kept me far too busy to visit or to even attempt to explore the city for possible escape routes. And even though I wouldn't have a clue how to break him out of an Unseelie cell, if the opportunity to flee ever presents itself, I want to know which way to run.

The thought of being stuck here forever almost makes me want to give up. But I'm not a quitter. That means I have to come up with a plan—even a bad one, if it will help me stay sane.

Every day from just after dawn, I work with Elas until sunset, then drag myself back to the White Tower to eat dinner alone before falling into bed to sleep like a log. I use the term *work* loosely because my presence at the Meritorium is nothing but smoke and mirrors. But who knew pretending to be productive could be so exhausting?

At least Elas isn't evil. Far from it, in fact. When I talk about home and how much I miss Mom, he always cheers me up, and he constantly saves my bacon by making me appear useful in front of his co-workers. Elas may look scary, but he's living proof that not all Merits are vile and wicked—this one might even be an ally.

That's where I'm heading now—to the Meritorium to pretend to work all day.

With a brilliant dawn dusting my skin pink and orange and thoughts of Raff spinning in my mind, I trek through the city with my eyes open wide, taking in the strange sights.

Hybrid animal-fae creatures move with purpose around an industrial fairyland made of glass beams and dark metals, the buildings encrusted with smoky and transparent-colored crystals. Shimmering insects as big as dinner plates flit through the sky, which is turning a pretty bronze-tinged azure.

From the center of the Meritorium's gardens city streets spread out, mimicking the rays of the sun, those on the outskirts lined with bustling stores. From what I can tell through the glass shop fronts, they mostly sell mechanical critters similar to Temnen's bird, tech gear, and all manner of magical charms and services.

If I wasn't always running so late for work, I could wander inside, inspect the wares, and chat innocently while I fish for information that might one day help Raff break out of the tower, shift into the firebird, and fly home—hopefully with me on his back.

As I pass the retail sector, merchants and customers bow and wave, and I smile back while my pendant flashes and accumulates new Merit points, validating my popularity with the courtiers. I try not to feel too pleased that they seem to like me because their good opinion definitely won't last long.

Soon they'll realize the miraculous life-changing device they're waiting for their new change-bringer to invent isn't coming, then I'll be far from the flavor of the month. I'll be chopped liver. Or, worse, toast.

Speaking of food, I haven't baked anything since the morning I left the Emerald Castle, and I'm suffering a terrible withdrawal from gooey-chocolate croissants. If I can't plunge my hands into a bowlful of sugar and flour soon, I'll lose my freaking mind.

Baking is the only thing that brings me peace. It's my one addiction. My solace when life turns to crap. With the Seelie heir rotting in a tower cell because of me, the two of us stuck here at the questionable mercy of the Merits, I'd say I'm in dire need of a major cooking session. I need to get on to that pronto.

When I enter the Meritorium's glass atrium, I find Elas alone and slumped over a long central table, shadows from the metal rafters in the roof crisscrossing the messy spread of plans he's currently frowning down at.

"That looks hard to read," I say, squinting in the bright light as I take a seat at a high metal stool beside him.

He's working on a new transportation system for the city, similar to an elevated railway, but sleeker and run on a combination of steam power and magic. "Why don't you move to one of the smaller workspaces with a roof? Then you'll be able to see better." I shuck my red cloak and gesture around at all the too-painful-to-look-at shiny white or glass-paned surfaces.

His mouth twitches, and he gives me a side eye.

"This building is huge," I continue. "You're spoiled for choice. Might as well get comfortable."

"Good morning, Isla," he finally says, smiling now.

I grin back. "Morning."

From what I've witnessed so far, for a Merit, Elas is warm and polite. When I'm with him, I feel safe and comfortable. Unlike Temnen. That guy is seriously creepy. But Elas already feels like a friend—trustworthy and supportive.

"Moving won't be necessary. The brightness of the atrium helps me think." His black nails tap the plans, tracing over the Merit castle. "The skyway's route around the palace puzzles me still. Until I decide whether or not to bypass it, I cannot move forward with the project. But if I consult with the king to ascertain his preference, the surprise will be ruined. I am at an impasse."

"Hey, why not do something crazy? Like..." Rubbing my chin, I drop my head back and gaze through the roof at the clear sky. "You could make El Fannon Castle a feature of the journey."

I wasn't surprised when I learned the vain king named the castle after himself. "You could put a station on the south side of the

Great Hall, then passengers could hop off there and look through the wall of glass straight down into the throne room. I'm pretty sure El Fannon would adore being on display like a gorilla in a zoo."

"I do not know what a zoo is, but your idea is most definitely a good one."

"I still don't get this project. Most Merits can shift into a creature or do that transfer thing and disappear and reappear somewhere else, and both methods beat walking if you ask me. The last thing a magical city needs is a transportation system."

He bares his fangs in a smile. "The skyway will be extremely popular because it will look extraordinary, stunning, and progressive. That is all our people care about—appearances. This will be the great change you'll bring to Merit society, Isla!"

I snort. "Hardly. Merits have known about mortals' trains and cars for ages. You've said as much yourself."

"Yes, but this will be different because you proposed the idea. Mortals paint pictures of possibilities. Merits mix magic and technology to bring about new realities. We could not have done this without you."

That idea is so ridiculous, I laugh loudly. In a think-tank session yesterday, I described the subways and railways from home, and the Merits acted like I was a genius. In love with the idea, Elas went into an ecstatic frenzy and stayed up all night sketching plans.

"Elas, this is nuts. You know I'm no change-bringer. It's okay to admit it when we're alone."

"Isla, you are wonderful company. I enjoy your stories about your work at Max's Vinyl City and other reports of Earth life very much."

He can't lie, so what he *doesn't* say speaks volumes. He knows I'm a fraud and, for some reason, he's helping me regardless.

"But if the king finds out I'm just a baker or, worse, Temnen does…" At the thought of the sinister green-haired prince, my skin crawls. "And, by the way, when are you going to tell me where the queen is instead of changing the subject every time I ask?"

He sighs. "She is dead."

"How did she die?"

"It is best we leave it at that. And, please, do not worry about the king. He will be more than happy with your skyway contribution. You must continue to tell me of your home—that is the only work you need to do here—and it will spark further ideas that my innovators can develop. Simply appear busy whenever the king or princes are present, and they will be satisfied. El Fannon loves to see you—his precious change-bringer—hard at work in the Meritorium. And your duty is simply to play a role—it is a performance."

"But why are Merits obsessed with human stuff? Your magic is way cooler than our technology. Take your pendants for example, how do they even work?"

The glass doors swoosh open, and Lidwinia glides through them into the atrium. "Our pendants work the same way all our devices do," she says, her spiky, green hair bouncing with each step she takes. "Magic and metal and crystal energy."

Which hardly explains a thing.

She looks amazing in another silver scale-covered dress, this one cut to her thighs, displaying more of the lacy, purple patterns that cover her skin. With her beside me, I feel plain in my beautiful royal-blue tunic, richly embroidered with silver suns and dazzling rays of gold.

As Elas drinks in the sight of Lidwinia, the tips of his wings shudder hard and flare out. Black feathers made of little metallic plates chink across the marble floor, and the princess ducks down to collect them. Instead of handing them back to the technomancer, she pockets them in her dress, grinning at his blush.

Face still flushing red, he stands and performs a clumsy bow. "Greetings, Princess Lidwinia. Your presence in my laboratory as always, humbles me greatly."

"Oh, be quiet, Elas." Her thin tongue flickers out. "Isla isn't blind. It's obvious I'm a frequent visitor."

Yeah, it sure is. Going by the sizzle in the air, these two have a major thing for each other, which makes me wonder if the king knows or cares what his daughter gets up to in her spare time.

"Nice to see you again," I say as she sits opposite and pulls the skyway plans around to inspect them.

"Oh, these look wonderful, Isla."

"I didn't design it! It's Elas you should be complimenting. As I was in the middle of telling him when you arrived, I don't understand why you want boring Earth machinery in your land. For the love of pizza, you have magic!"

"Except for my brother, Riven, we Merits have lost touch with our nature magic heritage. The Blood Sun sacrifice allows us to maintain our magic, but we need machines to mix the energy with. They are security against our failing powers. For now, we combine the two with great success."

I take a deep breath, not sure if I want to hear the answer to my next question. "What's the Blood Sun sacrifice exactly? It sounds...ominous."

Lidwinia's gaze locks with Elas's, a brief silent conversation passing between them, then she nods.

Elas turns to me. "Unfortunately, it is exactly what you fear it is. At dark of the moon, a courtier is chosen to be sacrificed by Draírdon. It is an honor to be selected, their life force and blood powering our magic until the next cycle."

Good grief. My stomach curdles at the thought of the water feature in the throne room, a river of red blood flowing through the marble. Gross.

Lidwinia grips my forearm, her touch light. "Elas, Riven, and I are likely the only three fae in the kingdom who wish to see the end of this ritual, this way of retaining our dark magic. Our hope for the future lies in Riven's ascension to the throne. If Temnen doesn't kill Riven first, when he is king, our land will not be so brutal a place to reside in."

Groaning, I drop my head into my palms. I feel sick. "How do the sacrifices get chosen?"

"The mage, Draírdon, always chooses..." Elas's dark eyes shift away from mine, focusing on his hands. "In consultation with Temnen."

"That's terrible. This place sucks. Now I really want to go home."

"You are unhappy here," Elas says, watching me closely. "How can we help you be more at ease?"

Over the last few days, he and Lidwinia have become my friends, but they're Merits, and I don't trust them completely. I can tell them the full truth—that I hate being here, that I miss home, my mom, and Lara and Ever, all of which they can do nothing about, and I'll sound like a major whiner. Or I can talk about the one thing they can actually help me with. Baking.

"I was training to be a pastry chef back home. It's my obsession. My one great love is baking crispy, fluffy sugary sweets. I miss it so badly; I even dream about cooking."

He looks delighted. "This problem is easy to solve. Tell me what you require to make these sweets you long for. I will have ingredients delivered to you chambers. You must do this thing you love, Isla. I do not know how long you will be a guest in our land, and you must find some measure of happiness."

"Because you think I might be here forever, right?"

His sad smile says it all, and my heart sinks to my stomach.

Lidwinia's orange eyes brighten. "Have you seen the fire prince yet?"

"No. I've been hanging out here at the Meritorium every day. Elas swears Raff's still alive, but I won't believe it until I see him with my own eyes."

"You must go right now," she says.

Her sly smile tells me she knows about the voice whispering inside my head, the one I refuse to listen to because all it does is remind me of the way Raff's eyes smoldered the day we played with fire together. The feel of his rough palm on my cheek, his warm breath caressing my lips. The way my limbs grew weak, not from the fire, but from the heat of the fae prince's body.

"Go to him," she insists.

"Now? I've got an awful lot of pretend work to get through today."

She laughs. "I will stay with Elas. If my father or brother come here, I will take care of them. I am highly skilled at reshaping the truth. Listen and learn."

A frown creases her brow, her expression one of fake concern. "You look pale to me, Isla. You need rest. You must return to your chambers, stay there for the day and recover." She smiles. "There, you see how easily it is done? Now I can repeat those words and speak the complete truth when I tell the king I advised you to rest, and you can visit your Seelie prince free from worries."

He's not *my* prince, but even so, I desperately need to see him. "Fantastic. I'll leave now. Just keep Temnen away from the tower if you can. I don't want him near Raff."

She takes a green stone from her pocket. "Give this to the guard. Tell him my orders are to leave you to speak with Rafael in private. The stone is my word. He will do as I ask."

"Thank you," I say.

As I get up, Lidwinia does the same and walks around the table to stand in front of me. She pulls me close for a quick hug.

"I'll see you both tomorrow." Or if Raff and I can devise a plan to bust him out of the tower, maybe I won't.

"Isla?" Lidwinia says. "A word of advice. You should seek out my oldest brother as soon as possible. Like me, Riven does not wish to be at war with the Elemental court. I feel strongly that you and he will be of great help to each other." She settles on the stool next to Elas. "And, please, take a fire torch with you to the Black Tower. The dark is deep there, even in the daylight."

I make a quick trip to the meal room, borrow a satchel, and stuff it with bread, fruit, and cheese. Who knows when they last fed Raff? Then I duck into my chambers and collect a torch before traipsing toward Raff's prison.

As I tread carefully over the spiked bridge, the waves smash the rocks below in time with the wild beating of my heart.

*Please let Raff be alive.*

It takes forever to scale the steps to the top of the dark tower. Torch light flickering, I climb and I climb and still the narrow staircase spirals upward.

There are no rooms or hallways leading off from any of the small landings I pass through. No signs of life. Like a remote and lonely lighthouse, this dark arrow points at the stars, but instead of saving ships from ruin, the tower's only purpose is to serve as a prison for wayward princes. If only it were Temnen in there instead of Raff.

Finally, I arrive at a slightly larger landing with torches blazing at four points on the walls. In one direction, a small window frames the blue sky. Opposite stands an arched-wooden door, an armored fae asleep on his feet, guarding the front of it. As I turn, the scrape of my boots across the stone floor wakes him.

"Change-Bringer," he greets me in a voice that matches his foreboding appearance. He's enormous with leathery skin and slightly mangled tusks curling from his jaw. "My name is Newt. You wish to see the prince of the Lesser Court?"

As I approach him, I straighten my spine and square my shoulders. Never show fear if you can help it. "Good morning, Newt. Yes, please. I would very much like to see Prince Rafael." I pass him the torch and fish Lidwinia's stone from my satchel. "The princess asked me to give you this and for my visit to be a private one."

Scowling, he takes the stone. When it touches his palm, it glows an iridescent green. He squints at it as though he's reading something, then sighs heavily, passing the stone back. "When you enter the cell, light the torch to the left with your own. Stay as long as you like, but remember, even in his current condition, the fire prince is dangerous. I will wait for you on the bridge."

He takes two steps, then turns back. "You must bar the door when you leave. If you don't, I will report your disobedience to Prince Temnen."

I nod, and he disappears down the dark stairwell.

*Even in his current condition...* Those words make me tremble as I take a few steadying breaths. What will I see on the other side of this door? Preparing for the worst, I adjust my bag of supplies on my shoulder, and step inside the cell.

The darkness seems to suck up the light from my torch, and I can't see a thing. But over the roar of my pulse in my ears, I can hear Raff.

Short, ragged breaths saw in and out. Boots scrape over dirt as if he's scrambling away from me.

I raise my torch and light another next to the door. "Raff?"

"Isla," grates a voice from the shadows. "You came. The poison told me you would."

# 14

## The Black Tower

### Raff

Day and night the poison whispers vile and hateful lies.

*The girl is here, it tells me now. Look and see; your fire queen has finally come.*

More lies.

Regardless, I crack my eyes open, flinching against a flare of bright light near the door. Sitting in the corner of this dismal cell, knees drawn to my chest, I cannot tell if it is night or day. Shrouded in darkness, to me, it's all the same.

The poison has sent another vision to taunt me, but I am still desperate to see it. Slowly, I lift my head, temples pounding. And there she is, her sunshine hair shining in the dark. Eyes twin blue flames. A creature of warmth and light materializing from the shadows.

*Save yourself and look away*, the poison says. *She can never be yours. Look away while you are still able to.*

"Raff?" says the ethereal specter, moving closer.

Interesting. The phantoms don't normally speak. Today, the poison seeks to torture me severely.

"Isla," I say, pretending for a moment that she is real. "You came. The poison told me you would."

The vision kneels beside me. "Your voice sounds terrible."

When she touches my face, I draw a sharp breath, my throat aching. "You're real."

"Of course I am. When did they last give you something to drink?"

I shake my head, my memories muddled. How long have I been here? Days? A moon's turn?

"I cannot remember." My throat burns. My eyes too. Not enough water. No warmth. No light. Chains clink as I reach and stroke her cheek, the skin so soft. So fragile. "You are well?" I ask. "They have not hurt you?"

"I'm fine. Compared to your situation, the Merits are treating me like royalty, which is ironic since you're the prince, and I'm the pauper."

Relief courses through my blood, quieting the vile whispers. "I have considered our situation from all angles, and I cannot fathom how to get you out of this land... These chains of iron, the curse. I am no longer the warrior I was. I wished to rescue you, Isla, but instead, I have failed you."

"No. I failed *you*. And Lara and Ever. I should never have wandered into the forest by myself. It was so stupid."

My blood stirs. *You are filth*, says the darkness in my veins. *No longer worthy to look upon the girl with your inferior gaze—you are a Prince of Five no more.*

At last, the poison speaks the truth. I am done for. Finished.

But I cannot help wondering what Isla sees before her. A broken warrior, ruined and trapped, unable to stop the shadows consuming him. Certainly not a worthy mate.

*Kill her, then*, says the poison. *Wrap her neck with chains. Pull them tight. Take her last breath, make it your own. End her now.*

"Be gone!" My head falls back against the cold wall. "I will not listen to you."

"What?" She grips my chin and tries to turn my head. "I've hardly said a thing! And I'm not going anywhere yet."

"I did not mean *you*. The curse lives and breathes inside of me. It is a demon dwelling in my blood, one that speaks through nightmares and tells me to end this worthless existence, tells me to hurt you, Isla."

"You won't hurt me. And you don't want to end anything, at least not until after you've had something to eat and drink. I have goodies in my bag."

My attention snaps to the lump of cloth on her lap. I scramble upright as she places items on the stone floor between us.

She raises a pouch. "Have some water."

I reach for it, but the iron that shackles my wrists and ankles has weakened my limbs, and it slips from my grasp. Shame fills me.

"Here, open up." She presses the pouch against my mouth, cool drops of water touching my tongue. I drink, spilling more than I can swallow, spluttering and coughing. When I finish, I release a long sigh, feeling strength return to my limbs.

"Better?" she asks as she tears bread from a loaf and adds slices of cheese between hunks before passing it to me.

"Yes. Thanks to you." I scan her body quickly. She looks well. Better than well. The beauty of sunrise and sunset combined. "Why are you smiling?"

"Because you're alive." A blonde eyebrow rises as she regards the cell. "I like what you've done with the place."

I laugh. The cell is vile. A bed of filthy straw with a single tattered blanket strewn over it, constant darkness the only comfort. Fury fills me, igniting the barest flicker of fire magic in my chest.

"Listen, Raff. I know I haven't been very friendly since I met you, and I'm sorry about that. But I really am glad that you're alive."

"Tell me the truth of how the Merits are treating you. When I break free from these chains, I will destroy all who have harmed you. I vow it."

"I'm their precious little human change-bringer. They won't dare hurt me while I'm working with Elas in the Meritorium. He's been amazing. Lidwinia, too. They're covering for me, Raff, keeping me safe."

Relief loosens my muscles, and I drop my head back against the rough stone.

A frown marring her brow, her gaze trails over my skin. "You should eat some more. You look like you need it."

I gorge on the food, plain but more delicious than the strawberries and truffles from the last Beltane feast.

She shuffles to sit beside me against the wall, her arm almost touching mine. A shimmery tunic covers her from wrists to knees, the colors of every metal in the seven realms glinting in the torchlight. My senses sharpen as I stare at her. My bright sunshine. My glowing firefly.

Her eyes find mine in the dim light. "Okay. What have they done to you? Tell me the worst of it."

I shrug. "They dare not torture me. If they did, they could never in all faith deny that they had done so to my mother and, eventually, a never-ending war with my kingdom would result. Mostly, they leave me alone and sometimes even remember to feed me. The worst is these chains—part cold iron, they have depleted my already weakening magic, leaving me at the mercy of the curse."

"Lucky I'm here to help then. What we need is a plan. We have to find a way to get you out of those chains and somewhere safe."

A wide smile curves my lips. Is she afraid of nothing?

"Don't do that! You're handsome enough when you're scowling. Please don't smile at me like you mean it."

I grin down at my torn leather pants, running my fingers over the remaining spikes and feathers embedded in my tattered vest. At this moment, I'm more akin to a ragged woodland creature than a prince, and she calls me handsome? Mortals are strange indeed.

"You have no magic." She kneels and tests the pins on my wrist shackles, then huffs a resigned breath, leaning back against the wall. "And those chains don't look like they're gonna fall off by themselves. It won't be easy to get you out of here."

"Since eating, a little of my strength has returned."

"The miracle of food and water."

No, it is her who affects me. She neutralizes the poison, stops its deadly flow. The miracle is the proximity of my fated mate—of Isla.

She squeezes my hand, sending heat licking over my skin. "I can't stop thinking about Lara and Ever, how worried they must be. They probably think we're dead."

I shake my head. "No. Our mages see nearly everything, and the Elemental Court knows we are safe enough. The Merit king is many things, but he is not an idiot. He will already have sent Mother a carefully worded message, promising our safety, describing it in terms of a diplomatic visit, yet at the same time subtly taunting her to war. But he will make certain that he does not give her an actual reason to set her warriors marching southward."

"So, it's a stalemate?"

"Yes. He's waiting for her to make the next move and dearly hopes it will be the wrong one. But Queen Varenus is both intelligent and callous, I can assure you she will take no action against the Merits. With Ever back at Talamh Cúig, she has no need of me. Should I die, he becomes heir once again, and the curse will pass back to his line. That outcome would be more than acceptable to her."

Shock flares in her eyes. "But what if the Merits keep you like this forever, barely alive, and the queen dies while you're trapped here? The Land of Five king will be a prisoner of the Unseelie court. She'd be nuts to let that happen."

"If by nuts, you mean of unsound mind, then you describe my mother well enough." I raise my head slowly and meet her gaze. "She won't allow that to happen. If this goes on too long, my mother will goad El Fannon or the mad prince into finishing me off. Then she won't have to wait overlong for the poison to kill me, and her line of succession will be assured with Ever and his children."

"Wow. Awesome mother you've got! And Riven, would he actually kill you?"

I smile. "Riven is a mercurial creature. I cannot profess to know what he would do. Temnen, however, is mad, bad, and predictable. And nothing would give him greater pleasure than to kill an Elemental prince."

Her lips twist. "What happened to the Merit queen? How did she die?"

"Beheaded while she slept."

She shudders. "Gross. Did they catch her murderer?"

"Yes—it was her husband."

"El Fannon?" she asks, grimacing.

"Of course. She only had one."

"Was he...punished?"

"The king punished?" Harsh laughter rattles my chest. "The opposite. Rumor has it that immediately after he committed this terrible deed, his popularity was the highest it had ever been. His wife, Ciara, was a beauty, but kindhearted and weak. Therefore, she was not a well-loved queen."

Isla blows out a long breath. "So, how do we get you out of here?"

At a loss, I shake my head.

"Raff? There must be a way."

"If there is, I do not know it. Look at me! Chained like an animal, my magic depleted. I am powerless."

She scrubs her face. "If only I were a fae and had magic of my own."

As the words spill from her lips, I remember that she does indeed have power, albeit latent, untrained, and raw. Nonetheless, fire magic it is.

My lips part to mention this as Isla shifts beside me, crossing her legs. Our knees touch. The poison in my blood slows, all thoughts of escape dissolving as my body ignites with longing.

Wild images dance through my head—flames flickering on golden skin, fingers tracing delicate curves and hollows.

I clear my throat. "Isla, when you saw my beast on the cliffs, were you frightened?" I must be delirious to ask such a foolish question, to burn for her while depleted and in chains. And, also, I am a prince—why should I care what a common mortal thinks?

But more than I need my next breath, I find I require her answer. Desperately.

"Your firebird? I wasn't afraid of it. I was awestruck. Amazed. And dare I say impressed?"

My eyebrows raise, the corner of my mouth curling as I absorb the sight of her. Silky hair tumbles over her tunic, now silvery blue in the shadows, and embellished with the Merits' beloved sun emblem.

They have honored her by allowing her to wear this dress, but she wouldn't understand the elevated position a change-bringer holds in Merit society, even an ineffectual one. And now that they have her, they will never allow her to leave.

Hugging her knees to her chest, she shivers. "You know what? Your firebird looked almost exactly like my tattoo."

I huff a breath. "Yes. What a coincidence. Or...perhaps not."

She rolls her eyes. "Don't start banging on about the fated mate thing or I'll have to leave you to talk to the shadows on the wall again."

"Wait. Not yet." My hand shoots out, chains clanging as I grip her thigh. "Please. Don't go."

She stares at my hand resting gently on her leg. I wait for her to brush it off. To move her knee. Scowl at me. But she shocks me with a smile so bright I can hardly bear it. I drop my gaze to the floor before I do something rash—something I will regret when she runs away from me screaming.

"What would you do if I kissed you now?" she asks.

"What?" My head snaps up, our eyes locking hard.

"You heard me."

"*Right now?*" I choke out an incredulous laugh. "Look at me, filthy, bedraggled, and as your rescuer, I have failed abysmally. Why do you wish to reward my failure with a kiss?"

She shrugs. "I don't know. I've always been one to test a theory. You know, jump first and hope I don't break any bones when I land."

"And if you kissed me, what theory would you be testing?"

"Whether you pay the price of your bargains. How solid your word is." She takes a quick breath as if there are more reasons, then sighs, deciding not to share them with me. Twisting her upper body, she rises onto her knees and leans closer until we're breathing the same air.

"You know I cannot lie."

She smirks. "Yeah, but I can. And if I want to, I have every right to call in the bargain we struck on Mount Cúig and make you kiss me."

"And you would be a fool to waste your command on something I would give you freely a thousand times over."

I pick up her hand, placing the palm on my chest. "Feel the pound of my heart, the heat of my skin, then look around and count the nightmares in this cell. This, sweet Isla, is not how I pictured our first kiss."

I touch her cheek, marveling at the silky texture. "I imagined a lavish feast in my chambers. A roaring fire in the hearth. Fine wine. Soft furs. I want you to feel like a princess when I touch you, not a prisoner."

"And I want warmth and comfort. And, just for a change, a zing through my blood that doesn't come from fear or confusion. I want heat and fun. So I'm asking you to give me this now just because I want it. Let me have power over *something*. Take my mind off our reality, Raff. I don't want to think about where we are anymore."

Even if I were dying, I could not deny her. As her cherry lips move slowly closer, I frame her face with my palms, losing my last scrap of sanity in the inky depths of her eyes.

Chains chink between us—but they may as well be fashioned from feathers. A soft palm cups my shoulder. Her lashes drop. Her mouth opens—an intake of breath.

I press my lips to hers and the poison sizzles in my blood, then stops, halting its progress toward my coal-black soul.

She presses closer, her hands going to my face. Our tortured breaths combine, panting in sync. Our mouths slide deliciously, pulses pounding, skin on fire. Minds combusting.

The cell disappears. I'm cleaved in half and dragged two ways—one part joins the endless galaxies that spin the fabric between worlds, the other melts slowly, and with every soft moan and ragged sigh, merges with Isla's being. This girl is mine. I am hers. Sealed with a kiss. My fiery queen.

I cannot—will never get enough of this.

Fortunately, before I can take more than I deserve, her lips leave mine, her face drawing back, and she smiles, indigo eyes gleaming in the dark. "Why do you still smell good? You can't have had a bath since you've been in the tower."

"Fae do not sweat. We only bathe for pleasure and to improve our looks."

Her hands drop from my face into her lap. "Lucky you. Or maybe in this case, it's lucky me."

"Isla." I breathe her name like it's a spell, entwining our hands together. "Do you feel it? Is this spark between us real? Or is it just the curse that forces me to think about you constantly."

"Nice way to ruin an intense moment. Blame it on the curse. Whatever. Look at it this way, you're stupidly hot. I'm probably the only girl who's ever said no to you. Of course we want to kiss each other. But reality check—I'm a human baker, and you're a cursed fae prince. Let's not turn this into something that it's not. Okay?"

My shoulders drop, and I heave a sigh. "If my blood is the poison that kills me, then your kiss is the antidote."

"Please don't speak like that. It's confusing as hell, and crap about the curse puts me off wanting to help you escape."

"Us escape."

"Yeah. Us."

I release her hands and lean back against the gritty wall as she rises and dusts off her clothing.

"I'll keep working on Lidwinia and Elas. They want to help us. Maybe the mysterious Riven does as well. I can't wait to meet him."

"You must ask the princess to come speak with me. As future ruler of Talamh Cúig, in return for her assistance, I can offer a pledge of everlasting peace with the Merit kingdom as incentive."

"As I said, she already wants to help. She's nothing like her worm-headed brother. I trust her."

She picks up her bag and stuffs the water pouch inside, her gaze already on the door.

"Isla, don't go yet. I am lonely here in the dark. Stay a while and speak with me."

Her arm drops, the bag now hanging loosely from her hand. "What about?"

"Anything."

Her eyes flick toward the door again. I will need to entice her, to challenge her.

"I dare you to tell me a secret," I suggest. "And I will tell you one of mine. Not a bargain this time, but a trade made as an offer of friendship."

My stomach clenches as she walks to the door, my muscles relaxing when she drops the bag, and then turns and walks toward me, her hips pendulous and her eyes hot and wild.

She sits opposite me, crossing her legs as she lifts her stubborn chin. "You go first."

"As you wish. I will tell you two secrets. The first one is this—when my brother, Rain, died in my arms, I cried for the only time in my life—hot, scalding tears of terrible guilt."

"Why? It was the poison that killed him, not you."

"But I should have been helping to find his mate, or searching for a way to end the curse, but instead, I spent my days and nights drinking and carousing and causing trouble at court. As far as I was concerned, there was not a problem in all the realms that couldn't be drunk or feasted away. The day Rain died, for the first time, I experienced the unbearable pain of losing someone I love, and I learned that no amount of wine or magic or laughter could cure it."

"Raff." Her fingers stroke my cheek, skimming over my lips.

"Tell me of your life back in the mortal world." I say, resisting the urge to nip her finger, to take it in my mouth. "Were you happy?"

Sadly, she withdraws her touch, her hand falling into her lap where she twists the material of her tunic. "Happy enough, I guess. I was always too busy working, and learning, and running from one thing to the next to really enjoy myself properly."

My spine straightens. "Were you a slave?"

She laughs, the sound sweeping away the darkness in my soul. "No, no. My life was fine. It was comfortable, and I was free to make choices. I know that's a blessing and shouldn't ever be taken for granted. It just always felt like something was missing, but I have no idea what."

I know what was missing from her life in the mortal world—*me.*

Leaning closer, I lift a lock of hair from her shoulder and rub it gently between my fingers. "Isla, will you tell me one thing that you have never told another soul before?"

The ragged sound of her breathing fills the silence. I count each heartbeat. One. Two. Three. Then four.

"Okay. Here goes..." She brings her knees to her chest, her arms wrapping tightly around them. "When I was seven, my parents divorced. My dad moved in with his new lover and quickly started a second family. He rarely bothered to visit me, but this one time when he did, I was a little older, and before he drove off in his car—that's like a carriage but without horses—I stole his wallet, made a small bonfire in the yard, and burned all his cards. And right then and there, watching the image of his smug face melt off the surface of his license, my love of flames was born."

I don't understand the meaning of every strange word she uses, but as my pulse drums in my veins, I have to clench my fists to stop myself from dragging her close. I can see her as clearly as if she stands before me, the young girl entranced by flames, terror and excitement dancing over her face, her body enveloped by a black, star-studded sky.

"It was night time," I say, certain that it was.

"Yeah. How did you know that?"

*Because you're mine.* I shrug. "I have my ways."

"Huh. Mysterious. So, what's your second secret? Do I have to do something wicked to extract it from you?"

I wish to answer *yes* because a few excellent ideas have sprung to mind. Instead, I quickly search my heart for a truth that won't cause her offense, finding one with ease. "Until recently, this was a secret I kept even from myself. Now I offer it to you freely. Never have I seen a finer shade of blue than the one that shines from your eyes, Isla. It is an azure sky flecked with golden sunshine that warms and lightens my heart, even in this cell full of nightmares."

A slow smile sets her eyes on fire. "Are you trying to tell me I make you happy, Raff?"

I nod.

"Wow. You sweetheart! I think I'm starting to see a glimpse of the man Lara spoke about."

My eyebrows rise. "You mean my brother, Ever? I remind you of him?"

"No, you doofus." Like a blunt knife blade, her finger gouges the center of my chest. "I mean you—the charming version of Raff."

"Oh, that is alright then."

"I like your smile," she whispers.

"And I yours." I purposely omit the word I cannot say aloud. Love. I love her smile. Its effect is the strongest magic I have ever felt.

"Stop using it," she says, her perfect smile growing. "It's too distracting."

"I cannot help myself," I admit.

"Me neither."

Then her mouth is on mine and the kissing spell begins again, only this time it is hotter. I am more desperate, determined to take enough heat and oxygen from her to keep my life force kindling until the next time she comes to this ghastly cell. I don't know how long I must wait before I'll see her again, so I take more. And more. And more. My palms holding her face, I moan into her mouth. "Isla."

Her hands on my chest, she pushes, making space between our bodies and gentling our kiss, slowing the pace. Nibbling. Calming. Soothing.

When her lips leave mine, she says, "I don't know why I keep doing that."

I think I know, but I'm not going to ruin this moment like I did after our first kiss by speaking of it.

"I should go before someone comes looking for me."

"Can't you stay longer?" I ask, wishing I could keep the pleading tone from my voice. When I'm with her, I do not feel like a prince. I am her supplicant, her servant. "If you do, I will tell you stories of Spark and Balor. I have many funny—"

"I'd love to hear them, but I really have to go." She kisses my cheek and gets to her feet.

Smoothing her clothes, she says, "Don't look so sad. I'll find a way to get us out of this, Raff. I promise. And next time I come visit you, I'll bring macarons."

"What are macarons? I pray to Dana that they can break open my shackles or this may well be my chamber of horrors until the end of time."

Her laughter arrows through my ribs, piercing my chest with warmth.

"They're cookies, not locksmithing devices I'm afraid." She walks to the door then turns back to me. "Hang in there, Raff. And don't start eating anything gross like rats or cockroaches. If I can't get

Lidwinia and Riven to break you out, I'm pretty sure Ever will come for you soon."

He won't.

He *can't*.

I take a breath to tell her this, but she slips through the door and closes it before I can speak, sliding the bolt into place behind her.

Burying my face in my hands, I release a groan of frustration. There are no windows in this cell from which to view the sky, but still, day and night, I feel the power of the moon waning. And, unfortunately, I know what the dark moon brings in this land.

Death.

I must warn her of the coming feast, the celebration we will both be attending—Isla as guest of honor, me dragged there fighting tooth and nail.

I know what is coming, and I failed to prepare her.

This is becoming a terrible habit—failing my mate.

Long ago, when I was a boy, my family visited the Merit Court, and I had the extreme displeasure of witnessing the horrors of this particular celebration.

The wicked *Grian Fola*. The Blood Sun ceremony.

Never again, I swore at the time.

And now never has almost arrived.

# 15

## *Blood Sun*

### Isla

On the night of the dark moon, the Merit court has gathered for a wild and decadent feast. On either side of the glistening channels of the Blood Sun altar, long tables covered in curling ivy, flowers the color of aging bruises, and a mess of left-over banquet food line the Great Hall, a host of gruesomely beautiful Unseelie fae seated at each.

Yesterday I learned the name of the water feature that's carved into the floor, and the combination of the words *blood* and *altar* sent a cold chill down my spine, filling me with dread about what might happen at tonight's Grian Fola ceremony.

Right now, I'm at a table positioned on the floor to the right of the dais, sitting with Elas and his innovators. I've only picked at the main dishes—eggs in blood-red shells, tiny bats floating in a thick crimson sauce, wriggly, gooey tripe—and instead nibbled the over-ripe figs and persimmons that were bursting from their skins all over my plate. Out of everything on offer, they looked the most likely to stay down.

If I can help it, I'd prefer not to vomit all over my lovely vermilion gown.

In the light cast by the numerous braziers and torches set throughout the hall, everything gleams red—the crystal goblets, marble floor, the black columns and fluttering palm trees, even the giant metallic beams of silver and gold behind El Fannon's throne. Red. Red. Red. Everywhere I look. Feeling queasy, I push my plate away.

Lidwinia glides down the steps from the dais, then weaves through the tables to lean between Elas and me, her purple-patterned hand squeezing his shoulder. "How was dinner?" she inquires with a knowing grin. "Isla, it appears that your favorite was the bog troll pudding stuffed in over-ripe fruit casings."

Ugh, bog troll. Really? My stomach churns again, but I hide my nausea by smiling brightly at her. "Yeah, it was delicious." *If you enjoy the taste of dead butt.* "Thanks for asking."

She nods serenely. "And now, Isla, the evening begins in earnest. Prepare yourself. No matter what happens, you must do your best not to react. Your focus must be to find a way to meet with Riven as soon as possible. Do not lose sight of your goal."

She sounds like my old basketball coach.

My gaze shoots to the fae seated at El Fannon's right—Riven—the Merits' mysterious heir. Since the moment he took his place at the high table, it's been difficult not to look at him. He's so compelling.

A pale warrior with an ethereally beautiful but serious face. A wavy curtain of snow-white hair. The bluest eyes I've ever seen, glowing as though lit from within. His clothes are black, his spiked crown too.

Perched on the back of his ornate chair is a rather large owl, its face and body divided vertically by two colors—one side white, the other black, wide eyes studying everyone in the room with an unnerving intensity.

Lidwinia flicks her tongue out, grabbing my attention with a quick lick of my cheek.

"Eww. Stop that."

Laughter tinkles. "Of course, he won't agree to a private meeting with you, but if you watch him closely over the next few days, it will be apparent where he spends most of his time and you can easily apprehend him."

I roll my eyes. "You know, it would be a whole lot easier if you'd just tell me where to go."

"If I disclose this location myself, then when questioned, I would have to admit I gave you this information. And that would not be wise. Also, Meerade is the one you must impress. Riven respects her opinion."

"Oh? And who's this Meerade?" I ask, searching for a stunning fae creature hovering somewhere close to the prince. "His girlfriend?"

Lidwinia and Elas laugh. "No," she says, gesturing at the owl. "It is his bonded creature."

I hide my shocked expression with a yawn. I wonder if it sleeps in his chambers? The owl is a magnificent looking critter, but I wouldn't want those knowing eyes staring at me while I slept each night. No thanks. I'd rather snuggle up with jolly Balor or mischievous Spark. Or the fire prince with the delicious lips.

Inwardly, I smack my forehead. Why did I let my thoughts travel back to that dark cell? His warm body. And the softest, sweetest kisses a girl could ever imagine. Remember—he may be a great kisser, but he's a supernatural pain in the butt who thinks I'm his fated mate. Weirdo, right?

"Isla, are you well?" asks Elas, his wing wrapping protectively behind my chair.

"Oh, absolutely. Don't worry about me. Just realized I forgot to put my croissant dough in the cooler before I left. Never mind. I'm fine—"

"Hush," says Lidwinia. "Look who comes." She waves goodbye and steps quickly up the red and black staircase to take her seat next to Temnen, who looks horrid dressed from head-to-toe in a nauseating, pale-green shade that perfectly matches his hair.

Flute music plays, a haunting tune drifting through the air. Perhaps there'll be dancing. A previously hidden silver door near the stairs stands open, and the leathery-skinned guard with the curling tusks from the Black Tower strides through it pushing a half-naked Raff before him onto the dais.

Panic closes the muscles of my throat, my hands rising to cover my mouth. Elas removes his wing from around my shoulder, replacing it with a gentle hand. "Be calm," he whispers.

Temnen goes straight for Raff, dragging him by a metal neck cuff to the center of the dais, then shoving him down the stairs head first. I can't contain my moan of horror as I watch him tumble down in a mess of clanging chains to land on the marble floor.

"Behold," shouts Temnen. "I give you Prince Rafael Leon Fionbharr, the fourteenth Black Blood heir to the Throne of Five. A guest in our land. Come and take a closer look. What think you of him, fellow Merits?"

Cheers and howls swell through the room as the fae crowd around, clambering for position, even hanging from rafters and columns, some peering between vines like shy children.

I shoot out of my chair and the restraint of Elas's arm and push my way to the front of the throng.

The sight of the Prince of Talamh Cúig so badly abused cleaves my heart in two.

Legs crossed and his back a steel rod, Raff sits on the floor, his bare chest heaving, hands braced on his leather-clad thighs, and his golden gaze burning a hole through one side of Temnen's smirking face to the other. Most likely murdering him over and over in his mind.

Still seated at the table, El Fannon smiles proudly while Lidwinia and Riven fix blank stares over the top of their brother's head, clearly unimpressed by his cruelty.

"Damn you to the hellfire realms, Temnen Prince of Merits. You are nothing but a coward," says Raff, spitting the words between gritted teeth. "Soon you will pay for every misdeed, every foul action. Do not dare think you won't."

"But how will you punish me? You are too weak, and besides I have your human. Would you like me to punish *her* for your impudence?" Temnen digs his fingers through Raff's neck cuff, shaking him roughly as he addresses the court. "Tonight, we are fortunate to have royal fae blood with which to mark the beginning of the beloved Blood Sun ceremony."

The courtiers cheer, Temnen's pendant blipping and flashing with their approval.

"Let us delay not a moment longer." He drags Raff back up the steps to the stone circle carved into the floor immediately in front of the throne, the beginning of the Blood Sun altar.

Draírdon materializes from nowhere, gray robes swishing, a ceremonial knife held glinting in his fist.

"No." I step forward. Elas appears beside me, pulling me back by linking our arms together, then holding me in place.

Outside a violent storm rages, the wind's howl audible above the music and the excited noise of the courtiers. Temnen raises a hand toward the ceiling. Silence drops like a guillotine, the wind outside stilling.

"Praise be to the favors of the Merits. The Blood Sun is all seeing, all knowing, and flows with vitality and strength through all who respect the ways of our kingdom. Blood is power. Let it run."

Draírdon's knife slashes, blood welling then flowing from Raff's chest. The fire prince hisses, the demon tattoo on his throat emitting a weak, throbbing pulse of light. As Temnen pushes Raff close to the altar, his blood drips freely, and the flutes begin to pipe again, their tempo frantic, nauseating.

"The fire prince's blood is thick and rich!" Temnen tugs Raff's wrist high, effectively dangling him from it like a puppet. "Cursed Seelie blood will make a superior sacrifice. Let us take a little more."

Raff kicks his bare foot out, tripping the Merit prince. Temnen laughs, quickly regaining his balance. "Yes, bleed the Seelie prince, High Mage. Then take a little more. No need to be gentle."

Rip, slash goes the mage's terrible blade as it crisscrosses Raff's skin—the soft side of his forearm, muscled back, then returning to his chest. Before long, he's covered in blood, tawny hair a wet tangle over his face and shoulders.

I gaze around the court, shocked at the gleeful faces on the dais, the stench of blood lust permeating the air. The king smiling a strange close-mouthed grin. Lidwinia still as a statue. Riven too.

Acid tears sting, dripping down my face as wild thoughts run riot inside my head, terrible, futile ideas of how I might put a stop to this horror. What I finally settle on is a question: When should I start screaming?

"What a handsome prince you make decorated in your own blood," Temnen crows. "I think our work has much improved him, Draírdon. Although, perhaps your cuts could be a little deeper and more precisely placed." He runs his claw slowly around Raff's throat. "Yes, I think you'd look wonderful, Rafael, with a long gash right here."

A burst of noise explodes near the throne—massive black and white wings spreading wide as they beat the air. The owl swoops over Temnen's head, talons knocking his circlet of emerald stones to the floor before it lands in front of Raff. Chest puffed, the bird's eerie eyes fix on Temnen.

"Brother," says a low gravelly voice. The silver prince now stands in front of his carved-black chair, his face calm and strange, night-deep shadows coalescing and moving around his body. "You have upset Meerade. She does not approve of your treatment of the Court of Five heir. It is beyond—"

"I do not care what your *owl* thinks, Riven. She is ever the killjoy whose only desire is to spoil my fun."

The king yawns and raises his hand limply. "Nonetheless, Temnen, Meerade and Riven are correct. You know you cannot kill the Elemental prince, and if you toy with him much longer, you surely will. War with the Elementals will commence when I say it is time and not a moment before. Release your plaything at once."

Temnen bows. "As you wish, Father." He lifts Raff by the chains and throws him down the stairs for the second time this evening, following and kicking him until he lands right at my jeweled slippers.

"There." Temnen grins and pushes me onto my knees beside Raff. "Now you may take a seat next to your brother-in-law, Change-Bringer, and watch the rest of the proceedings."

"Lara isn't my sister, you jerk, she's my cousin."

The king laughs. Elas hisses a warning. But I can hear each one of Raff's ragged, death-rattle breaths, and they make me not care what the Merits might do to me.

"Cousin. Sister. Details, human, they bore me immensely." Temnen prances off, rabbiting on in his nasally voice about Blood Sun this, sacrificial honor that. I couldn't care less about his stupid ceremony. I just want to find a way to help Raff before he bleeds out on the pretty marble floor.

"Are you okay?" I whisper, my fingers itching to smooth his cheek, to comfort him.

He grunts, then winces. "I shall live."

The noise of the court rises around us. It sounds like they're engaged in a bidding war, an auction, and it provides a convenient cover under which to speak to Raff.

"I think the silver-haired dude, Riven, wants to keep you alive. That's at least one positive thing, right?"

"What is a dude?"

I shrug. "It just means a guy. A man who..." I let my words trail off as Raff's brow twists in confusion. "Oh, forget about it."

He snorts a laugh, his palm pressing against the nasty gash bisecting his ribcage. "Riven just saved my life. Surely he deserves a more respectful title than *dude*."

"Actually, I think his owl saved you. Riven looks about my age. How can he be older than Temnen who looks like a sour, old wrinkled prune?"

"Riven is three years older than Lidwinia and she has two years over Temnen. As is typical for the youngest brat in a royal line, Temnen always seeks attention and is willing to behave despicably in order to receive it. Before my brother Rain died, I was the youngest of three siblings. I understand Temnen's desires all too well."

"If I didn't know Riven was the heir, I'd easily pick him as the baby of the family. He reminds me of the beautiful music majors I see skulking around the school campus picking up girls with nothing but the power of their tragic stares."

Raff scowls at the word beautiful, then cocks his head. "I do not know the word *campus*, but if girls can be picked up by the powers of music mages, does that mean humans have magic, too?"

"*Majors*, not mages. They're students—" I shake my head, bringing my focus back to the Merits. "Don't worry about it, I'll explain later. Why does Riven look so young?"

"Since the moment he turned one and twenty, he has not aged a day. A dark spell suspends him in time. It is said when he meets his match, he will begin to age at the normal rate of a fae male. And in Temnen's case, there is no magic that ages him beyond his twenty fae years, only his foul nature."

"So Riven is cursed?"

"No, quite the opposite. The spell was bestowed as a blessing. At Riven's birth, the court's High Mage foretold that he must wait many years for his mate to be born and come of age. Riven is not one to share his secrets, but according to Lidwinia, her brother despises this meddling with his life's natural processes. This dubious blessing has made him the reclusive creature you see before you."

"I thought Merits adored unnatural things."

"Riven is different. El Fannon longs to make Temnen his heir because they are so similar, but Merit laws forbid it. Riven will rule, and my people sincerely hope he will indeed live to ascend the throne. The silver prince represents the greatest chance for peace between our kingdoms in several hundred years."

"You seem to know a lot about the Merit royal family."

"We fae like to be well acquainted with our enemies."

A loud cheer rises above the general ruckus, and Temnen pushes a young man past us toward the dais, stripping the fae's clothes from his wiry body along the way. The Merit prince backhands the boy's head, making him stumble, before tearing translucent wings from his shoulders with a jubilant roar.

Silence drops like a machete blade cutting off the crowd's laughter. I let my arm sneak around Raff's shoulders, squeezing him tightly, for both of our comfort.

Grinning like a madman, the Unseelie prince turns to address the court, his orange gaze falling on me and Raff.

"Father, look!" He pushes the trembling boy aside. "Do you see how your change-bringer protects the Elemental, fawning there at his side? What use is she to us when her loyalty so clearly lies elsewhere? Methinks we should pass over this woodland elf and instead make the Blood Sun a truly outstanding gift—a human sacrifice!"

The king considers me, hunched as I am beside Raff, his thin lips pursed and brow pinched. He leaves his throne, joining us on the floor in front of the dais, circling us with his fingers steepled under his pointy chin, black jewels glinting like knobby knuckles. "Perhaps you are correct, my son—"

"Your Majesty," calls Elas, stepping toward the king and waving a scroll through the air. "Before we move forward with the ceremony, I have a special surprise for you and the court, if you will allow it."

"Oh? A surprise for me, Elas? How thrilling." El Fannon's curls bounce as he gestures his technomancer closer, forgetting that

Raff and I exist. "Of course. Come quickly. You must reveal your surprise at once. The court is eager for new amusements."

Elas bows low, and as he straightens, he flings the scroll into the air. Wrapped in a diaphanous bubble of silver it tumbles slowly into the giggling king's outstretched hands.

Clearing his throat, Elas flares his black wings, the metal feathers jangling musically. "King El Fannon, with the express blessing of Lady Isla, our esteemed change-bringer, I bring you her vision for our city."

The courtiers gasp and hiss, squeal and growl.

The king unravels the scroll, his beady eyes scanning the contents. A jagged black gash grows across his face, his version of a delighted smile. "Praise the Merits! It is called El Fannon's Royal Celestial Skyway, and if I am not mistaken, it is a complete transportation system, yes?"

"Your Majesty is correct, and it is our change-bringer's design," says Elas, flourishing his palm in my direction.

A lie. But, like all fae, Elas is a master of stretching the truth.

"How wonderful!" the king holds up the plans. "I see there is a point to disembark above the throne room. Courtiers will have the pleasure of witnessing my private audiences." He beams at Elas. "Yes, this is a genius idea. Temnen, come quickly. Pass the plans around the court so that everyone may be filled with delight."

Scowling, the prince strides over, his antennae quivering and coat tails flapping. He rips the plans from his father's fingers, his pinched gaze devouring them, clicking his tongue and sighing as his frown deepens. Finally, his head turns my way, his orange eyes now black.

"*She* did this?" he asks Elas, pointing a claw at me. "That one there? The human?"

"Yes. The Celestial Skyway is Lady Isla's invention. Without her, the project couldn't have been conceived."

I smile sweetly at Temnen.

I curtsy as though I'm a brilliant innovator whose every single braincell is awash with technological genius.

I puff my chest out, tilt him a challenge with the jut of my hip.

Something wild burns at my core—triumph, rage, the stupid overconfidence of a fleeting victory—perhaps all three? I feel Raff shuddering beside me, see the flash of Draírdon's blade across his skin. I'm on the brink of madness, about to explode any second. And when I do, it's going to be ugly.

Temnen gawks. I stare back, silently cursing him.

That's right, you nasty green-haired Merit, check me out. My bones might be frailer than yours, but the marrow inside hides my special talent. You can find it in my smile. Hear it in my words. If you kneel at my feet and lick my tears, you'll taste it in my sweat and sorrow.

Because I am something that you can never ever be, not even in your wildest dreams—I'm a freaking awesome liar!

His slimy antennae vibrate, and I grin so widely it hurts. I hate him—he's nothing but a bully, and at their core, bullies are always, always, *always* weak, sniveling cowards. Do you really want to mess with *me*, you jealous, worm-headed sook?

A lake of fiery lava rolls through my body.

I've never been so mad before. So ready to punch someone in the face.

Heat sizzles from my brain to my chest, building and building until it explodes outward in a flash that blinds me momentarily. A pulse tingles over my palms, scorching my fingertips, and blue flames dance around my knuckles.

What. The. Ever. Loving. Hell.

I squeeze my eyes shut. When I open them, the flames are still there.

I've made fire!

Oh, shit! This is new.

I thrust my hands behind my back, blowing out a slow, cooling breath. I quickly scan the courtiers, checking who might have seen the unbidden magic bursting from my hands.

My blood begins to cool. My limbs grow steadier. Thank God no one noticed! Not even Raff.

At the moment, he's too busy rearranging his battered limbs, inch by painful inch. And the way he's staring at the Merit prince, I suspect he's getting ready to pounce on him like I am. But I hope Raff saves his strength. In his current condition, he couldn't tackle a kitten.

The skyway plans circulate around the courtiers, and my pendant takes on a life of its own, incoming data lighting the screen in bright pulses. Tilting my pendant toward my face, I see my approval rating is soaring like crazy! Unfortunately, Temnen notices, and his squirmy feelers straighten in my direction, pointing at me with interest. Ugh. It's a truly disgusting sight. No doubt he's burning with jealousy. Consumed by fury.

Rolling back his shoulders, he smiles right at me. Not a wicked smile. Not a creepy smile or even a particularly cunning one. It's just...eager and hungry, like a child plotting how to steal his best friend's special toy right out from under their eyes. And I have a horrible, gut-sinking suspicion that I'm the shiny new toy he wants to get his claws on, which is an incredibly disturbing thought. But...wait. Hmmm...

Even as bile rises in my throat and fear weakens my legs, I flash him a forced smile, a terrible idea sparking in my obviously demented brain, a really, *really* bad plan forming.

I keep the fake smile plastered on as Temnen angles his body my way. Oh, crap. He's thinking about coming over. I quickly shuffle through opening lines—something cheeky, but friendly. Yikes! Am I really doing this?

Yep.

Yeah, I am.

Merits go crazy for what others cherish and admire. And, thanks to Elas, I seem to be pretty popular. This is the perfect chance to earn Temnen's trust before the whole court discovers what a faker I am.

Whether he likes it or not, the frog prince is going to blab information that will help me hatch an escape plan. Then Raff and I can get out of this place forever. And soon, too. It's a good plan, mainly because it's better than no plan.

The hardest part? Having to pretend to like Temnen.

As I take my first step toward the Merit, trumpets blare from each corner of the hall, a fanfare of sorts, silencing the chatter and drawing attention back to the king, who's standing in front of his throne, arms raised high like a pompous ringmaster.

"Gather around, dear courtiers," he commands. "The moment you have been waiting for has finally arrived. The Blood Sun ceremony commences!"

The poor, naked faery that Temnen de-winged is pushed forward. His eyes go to an older woman standing at the front of the crowd. Her features are similar to his, so I'm guessing she's the boy's mother. She wrings her hands, but doesn't cry out or reach for him, her only protest the silent tears streaming down her cheeks. Whatever is about to happen to her son, it seems she's already accepted it. Or knows there's no point in appealing to the Merit king.

Drums pound. Faeries chant. Draírdon drags the young man to the altar carved into the floor of the dais. When the fae's throat is slashed, his blood will flow along the channels, down the stairs, and become part of the hall's glistening water feature.

Water feature, now that's a joke! Filled with horror and death and misery, it's nothing but a monument to terror.

Eyes filled with blood lust, the king raises his head. "Change-Bringer, come!"

What? Me?

Temnen offers me his arm and guides me up the stairs. As we climb upward, my head spins, and I try not to lean too heavily on him. At the top, he positions me between his father and Draírdon. El Fannon places an obsidian knife in my hand, my fingers closing reflexively around the bejeweled handle.

*It's heavy*, is the first thing I think.

Then: *what am I supposed to do with this flipping piece of shit?*

The High Mage warbles on in an ancient language, the words *Merits and blessings and blood* being the only ones that make sense to me. The court is working itself into a frenzy, leaping, howling, spitting, and some writhing disgustingly together like this is a spring festival. I'm no prude, but a ritualized killing would have to be the farthest thing from sexy-times that I could possibly imagine.

The king silences the court with a flourish of his hand. His gaze burns through me. "Tonight, our change-bringer has the honor of making the Blood Sun sacrifice. Praise be to the Merits and the beings who have brought her to us." He nods at me. "Now, girl. Use the blade."

Temnen's face is a horror-mask—his gruesome smile taunting and cruel. He lives for moments like this.

Seizing the boy's hair, the mage jerks him around, revealing the soft flesh of his throat, the terror-stricken whites of his lovely violet eyes.

As I open my mouth to say *no, no way*, a strong hand covers mine and slashes it over the boy's neck. Blood splashes rich and red, the fae's body thrashing its wild, final protest.

Swallowing vomit, I step back into Elas's chest. "Smile like you mean it," he whispers over the din of the roaring crowd.

Drums and flutes begin playing with renewed vigor. The knife still entwined in our hands, Elas lifts it high, blood dripping from the blade down the sleeve of my dress. With a smile frozen on my face, I silently beg the tears threatening to spill down my cheeks to hurry up and reabsorb into my trembling body before they expose me as a fraud.

What the hell just happened?

What have I done?

The fae scream and howl, loving every sick and violent moment.

I don't turn and thank Elas for saving my life, even though that's exactly what he's done. If he hadn't moved my hand, I would never have killed the fae myself, and I'm sure the king would have dealt with me swiftly. And, now, thanks to Elas's intervention, I'm an accomplice, not a fully-fledged murderer, which is great, and we can both go to hell together.

I refuse to look down and watch the river of red pulse along the stone channels. I won't look at the king or the mage or Temnen or the poor boy's mother.

And I definitely won't look at the courtiers dipping fingers into the warm liquid and smearing it over each other's lips and chests. Instead, my gaze flits around the room like a startled butterfly, finally settling on the warm amber eyes of the Court of Five prince and it stays there, stuck on his kneeling form as if my life depends on it.

Perhaps it does.

Raff's fists clench and unclench. His chest pumps, his expression unhinged as if he's about to do something extreme, something very, very stupid.

"It's okay," I mouth, even though it's a lie. Nothing will ever be okay again.

"I'll kill him," his lips shape back, and I wonder who he means. Temnen? El Fannon? Elas?

Temnen peels the knife from my fingers, then lifts the blade to his mouth, licking it clean.

"Very well done, Change-Bringer," says the king. "Your actions have secured your position for another moon's turn. Yes, well done indeed."

Right. So that means I have roughly four weeks to make progress on Temnen and get the hell out of here before the next Blood Sun ceremony, because there is no way I'm doing that again.

Ever.

"Yes, you surprised me, little human," says Temnen. "But tell me, Elas, why did you help her? Did you wish to share in the Blood Sun glory?"

Elas bows. "No, my prince. I wished her first cut to be magnificent and for the blood not to be wasted. But do not fear. By the time of the next ceremony, with my assistance, her skill with the blade will be much improved."

"Yes, indeed. That was very wise of you. You may take courtiers of your choosing to practice on. And, at this time of year, the woodlands are teeming with nymphs, perhaps you can cull their population. It would be a service to your king."

El Fannon takes a dish of blood from a platter and gulps it down, waving a hand at me. "You may take her away, Elas, before she falls asleep on her feet. A mortal's first Blood Sun is a taxing one."

Temnen captures my arm. "I will escort her, Father."

"No, no. Elas will do it. She requires rest, and I do not believe the likes of your attention will be particularly restorative. You can take the Elemental fae back to the tower instead. And, yes you may play, Temnen, but please do not kill him. He's far too valuable alive."

"Perhaps I could visit you tomorrow, Temnen," I force myself to say, still sick to my stomach. "If you will allow it, of course."

Those wriggly antenna quiver, and he does his best impression of a charming smile. "I would be delighted. The aviary at noon would suit me well."

I curtsy. Elas bows. And then we hold our heads high and walk slowly down the stairs. I count each step—a red one, then a black—on and on until we reach the marble floor.

As we push through the crowded hall, a hand reaches out and squeezes mine tightly. I look up into Lidwinia's kind face, every word she dare not utter clear in her eyes.

At the doors, Elas says, "To the White Tower, My Lady?"

"Yes, please. But no shifting. A long walk in the fresh air will do us both good."

Then we leave the hall and hurry through the empty streets of the Merit city—a city that runs on pain and blood and terror.

# 16

## A Plan

### Raff

For the Merits, the day following the Blood Sun ceremony is one of rest. I can tell this from my windowless cell, high above the crashing waves of the Obsidian Sea, because the fetid scent of the guard's lunch isn't wafting through my door, a welcome relief. I was never much fond of offal.

Overnight my knife wounds have healed remarkably well, and the anger boiling in my blood gives me energy to crouch against the wall and plot the frog-like Temnen's death.

I long to make the Merits pay for what they did to Isla at last night's ceremony. Weak and chained like a rabid dog, I cannot run or fight or shift into my firebird, but nothing can stop me dreaming of it.

So I concentrate, not on the spurt of the woodland pixie's blood after the slice of Isla's knife, but on Temnen's after mine.

I hear the crunch of windpipe, the gurgling gasp of air. I feel every wracking shudder, every kick of his boot and desperate claw at life. I snort at the stench of urine as it pools around his body. Stare into salmon-colored eyes rolling backward into forever darkness. Revel in his limpness followed by the cold, lifeless flesh, growing rigid under my touch.

Yes, Temnen's death will be a glorious thrill to savor.

*Revenge*, whispers the poison. *When you do it, take your time. Make it slow. Think of—*

"Raff? I come bearing sweets." Isla's voice penetrates through the ancient wooden door, clear and strong, waking me my from my violent fantasy. "Are you decent?"

Decent? What could she mean? My thoughts of murder certainly aren't. While I struggle to make sense of her question, the heavy bar grates across the door.

"I'm coming in." Then like a blast of sunshine, she enters bearing a torch in one hand, a wicker basket in the other, and a bright smile on her lovely face.

Swallowing hard, I straighten my spine, wishing I could conjure a glamor of princely strength and vigor. It pains me that she must see me so badly diminished.

After lighting the wall torches and setting hers on a bracket, she places the basket on the ground and kneels next to me, her brow pinched. "Are you okay?"

"I'm fine, but after the horrors of last night, I fear that you cannot be. When I finally get Temnen's vile neck in my grasp, I shall delight in breaking it. Then I'll tear his feelers from his forehead like he did that pixie's wings and stuff them up his—"

"Raff! Thanks to Elas, I'm fine. I promise. Don't waste what little energy you have on that creep Temnen. Now let me see your wounds."

I lift the tattered tunic the guards tossed me last night and reveal my healing skin. She delves inside her basket and withdraws a small clay jar. Cool fingers press against my flesh, chill bumps following in the wake of her soft caress.

A sharp breath hisses between my teeth. Her touch is pure agony and not because of my knife wounds.

"Relax. It's only calendula cream. Those cuts look good. Your magic mustn't be entirely depleted yet. It's helping you heal."

"But it may as well be spent for all that I cannot do."

She smiles sadly. "Poor Raff."

"Isla." I lift my hand and stroke her velvety cheek. "I have never felt more powerless than I did last eve watching you with that knife in your grip. Those moments of the pixie's death will forever torment me. But if I could take the memory from you and make it mine to bear alone, I would do it in a heartbeat."

Unshed tears shimmer in her eyes, the corner of her mouth quivering. "Elas did what he had to do to keep us all alive."

"The boy would have died regardless," I confirm, wishing to remove her guilt. She is blameless in the matter.

She closes her eyes momentarily, releasing a long sigh. "You're right. Let's not dwell on it." She hands me a water pouch and then lifts a bundle wrapped in checkered cloth. "So, I think for energy, you should go with savory first, followed by a sweet treat for seconds."

After gulping water, I eat salty cheese and olives pressed between slices of crusty bread, a sandwich she calls it, as I groan in pleasure. Then she passes me the strawberry-colored cookies. On the outside, they're crisp and chewy, the insides light and fluffy, and I eat six in quick succession. As I chew, perfect joy blossoms inside my chest.

"Good, huh? They're the macarons I promised I'd make you."

I nod, and then speak with my mouth full. "You were happy when you baked them."

"The happiest I've been since that idiot kidnapped me. Baking helped me stop thinking about that poor boy...and his mother..."

Fury turns my vision red, but I wrestle it into submission and force a smile. "I've never tasted anything so pleasant. I would eat these red sweets every day if I could. What are they made with?"

"Well, the shells are egg whites, almond meal for the—hey! Don't try to distract me." She laughs, pushing my shoulder as she sinks next to me against the wall, our arms touching lightly. "Why haven't Ever and Lara come for us?" she asks.

"Lara? There is no chance in any realm that my brother would dare to bring her near the Merits, even under the pretense of a diplomatic mission. First of all, if something went wrong and they couldn't leave, he would not trust our court to care for Merri because she is only a half-fae child. And since he has been free of the curse, it is Lara's love that runs through his veins and gives him purpose. He would never risk her life."

"And if you die here? Do you really think the curse will return to Ever?"

"I suspect it will but do not know for certain. When I'm gone, perhaps you will find out."

She squeezes my arm. "What do you miss the most from home?"

"Spark. I miss her terribly and pray to Dana she is keeping out of trouble."

"Here, have another macaron and try to picture her romping happily with Balor."

An image of Magret and Ever's horror-stricken faces after eating Isla's cookies fills my mind. I jerk upright, the chains clanking. "Those cookies you shared on the first day of the procession, they made anyone who ate them cry, including me."

Her blue eyes widen. "Yeah, they did, didn't they?"

"We were overcome, not with simple sadness but a sorrow so profound we could do nothing but surrender to it. This ability to imbue food with horror is powerful, Isla. It is a weapon, and if you know how to wield it then—"

"Then I can use it against the Merits. All of them at once. I just need access to their kitchens at a feast which...would be impossible. They'd never trust me. Damn."

She sags beside me, picking up a stone and throwing it against the opposite wall. "Wait... Temnen was so excited by my booming Merit pendant's statistics last night that he wanted to hang out and share in the glory. I know you'll think this was too risky, but I had to do something to try and get a plan started, so I met him at the aviary earlier today. I tried to grill him for information. It was horrible. He's so into himself."

"What does that mean?"

"It means he's pompous. Basically, he's an ass."

"True, but he is a dangerous ass. You must promise to keep away from him."

"I can't. Right now, he wants me to like him, and I need him to trust me, which, unfortunately, means lots of fun times hanging out with the Frog Prince." She sighs, shoulders dropping. "Yeah, I'd rather not be buddies with Temnen. But, I think it'll be the key to getting us out of here."

"No, Isla. Do not encourage him, I beg you. He is unpredictable and cruelty is his favorite game."

"It's fine. Because he's vain and obsessed with being popular, it makes him easy to manipulate. All he wants is for me to tell him stories about my home that he can spread around the court. Temnen's a joke." She laughs, shaking her head. "He's already flapped his mouth and told me that each night after dinner Riven disappears beneath the castle alone and is down there up to no good."

"Precisely! It would be foolish for you to follow Riven."

"Maybe, but I trust Lidwinia, and she keeps insisting I need to speak with him. Riven can help us, Raff, I'm sure of it." Her expression changes, her eyes gleaming with excitement. "And this might be useful, too. Look..."

She holds her palm out flat between us, closes her eyes and grimaces, concentrating hard. One, two, three moments pass, then blue flames burst from her hand, curling along her fingers.

Grinning, I lean over her fire magic. "Make them dance."

She squints hard, and the flames rise, then disappear. "Dang it. It works best when I'm really angry. I practiced a *lot* last night, and I think I'm improving."

"You are a wonder."

She screws her pale eyebrows at me, as though she suspects I lie. Has she forgotten I cannot?

Her eyes drop to my mouth, scan my face, then focus on my lips again before flicking away. "Okay." She stands and brushes dirt from her tunic, stepping backward. "I'm leaving before I do something stupid, like kiss you again."

All my senses sharpen. "Yes! You should do this stupid thing. It is a most excellent idea." I leap to my feet and lunge forward, the chains jerking me back when I almost touch her.

I'm close but not close enough. Pain tears through my shoulders as my weight hangs from the wrist shackles behind my back, and, straining my muscles, I fall forward until my lips hover only a breath away from hers.

Soft as a butterfly alighting on a flower, she kisses me once, then strides toward the door.

"Wait! Get back here, Isla."

She laughs. "Next time I see you, I'll have a fail-proof plan to get us out of this dump. Just you wait and see."

"*Isla*," I growl. "Stay away from the Merit princes."

She plucks a torch from the wall, leaving the other burning, and throws me a smile. "Okay, Raff. I'll see you soon."

"Isla...promise me—"

The door slams shut, the bolt screeching as she slides it across. "Sure," she says through the slab of wood. "I promise."

I sink onto my haunches, dropping my head into my hands.

She lies. She lies.

And besides, she did not even specify what she was promising anyway.

# 17

## Betrothed

### Isla

"I sla, I must speak with you," calls a voice from the aviary's entrance. The loud, grating tone frightens the bluebird on my shoulder, sending it fluttering and chirping into the branches above my head.

Excellent. Just as I'd hoped, my new buddy, Temnen, has come seeking another friendly tryst.

Over the past week, we've had quite a few cozy chats, which is thrilling for him, droning on and on about his favorite person—himself. But for me, it's about as fun as one of the lectures Max gives me when I leave the grill on overnight after a shift.

So, yeah, I kind of sorta lied to Raff—I've only been staying away from *one* of the Merit princes, and that's only because I'm still working out how to get Riven alone. Once I do, I won't be staying away from *him*, either.

"Human?" says Temnen as he opens the aviary's curling metal gates and prances inside.

Hiding behind a feathery gray bush that's dotted with bright-gold berries, I stay silent. *Come find me, Merit.*

"Human, I know you're in here. The bird attendants saw you enter."

Because I made sure they did.

I paste a phony smile on my face, then pop out from behind the branches like a demented jack-in-the-box. "Good morning, Prince Temnen. I am aware which species I belong to. No need to keep reminding me." I force a tinkling laugh.

"Ah, I see you there by the stream!" He struts forward, hands clasped behind his back, wearing a haughty expression and a black cloak made of noisy, swishing fabric covered in green-copper points.

He looks impressive until you notice the mile-high platform heels at the end of his black boots that tell you he's overcompensating for something—most likely his tedious personality.

As he kisses my hand, I suppress a grimace and arch a cheeky eyebrow. "If I addressed you as *fae* Prince Temnen all the time, it might start to annoy you eventually."

"True. It would become a bore and you would need to be dealt with."

Dealt with? Hm. That sounds unpleasant.

"When I decided to look for you after breakfast, this was the first place I came. You seem rather fond of the birds."

"They're amazing." The aviary is a wondrous place, strange and beautiful, teeming with exotic, colorful birds like macaws and parakeets—the whir of their mechanical wings a comforting sound as they flit through the pastel trees.

"And these little guys are hilarious." A group of otter-like creatures with long fangs frolic in the stream that meanders through wild grasses, shrubs, and rambling flowers, leaping and rolling as they dunk each other under the water.

"Yes, the river reapers are most entertaining."

"Reapers? That's a ridiculous name for the sweet, little furballs."

"If you saw what they change into at night time, you would not say that. The cage around the aviary exists to keep more than the birds in."

The entire complex is roughly the size of a large concert arena. Under the spectacular, metal-filigree domed roof are bright sections, expansive and alive with color, while others are dark and shadowed and riddled with secrets.

While I wait for Temnen most days, I like to spend a little time in both areas, listening and watching closely. Light and dark—they both have things to teach me.

After my first meeting here with the Merit prince the day following the horrific Blood Sun ceremony, I realized the aviary is the perfect place to continue to lure him to—the birds and tiny animals keep me from falling asleep while he prattles on about himself and his ever-rising statistics.

"This is beautiful," I say, for once not lying to him. "Where's Olwydd today?"

"He eats too many of the smaller birds, which is amusing but nearly always gives him indigestion. Therefore, I've banned him from accompanying me today."

Shame. Olwydd is better company than his master.

My arms splay wide as I spin in a circle, stopping to watch a group of fluorescent-orange birds fly through the twisted branches of a golden oak. "Most of the city's outdoor spaces are ordered and industrial, but the aviary is wild. Untamed. It's perfect."

For a moment, he looks annoyed by my opinion, then his creepy eyes scan my pendant again. "Your statistics are marvelous! Your approval rating has tripled this week. I admit I am surprised a human has become so popular with my people."

I smile, turning toward a sculpture of a sundial so I don't have to look at him. Every time I do, I can't help picturing his violent expression as the blood gushed from that poor pixie's throat.

Swallowing my rage, I say, "Well, I guess you Merits have good taste."

He gestures to a woven-branch bench seat nearby. "Do you wish to sit?"

"I'm happy standing." That way I don't have to get too close to him.

"What do you imagine your next fabulous invention might be as our change-bringer?"

"Well...let's see..." I have no idea, so I say the first thing that enters my head. "I think I'll design special airplanes and an airport."

His orange eyes widen and glow. "The flying machines from your world? Yes, I have heard tales of them. Father will adore this new venture."

To stop myself from laughing, I squeeze my eyes shut, picturing Raff in that lonely, dark cell. When I open them a moment later, Temnen is way too close, his black-tipped fingers reaching for my hair.

He picks up a long strand and tugs it painfully. "For a human, you are exceptional. My father and Lidwinia are extremely impressed with you. Do not mind what Riven thinks. His opinion is worth less than the cooks who toil in the kitchen."

Little does he know he's speaking to someone whose favorite pastime is *toiling* in a kitchen.

Expression intense, he clutches his pendant like it's his most beloved possession, his gaze sliding over my body. "Isla, even now, as the pet I stole from the Elemental court, you add great value to my status. But if you were to be my bride, I would be the envy of every male in the court, and my father would have no choice but to reconsider which of his sons truly deserve to inherit the Throne of Merits."

"But I thought your laws specified that only the oldest son can—wait, did you say *bride*?"

"Yes," he whispers, antennae pointing at me rather vulgarly. "I am suggesting you become my betrothed. It will be advantageous to us both and a perfect revenge against the Elemental Court."

Oh sweet Lord. If on pain of death, I had to choose a Merit to marry, I'd pick Lidwinia every time. We'd get along fine.

He steps forward. I step backward, stumbling over a tree root. The backs of my knees hit a bench seat and I sink down onto it, grim reality heavy on my shoulders. Why did I beg Sally Salamande to send me through that portal?

Worst. Mistake. Ever.

"Are you quite well?" Temnen asks as he sits next to me, his hand draping across my thigh like a limp octopus tentacle.

I can't get a word past my seized-up throat muscles, so I just nod.

"Good. Good. It is understandable that you are overcome with excitement, for it is a great honor to secure the affections of a Merit prince. Now, what was I saying?"

I can't remember. No doubt something shockingly boring. Or just shocking.

"Oh, yes. I was pointing out that since you are a change-bringer, you will bring me great renown and fortune. Are you pleased with the idea?"

Nope, terrified. And extremely cheesed off at this bizarre turn of events.

Antennae bristling, he leans in, his lips parting like moist black slugs waking up and rolling over for breakfast.

"Noo..." I turn my head away and attempt to look flattered, but shy, as if my greatest desire is to lock lips with the dreadful prince if only my virtuous nature would allow it. "Please, Temnen. You mustn't do that."

I use my best judgy tone, the one that makes rude customers at Max's diner turn red and apologize for their half-sweet, non-fat, vegan caramel macchiato orders. Just FYI, I never guilt trip the polite customers, no matter how annoying their orders are.

"You do not find me attractive?" He pouts in disbelief.

I've never been more grateful for the ability to lie. "Of course I do! It's just that...we don't do that back home. I mean, before the...ceremony. If my mother found out, she'd murder me in my sleep."

So, so, so not true. I swallow quickly as I realize how close my comment cuts to his mother's death at the hand of the king. Luckily, he's too obsessed with himself to notice.

His pupils dilate to the max, turning his eyes a creepy black. "Your people do not enjoy their partners prior to marriage?"

"No," I lie again. "And we don't kiss each other either."

"But I've heard reports from fae who have visited your world, Merits even. They say many humans indulge in bed sports without marriage vows."

Crap. "I didn't think you could travel to my world."

"I admit it is difficult, but not impossible. Your moving films—wonderful inventions, a true melding of magic and technology—provide evidence of humans' love of debauchery."

"Really? You've seen a movie?"

"No. But when I was a child, I met a fae who had been to a mortal house of films."

"You mean a movie theater."

"Yes, a moving theater; that is what I said."

I stifle a laugh, and he leans closer, extinguishing my tiny flash of humor.

"We Merits follow our passions wherever they may lead us. The more depraved the better."

My heart flips, then sinks to my stomach as my frozen smile melts away. "Where I come from, our traditions are different. Suitors who force unwanted attentions onto their betrothed are reviled and looked down upon."

"I see. They are disliked and unpopular. Since you are such a prize and your approval rating is soaring, I will cede to your wishes, my dear mortal."

Relief flows through me. "You will?" I bite back my elated smile.

"Yes." He stands and struts around like a rooster, flicking his cape behind him. "If you will seal our betrothal with a chaste kiss, then you have my word—I will wait until our wedding night to avail myself of your charms."

Ugh. Do I really have to kiss him? I'd rather make out with a cockroach. Or an iguana. Am I really going to go through with this and pretend to be betrothed to Temnen?

A pair of amber wolf eyes appear in my mind. A Wild mane of chestnut hair with delightfully pointed ears peeking through it. Warm, soft lips. That intense haughty stare. Raff.

I mentally push those images away and let a plan form, one that involves banquets and guests and distracted pompous Merits. This may be the best chance I'll ever get. I'll be damned if I'm going to let it slip by.

"Have you fallen in love with me?" I ask, fluttering my lashes like a dummy.

His gaze flicks off mine and dances over the leaves of the golden oak tree. "I have fallen in love with the idea of what we can become together."

Ha, ha. Good save. I pout. "Do you at least think I'm pretty?"

He swallows, his Adam's apple bobbing. "You are plain but pleasant enough to look upon, for a human."

"Under your guidance, perhaps I will improve in time." Ugh. Vomit. "Will there be a feast to celebrate our betrothal?"

"Yes, of course. The grandest affair you can imagine. Everyone in the land will wish to attend. Sea witches. Brags and boggarts. Shades. Pookas. Ogres and skinwalkers. All the kingdom's Dark Bringers! What a triumph it will be."

I peer around his shoulder, pulling an amazed expression at the sundial behind him. "Oh! The time's gone by so fast. I'm so sorry, Temnen, I have to race. I forgot your sister is expecting me."

"Lidwinia? What could she possibly want that is more important than speaking with *me*? My sister can wait."

"Actually, she can't. She wanted help to choose a design for a Solstice festival gown. There's a particular fae coming from the Shade court, and she wants to impress him. Exciting, isn't it? Maybe she'll be betrothed soon too."

It's not exciting. Utter baloney is what it is. Lidwinia couldn't give a fig about gowns, and as I suspected, Temnen doesn't know his sister very well because, if I'm correct, annoyance is making his antennae wriggle, not anger at my latest lies.

I feign wide-eyed innocence. "Would you like to come with me and help? I'm sure she'd appreciate your advice. She's deciding between two awesome designs. One is a russet organza with tiny machines—"

"Enough! I have no desire to hear the details." He sinks back onto the bench and waves me away with both hands. "Hurry along. You are already late."

"I understand, my love. I can't wait to tell Lidwinia our news." Ouch. Those words scalded my tongue—now I know how Raff must feel when he tries to lie. "You have more important things to do." Like tear wings off helpless creatures.

My skin crawling, I leap up, curtsy, and then lean in to peck him on the lips, nausea churning my stomach.

Forcing a saucy wink, I step back and say, "There. Consider our betrothal sealed."

He grips my tunic, pulling me into his face again. He bites my bottom lip, drawing blood.

"Ow!"

Licking blood from his lips, he smirks. "I look forward to announcing our engagement to the court after dinner tonight."

I smile sweetly, wiping my mouth. Then I lift the hem of my tunic and dash through the aviary and exit into the walled garden surrounding it, my pulse roaring in my ears.

Outside, the sun blazes high in an azure sky scattered with puffy, purple-tinged clouds. I draw the sultry air deep into my lungs and walk quickly toward the wall and a set of thorn-covered gates, closing them behind me with a loud click before I rush along the ordered streets that surround the Meritorium.

Then, with my gaze fixed on black spires and the massive ornately framed glass panels that make up the back wall of the castle, I scale the winding alleyways, crowded with fae going about their business, and head for the servants' entrance.

When I enter the kitchens on the bottom level, the smell of roasting meat makes me dizzy, and I yell cheery greetings to the cooks, so I'll be heard above the clank of pots and general hustle and bustle.

Thankfully, no one stops me as I duck up the servants' stairs and breeze along back passageways until I reach the floor Lidwinia's wing is situated on.

I stride through a grand hallway that's lined by green columns marbled with gold, thinking of Raff bored out of his mind on the stone floor of his dark cell, the cruel contrast of the castle's luxury making anger swirl hot through my veins.

As my supposed fated mate, how will the fire prince react to news of my fake engagement? Truth be told, I'd rather be stuck with arrogant Raff forever than horrible Temnen. Even in a cell. And especially in the dark.

In fact, if I didn't know about the dumb curse and the prophecy Raff is obsessed with, I'd probably have a major crush on him. But I have no desire to be with a guy who only wants me because I can allegedly fix all his problems.

I don't have a savior complex. I want to be loved in my own right, on my own terms—and maybe for the rhapsodic delights of my baked pastries.

By the time I reach the princess's chambers—a series of black crystal-lined rooms decorated with tumbling green vines and deep-red furnishings—my mind is full of images of what life with Temnen might entail. Sitting next to him at every single meal for the rest of my life, his sour features my first sight each and every morning, kissing him while those slimy antennae-things stroke through my hair or suck out my marrow. No thanks. I must take great care I don't end up living in that particular alternate reality. I'd rather die.

Me a Merit princess? Nope. No way.

When I burst into Lidwinia's sitting room, she takes one look at my face and sends her ladies scampering like mice out the double doors, their giggles trailing behind them.

"What has happened?" she asks as she stops sharpening a bone arrowhead, laying it down on a pile of split shafts and feather fletching.

The girl loves her weapons, and going by the leather outfit she's wearing, I'd say she's not long returned from a hunt.

"Temnen wants to marry me," I announce without preamble.

"What?" She covers a laugh with one hand, the other beckoning me forward. "Come sit beside me. That is the most absurd thing I've ever heard."

"For me, it's the most disgusting. Sorry, no offense meant to your family. You're perfectly wonderful. Your brother, not so much."

"None taken."

I contemplate the metal spiders decorating her leather corset, while she frowns and scratches her neck. Long gold legs wriggle as the largest one crawls to her shoulder. "Lidwinia, I don't want to freak you out, but that spider's moving."

"Oh that's just Rothlo. He only hurts flies. Do not fear him."

Eight emerald eyes swivel my way, each one of them glaring at me.

"Hi Rothlo," I say, just in case he can understand me.

Lidwinia gets up and paces across the room. "Isla, this is grave news indeed. I cannot let you marry my brother. Cruelty is his greatest pleasure, and I will not let you suffer at his hand. You must speak with Riven tonight and put a plan for escape in place. It is decided—I must tell you how to find him."

"But Riven has barely bothered to look my way. Why would he care what happens to me and Raff?"

"Believe me, he cares. He desires lasting peace with the Elemental princes and their heirs. He will help you. As soon as he rises from the dinner table this evening, you must do the same. Move quickly and go to the arched stairwell behind the dais. It is on the left as you look at it. Wait there and Elas will meet you with a torch. After Riven passes by, take the torch and follow at a safe distance."

"Where will he be going?"

"Down. I can say no more. When he discovers you, plead your case. He will listen, and I promise he will not hurt you, Isla. I know my older brother well. He is nothing like Temnen."

"Thank you," I say as I approach Lidwinia. I place a hand on her shoulder, and the spider races up her neck, disappearing into her green hair. "Sorry, Rothlo. I didn't mean to squash you."

Lidwinia draws me close, squeezing the breath out my lungs with a quick hug. "Don't worry about Temnen. Ultimately, he's a coward."

"And *you're* very strong." I laugh, rubbing the ache from my ribs.

Leaving the princess to tinker with her weapons, I hurry back to the White Tower. Once there, I make strawberry crepes for an afternoon snack and then move to my bedroom to consider the clothes in my over-stuffed wardrobe.

Tonight, I need a special outfit. Something charming to wear on the dais beside Temnen but practical enough for chasing Riven into the cobwebbed bowels of the castle. I hate to think about what I might find him doing down there, but I'm praying it's nothing violent.

Either way, I think a dress with a floor-scraping train is out of the question.

# 18

## The Crystal Well

### Isla

Just as Lidwinia predicted, as soon as Temnen has announced our betrothal and brought an official end to dinner, Riven rises from the royal table, the sharp points of his silver shoulder pauldrons flashing as he adjusts a jeweled sword belt over his black tunic.

I watch him hurry down the stairs onto the marble floor and then make a hard right behind the dais. Chin raised, he speaks to no one, staring ahead as if in a trance, his expression cold and regal. His shock of silver hair is the last thing I see before he disappears.

Throughout dinner, I was surprised to find myself left in peace to eat my meal with Elas and his Meritorium crew of sweet-faced light elves. But for the betrothal announcement, I had to stand by

Temnen's side, grinning at the courtiers until my cheeks hurt, as both our pendants strobed wildly.

Still seated at the high table, I put down my cup of wine and glance at my new fiancé. "Temnen," I whisper near his ear, rubbing my stomach like an alien might explode out at any moment. "I'm sorry, but tonight's excitement has completely overwhelmed me. I'm feeling unwell. Would you mind if I returned to my chambers early?"

Black brows pinch together. "If you must. Humans have weak constitutions, and I suppose I must learn to tolerate yours. A guard will escort you to the tower."

Leaning close, I squeeze his arm. "Thank you for the offer. But while you announced our betrothal, you sparked an incredible idea for an invention, and I can't wait to run it by Elas. He can see me home."

His eyes widen. "You must tell me about it now."

I suppress a shudder at his quivering wet lips. "A fiancé must keep some secrets. This may well turn out to be your wedding gift, so you must be patient." I kiss his cheek, drop a curtsy, then flee toward Elas who will by now be waiting in the archway through which Riven has disappeared.

"Quickly," says Elas, passing me a torch and opening a metal-strapped door.

"Thanks. I took far too long to get away from Temnen. Riven will be way ahead. How will I know which way to go?"

Black wings flare out, one wrapping around my shoulders and nudging me through the doorway. "There's a secret door off the second landing. Look for a triangular recess in the bricks and press it. Simply follow the stairs downward. And for Merits' sake, don't trip."

Grimacing, I suck on the corner of my lip.

"Go. You will be fine." Elas waves his hand and the torch bursts into flame. I step through the archway. Light spills over the jet walls as the door closes behind me, cutting off the noise of the Great Hall.

I take a few slow breaths to steady my nerves and then start walking.

A narrow, gently inclining passage leads me up to the second landing. I pass the torch over the walls and find the triangle above my head. Cold fear seeps into my bones as I press my palm against it. A door appears, cracking open to reveal a narrow stairwell.

I listen for Riven's footsteps, for rats, for monsters sharpening their claws in the shadows but hear only the ragged sound of my breathing echoing off the walls.

Down to the depths I go, my heart in my mouth, my mind racing as I try to form a compelling case to present to the severe silver prince.

The damp, musky air is heavy in my lungs. I keep my eyes on my slippers, not looking too closely at the walls around me in case lots of friends of Rothlo's are hanging from webs above me ready to drop inside my dress, crawl into my hair, and lay eggs that will hatch a billion tiny baby spiders and—arghhh! Stop it, Isla. Focus.

Finally, the passage widens, and a stack of boulders probably three times my height blocks the path forward; all but a tiny section I could probably squeeze through if I had to. I peer around the wall of rock, my eyebrows leaping at what I see.

Four torches burn at the curved corners of a large cavern, the walls and floors dripping with sparkling limestone—stalactites and stalagmites reaching eternally toward each other like parted lovers.

Water floods the bottom of the cave. A small island of jagged stone stands in the middle from which a quartz-colored column grows into a chest-height well or font, its surface glowing brightly with a magical, mercurial liquid.

This must be the druid's well that King El Fannon spoke of.

From where I stand, I have a perfect view of the silver prince, his hands fisted against black-clad thighs as he stares into the mirrored surface. Rainbow colors flicker and dance over his face and the cavern's walls. Other than the sound of dripping water, an ominous silence fills the mystical space.

Next to the crown's black spikes, the owl, Meerade sits on Riven's shoulders. She swivels her head, the black-scaled half of her face and penetrating green eyes now aimed in my direction. Despite the deep shadows enveloping me, I'm certain the creature can see me.

For long seconds, my heart pounds hard, then the owl turns away, ruffling her black and white feathers. "The future comes close. It creeps in dark shadows," says a raspy voice that sounds like it's coming straight out of the owl's hooked beak.

"What?" says Riven, flicking his gaze up to Meerade who's still perched on the sharp silver plates covering his shoulders. Yep, his creature definitely speaks!

Frowning, Riven peers back into the well.

"A girl! A girl!" says the bird.

"Yes, I am not blind, Meerade. I can see she is here again."

What? Can he see me? I jump backward, my ears straining to hear their conversation. And what does he mean by again? I've never followed him down here before.

"And each time I look into the druid's well," Riven continues, "she grows older still."

He's talking about a girl he can see in the well, not me, thank God. I creep forward, wedging my body into the gap between the rock and wall. The owl rotates its head again, and this time looks straight at me. "Come," it says.

"Yes, Meerade," says Riven answering distractedly. "I hear you."

But the owl wasn't speaking to the prince. She's telling *me* to come forward, to reveal myself. I shake my head no. I'm not ready for Riven to discover me snooping in the shadows.

"Come. Come quickly," she repeats.

"Be quiet, Meerade. I cannot focus with your prattle."

She bobs her head, beckoning me forward.

I pad carefully around a narrow shelf of silt and fine rock, skirting the outer edges of the cavern until I'm directly behind Riven, but at a safe distance. Arms braced on the edges of the well, he's so absorbed in the image reflected upon its silver surface that he doesn't notice my intrusion.

I wait a few moments then dip my toe into the water, testing its depth. Ankle deep, I wade closer, my pulse pounding in my throat. If I can hear the soft swish of water as I move, then surely the prince can too. This is risky, but I need to see what he's looking at and can only pray he isn't too angry when he realizes I'm here.

A blurry image of a girl passes over the water, and his knuckles whiten as he grips the edges of the well.

Before the image vanishes, I need to see who the girl is. The intense heat building inside my head and my gut, tells me it's important. Maybe fatally so.

To get a better view, I move a little to the side. Something about this scene strikes me marrow-deep, and I know I'll never forget how Riven looks at this moment. A curtain of silver hair falling over one high cheekbone. His expression full of agony. The hopeless curve of his shoulders. Sorrow washes through me, tears stinging my eyes.

I wade two steps forward, the water cold on my legs.

The bird watches my approach, but deep in a trance, Riven remains statue-still, frozen in his grief. Two more steps and I'm standing directly behind him, peering around his broad shoulders. Instantly, the image of the girl reflected in the well sucks me in.

First, I'm captivated by a delightful spread of freckles, then the long tips of fae ears parting bright-red hair, my attention settling on a brilliant pair of silver eyes. It's unbelievable, but this girl looks exactly how I imagine Lara's child will look when she's grown up. A terrible thought leaps into my mind.

"That's Merri!" I blurt.

Slowly, the black crown turns. Blue-tourmaline eyes skewer me, the shock and anger flickering in them terrifying. Oh, shit! This wasn't how I planned to announce my presence.

Wondering how he'll punish me for invading his privacy, I cover my mouth with a shaking hand.

"You!" growls Riven, the angry vibrations of his voice cracking stalactites from the roof. With great splashes, they pierce the water around me like sharp spears, forming a cage around my body.

Like a real-live deity, he steps toward me, black boots barely dinting the water's surface. Creepers—he's walking on water! Grasping the bars of glittering limestone that surround me, he leans in close, and I look up, up, up to his furious face. Hulking body shuddering, his lips compress, a deep scowl marring his ethereal beauty.

Prior to this moment, I've only seen Riven from a safe distance across a crowded banquet hall, and it's quite another thing to be this close to both him and the intense, all-knowing stare of his owl.

Right now, I'm in a perilous position, and my stomach fills with dread as I prepare for anything. Possibly even death.

Seconds pass and he and the owl stare into my eyes.

Drip, drip, drip goes the water.

Bang, bang, bang pounds my heart.

"Speak," he shouts, and I nearly leap out of my skin.

"Riven, please... I'm sorry to disturb you, but Lidwinia sent me here to speak with you. She promised you wouldn't hurt me."

"You lie. My sister would never send a human into the sacred druid's chamber. You are my brother's betrothed, a spy sent to report on the family's bad seed."

I take a quick breath, then a small risk. "And you're that bad seed?"

Those glowing eyes narrow further. "Some refer to me as this, yes."

"I'm not a spy. I've come for your help. I know you want peace with the Elemental Court, and because of that, you'd probably like to set Raff free. But I also know that because of your father, you can't just let him walk out of here. But if you were to help me plot an escape, the king wouldn't have to know. Temnen won't—"

"Temnen!" he scoffs. "What vile creature plots against their beloved's wishes?"

"Whoa—hold up! I don't want to marry him! He suggested it, and I only agreed because I'm desperate to get information about how to get the hell out of here before the curse finishes Raff off. As a wife, I'd make Temnen miserable. The betrothal is nothing but a necessary ruse, Riven. I couldn't see any other option."

Hopping from one leg to the other, the owls says, "The girl speaks true. Isla tells truths." It punctuates each word with three hard bounces on Riven's shoulder, then screeches, "Truth. Truth. Truth!"

Fists releasing the limestone bars, Riven turns and strokes the owl, a wide grin splitting his face. "Yes, Meerade, I heard you the first time. I am not deaf."

Beautiful when he's scowling, Riven's smile is like the sun bursting through storm clouds to drench the land in warmth. It settles my pulse, calming my terror. Perhaps he won't kill me or leave me to wither away in this cavern for all eternity after all. My shoulders sag in relief.

The corners of his lips curve gently. "Tell me what you want."

"I want to get Raff out of that cell. Do you know they've got him chained to the wall in the Black Tower, his power being constantly drained by the iron? They're barely feeding him while they let the poison slowly kill him."

Riven's lips part with a sharp intake of breath. He shakes his head, silver hair cascading over black leather.

"When you're king, is this what you want the Land of Five fae to remember? The way your people degraded their heir? If he dies, you'll be at war with them forever. And his death will be the legacy you build your rule on. Is that what *you* want?"

"No," says the owl. "Meerade wants to help the fire prince." She sinks her beak into the point of Riven's ear.

"Fine." He reprimands her with a gentle tap on the head, then waves his fingers through the air, dissolving the crystal bars of my cage. "I will help you." The prince beckons me forward. "First, you must look within the druid's well."

I take a breath and gaze down. The silver surface ripples, and when it clears, the red-haired girl is there again. Merri.

"As you see, you are correct. The girl who appears in the vision is Prince Everend's daughter fully grown."

"That's just...weird. Why? And why are you in pain when you look into the well? Does scrying hurt?"

He flinches. "No. It does not hurt. But..." His gaze slides away.

The owl slaps his head with its white wing. "Tell her and you will help yourself, Riven."

The prince shoots a death glare at the bird, but draws me closer to the well, waving his palm above the silver liquid. I get the feeling that only the silver prince understands Meerade's riddles. Understands and obeys.

The image of the older Merri's face melts away, the water darkening. Then she reappears, this time seated on a black horse that looks like Jinn, riding through a gray, dismal land, her face pinched and body slumped. She doesn't look happy.

"Is she okay?"

"What you see is only a possibility. It has not happened yet."

"This is the future."

"Perhaps. Are you aware that the Black Blood curse has a final verse, one which Merit druids have kept secret for hundreds of years?"

"It's not a secret. Ever says his court has always known it. Their heir must marry their fated mate to keep the curse from killing him, but there's a rumor that if the prince should kill her instead, it might end the curse forever and stop it passing to their sons. Ever had actually planned to test this theory and murder his mate but, luckily for my cousin, Lara, he fell in love with her first. Maybe Prince Raff will try to break the curse by killing his girl."

What am I saying? Apparently, that girl is me!

Riven's chest rumbles with a humorless laugh, the sound setting my teeth on edge.

"Ah, yes, of course. I believe this is the part of the curse you refer to: *If by another's hand the chosen dies, then before their blood fully weeps and dries, black will fade to gray, gray to white, and white to never. Never was the darkest taint and never will it ever be.*"

I nod. "Yep, I think that's pretty much how it ends."

"It does not. Look into the scrying waters." He moves to the opposite side of the well and waves a hand over it.

Another image of Merri emerges, but this time, she isn't alone. A smiling male faery stands close, his fingers entwined with hers. His crown is black and twisted, long silver hair tumbling over his shoulders. It's Riven, and shock-horror, he looks extremely happy!

I gasp, and his gaze flicks to mine, the corner of his mouth lifted in a wry smile. "Listen closely. This is the final verse of the Black Blood curse." In a crisp voice, he begins to speak.

"A *halfling defies the Silver King,*
*From dark to light, her good heart brings.*
*Enemies unite. Two courts now one,*
*Should merry win, the curse is done.*"

Bumps break out over my skin, prickling like tiny needles. "Oh, my God. Could that... Do you think that's about Merri and you?"

"Yes. I believe so. For many years, I did not understand those words. I knew they were about me because my court likes to call me the silver prince. When my father dies—a Silver King is what I will be."

"And Merri is the halfling?"

"I first saw this verse as it was presented to the druids, written on a stone tablet, and I must admit that the spelling of the word *merry* misled me... I thought its meaning was to be joyful, happy. It made no sense in the context of the curse. From the exact day of Prince Everend's child's birth, I began to see the scarlet-haired woman in these crystal waters. And, of course, Ever's daughter is called Merri."

I blow out a long breath. "I can't believe that you and Merri—"

A silver eyebrow rises. "I too was skeptical. But then I was informed of Merrin's full name."

"Merrin Airgetlám Fionbharr," I say.

"Yes, and do you know the meaning of her middle name?"

"Nope."

"Airgetlám means silver hand or silver arm. Fae kings and queens rule by the power in their dominant arm, the hand their magic moves through. At the beginning of time, when Faery was an incorporeal land, the first king, Nuadu Airgetlám, brought the Tuatha Dé Danann, or the fae as we are commonly known, from the land of spectral mists. I believe Merrin's middle name is a sign that she may be the queen to rule by the power of a silver hand. I will be Merrin's hand, this Silver King the curse refers to, and she will control me. But whether by good or evil, for better or worse, remains to be seen."

Riven's eyes are filled with sadness and pain, as if he's unhappy about the meaning of the verse. But I'm not. Warmth fills my chest—and a strong feeling of hope.

Merrin is good through and through, and I'd bet my life, no matter what her future holds, she will remain so. An alliance between Merri and Riven could bring about the end of the curse, and if what I suspect the true nature of their relationship is turns out to be true, then it could bring everlasting peace between the Elementals and the Merits. Their courts will become one. No Black Blood curse. And no more horrific Blood Sun ceremonies.

Holy cow—this is huge! I can't wait to tell...but, no, I can't tell anyone.

My promise to Sally Salamande ricochets around my brain. *"You will come to know the cure. But you must promise never ever to share this knowledge. Not with your cousin. Not with her husband, the Prince of Air. And certainly not with the cursed Prince of Fire himself."*

But how can I keep this from them without going insane? And when Merri's older, how will I manage to not very strongly hint that she should go and hang out at the enemies' kingdom, fall in love with a possibly insane Unseelie prince, and be doomed with Temnen as a brother-in-law forever and ever?

And what if Riven's interpretation of the vision and the curse is wrong? What if I were to send Merri into the cruel hands of the Unseelie court, sentencing her to life as a prisoner? Or worse to a horrible death.

God, I hate the games faeries play.

"After seeing the vision of you and Merri, the thing with you not aging makes a lot more sense."

An icy stare is his only reply. It lasts so long and is filled with such dark emotion that my knees tremble in response. I force a smile and surprise flickers in his eyes.

Feeling daring, I lay my fingers on his chest, and he flinches as if my touch burns. "But, Riven, think about what that vision means. All you need to do, is find a way to keep peace between your courts until Merri is older, then simply go to her. Meet her. Maybe if you let yourself fall in love with her, Aer's terrible curse will be destroyed, and your union will bring lasting peace between your courts. Everyone wins." Except Temnen. But who cares about him?

Anger spikes in his iridescent eyes. "No. That will never happen. Merrin is the daughter of my father's sworn enemy, and in addition, she is half human! The pictures that float like dreams across these waters are nightmares. Untruths sent to torment and torture me."

"If they're so horrible, then why do you look at them? I know you come down here every night. If you don't like what you see, then why put yourself through it?"

His gaze drops. "I do not know. It is an addiction. A sickness. And, for some reason, I cannot sleep unless I come here and look. In these images, I see myself smile at this girl. I cannot believe that I appear happy. But I do not wish to be wedded to a halfling Elemental or to bring further harm to the Prince of Fire. But I *do* wish for there to be peace between our courts."

Okay, so he's obviously in complete denial. But I can work with that.

"So, the perfect solution is for you to help me and Raff get home. If you do that, you'll have the Elemental Court's undying gratitude. And I can vouch for the fact that you had nothing to do with our capture and Raff's imprisonment."

The owl's wings stretch and flap. "Sorrow comes in tear-sweet cupcakes. Anger baked in flames."

Riven and I turn toward Meerade.

"The Fire Queen. The Fire Queen's banquet!" she squawks.

The prince silences her with a hard scowl, but her words tumble around my mind.

Riven paces over the water, a real-life miracle before my eyes. "For the sake of the girl in the vision, and for future peace, I must help you and think of a way for you and Rafael to escape. You will need to trust me."

A warning twangs through my blood. In the old tales, faeries are always fickle and full of tricks. Untrustworthy. Everything Lara has told me confirms this. But Elas and Lidwinia have sent me to Riven, and I'm certain they wouldn't lead me astray.

"I do trust you. One thing that's bothering me though... What happened to the Merit druids?"

Fury twists his handsome features. "When techno-magic first flourished in our land, my father had the druids poisoned. While they were unconscious, every last one of their throats were slit. The king is a coward. And now I am the only Merit who possesses enough natural magic to scry in the priests' well."

"It's only a matter of time before he realizes I'm useless and tries to get rid of me. That idea makes me incredibly keen to get out of here."

"A wise wish." He spins and faces me. "Now, I imagine your prince is iron-sick from the chains Temnen has him wrapped in."

"Yes, and the black poison isn't helping either. He's in a bad way. Why doesn't the metal in your city make you Merits ill?"

"It's not the same as the iron in your human cities. If it has been dug from the ground, it does not affect us. But Rafael's chains contain a mix of metals, one of them being cold iron, forged in the hearts of stars and rained down into our realm from the skies. With prolonged exposure, this type makes all fae sick. High enough doses are fatal."

"His weakness will make it so much harder to get him out," I say, despair curdling my stomach.

"Yes, but it is not impossible." Hands linked behind his back, he resumes his silent pacing.

I take a moment to muse over my unfair plight. Just as the fire mage predicted, I now hold the answer to the riddle of the curse—I know how to end it yet can do nothing about it. If I don't keep my lips zipped, Raff will die. He may drive me insane, but I don't want him dead. He's not that bad. And I wouldn't even mind kissing him again—just the once. Okay, maybe twice.

The idea that I could take away the Elemental Court's worries by speaking a few sentences fills me with gloom. To be fair, maybe it wouldn't be quite that simple. If Ever heard his daughter had to hook up with a Merit prince to save the realm, I can only imagine the damage the ensuing hurricanes and gales would wreak upon the city, and that's if he'd even believe me.

Oh, but if an escape bid doesn't kill me, keeping this a secret from Lara surely will. How will I manage to keep my promise to Salamander?

The more I contemplate the complicated fix I'm in, the hotter frustration burns at my core, spreading to my fingertips.

A sudden laugh shocks me out of my self-pitying trance. "You have fire magic!" says Riven.

I look at my hands and see blue flames curling around them.

"Maybe. Just a little." I shrug. "I can barely control it. But what I *can* do that might be useful is to make people feel strong emotions when they eat the food I cook. I can render them weak with sorrow and pain and all manner of debilitating horrors. So if you can think of a way to get me into the kitchen at the right time safely…"

"Yes." His lips curve into a smile. "If we are plotting the same path, and I believe that we are, the night of your betrothal feast will be perfect." He rubs his hands together. "A plan forms! Let me think through the details. Meet me here tomorrow night, for we have much to discuss."

Boy, do we ever.

I can barely wait to tell Raff!

# 19

## *Respite*

### Raff

"**B**e careful, Elas. Please don't drop him!" yells Isla, waving her arms in the meadow below.

From my view above the treetops, she looks roughly the size of a moss elf, but unlike the demure little forest dwellers, Isla is a force of nature and blazes like a wildfire.

With each beat of Elas's wings, hair whips over my face, and I lose sight of Isla on the ground. One moment I catch a flash of gold hair—then it's gone. Her tunic flutters like a bright turquoise flag, then the world tilts and all I see are the mottled gray and bronze tops of the beech trees growing ever closer as we swoop toward the mountainside clearing they enfold.

As we descend, wind tears at my clothing and my eyes water. I've never felt as weak as I do right now with the technomancer's arms banded around my chest, my body swinging loosely.

In the form of my firebird, I love to fly. Primitive instincts take over, and the freedom is exhilarating. No other feeling comes close—not hunting, not feasting and drinking, nor bedding the rarest fae beauty. Not even setting an inferno ablaze. But this, being transported through the air like a wretched puppet, this is pure torture.

"Brace yourself," says Elas. "We are about to land."

Wind roars in my ears, tearing at my limbs, then moments later my body thuds against the earth. I tumble along the grass, pain exploding inside my skull as the loose wall shackles fling about and strike me repeatedly. White light flashes in my mind, then I see stars spinning, Elas skidding to a halt in front of me, and then Isla—Isla bouncing on her toes, hands covering her face as she squeals.

"Pardon the rough landing, Prince Rafael," Elas says, ruffling his wings, the metal feathers chiming. "I misjudged the distance and came in too fast."

"Maybe you should have practiced that," says Isla, running to where I sit with my arms bracing my drawn-up knees as I wait for the mountain to right itself.

"You could've killed him. Those chains have made him as weak as a baby," she scolds as she checks me for injuries, patting over my body.

"You must be referring to human ones. Fae babes are born strong," says Elas.

She scowls at him and then grips my chin, pulling my face close. "Are you okay, Raff?"

"I was perfectly fine until you referred to me as a weakling." My frown turns into a broad grin. "But as I sit in this meadow, I already feel my strength returning." Sunshine warms my skin, its healing power seeping into my blood.

Used to the deep blackness of my cell, outside in the brilliant light, my eyes feel like they're bleeding, full of shards of glass. But I do not care. As I stare into the bluest of skies, the pain almost unbearable, hope blooms in my chest. With green grass and wildflowers beneath me, birds and insects drifting on the warm breeze above, I could not be happier.

"How did you convince the Merit king to agree to this outing?" I ask Isla.

Brushing off her clothes, she gets to her feet. "I told him the lack of sunshine and fresh air was killing you and that you'd be dead in a matter of days if you didn't get a medicinal dose fast. He trusts Elas and knows that in your current condition, you couldn't possibly escape on foot. I guess he needs you alive."

"For now," I add.

"Can you stand?"

Shielding my eyes from the sun, I squint at her. "I can try."

Elas hurries to my side and helps me rise. Muscles burning, my head spins, the sun's rays warming my poisoned blood.

With my face tipped toward the sky, I turn in a slow circle, my arms stretched wide as I concentrate on the tiny ball of heat kindling at my core, shaping it into elemental magic.

Tiny yellow flames dance over my open palms, but no matter how hard I try, I cannot make them grow. Fury roiling in my gut, my chest, I glare at the cold iron shackled to my ankle, the loose chain dragging behind my right leg.

The pity evident on Isla's face makes me even angrier.

"I'm sorry, Raff. I wish we could take it off and smash the damn thing to pieces." Her brow smooths. "But, finally, I have some good news for you. Elas has a potion that'll hold off the iron sickness for a few days. It won't help with the poison in your blood," the effects of which reduce every time she is near, "but it'll give you enough strength for an escape bid in three night's time."

"Escape?" I trip over a small rock, stumbling like a fool. "How?"

She folds then unfolds her arms, flicking a worried glance at Elas. He nods.

"Well?" I demand. "You had better tell me quickly."

Her leather boots scuff the grass as she shifts her weight from foot to foot. "Um...you aren't going to like this much, but it's the only way."

Advancing toward her, I watch the pulse flutter at her throat. "Speak."

Fingers clasped together at her chest—a pleading gesture I'm very familiar with. Whenever her diabolical pranks cross the line, a daily occurrence, Spark uses this exact posture to avoid my wrath.

"I know I said I'd stay away from Temnen, but...well... Now don't get mad—we're betrothed."

"Betrothed?" I roar. "You have lost your mind—"

"Whoa. Take it easy. It's only for three more days. Then we're going to take the Merits out in one fell swoop and beat it fast."

"*Isla.*" My voice rumbles a warning.

She rests her hand on my bicep over the clean leathers Elas gave me before we left the Black Tower. "It's fine, Raff, I promise. Lidwinia wouldn't let me do anything stupid and neither would Elas. Would you?" she asks, turning to the winged Merit.

"This is true, Prince Rafael. In three night's hence, Isla will imbue the main dish at the feast with terror and sorrow. While the court is busy wiping their tears, Riven will free you from the iron chains and transport you to Ithalah Forest. His owl, Meerade, is on her way to your land now to advise the Elementals of the plan. Members of your court will meet you in the forest and return you home safely."

"Riven?" The chain about my leg rattles as I swing around. "That fae is not entirely sane. He's dangerous and is not to be trusted."

"Riven is fine. Come," says Elas, beckoning me forward. "We must return to the tower before Temnen hears of our excursion and seeks to join us."

I tip my chin at the two swords hanging from the technomancer's belt. "Give me one of those."

Elas bows before walking up to me. "Of course, but drink this first."

He hands me a tiny translucent capsule—the iron-sickness antidote. As I bite into the crystalline casing, bitter liquid floods my mouth. I swallow and warmth flows through my veins, instantly clearing my head. "This is amazing. What is in it?"

"Secrets." Smirking, the Merit passes me a sword, then watches as I test the grip and balance, swiping it through the air.

It feels good to use a blade once again. Although I am not Talamh Cúig's finest swordsman, only one fae can best me—my brother Ever.

Moving fast, I lunge twice, thrusting hard. Quick to respond, Elas draws his sword, parrying, then slicing his blade. I strike his shoulder and wings clank and rattle.

"Raff," yells Isla. "What are you doing? Don't hurt him!"

Elas and I laugh as our blades clash together, and I reply, "I wouldn't dare. I need him alive so he can take care of you."

I slash more fiercely, the brutal clanging sound music to my ears. I have badly missed daily combat training in the onyx courtyard—the addictive violence, working my muscles until they shake, and kicking Kian's butt to the ground.

"But if Elas fails in this task, when I am free, I shall show him no mercy."

Elas moves faster, silver blade flashing in the light. Clang. Clang. Clang. Metal strikes metal, our lungs laboring hard. We back away, circling each other.

"You are fortunate I will not strike a killing blow to one in so weakened a state, no matter how ungrateful he is," Elas taunts.

My face raised to my beloved sun, I sprint, then close my eyes and spin through the air, kicking the sword from his grasp in one strike. It skitters along the grass. From somewhere behind us, Isla cries out.

Blade pressed against Elas's throat, I say, "Do you yield to me, Merit mage of metal and darkness?"

His breath pants over my face. His eyes are black, skin ivory, and when he grimaces, needle-sharp fangs press into his bottom lip.

He's a blood-sucking fae, rare in the Seelie Court but common in the Land of Merits.

He snarls. "Were it not for my potion, you wouldn't have succeeded in lifting the sword off the ground."

Laughing, I release him, collect his sword and throw it toward him. He catches it with ease.

"True," I admit. "And I thank you for this glorious reprieve from my vile cell and the ghastly iron sickness. And most of all for the gift of friendship you've given to my human."

Elas snorts. "Fortunately for you, she cannot hear you speak thusly. These last weeks, I've come to know her well. Claiming ownership is not the way to gain her affection."

"Correct again." I clap his back, pleased to see him stumble from the impact. "Your words are like arrows, aimed straight and true. I see why Isla likes you."

"Okay, guys. I'm sure you're both awesome warriors." Isla hurries toward us, her hair rippling like gold silk in the breeze. "It's wonderful to see you looking more like yourself, Raff, but Elas is right, we need to get you back to the tower. I still haven't convinced Temnen to let the cooks prepare my special recipe for our betrothal banquet yet, and I need to spend some time working on him."

Anger spikes in my blood. "Yes, you must work hard on your thoroughly irrational plan! You are both deluded. As soon as the Merits realize you have left the Great Hall, the king will have his guard after us. What man wouldn't notice the disappearance of his intended at their betrothal feast?"

"Temnen," Elas and Isla both declare.

"The plan may not be perfect, Raff, but it's all we've got. You're not going to survive in that cell much longer. And I'm not hanging around to endure another Blood Sun ceremony."

"Elas can fly us out of here. It would be far simpler."

"It would be if he could carry more than one person at the same time," says Isla. "And if he helped us escape, he could never come back to his home again."

I raise an eyebrow. "And that would be a problem? Personally, I see it as a benefit of the plan. Elas can be rid of this dreaded place forever."

"Not everyone wants to live where nature magic rules, Prince Rafael." Elas flaps his wings, his body hovering a couple of feet above the ground. "Some of us quite like machines." He only says that because he is one.

Isla lays back in the grass, her gold locks threading through purple and red wildflowers. "What a beautiful day! I'm just gonna lie back and enjoy it while you two argue. Let me know when you're ready to leave."

She looks as pretty as a river nymph.

"One moment," I tell Elas as I crouch beside Isla. "Before I agree to go along with your outrageous plan, answer me this—will you finally admit that you are my fire queen? That we are destined for each other, and that you will never allow yourself to be joined with the Merit frog prince? Have you accepted who you are yet?"

Fire flashes in her eyes. "And what about you? Do you admit you've fallen in love with me?"

I open my mouth to speak, but no words come out. I barely comprehend what I feel, and I certainly can't explain it to her.

Her brows pinch together. "Just as I suspected. You haven't got a clue, have you? Therefore, I'm still not interested." She offers me her hand.

What? Are we making a bargain? My mind whirls in confusion. I cannot remember what I agreed to. Regardless, I clasp her hand. Instantly, hot flames leap along my arm. "Damn," I say, wrenching it away. "Amazing. You are making fire without even trying."

"And for your information, that means I'm really angry. Oh, and I nearly forgot—to be crystal clear and answer your stupid questions, I'm not yours, and neither am I Temnen's plaything. I'm a good person, an awesome cook, and I even possess a wicked bit of burgeoning fire magic. So listen carefully, I don't need either of you two knuckleheads to complete me. I'm doing fine on my own. Okay?"

"But, Isla—"

"No buts. This is the plan: I'm going to ruin Terrible Temnen's engagement bash by making everyone cry. While the Merits are distracted, with Riven's help, I'm going to set you free. So if you think about that carefully, you'll find that it's actually you, Prince Rafael, you obnoxiously self-centered, fickle faery who needs *me*. A human—imagine that!"

For the first time in my life, I find myself utterly speechless and completely in awe of someone besides myself.

Thanks to Isla, wonders will never cease.

# 20

## Bed of Flowers

### Isla

"**C**urse the Merits, my pendant's data is scrambling!" says Elas, stopping in the middle of the meadow and studying his statistics.

"What?" Raff and I say, both jolting upright on the grass.

"Pardon. I should not have taken the Merits' name in vain, but I was surprised into doing so. There is only one thing that causes a glitch in the technology in a natural setting such as this...Lidwinia."

Lidwinia? What's she got to do with anything?

"She is nearby, and I must speak with her. I know you wish to leave straightaway, Isla, but I promise I will return for you quickly." He smiles and fans out his wings. "Please do not murder each other in the meantime."

From my seat on the grass, I swipe my hand at him, clutching only air. "Elas! Wait..."

Without looking down at us, Elas bends into a deep crouch before leaping into the air just like Superman—except with glittering black wings instead of a shiny red cape.

Damn. This isn't good. What if Temnen arrives or Elas never comes back? What if Raff starts spouting curse-crap to me again? I might punch him smack bang in the middle of his regally handsome nose, and it would be a mighty shame to spoil it.

The moment Elas's sleek form disappears behind a bank of puffy white clouds, I feel Raff's gaze on me, scorching patterns over my skin.

His large hand wraps around my wrist. "Isla. I am sorry that I upset you. It would please me a great deal if we could be friends. Despite what the prophecy claims about us, I enjoy your company for its own sake."

But do I enjoy his? The butterflies taking erratic flight in my belly are evidence that I do. I open my mouth, and his palm shoots out as he leaps to his feet. "Wait. Before you speak. Let me explain further."

With his chain and shackle dragging behind, he paces over the grass, stretching his arms above his head and then behind his back, his impressive muscles flexing.

I lean on my elbows and enjoy the show.

"Get to know me, and you will find I am not so bad."

I raise an eyebrow.

"You've called me arrogant—well that is simply the way of my species. We can no sooner pretend humbleness than lie about our vigor and beauty. And besides, I am a prince of the fae—and we never have cause to doubt the importance of our station."

Now I roll my eyes, which stops him strutting back and forth, his heart-melting smile wavering.

"Before the poison fouled not only my blood but my spirits as well, I possessed many attributes that you might consider favorable to have in a friend." Moving closer, he lists points off on his fingers. "I was a storyteller. The life of every feast and revel. A lively friend who was ever devising entertaining misadventures. A skilled lover. An accomplished fighter and hunter."

"Why are you telling me this? People don't care if their friends can bring down a buffalo with one shot of an arrow. Or kiss like—"

"What is a buffalo? No. Do not answer. I don't care to picture you with one."

"What?"

Three tiny bright-green birds swoop over his head as he bends to pick a silky purple wildflower, then drops to his knees at my feet, holding it out. "Isla, a token of my affection."

"Oh," I say, taking the flower and inhaling its honey-sweet scent. "Thank you."

He leans close. From only an inch away, his wolf's eyes smolder at me. "I care for you, Isla. I feel...many things..." He shakes his tawny head, letting his words trail away.

"Um..." My gaze drops to his lips and stays there. "Thank you."

"Thank you? Is that all you have to say to me?" he asks with a sigh.

No. No, it's not. I can think of many things to mention. I could start with all the items carousing through my mind right now—the mouth-watering golden hue of his skin, the heart-pounding intensity of his fiery eyes, his tousled hair streaked with every tawny, coppery shade imaginable, those lips... When my gaze lands on his lushly curved mouth, I don't want to say anything at all.

I want to throw caution into the flames and laugh as it burns to ash.

Grabbing him by his studded leather top, I drag him forward until our noses bump, his blown-out pupils staring into mine. "Shut up Raff and kiss me."

Without a word, he obeys, and it is glorious. The fireworks exploding in my chest and belly, the delicious taste of his sighs. The low, rough sounds he makes. I stroke his pointed ears the way I wanted to the first time we kissed in the tower, but didn't because it felt too intimate. This time, *wrong* feels so *right*, and I let his heavy shudders move through me and delight me.

With his weight, he pushes forward, lowering me carefully to the ground, and the entire seven realms that he's always banging on about, narrow to the fire prince's lips, the tracks of sparks his calloused fingers make along my throat, then my collarbone.

The sun glows, birds sing. The meadow beneath us feels like an undulating wave. And I breathe and whisper and feel every cell in my body ablaze with desire for the first time in my life. *This* is how it's meant to feel.

Long minutes pass in bliss. Or perhaps it's hours that we idle away stoking flames, then banking them only to raise them high again. Over and over.

I really hope that it's been hours. And if it has, I'm still not ready for it to stop. I could stay here forever, kissing Raff, floating and melting in his arms.

When Elas returns, I don't hear the steady beat of his wings, nor feel the thump of his boot as he kicks the sole of mine. I hear nothing until his laughter booms out, echoing over the valley.

"So," says the technomancer. "This is how you occupy yourselves when I am not here to act as chaperon. Very interesting indeed."

Raff smirks at Elas. "We were only making friends. You cannot blame us for that."

"I see. And is that what humans call it, Isla, *making friends*?"

"No, Elas, we don't. How was Lidwinia?" I ask, in a quick change of subject.

"Very well. I will explain what she wanted later. Now we must hurry and get you back to the tower, Rafael. Please stand and ready yourself for flight."

Leaning back on his elbows, the prince chews on a dandelion stem, and says, "Take Isla first. I shall lie here and bask in the sun—and the memory of Isla's friendship. I can't think of a more pleasurable way to spend the last moments of my freedom."

Elas beckons me onto my feet. "Come, Isla. Let us hurry."

As Elas wraps me tight in his arms, I look over my shoulder at Raff sprawled on a bed of multi-colored wildflowers, a crooked grin on his face.

He winks at me, a thing smarmy guys do that I usually hate with a passion, but not now, not when Raff does it.

Perhaps the Prince of Fire is right after all—he's not so bad. As he so helpfully pointed out, all things considered, there's plenty to like about him. If only he didn't think I was his stupid fated mate, I could throw myself into exploring this interesting new friendship of ours.

Possibly quite frequently.

# 21

## Sorrow

### Isla

The first thing that hits me as I enter the castle's kitchen, is the mouth-watering smell wafting from massive pots on the wood-fired stovetop that runs the full length of a white-washed wall. Inside the pots is my favorite dish, a delicious French stew made of garlic, fish, vegetables, and herbs.

The second thing is Riven's hard body as he skids to a stop and slams into me, his crystal coat buttons stabbing me in the back of the head.

"Ow!" I scowl at him over my shoulder. "What were you running for? This isn't a race."

"I'm sorry. You disappeared in the stairwell, and I wanted to catch up. You are very fast for a human."

Grinning to myself, I give my rock-hard thighs a mental pat and quickly scan my surroundings. Mesmerizing me, steam curls in odd shapes toward the high, vaulted ceiling. But other than cooking equipment, several scarred wooden benches and tables, and bunches of fragrant herbs hanging from pale beams, the room is empty.

Riven nudges my ribs. "Stop gawking like a dryad attending court for the first time. You need to act quickly and infuse the food with emotion. And when the servants return shortly, you must strive to look blissfully happy, just as any girl coming to supervise the preparations for her betrothal to a prince would."

Riven mustn't know too many girls if he assumes we all want to marry princes. So far, I've met four of them, and honestly, they seem like hard work.

"Yes sir, I'll get right on it." It's difficult to pry my eyes from the steam above the bench that, weirdly, is starting to resemble a mire fox, growing from thumb-size to life-size before my eyes. The steam-beast winks at me and promptly turns into a flesh-and-blood creature, part monkey, part fox with silky red fur and pointy white ears. Spark!

"Good Goddess, what is *that*?" says Riven as Spark drops to the floor with a thud, then scrambles toward us and climbs up my body, screeching as she clings to my neck.

"I think it's Raff's mire fox. Unless your land happens to have them as well?" My heart flips then pounds erratically. This is bad. I cover Spark's mouth with my palm. "Be quiet, you little terror. How did you manage to morph out of the cooking steam?"

"The Elemental's water mage would most definitely hold the power to send her through it," Riven suggests.

Spark leaps from my arms into Riven's, squealing in his face.

"Yes, yes. I understand your point, furry creature. Rafael is fine. But if you do not cease your shrieking, you will ruin our plans to help him." He glances at me. "Go now, Isla. Do your work. And you, little complainer, must hide beneath my cloak. You shall see the fire prince soon. I promise."

Blinking adorably, Spark nods and allows herself to be tucked under black velvet lined with white fur.

I head over to the pots and commence stirring. As the sorrow of missing home flows through my veins and trickles over my skin into the stew, I force my mind to wallow in nightmares made of murder and grief, and the persistent hauntings of vengeful spirits, tortured souls, and ever-hungry ghosts. Cold terror drips from my fingers, the kind that chills a person to their bones and freezes every muscle, so all they can do is stare.

Stare and weep.

Right now, I'd like to thank my ex, Sam, for all the Saturday nights he made me watch horror movies. Not the gory slasher types, but the ones filled with the kind of psychological terror that makes a grown person want to sleep with the lights on for two whole weeks after seeing them.

Chatter and footsteps sound in the hallway, and then the kitchen staff enter, three green-skinned hob goblins and the head cook, a tall elf called Estel with baby-pink hair coiled into a towering bun. At first glance, she seems far too graceful to be slaving over hot stoves, but then I notice the dead chickens she has hanging from her hands and the proud expression she wears that tells me she strangled them herself.

"Ah, the cooks have returned," says Riven, stepping forward. "Good evening, ladies. May I compliment you on the stargazer pie? It was divine."

I wouldn't call those cute, little fish heads that were peeking through the pastry divine. Gross might be a better description.

"Pardon us for intruding," says Riven. "Lady Isla wished to cast her love and best wishes for her marriage into the dish, her favorite meal, that you are so very kindly preparing for her tonight."

True. Bouillabaisse is my favorite dish.

"Betrothal wish-casting is a tradition in my home city." Definitely not true. I give them a wave and let a bland smile settle on my face as I keep flitting between pots, stirring and stirring.

The hob goblins curtsy, and Estel inclines her head. "Welcome, Lady Isla. We are honored to have you visit our kitchen."

"Your Majesty," says a hunched-over cook, pointing at Riven's cloak and the wriggling lump that is Spark. "You are possessed by a demon. Shall I call for the High Mage?"

We all stare, the cooks whispering and giggling.

Riven's eyes glow an unearthly blue, and the staff's expressions turn vacant, their gazes clouding over. He's using some kind of magic on them.

"No need to involve Draírdon," he says in a calm, deep voice. "What you see moving beneath my cloak is an abhorrent creature, a magical experiment gone awry. I hide it to spare you the alarming sight."

His words are a stretch, but true enough—the mire fox's bad behavior can be quite shocking.

Riven clears his throat. "Look instead at the lovely princess-to-be, brimming with anticipation for her coming wedding and so full of emotion."

While the cooks smile coyly, probably imagining me frolicking in Temnen's bed, I grin back, continuing to stir the pots and fill them with dark horrors.

Striding over to the stove, Riven says to the servants, "Lady Isla has brought a special ingredient to add to the meal, a present for her esteemed lover."

What is he up to?

Delving into a pocket, he withdraws a tiny, silk-wrapped parcel. "It is precious spun gold." He opens it, holding it out for the cooks to see. Impressed, they ohh and ahh appreciatively.

He places the golden threads on my palm, and I hold them for a few moments, my eyes closed reverently. Then I sprinkle a little into each pot, holding a strong image in my mind of the entire court frozen with grief.

Clunking the spoon against the last pot, I meet Riven's intense gaze. "There," I say. "That ought to do it. It looks perfect. Is the second course nearly ready, Estel?"

"Yes," she replies. "We are about to serve it."

The three hob goblins scatter to the various ovens and benches, piling platters with all manner of interesting finger food.

Riven leans close to the tall elf. "Thank you, Estel. May I remind you that Lady Isla's betrothal wishes are a surprise, and they must remain so. If any of your staff's tongues prove loose, I shall be happy to point them out to Draírdon at the next Blood Sun ceremony."

She blanches and drops a quick curtsy. "Oh, no, Prince Riven, we would not breathe a word. Who are we to meddle in true love's games?"

Ugh. Barf. I lift my brow innocently, a sweet smile on my face. "Thank you, Estel, for recreating my special recipe for the occasion. I can't wait for everyone to try it."

"We will return to the hall." Riven gives them a rare grin. "Ladies." Then, with his arm on my shoulder, he herds me through the door.

"Did it work?" he hisses as soon as we're in the passageway.

"I don't know. It's not a spell, more like a...freaky accident that nearly always seems to work. When I was back home and it happened, I didn't even realize I was doing it. Since I've been here, I've tried experimenting on the castle guards. As long as I concentrate hard enough, it doesn't fail."

"Good." He pulls a sleeping Spark out from under his cloak. "And you, little fox-ears, you must wait here and hide in the shadows. I promise we will collect you on the way to release Rafael." Placing her on the floor, he asks, "Can you be quiet? If you believe it is beyond you, I must use a druid spell to keep you mute and still."

Spark squeaks, shaking her furry little head hard.

"Isla, you must rejoin the festivities before my brother comes looking for you. I will follow in a little while."

Plucking nervously at the black jewels sewn into blood-red slashes in my gown, I grimace.

"Go. It will be fine. Like any nightmare, this will end, and before long you, and Rafael will be returned to your families."

But first, I have to make it through the main course without slapping Temnen's lecherous-weasel face. It'll be a challenge.

The second course goes well, and immediately after it, I waltz before all the court with my supposed fiancé. The dance leaves bruises blooming on my skin and my pride. Everything about it is horrible and wrong and so very different to my first dance in Faery the night I met Raff.

It seems like another lifetime ago, but I can easily recall each detail—the way my skirt wrapped around our legs, binding us together, Raff's wolf-like gaze, arrogant and intense, his skin-tingling embrace as we whirled around the Great Hall, wildfire trailing in our wake.

Trumpets blare as Temnen leads me off the dance floor and back onto the dais. As I walk around the high table, servants crisscross the hall, serving the bouillabaisse. Excitement and fear spike in my blood, making my mouth dry, my pulse pound. I fix my eyes on the stars sparkling through the glass behind the throne and take my seat between Lidwinia and Temnen.

She pats my hand and leans close to whisper, "Keep smiling, Isla, not much longer now. Look, Riven and Meerade are excusing themselves."

Face a solemn mask, the silver prince bows to King El Fannon who's too busy scratching his cat behind the ears to do more than nod at his son's departure.

Temnen chats to Draírdon on his right. His bird is perched on the back of his lavish chair and peers around their heads to ogle me with its sinister black eyes.

"Thank you for everything, Lidwinia," I say in a low voice, squeezing her hand. "I don't want to say goodbye to you. I wish you could come with us."

"I will miss you too. The cruelty of this land weighs heavily on my heart, but I know everything will change when Riven rules. And he will need someone by his side who loves him and who will help to keep him sane. This will be my role. My duty."

The tip of her black tongue darts out as she smiles, arching an eyebrow at the technomancer. "And look at those beautiful wings—I could never leave Elas. Who would protect him from all the wicked ladies of the court?"

"Will the king let you marry him one day? His statistics are pretty high."

She laughs bitterly. "No. Father will never allow it. My husband must be of royal blood. Just like Riven, I am doomed to live a life of sorrow. My brother pines for something or *someone* that he believes he shall never have. I wish he would share the burden and confide in me."

The image from the well of he and Merri together appears in my mind, their gazes locked, hands entwined like vines of ivy.

Lidwinia notices my frown and says, "We shall see each other again soon, Isla. I'm certain of it."

"As long as I'm not chained to the wall in the Black Tower when it happens, I hope we do. Can you thank Elas for me? I couldn't have survived my time here without both of you. I'm so grateful for your friendship."

Looking like a warrior queen in an emerald and black outfit made of alternating plates of hard leather and metal, she smooths her spiked green hair. "And I for yours."

"Nice outfit," I say. "More appropriate for a battle than a fake engagement feast, though."

She shrugs. "I am prepared for all possible outcomes."

That makes me spurt wine back into my goblet. What does she think is going to happen tonight?

Aquamarine bowls brimming with fragrant stew are placed in front of us. Temnen leans over his and wrinkles his nose.

I pat his hand. "This is my betrothal gift to you, Temnen. It's my favorite dish—bouillabaisse. May it make your dreams a reality. I hope you like it."

He regards me with a cool gaze. "I am not fond of fish, but for you, my little innovator, I will try it."

Thank the powers that be in this screwed up land! I breathe a soft sigh, closing my eyes for two heartbeats.

Picking up a jewel encrusted spoon, Temnen's mouth twists cruelly. "And in return, on the night of our wedding, you will be privy to my favorite dish. Picture this: I will open the doors to my hidden chamber, take you below, and introduce you to the sweet treats I have strung up there, basting slowly. Painfully alive and all the more tasty for it." He pauses to lick his lips. "And if you do not please me as a wife, perhaps you shall join them."

Yuck.

And did he just threaten to eat me?

My tightly braided hair, threaded with gold and ebony silk and black diamonds, pulls at my temples as I smile serenely at Temnen, which only increases my headache.

The bird dips his beak into the bowl, pecking at some fish.

"Olwydd likes to taste my food first. He checks for poison and flavors of ill intent."

Oh crap!

Copper feathers ruffle then smooth, and Olwydd stares ahead, composed and calm. Either my fledgling magic has failed, or the bird has no fears to haunt him.

Temnen nods, and I hold my breath as he slurps a big mouthful of stew.

*Please work. Please work.*

Beside me, Lidwinia pretends to eat, and I can't bear to watch. I stare blankly at the burning braziers, swaying palm fronds, and the glistening waters of the Blood Sun fountain, all blurring together like a foggy dream. A nightmare enfolding.

And all around me courtiers gulp down my stew of sorrow, their eyes slitted with laughter.

My hand shakes as I grasp my spoon, a loud splutter sounding beside me. Temnen! His head is bowed, the long antennae flopping limply over his brow. Tears track down his face, and his sharp black nails dig into the female heads carved into his armrests, their mouths open in gruesome, silent forever-screams.

Standing quickly, I squeeze his shoulder, fixing a mask of fake concern on my face. "Temnen, what's wrong with you?"

He coughs and croaks as his fingers tear at his throat, eyes wide with terror. For a morbid moment, I wonder what kind of visions he sees, then quickly shove the thought away. I don't want to know what frightens monsters.

Behind me, the bronze bird squawks miserably, and in front of me, is chaos. Squeals and howls and monstrous cries rip through the air, prickling my skin.

I rub slow circles over Temnen's back. "Let me find Riven. He'll know how to help you." He doesn't even glance up as I leave the dais and descend the stairs one quick but careful step at a time. Black. Red. Black. Red. Black. Red. And so on.

Now, to meet a silver prince and rescue a fiery one.

As I weave through tables of sorrow-stricken fae and stride across the dance floor, a million horrible thoughts of all the ways this plan could go wrong whir through my mind.

Picking up speed, I smooth the flame-colored tulle of my elaborate dress. The leather corset and metal shoulder pads Lidwinia stuffed me into earlier constrict my breathing, adding a layer of claustrophobic panic on top of the already considerable stress of an escape attempt. An attempt that could so easily fail.

*Breathe. Just breathe.*

As arranged, in the torch-lit narrow passage behind the kitchen, I find Riven, Spark clinging to his back like a frightened child hoping to be piggybacked to safety. Except we're heading in the opposite direction—toward untold danger.

"Come, let us move quickly. Someone waits patiently for us at the entrance the servants use to bring market supplies into the castle."

Meerade perched on his shoulder, says, "Fire Queen. Fire Queen," and pecks rudely at the mire fox's fingers.

Maybe she thinks Spark is Raff's fated mate. The idea amuses me greatly and fixes a stupid grin on my face as I rush headlong into peril. I must look insane. For daring to think I can beat the Merits with nothing but bowls of fish stew, I'm sure I am.

Riven leads us down several winding hallways and three sets of crumbling staircases before cracking open a thick metal door into a courtyard that's surrounded by high vine-covered walls. While I wait for my eyes to adjust to the darkness, I listen to the near-constant clank and grind of the Merit factories, lights from the courtiers' apartment towers twinkling in the distance. Then I hear a snort and a whinny at the same time as Riven steps close. Don't tell me he turns into a horse too!

"This is Tulpar," he says, and a blood-red horse with black wings similar to a bat's, but much larger and covered in metal scales, morphs out of the shadows. "She will deliver us to the tower quickly."

"Hello," I say, waving at the beast.

Without warning, Riven throws me into the saddle, then leaps up behind me. With a click of the prince's tongue and a loud screech from Spark, we're airborne and flying high, Meerade traveling beside us and a bright moon watching us flee.

When we land on the spiked bridge near the Black Tower's entrance, Riven dismounts and tells Tulpar and Meerade, "Please wait for us here. We won't be long."

He lifts me to stand beside him. "I'm sorry, Isla, but we must transfer to reach Rafael's cell with speed. It will not be pleasant for you. And Spark, you disobedient creature, you must come with us."

He shifts Spark around to his chest and draws me into a tight embrace. The ground shakes, and I lose consciousness, waking in the foyer in front of Raff's cell, my head pounding and stomach churning.

"Crap," I say. "I wish that got easier with practice."

The guard is out cold on the floor, his limbs spread wide as if he's fallen asleep while making snow angels. "Is he dead?"

"No. Thanks to Elas he still lives." Riven grabs the torch to the left of the door, and we enter Raff's cell.

There's a rustle in the dark, then a moan.

I kick Raff's boot. "Wake up! How can you sleep at a time like this?"

Spark releases a blood-curdling screech and scampers over to the fire prince. She climbs his body and smacks his shocked face, the sound echoing against the stone walls.

Raff shakes her by the shoulders. "You little beast! How dare you follow me to this terrible land. Do you want to die? Tell me whose magic caused this and your words will sign their death warrant."

Spark replies with angry chirruping noises.

"*Undine*? I will burn every strand of her flowing blue hair. Then I will—"

Spark throws her arms around Raff's neck and peppers his throat and face with little mire fox kisses, making him laugh. It's a wonderful sound, and the adorable sight of them melts my heart.

"I was awake, Isla." Raff's gaze flicks toward me. "I leaned on my injured arm, that is why I made a sound. Perhaps it is broken."

"Broken?" Riven and I say.

"It seems your guards are very brave when an Elemental is straining at his chains and unable to reach them."

Unlocking the wrist and ankle shackles, Riven says, "Do not worry. They will be held accountable for their abuse."

Frowning, Raff's eyes scan my body as he scrambles to his feet, Spark clinging to his neck. "Look at you!" He points at the flames painted on my eyelids, the orange and red layers of tulle and silk frothing around my legs. "They've dressed you like a fire queen to celebrate your betrothal to a Merit frog prince. They insult us both."

Legs braced wide, he cradles the mire fox against his bare chest, leather pants molding to his muscular thighs. He wears knee-high boots and a cocky twist to his lush lips. The vision makes my mouth water. Stupid, stupid saliva glands.

Ready to sass him, I take a breath, my attention sliding to Riven who's pulling leather armor from a bag, followed by a sword, a dagger, and a belt, which he throws to Raff. "Put these on quickly, Rafael. And, Isla, take this sword. It's light. And you should unfasten the skirt that so displeases your Lord of Fire. Without it, you will be better able to fight if necessary."

"Raff's not my lord of anything."

Riven's blue eyes glow, a smile tilting his lips. "As you say, but still, when you return to your land, you two should marry as soon as possible. The druid's well tells me the Queen of Five is not long for this world, and your marriage will restore his powers."

Raff starts at this news but remains silent.

"Pity I'm not interested in him. I deserve better than a conceited fae prince for a life partner."

Raff's molten wolf eyes freeze over. "And I have no desire to be married to a human forever either. But duty must be done, and Isla must grow up and accept the fate she has been chosen for."

This is exactly the attitude that douses the attraction that burns between us, quelling the flames as my heart fills with ashes. He doesn't give a fig about me. All he cares about is halting the curse, saving his land. He may be the most gorgeous looking creature imaginable, but he can take his colossal-sized ego and go suck a barn-full of eggs.

I don't need the Prince of Fire in my life. As long as I've got my family and my amazing oven, I'll be fine.

With violent movements, I tear the skirt off, revealing the leather leggings beneath it. "I may have been chosen, Raff, but there's nothing you can do to make me accept it."

Raff stares at me in my outfit of buckled leathers and the sword belted at my hips, and I find myself doing the same to him. I note we're both dressed for battle rather than a speedy flight into Ithalah Forest, and that worries me more than the disturbing fact that I find him so attractive.

"Good, you are ready," says Riven, giving us a once over. "To get back to the bridge, I can transfer with the mire fox and one other person. Rafael is still weak. Go now, Isla. You must descend the stairs as quickly as you can. See you outside."

Without another word, I snatch the torch, leap over the sleeping guard, and race down the winding stairwell, my body scraping against the ancient stone walls all the way to the bottom.

As I burst through the exit, Tulpar snorts and paws at the earth, Raff and Spark already in the saddle. Riven takes my arm, steering me over, then places me in front of Raff. Despite his earlier insults, I take great comfort in the feel of his big, solid body behind me.

"You must leave before Temnen recovers from your magic. Tulpar knows the place in the forest where you will meet your people. All you need to do is hold on and not fall off."

Riven grips my arm. "What you have learned, Isla, you must keep to yourself. Please do not meddle in the fates of others."

"Of course," I reply. "Thank you for everything. I hope your family doesn't find out you helped us."

"Even so, I will be fine. Goodbye, Isla, Prince Rafael. I hope we never see each other again."

Err...same...I think?

"You have my deepest gratitude for taking care of her and also for helping us escape." Raff's deep voice rumbles over my head. "Queen Varenus will no doubt be speaking to your father. Henceforth, I imagine the Merits' safe passage through our land to visit the sea witches this year will have been rescinded."

"At the very least," says Riven, bowing.

Raff nudges the horse, and she springs into the night sky, dust-colored clouds rising around us as we begin our flight to freedom.

*Freedom!* It's hard to believe this is happening. Could it really be this easy?

The wind blows our hair around like ribbons in a wild maypole dance, dark mixing with light, carrying Raff's words along with it. "What was the Merit prince referring to when he spoke of a secret you had learned, something that could change the fates' of others?"

Crap.

"It's about Lidwinia and the king's plans for her to marry some fae from the Shade Court. Forget about it."

Closing my eyes, I lift my face to the wind, its caress soothing away my guilt. Lying is bad, but not when revealing the truth could do greater damage.

That's what I'm telling myself, anyway.

# 22

## Escape

### Raff

As usual, Isla's mouth spews lies, ones that plague me the whole journey to Ithalah, and as the winged beast's hooves set down in a small clearing on the southern edge of the forest, I find I cannot let it rest.

I ask her again, "You said earlier that the secret Riven mentioned concerns the Merit princess, but I know this is a lie."

Sighing, she leans her weight back, squashing Spark against my chest. "Okay, if you must know, Mister Nosey, the gossip was about Lidwinia's plot to escape marriage to this Shade Court guy so she can marry her true love. It doesn't concern you at all. It's girls' stuff."

Three more lies to add to her growing pile of untruths.

I dismount with Spark clinging to my neck, then pull Isla onto the ground as I survey our surroundings.

Shrouded in darkness, the clearing appears empty, but since my night vision is not what it used to be, I can't be certain we are alone.

How I wish the moon tonight was larger and brighter. Besides being easier to pick members of my court from the shadows, it would allow me a better view of Isla. Her face painted with spiraling flames, she looks entrancing. Mesmerizing.

*And I have no desire to be married to her forever...*

Those words I spoke to Riven taunt me now, so close to a lie, so impure a form of truth that pain blinded me as I uttered them. What do I truly feel for this human? Why do I reject her with harsh twists of the truth when I need her—when my *kingdom* needs her so badly?

Pride. Foolish, wounded pride.

"Raff, look." Isla points to the horse, Tulpar, who must have leaped silently into the air while our backs were turned and is now flying away, abandoning us to our fate.

An owl hoots in the distance, a mournful sound. I sigh and take Isla's hand. "Come, let's move under the cover of the trees while we wait for our rescue party."

As we take our first steps, a horse neighs and four figures walk out of the forest, moving quickly toward us. My muscles uncoil as the darkness falls away from their bodies, revealing their faces.

The queen has sent Princess Lara's personal guard, Orlinda, who is the best archer in our land, and three strapping, blue-skinned warriors from her below-mountain tribe, their horses walking beside them.

My own horse, Flame, trots toward me, snorting and whinnying, his white mane trailing behind him like wisps of smoke. I inhale his warm, comforting scent as I rest my forehead against his nose and rub his neck. "I am glad to see you, old friend."

Spark scrambles up into Flame's saddle, and my horse bucks three times, snorting like a devil, to make my mire fox screech—an old game they both enjoy.

Orlinda and the guards bow low, armor and weapons clanging. "Your Highness, Lady Isla. Thank the Elements you are safe. We must ride—"

"Wait," says Isla, shaking my arm and pointing over her shoulder. "Is that Tulpar coming back?"

I peer into the sky. A black-winged shape swoops through the clouds heading downward fast, its strange white lumps and bony projections glistening in the scant moonlight, a smaller bronze bird beside it. That's not Tulpar...it's—

"Temnen!" cries Isla. She screams once and tries unsuccessfully to mount Flame as the rest of us draw our weapons. The time to flee has passed, now we must fight or die.

Wind gusts as the beast skids to a landing—part flesh and bone, part mechanical, it is most definitely the Merit prince's monster. His bird, Olwydd, alights on a nearby branch, a beady-eyed spectator.

Hot steam shoots from the beast's skeletal nose, and he rears up, shrieking like a soul-stealing sluagh, its front legs paddling. Thick rivulets of red stream down its broad chest as magic thrums through the air. Clearly, Temnen has been using blood magic to strengthen his power!

I send a shaky bolt of fire toward the stallion, but my curse-weakened power is next to useless, and in a flash of green light, every being in the clearing freezes solid, bound by the prince's dark magic. Everyone except Isla and me.

Fury writhes in my gut, roiling and boiling through my veins. Hate. Revenge. Murder. These notions fill me. These feelings transmute into fire power, the strength to call upon my firebird burgeoning.

"Will they be okay?" asks Isla, her fingers digging into my forearm. "Oh God. Oh God. Tell me what to do, Raff."

"Draw your sword. Hold it up. Cut the stinking beast to pieces if you can."

Elas's potion may have rescued me from near death, but I am still weak, my magic barely functioning, my muscles far from fighting condition, but I need to change and face Temnen beast on beast. It is the only way we will survive.

Pushing Isla behind me, I clench my eyes and fists, begging the phoenix to not forsake me. "By *flesh, bone, wing, and fire*—"

"Raff! Hurry up! Please. We're running out of time."

My breath heaves in and out, growing hotter, burning my lungs. "*The Five gives life. The Five changes all. Lig é a dhéanamh.*"

I tense each muscle, beg every god I can think of in all the seven realms, but nothing happens.

Not.

One.

Thing.

*Happens.*

I do not change or send fire from my palms in violent purple plumes. I am wrecked. A wholly inadequate, useless Elemental fae and an even more worthless Prince of Five. Regardless, I will not let Temnen have my fire queen—he'll have to kill me first.

My only option is to goad him to fight me sword on sword. Flesh on flesh. Bone on bone.

"Temnen, you quivering sack of entrails," I yell. "You have long been a coward, and now you hide in the sinews of your metal beast, content to squash your enemies like insects. Is this a worthy act of a Merit prince? How would your statistics fare if your court could see you now?"

His head cants to the side, body going as still as he has rendered the Elemental warriors around us.

The wet grass beneath my boots smells like home as I stalk toward the creature. "Long ago, when we roamed together in packs of children at festivals, we would always seek out the weakest creatures in attendance or of the surrounding forests. Do you remember?"

He paws the ground, blowing steam through his gaping nostrils.

"My brother Rain wished to lecture these unfortunate beings, Riven to study them, Ever to save them, me to play amusing games with them...and *you*...all you wanted was to maim and torture and abuse. But only the ones who couldn't fight back, of course. The sickly. The powerless. Your fights are not battles, Temnen. They are *atrocities.*"

Roaring like a passel of stuck hogs, he gallops past us, knocking Isla to the ground. She quickly scrambles to her feet.

I whirl toward the beast, casting my arm back at the human. "See? You illustrate my point perfectly. Strike the weakest. Do you even know how to fight fairly?"

When he is a good distance away, he spins around and gallops for us once again, a black shadow gathering dust clouds and speed. Gripped tightly in two hands, I hold my sword high, ready to cut through the horse's neck, but Temnen changes back into his fae form as he moves, metal striking metal as his blade clashes with mine briefly before he ranges past us.

Then he turns and marches forward, his red-rimmed eyes full of evil intent and fixed on Isla. He snarls, shaking his head in a manner meant to instill terror in her heart. "Did you think your novice elemental food magic would restrain me long? You foolish girl! You lying, deceitful, pathetic human child. I will take you back to court, hang you in my chamber of terrors, and keep you alive forevermore. My wretched pet. My hateful toy. You will—"

In three long steps I am on the Merit, my sword arcing through the night sky, his rising to meet it, those foul eyes still locked hard on Isla.

"Can you not speak?" he asks her. "Do you have nothing to say for yourself?" With brutal force, his sword strikes twice across my shoulder guard, and I stumble backward, leaving him free to hunt Isla.

Her thin sword raised, she trembles as the Merit advances. "How did you find us?" she asks, likely hoping to distract him by prompting him to brag about his cleverness—his favorite occupation.

"As I have previously told you, Olwydd is a master tracker. He can locate anything, in any realm, even the lowest riffraff."

Unable to bear his petty games, I taunt him back. "Come, Temnen, what joy is to be had in conquering a human who has never had a sword lesson in her life?" That will change if we leave this clearing alive. "Are you a warrior or a flea-bitten cat chasing a barn mouse? I can use a sword. Fight *me*!"

"With pleasure." He runs at me, and I hold my ground, stepping swiftly aside at the last moment. His body spinning back, his blade slices through a gap in my vambrace. I kick him off balance, then advance, slashing and pushing him to retreat.

He lowers his sword, calls Isla's name so I look behind me, steps forward and punches my face. Galaxies spin. I wipe blood from my nose and lunge, then, muscles screaming, thrust my sword with all my might. Lift. Hack. Lift. Hack.

Olwydd flies above us screeching and flapping.

Clang. Clang. Clang.

Our elven steel blades spark, but no matter how I try, I—the supposed Prince of Fire—cannot muster a flicker of fire magic. Nothing.

As I fight, under my breath I pray to the gods, to blessed Dana for strength, for fury and might, but it seems they have all abandoned me. I have naught to rely on but my muscles, tendons, and bones, all straining near to breaking point. And if they fail me, as sure as night becomes day, we are done for.

But not before I break.

I turn and pump my limbs hard, running across the clearing in the opposite direction of Temnen.

"Who is the coward now, Rafael?" he yells. "Run little prince. If you try hard, perhaps you can make it all the way back to your mother."

As I pass Isla, I hiss, "Follow me." Wonderful girl that she is, without question, she turns and falls in step, jogging alongside me.

"Is this what we're trying? Running away?"

"You are. I'm not." I whip around and face Temnen.

Emanating fury, he stands in the distance, arms crossed over his black metal chest plate, no doubt preparing to change into his creature. To finish us off.

This is my final hope. I put every scrap of energy, every breath, every wish and desire for Isla to live—to *live, to love, to be happy*—into my effort, my speed, running at the Merit faster than I've ever moved in my life.

His sword is raised, and as his boot leaves the ground ready to bolt forward and meet me in the center of the clearing, I count four heartbeats than launch my body into the air, sword raised like a demon slayer.

A long battle cry leaves my mouth as we meet mid-air, my strength borne of a desperate fury. We clash, we tumble, and by some miracle, I land on my feet before Temnen does.

I strike as he leaps up and blocks my blade. I step back, then feint, and he lunges forward, leaving an opening for me to plunge my sword in. I aim for the lungs, but he trips me, and I merely stab his side as I fall to the ground again.

"Olwydd, *ionsáigh!*" the Merit yells. "Now!"

And then the bird is on me, its metal beak gouging at my skull as I roll and cover my eyes, struggling to get up, to save Isla. Damn Temnen! He has always been a cheater.

Isla yells a string of unfamiliar curse words while slicing her blade over the prince's leathers again and again.

A coward like his master, Olwydd squawks off into the trees, and while the Merit tries to wrestle Isla away without killing her or freezing her solid, I get to my feet, collect my sword and raise it high.

He wants to take her alive, and he most definitely wants to make her watch him kill me. But Isla seems determined not to let that happen.

"How's that caress, Boyfriend?" Isla says as she stabs through a tear in his armor, wounding his other side. "Rough enough for you?"

His sword clashing with mine, he roars in pain, the air shimmying as he thrusts one arm high, the palm outstretched, and manifests an accursed chain. I leap into blackness, slashing at the metal as it spirals downward, then wraps around my chest, binding my arms to my side.

Twisting and turning wildly, I flex my muscles, magic churning in my gut, but the little I manage to conjure is barely enough to sneeze with let alone break the links.

*I'm sorry Isla. I'm so sorry.*

Dread hammering through my veins, I look at Spark and Flame, Orlinda and the three warriors, all staring vacantly ahead like grotesque statues. Is this how it ends? Will this be my last memory of them all, of Isla fighting, as I descend to the underworld for eternity?

Isla roars, a surprisingly guttural sound, and fire leaps down her arms, then her blade, and she lunges and slices at Temnen's chest.

He looks down, laughing. "Your little cuts are foreplay, mortal. They thrill and excite me. Time to surrender quietly until we return to my chambers. Look at your prince, chained like a felon, bleeding like a Blood Sun sacrifice. Hm." He taps his chin in an infuriating manner. "Now that's an appealing idea. Should I kill him now or save him for grander, more gratifying torments?"

Gaze dropping, Isla flinches and points her blade at something on the ground. On the grass lies a Merit pendant, flashing and sputtering weakly from within its ornate frame. "I may not have struck a fatal blow, Temnen, but look at your pendant. Do you think it'll be okay?

He screeches like a thwarted child. "You foul, dung-faced human hag! I'll crush your bones one by one. I will skin you alive." Isla's sword hand moves closer to the pendant. "I shall—wait, human! Noooo!"

Flames shoot from the tip of her blade, enveloping and then burning the pendant until there's nothing left but a melted puddle of darkness on the grass.

Shaking and shuddering as he stares at it, Temnen doesn't move to strike us down. He's using all his energy to change!

"Isla, run," I command as her shoulders heave, tears streaming over her face. "Run," I repeat. "I beg you. Do it now."

Slowly, Temnen's head lifts, tracking toward her, his body shuddering violently.

"Isla, he's changing. He will destroy you. Run!"

While Temnen's body is locked in the transformation, she has one brief chance to flee. My only hope is that she can make it to the forest—to *my* forest—where there are beings, long asleep, who will wake to her cries for mercy and respond with aid.

As Temnen's eyes roll back in his head, wind gusts suddenly from above, sending our hair flying behind us like wild kelpies' manes.

Isla laughs. "Look. It's Rothlo!"

"What?" Rothlo is a spider, and Isla has lost her mind, understandable given her current predicament.

"Oh, my God, Raff, look!"

Riding a giant spider with two sets of whirling translucent wings, Lidwinia lands in the space between us and the still-transforming Temnen.

That creature she rides is little Rothlo?

She slides off the beast in one smooth move and in three steps, is at Temnen's side. His mouth gapes wide. The sight of her shocks him from the change, his body convulsing and warping—leathery skin, bleached-white bone, then flailing limbs.

Her eyes brightly glowing orange orbs, she turns to us. "Isla, I saw what you did to his pendant. Raise your fury and let it flame. Burn him. Burn him now."

Isla shudders beside me. Flames lick down her arm, tendrils curling around her fingers.

The Merit Prince laughs, a terrible sound that makes the earth quake beneath my boots. "A firefly could do more damage than that mortal's childish, incompetent tricks, Sister."

Arms splayed wide, Isla marches forward.

Lidwinia snarls. "He keeps creatures hanging in his chambers, paralyzed but conscious for as long as possible, some for years, so he can eat them slowly, piece by piece."

My fists clench, every muscle strung tight as I watch Isla break into a run, an explosion of color bursting around her body and shimmering like an aurora.

Chest laboring, Lidwinia continues stoking Isla's rage. "This is the gruesome end he plans for Rafael. And for you as well, should your popularity wane. Take your revenge. Take it now!"

Flames shoot from Isla's palms as she lifts them, thrusting them in front of her chest.

Leaning on one elbow, Temnen laughs. Isla's body flashes blue, green, red, then she yells, hurling small fireballs at the prince as she bears down on him. One hits its target, setting the grotesque black skin and bone protruding from his chest alight, melting the smirk from his face.

Temnen howls and writhes, claws reaching for Isla, who stands over him panting, watching the flames envelop him. Those flames will not burn long. Isla's magic is too new and untrained.

I curse the chains binding me to the spot, a mere spectator when I would give almost anything to be a player. To finish off the Merit Prince.

"You dragon-breathed, traitorous little bitch," Temnen growls, his voice a bubbling crackle. "I am going to—"

"Shut up and die," says Lidwinia with one kick sending him sprawling onto his back, his charred flesh sizzling. She shoves a boot in his chest and plunges her long blade into his heart. More dark magic has been used to so easily pierce through the layers of his armor, but this time, like Temnen's howl of pain, it is beautiful to witness.

Lidwinia twists the blade. "This is for my favorite nursemaid who you tortured to death when Mother took me to visit the Shade Court when I was seven."

Temnen groans as the sword is dragged out, and then pushed deeper into his chest. "This is for my second nursemaid, the river elf who you terrified into running away after Mother's death when I needed her most."

A squelching sound curls my lip as the blade is withdrawn and plunged deep for the third time. "And this is for every creature you bullied and betrayed and maimed and killed, and most of all it is for Riven, for every hate-filled look, word and move you made against him, your own brother and future king." She leans onto the sword hilt. "Take that you worm-headed cretin!"

Temnen, silent and unmoving, makes no comment.

A dark smile slides over Lidwinia's face. "Sorry, Brother Dear, but it looks like you won't be attending Riven's coronation," she says, releasing the sword, leaving it wobbling from Temnen's chest. "I'm sure you had something nasty planned to ruin the day. Can't do much when you're dead though, can you?" She circles his body and spits on the ground beside his head. "That was nice work before, Isla."

Chest heaving, the princess glances up at me, wiping hair from her face. "Hello Rafael," she says far too gaily. "That felt wonderful, finally giving Temnen what he has long deserved."

"Is he actually dead?" asks Isla, her voice shaking. "Did we kill him?"

"Yes. Thank the Merits." Lidwinia rises, wiping her blade on the grass. She flicks her thumb over her shoulder. "Look what has happened. With his death, your people are released from their thrall and now moving toward us, and you, Rafael, are bound no more."

I glance down and find the chains coiled at my feet, intense relief flooding me. Isla has survived. We will make it home.

Flame trots over looking none the worse for being briefly turned to stone. Spark, who sits in his saddle, is whimpering like a lost moss elf babe. Arms outstretched, she drops onto Isla's chest and is enveloped in a tight cuddle.

Orlinda and the men gather around. Thankfully, I remember their names—Marlin, Nerina, and Osprey—and we check that everyone is well.

"Holy crap!" says Isla, interrupting our relieved laughter. "What are you guys doing just standing there? We've got to get out of here right now! Won't the king be coming after us? This will definitely start that war you've all been trying to avoid. Let's not be the first casualties if we can help it."

Eye's calm and serious, Lidwinia walks to Isla. "I will do everything I can to avoid war between our courts. Despite your worthy assistance, it was I who killed Temnen in the end. You did not. Elemental fae did not. You have nothing to fear."

"No, Lidwinia, don't go back there. They might lock you in a cell forever. Come with us. Please," begs Isla.

"It is alright." Her palms brace Isla's shoulders. "You forget that Riven will soon be king. Do not fret, dear Isla. All will be well. But I'm afraid we must say our second goodbye for the night."

"You saved our lives. How did you know we needed help?" asks Isla.

"There were many members of the court on whom the sorrow spell did not last long. Temnen was unfortunately one of them. I followed him when he left the hall with Olwydd, both clearly on a mission to murder."

I grasp her gore-splattered hand. "Thank you, Princess. I am forever in your debt. Name your reward and you shall have it."

She smiles. "Peace, Rafael. That will do nicely."

The ladies embrace, then Lidwinia vaults into her saddle, whistling for Olwydd to join her. I lift Temnen's body onto Rothlo who caresses me with her rough, hairy legs, emerald eyes sweeping over my body in a strangely lewd way. This is a surprising time for a gigantic arachnid to engage in flirting. Winning battles can have unusual effects on fae creatures.

We mount our steeds, Flame nickering happily, and Isla leans back against my chest, a traumatized Spark already sleeping in her lap.

"Rest," I say, smoothing Isla's hair with my palm. "You should sleep as well. The journey home will be uneventful. We are safe now."

She yawns loudly. "You know, I can't wait to get home to the human world because then I'll never have to see you again."

Shock tightens my gut. "Why do you not want to see me again? What have I done wrong?"

"Just because we both nearly died tonight, don't think I've forgotten how you told me to grow up and pretty much admitted that you don't care one bit about me. And despite that, you still think I'll agree to a loveless marriage. I'm not the simpering idiot you seem to think I am. And, also, you haven't even thanked me for risking my life to get you out of that cell. We weren't friends before you went into that tower, and your little speech when Riven and I broke you out has reminded me exactly why. You're an arrogant ass. From now on, I think it's best if we stay away from each other."

I am an ass? And when did I say I do not care about her? I sift through memories of our escape and still, I cannot recall it. Baffled and weary, I hold my tongue, then click it so violently that Flame takes off at a canter, most likely wondering who is chasing after us.

After a few moments pass, I say, "Thank you...for breaking me out of the tower." Somehow, my tone doesn't sound very grateful even though I am immensely so.

I am forever in her debt when where I want to be, is in her heart. Right now, I am glad to be alive, but beyond frustrated.

Mortals are baffling creatures.

I give up trying to win this thorny girl over.

The curse rumbles inside me. *Rightly* so, it says. *She is dispensable. Inconsequential. A thorn in your side to be plucked out and stood on, crushed beneath the heel of your boot.*

The poison is right.

Who needs a human curse breaker anyway?

Her small hand grips my forearm as we gallop through the trees, a dark shiver tracing my spine.

Me, unfortunately, I need her.

And the entire Kingdom of Five does as well.

The poison is filth.

The poison lies.

# 23

## The Runaway

### Isla

"**H**ave you heard the news this morning, Isla?" asks Ever, his eyes on the hnefatafl board that rests on the table between him and Lara.

"Wait...don't tell me." Grinning, I pad barefoot across the grass of the royal family's private garden. "You've finally developed some humility. Is that it?"

He smirks, and Lara laughs, moving her rune and capturing one of his men. "Don't be silly, Isla," she says. "Arrogance is his most potent power. Without it, the Prince of Air disappears in a gust of wind."

"Ha, ha. As always, your humor delights me, wife."

"As you delight me, Never, my love," she teases back.

I sink into a deep cane chair pulled up to the table, my gaze following Merri as she tows Balor around a tree trunk by a golden leash, a white apron and an embroidered bonnet hanging from his neck.

Since he's wagging his tail like a well-trained puppy instead of a red-eyed hell hound, I think he's quite happy being dressed as a kitchen maid.

Ever stretches his arms above his head, knocking over a coffee pot with his leather-clad knee. He's wearing a black, gossamer-thin shirt with detailed silver embroidery that depicts scenes of a girl hanging out with his seven órga falcons—Taibsear, the biggest, perched on her arm in every one.

"El Fannon is dead," he says, leaning over the table toward me. "And your friend the silver prince will soon be made King of Merits."

"What?" I pick up a set of silver knuckle bones and flip them to the back of my hand.

The girl on his shirt is Lara. How adorable. Raff, who's not the least bit adorable, would never dream of having images of me embroidered on his clothes. Nope. Never.

"It is true," Ever continues. "Two days after the return of Temnen's body, the king was found dead in his bed. Lidwinia wrote to Mother. She stated the cause of the king's death as grief and, of course, she cannot lie. But the way she worded the letter...well, let's just say we may never truly be certain how he met his end."

I flip the knuckle bones again. "Are you suggesting Riven killed him? Or that Lidwinia did?"

He shrugs. "The Unseelie are capable of terrible crimes against their own family. Consider how El Fannon's queen, kindhearted Ciara, met her end."

Beheaded by her husband for not living up to his expectations. Harsh. Still, Riven and Lidwinia are different creatures. Aren't they? Then I picture her a few nights back, a pointed boot on Temnen's chest and that blade plunging in over and over. She's certainly capable of killing her father.

Sighing, I scatter the bones across the table, then sit back to survey the magical secret garden, wondering why I feel empty and depressed when I've recently achieved the near impossible—busted a fae prince out of a creepy Unseelie prison.

"Lara, I swear I did not," I hear Ever say, his voice dragging me out of my morose thoughts. "I merely used air magic to rearrange the board, and if that turned the game to my advantage, well, I could not help it."

"Which means you cheated!" she replies, swiping the hnefatafl pieces onto the grass.

Delighted with her reaction, Ever laughs.

Taking Lara's side in the argument, I decide to annoy him with a pointless question. "So why weren't you with the rescue party the other night? Too busy to come help us?" I already know the answer. But it's better than asking about the real issues that are currently plaguing me. Which are: Where's Raff? How's he feeling? And if he's not back home yet, when the heck will he be?

After leaving Ithalah Forest the night of our escape, Raff and the three guards stopped overnight at Mount Cúig for a fae version of a health spa, so he could replenish his magic at the Lake of Spirits.

Wishing them luck, I continued the journey with Orlinda, and ever since arriving here at Talamh Cúig, I've been sadly, stupidly miserable.

I want to go home, see Mom, and indulge in a massive bake-a-thon. Chocolate-dipped madeleines are at the top of my to-do list. They'll make me feel better.

"Mother used her water magic to prevent me from leaving my chambers," says Ever. "It was immensely cruel of her to forbid me from helping my brother and forcing me to miss the Merit prince's final breath. I would have given much to witness it."

Distant thunder rumbles, its intensity matching Ever's scowl. He huffs a long breath, then says, "Long have I admired Lidwinia. For an Unseelie, she's a powerful and sensible fae, and whenever she resolves to do something, she acts decisively."

Lara reaches across the table and pats his cheek. "I'm glad the queen bound you to our chambers. Your reckless nature may have got you killed. And we found fun ways to pass the time while we were in lock down. Didn't we?"

His wicked smile makes me blush, and for some reason think about his brother again. Sometimes their happiness is too much to bear, and, feeling guilty, I focus my attention back on the garden.

It's a beautiful sunny day. Dragonflies flit through rainbow-colored flowers to skim across the pond where tiny moss elf children play along the edges. Birds chatter and sing. The breeze is light and warm. It couldn't be more perfect.

I'm safe. My family is safe. The heir of Talamh Cúig is free and recovering. All things considered, I should be happy. But I'm not. Instead of being content with this gorgeous day and wondrous place, I feel irritable and unsettled. And, yeah, never thought I'd say this, but I really, *really* want to go home to Blackbrook.

I've only been away from Merri for a few weeks, and she's grown so much. Bright red curls fly around her sweet face as she hurtles around the garden, Balor still following close behind.

"How do you deal with that?" I ask my cousin.

She pops a scarlet strawberry from a nearby platter in her mouth. "With what?"

I nod at Merri. "Her non-existent babyhood. Now she looks like a four-year-old. It's mind-blowing."

Merri skips over, her hands raised, and fingers spread toward the sun as she conducts the wind, leaves of gold and green swirling around her. When she reaches the table, she stops, giggling as she pushes a strong burst of air magic at us. Our hair billows behind us. Black grapes, wafer-thin biscuits, petals, and drops of red cordial float in rotating patterns before our eyes.

"Stop that, cheeky Princess of Air," says Lara as she attempts to capture and smooth her red waves with her palms.

Smiling, Merri shakes her head—*no*.

Lara raises an eyebrow and takes a big breath. Then she begins to sing a fast tune that grows louder with each clap of her hands. The song's magic changes the wind. Rushing about us like a mini tornado, it collects the petals and food crumbs into a neat column and sends it spiraling in the direction of the empty platter.

"No, Mama," complains Merri as she giggles.

The food settles back on the platter, and Merri collapses into Lara's arms for a cuddle. "When I first met your father, he tried that little trick on me. Since then, I've worked out how to deal with it."

"Guys, I'm going home," I blurt.

Ever and Lara's heads jerk up.

"What?" says Lara.

"You can't go home." Ever growls and lunges at Merri who's just taken off with his barbed silver crown. "Careful that one's sharp," he calls to her, chuckling fondly. His glowing, metallic eyes return to me. "The portal is closed, and only Ether can open it."

"What about Salamander?" I ask. "She sent me here in the first place. She can definitely open portals."

"She hasn't allowed herself to be seen in this realm for many moons." Lara picks up her goblet and sips, the sleeve of her elaborate tunic falling down her forearm.

"What do you mean by she hasn't allowed herself to be seen? Doesn't the court know she's living in the human realm?"

Ever says, "She can't be living there exclusively. The kingdom's powers would falter without her remaining tethered to it in some fashion—even irregular visits to our land would suffice. But one who seeks refuge in flames and coals is not easily found."

Lara squeezes my hand. "What about Raff, Isla? If you leave Faery, you might never see him again."

I blow out a breath. "For fruit's sake, spare me the fated mate nonsense."

Ever's brow rises. "So you truly don't believe you're his chosen one?"

"I don't know. Maybe," I admit. "But I'm not going to marry anyone who doesn't love me. End of story."

The smile Lara gives me is entirely annoying. So smug and knowing. "And you feel nothing for Raff?"

I roll my eyes. "Okay, I wouldn't say nothing exactly... I mean, there's no denying he's incredible to look at but—"

"But," interrupts Ever, "you believe he does not love you."

"Exactly. So if I can work out how to get there, I'm going home. But who knows, I might come back and visit one day to see how you're all getting on."

"And when you do, you probably won't see my brother, because without his queen, the curse will have killed him."

I pull a face at him. Then, brushing crumbs off my leather leggings and blue-velvet jacket, I get to my feet and roll the kinks out of my shoulders. "Remember in Blackbrook how you used to try and guilt trip me into not eating the ice cream in our freezer so you could have it all to yourself?"

Looking wistful, Ever nods. He's probably thinking about cookies and cream and Saturday night Netflix binges.

"Did it work?" I ask.

"No," he admits. "Because to spite me, you would always finish the tub as soon as I was occupied elsewhere."

"That's right. Guilt trips don't work on me, so back off. See you guys later. I'm going to check out the Moonstone Cave. Maybe if I hang around there long enough, I'll eventually bump into one of the mages, and I can talk them into opening a portal."

"See you, Merri," I call out, interrupting her play with the moss elves, an image of sweet, joyful innocence.

"Bye Lila," she answers in her cute lispy voice. No matter how hard she tries, she still can't say my name properly.

I try to picture a grown-up version of Merri ruling the Merit Court at the side of secretive, solemn Riven, and a shiver skitters down my spine. I turn my attention to Lara and Ever, drinking in the sight of them, so content and in love.

Could their daughter find similar happiness with the silver prince? He seems like a nice enough guy, but over and over history proves that power has a habit of turning good men into oppressors. How will the weight of a king's crown change him?

The lost end to the prophecy Riven recited rolls through my mind:

*A halfling defies the Silver King,*

*From dark to light, her good heart brings.*

*Enemies unite. Two courts now one,*

*Should merry win, the curse is done.*

Should Merri win, the curse is done. Wow! How I wish I could share those words with Lara.

Holding back a big sigh, in case I don't see them for a while, I give my faery family massive rib-bruising hugs and then begin my desperate mission to get out of this place stat—first stop is the kitchen.

After I've swapped a couple of recipes with Estel, I fill a cloth pack with food and water, then trek through the forest toward the ancient ruins of the Black Castle.

The pungent, sea-scented air crinkles my nose as I go around the old jet walls then cross the grassy tournament arena where Ever kicked Temnen's butt in an awesome sword fight when Lara first came to Faery. Boy, I wish I'd been cheering on the sidelines for that one!

Above the sound of waves smashing into the rocks far below, a sinister cackle travels on the breeze toward me. Curiosity trumps good sense and, instead of climbing the hillside to the cave, I swerve toward the cliffs so I can check out who the evil-sounding chuckler is.

Behind a line of sacred hazel trees, a circle of women sit chatting on the cliff edge. Not just any women, but the three mages—the supposedly missing Salamander, better known to me as Sally Salamande, Terra, and the High Mage, Ether. And judging by appearances alone, with her red eyes and white hair braided with strings of dark seaweed, the fourth creature, who's currently laughing like a maniac, must be a sea witch.

Salamander looks up and waves cheerily as I reach them.

Folding my arms across my chest, I say, "Hi Sally. Decided to come out of hiding, have you?"

"Hello, Isla. For those who need to see me, I am always in plain sight." Her flaming hair glows as bright as her shrewd, scarlet smile. "What took you so long? We've been waiting for you all morning."

What the crab apples? They knew I was coming?

"Welcome, Isla," says Ether, her downy-white hair levitating around her ethereal face. Pale fingers point to the sea witch. "This is Ezili from the water realm, newly crowned queen of the sea hags. With our sister Aer in disgrace, we mages prefer to meet with a fourth power on matters of importance. Ezili's wisdom assists us greatly."

*Thanks for the insight into the fascinating affairs of Elemental mages.*

"Duly noted. Hi, Ezili." I give a casual wave, and the witch reaches across Terra's lap to seize my hand and tug me down beside her.

Her smile reveals pointed black teeth. "Nice to meet you, Isla. I am very fond of your cousin, Lara. When I first met her, she allowed me to receive her princeling's kiss of fine oxygen. I wonder...If I asked nicely, would you let me kiss *your* prince?"

"Last time I checked, I didn't have a prince, and that's not about to change any time soon."

Ezili throws her head back and cackles. "Such pretty lies."

"What am I lying about? What I said is the truth. If you're referring to Raff, he means nothing to me."

"Oh? Then why do you seek us today?" asks Ether.

"I want to go home, and I need the portal opened. One of you guys can organize that for me, right? If possible, I'd like to go now, please."

"Give me your hand, and I shall speak plainly to you." Ezili tugs my palm up. "Ah, ha! The lines do not lie." Damp fingers trail over my skin as she mutters to herself.

The wind rises, whipping our hair and clothes around, drenching us in sea spray. After a few moments, she lets my hand drop. The wind settles, and she gives the mages a smug nod. "As you suspected, Ether, this girl loves the fire prince."

Salamander leans close, the heat from her skin searing mine as she grips my knee. "You truly wish to resume your human life of drudgery and leave your fated mate behind, relinquishing your right to be a queen of the Seelie fae?"

Rolling my eyes, I blow out a frustrated breath. "If he loved me, things might be different but—"

324

"But you have not seen him since you returned from captivity. How can you be certain he does not love you?" asks Terra, brown dust glittering on her cheeks.

Ezili gathers me close, her briny smell strong but not unpleasant. "Listen carefully, child, and answer me this. Do you know what you must give to the one who sees sorrow behind your smile, love behind your anger, and reason behind your silence?"

"Um...my thanks?"

"No. Your trust. Don't you see it? You would trust this person with your life, and I am here to tell you, Isla, that you can trust the Prince of Fire. This man was made for you. Your connection to each other is elemental and everlasting, but you insist on telling yourself that you doubt him when deep in your heart, you *already* trust him. You understand that he is yours."

As I open my mouth to disagree, Ezili cuts me off with a hiss. "You see? Still, your narrow human mind needs proof, and it is only through an act of great faith on the prince's behalf that you will believe his love is real."

A heavy heat kindles deep in my belly. Weirdly, the sea hag's words make sense. They feel right. A little frightening. But mostly exciting.

Salamander takes my hand. "Child of fire, as intensely as you wish to run from Rafael, he seeks you now with thrice the fervor."

He does? He's probably been back in town for days, but have I heard a word from him? Nope. Not one. Nada.

Flame-colored silk dances over Salamander's body, her red and emerald gaze earnest. "As the fire mage, I feel every beat of his phoenix's heart. And I feel yours too. For you, Isla, the flames are the portal to freedom. I know how badly you desire to be free, and to achieve this...you must burn. Rafael must prove he has faith in you. And how will he achieve that, you wonder? Well, he must stand by and watch the fire consume you."

*Watch the fire consume me.*

*Watch the fire.*

*Fire consume me.*

*The fire.*

*The fire.*

*Fire.*

Images flash through my mind—me flambéing crepes in the kitchen, toying with the flames, those flames leaping, roaring. A pyre forming. Me at the center of it, spiraling slowly, my arms outstretched as I worship the elemental force. The power of fire.

A deep knowing bursts to life inside my chest, a crystal-clear sense of purpose. The secret I've long kept hidden whispers in the fire mage's blood—my terrible desire to let the flames have me. To rise like a phoenix from the ashes.

"Yes," says Ether, a slow smile warming her face. "Look, Sisters. Isla finally comprehends. Should we let her leave Faery? What is your opinion, Ezili?"

Ocean-deep eyes pin me. "Perhaps she no longer wishes to leave us. What do you think, girl?"

The world around me stills. The wind disappears. The sharp smell of the ocean. The violent, gold-tinged sky. The four otherworldly creatures before me. All of it merges with my pounding pulse, my panted breaths.

"No." I shake my head slowly. "No. I don't want to go. What you said feels true. It feels right. So, I guess that means I need to find Raff and test his faith in me."

The mages clasp their hands together, nodding with satisfaction.

"The prince is home but avoiding you," says Salamander. "He can no longer bear your rejection and has been listening to unwise council. You must be brave to counter it."

That sounds like he's been hanging out with Kian.

Ezili smooths a rough palm down my hair, the gesture maternal, but the feral look in her eyes quite the opposite. "Before we bid you farewell for today, answer me this. Can you tell me what it is that you must keep after you have given it to someone else?"

"That's easy. A promise."

She grins. "Yes. You have made one promise to two different creatures—Salamander and the Silver King—see that you keep your word on pain of death, not yours, but the death of the one whom you will come to love more dearly than your own life."

"I know. Salamander has already warned me. I'll keep those promises." Even if keeping my secret from Ever, Lara, and Raff breaks my little liar's heart. "Thank you," I add, getting to my feet.

"One more thing," says Ether. "Imagine for me now that you are in a dark room, alone, and cut off forever from all chance of finding love and happiness. How do you get out of this room?"

Another pointless riddle. My shoulders sag. "I don't know."

"Simply stop imagining it."

Right. That's a pretty dumb answer... Or maybe it's actually brilliant.

Stop allowing pride and fear to rule my decisions. Stop thinking that Raff could never love me while I wait for some big romantic declaration like a sulky child. Instead, trust the connection that burns between us whenever we're together. Trust the fire. The flames tell me he does want me, and not just because of the Black Blood curse.

Raff is mine. I'm his.

"Once again, your advice is good, and I'm grateful for it. See you round, mages, witch queen. Don't laugh yourselves off the cliffs in a fit of righteous smugness."

By the time I've jogged through the forest and am back in the meadow outside the city's rear walls, I'm dripping with sweat.

Folk working in the fields pay me no mind as I hurry past, but a few of the striped okapri cows stop eating grass to greet me with loud bellows, their yellow eyes seeming to judge me harshly—*there goes the human who lies to herself, we don't do that. We love grass, we just shut up and eat it.*

Time for confession.

I have feelings for Raff that may or may not be love—okay—they're probably love. Does he feel the same about me? I think he might.

Awesome. That wasn't so hard. Me and my stupid self should have had this talk weeks ago.

As soon as I get back to my room, high in the Emerald Castle, I'm going to write a very important note.

I just hope he'll read it.

# 24

## Moping

### Raff

"Oh, please do not chase the girl like a lovelorn sap," snarls Kian as our swords clash, his face turning as scarlet as his flowing hair. "I beg you to do anything but that."

I growl and push forward with all my might, sending his sword clattering over the black stones of the onyx courtyard. "It is time for you to shut up about, Isla. Anyone who heard you would think that you were the heir to the Crown of Five, not I. But in case you are still confused, let me make myself clear." Nodding at his sword on the ground, I say, "I am the future King of Talamh Cúig, and I shall do as I please. Now cease your whining."

Face wrinkling like an old plum, he paces before me, his blue-velvet cape billowing like a sail. "Even if it means binding yourself to an ill-tempered human for all eternity?"

"Yes, even that." I incline my head and hurry toward the exit, rushing through it as I ignore his shouted requests for me to return and listen to his dubious version of sense.

I must find Lara. She will know where Isla is. Squinting, I search the skies until I spot the órga falcons eddying directly above my brother's not-so-secret garden. Of course. On such a beautiful day, where else would they linger?

As I stride toward the eastern walls of the castle, I stretch my aching arms and shoulders. On account of my recent swim in the Lake of Spirits, the source of our land's nature magic, my full strength has nearly returned. And due to Isla's presence at Talamh Cúig, the effect of the poison in my blood diminishes. Since my return three days ago, I haven't seen my human mate, but thoughts of her have plagued me.

I've fought with myself—give her space, or go to her and beg for a few moments of her company, my shifting opinion on which course to take more erratic than the flight of fireflies.

When Ever was the Black Blood heir, my life was very simple with only two things on my mind—having fun and making trouble. Now, everything is muddled and complicated, made worse these past few days by lack of sleep. But amid the turmoil of my buzzing thoughts, one thing is clear as a silver flame—I must speak to Isla. And soon. I hasten my pace accordingly.

Moments later, I burst into Ever and Lara's garden, finding them deep in a game of hnefatafl. "Alright. You had better tell me where she is," I demand.

"Who?" asks Ever, pretending he doesn't know.

"Isla of course. Oh, hello, sweet Merrin. I didn't see you there behind Balor's over-sized form. What in the realms are you feeding your hound, Ever? He has grown wider since I last saw him."

Balor whines, rolling onto his back like a pup.

"Sorry, old friend," I tell him. "We will take you hunting soon. You've been playing dress up with the children for far too long."

Smiling, young Merri waves in greeting then continues to braid sections of Balor's shaggy coat, weaving tiny silver bells throughout. Tongue lolling in a foolish grin, the dog looks more like a court jester than a fierce beast of the Wild Hunt.

"Hello, Lara, how are you on this fine day?" I inquire. "And where is your cousin?"

Lara gives me a dazzling smile. "I couldn't be happier now that you and she are safe and well."

"Why do you need to see Isla?" my brother asks, employing his most annoying tone. The one that suggests he knows everything and is far superior to me in all ways. One day, I shall enjoy making him call me Your Majesty. Even if it's just the once.

I pace back and forth before their table. "I do not fully know why I want to see her. And if I did, it would be my business. Perhaps I am curious to see how she fares."

"In that case, I may be of assistance." Ever grins. "Because I can report she is hale and hearty. Now there is no need to waste your time visiting her, and you may thank me for saving you the effort."

"You sound alarmingly like our mother." I try hard but fail to suppress my scowl. "And even so, I need to see her. Do you know her whereabouts or not?"

"Yes, I do," he says, placing a grape in Lara's mouth, the corners of their lips quirking, their eyes smoldering at each other.

Anger spikes hot inside me. "Well hurry up and tell me then!"

Slowly, Ever's gaze slides from Lara's to mine. "Calm yourself, Brother. First, I have a question for you. Do you love her?"

I glare at him. How dare he ask the very thing I have refused to ask myself.

For three days now, I have moped around my chambers, stalked through the forests, growled at servants and friends alike. The court is ablaze—bright with joyful celebrations—yet I remain shackled to the shadows of a tower cell, heated lips sliding over hers.

What is the truth anyway? Elusive. Subjective. Unutterable.

I can manage one truth: I love the taste of red-wine summer lips.

Another: I am obsessed with her.

And the third truth...

"Raff? Are you okay?" asks Lara. "Ever, look at him. I've never seen him look so unhappy."

"That is because he cannot answer my question." Turning to me, Ever sighs. "I'll ask it again. Do you love her?"

I shake my head.

"Then say you do not," he insists.

My mouth opens. I draw breath. "I do not..." Words trail away as I grimace down at the grass.

"There. You cannot speak the lie. It is obvious you possess feelings for her. And if my hunch is correct, to make her yours, you must prove your feelings to her. What woman truly desires a marriage of mere convenience? Certainly not Isla, a girl of rare courage and independence."

"Perhaps I do feel something," I cautiously admit. "So what if I do?"

"So *what*? Are you a fool? You've been home three days and not once tried to speak to her!"

"Kian advised me—"

"Oh, for Dana's sake!" says Ever. "Since when has Kian's advice been of use to anyone but himself?"

"Well... Never."

"Precisely. Brother, you know what you must do."

Yes. I do.

I finally do.

"I have been more stupid than a brainless draygonet. But I promise I will fix this as soon as you tell me where she is."

"Gone," Ever and Lara say.

"What? Where?"

Merri tugs my leg, squeezing her eyes shut as she looks inward and uses the sight she was born with. "Near the hazel trees," she says in her bell-like voice. "Lila and the mages three."

"She's trying to go through the portal and return home without speaking to me. I cannot believe it!"

Lara laughs. "That's Isla. Always a rash one. You'd better hurry."

"And she had better still be in our realm," I say, striding toward the gate that leads into the meadow behind the castle.

They have the gall to laugh at my back. "And what will you do if she isn't?" calls Lara.

I walk through the gate, then leaping up, grip the wall and peer back over it. "I don't know. Possibly cry."

I let go and drop to the ground. Without looking up, I begin to run and slam straight into Magret, Lara and Isla's closest confidante in Faery, who is now scrambling on the ground like a beetle trying to right itself.

"Prince Rafael! Greetings," she says as I lift her back onto her feet. "I've been searching for you."

Mustering up a charming smile, I sketch a hurried bow. "I am flattered to be in your thoughts. How can I assist you? You must speak quickly, however, for I am in a hurry."

Antlers quivering, she grins and passes me a folded piece of parchment. "It is a letter from Isla. She bids you to read it immediately, so I may return with your reply."

A letter from Isla? To me? Perhaps this is her farewell, and if that is the case, I'm not sure I want to read it.

Mouth dry, I open it and scan the words.

This is...unbelievable.

Perhaps this is a trick of Kian's. Every muscle drawn tight, I read the words again:

To the Fire Prince of Talamh Cúig,

Cloaked in a midnight sky,

Beneath a sea of stars,

On a field of moonlit poppies,

From a girl to a boy, words must be spoken.

Truth must be told, and truth must be heard.

*Tonight is this night.*

*And you are the boy.*

*Raff, will you meet me?*

*Please.*

*I'll bring cookies...you bring the fire.*

*Yours,*

*Isla.*

Swallowing hard, I meet Magret's pale gaze. "This is truly from Isla?"

Magret's smile is sweet but tinged with pity, as though she converses with a fool. I'm certain she does. "Of course it is. I saw her write the note with my own eyes."

"Look at me." I grip her chin, dragging her close to search her eyes for signs of tricks and glamor. Finding none, I release her gently. "Yes. Please tell Isla I shall be in the meadow at midnight as she requests."

Meet my Fire Queen under a starlit sky?

Only death could keep me from her.

# 25

## Reborn

### Isla

I've been here nearly half an hour and still, there's no sign of Raff.

He's not coming.

My note was too silly, too cryptic, not enticing enough. He's given up on me entirely or met a stunningly beautiful fae with fire magic who knows exactly what she wants—*him*—and isn't afraid to grab hold and never let him go.

Okay, that last one's a little on the ridiculous side. I wouldn't be surprised if he's hooked up with someone since his return, but I'm his fated mate. I know it now. The fire in my blood tells me it's true.

I drop to my knees on a soft cushion of wildflowers. Moonlight shines over the meadow, outlining the Emerald Castle and the forest trees with an edge of glimmering silver. I pick flowers and crush them between my fingers, sighing as I lay back on the grass, the balmy breeze caressing my skin.

Disappointment and longing fill my stomach.

Why was I so mean to Raff the last time we spoke, my words careless and spiteful after our escape? If I'd chosen them more wisely, maybe he would have turned up tonight like he told Magret he would.

A line of glowing lights moves up the hill toward me. I rise onto my elbows to watch them. Fireflies, I realize as they grow closer, closer, closer, then circle wildly above me. They flit over my arms and chest, and then disappear.

A blaze of light appears in the distance near the city walls. Hope sparks in my chest. Could it be...? I squint through the darkness at two columns of flames, hovering mid-air and moving toward me.

I stand quickly, the hem of my long dress tickling my bare feet. Yes! It's Raff, dressed in the usual black and red leathers, an unbuttoned dark-colored shirt flapping in the breeze, and fire dancing on each palm, reaching for the heavens.

He stops about a meter away, lighting up the night sky around us. His fire magic crackles like a campfire, but it smells different, cleaner and sweeter.

"You came," I say.

"How could I not?" In the moonlight, the intense brightness of Raff's smile competes with the beauty of the flames. "I will always come when you bid it."

As he moves closer, the fire reaches for me, licking my bare arms. "Sorry," he says, and flicks his hands, the lovely flames disappearing. "You asked for fire. I brought it."

"Yes, you did. And I promised cookies." I withdraw a parcel from the pocket of my long linen dress, the soft wheat-colored fabric shining like gold. "Would you like a chocolate macaron?"

In two steps he closes the distance between us, so close now I can see every movement of his chest, the way it labors like bellows.

He grins down at me, his gaze on my lips. "I think I'll pass on a dose of your baker's magic. Tonight, I wish for my thoughts to be clear. And there is something I crave much more than chocolate."

I raise an eyebrow. "And what is that?"

"Your kiss."

The earnest look in his amber eyes, the rakish angle of his circlet on his forehead with its sunstone pulsing brightly, he's so adorable, I can't help but smile back.

"Words first," I say.

"Ah, yes. You enticed me here with the truth—a precious gift indeed from a mortal. Tell me; I am ready to hear it."

A flash of nervous energy rushes through me, my mouth going dry. I gently grip his forearms and step even closer. "I think I..." Taking a deep breath, I let my words trail off.

Raff's focus is intense, like a hunter preparing to leap on his prey and devour it.

I promised the truth, and he deserves to hear it. "I think I might be in love with you."

Even in the darkness I see his eyes flare, a rush of breath parting his lips. Before he can speak, I continue, my words tumbling over each other. "I think I felt it—a strong connection—the very moment you walked onto the dais the first night I arrived in Faery. And I've been fighting it ever since."

"But why fight it?"

"Because I wanted to be safe, to protect myself from pain. Before I met you, I had this awesome life plan to prevent myself from ever being heartbroken, like my mom was when my dad left. That plan was to make sure I only ever loved people who loved me back."

"Your plan was flawed. Only those who love you hold the power to break your heart in the cruelest of ways. I have realized the hard way that you cannot protect yourself from the pain of love. Open yourself to it and the greatest joy will be yours."

"It sounds like you've been in love a lot then."

He laughs softly. "No. Like you, I am only experienced in running from it. These wise words I recite to you are my brother's. This is what he has learned, the advice he gave me when he returned with his family from the human world, which I, of course, have long ignored."

"So, you don't see yourself ever loving anyone?"

"As your note promised, the truth must be both spoken and heard. It is your turn to listen." A warm smile softens the sharp fae angles of his face. "Each moment I spent chained, wrapped in the darkness of the Merits' cell was in your company. Thoughts of you never once abandoned me." His palms bracket my cheeks, his words whispering over my lips.

"And when you kissed me, I have never known such powerful sorcery. This magic that flows between us is love. I was too stupid to see it. Too proud to admit it. But I love you, Isla. Ask anything of me and I will give it to you. Should you wish me to forsake the crown and live with you in the human realm, I would do it in a poisoned heartbeat."

Tears sting my eyes, wild, crazy hope soaring. "I would never ask that. Before I even met you, Ever spoke about you often. He told me that you planned to face the curse head on. Well, I admire your bravery, and I want to stand beside you and help you do just that."

Forgetting my true purpose for meeting him here on the hillside away from the revels of the court, I press my lips to his, entwine my arms around his neck, and lose my mind in the blistering heat of his tight embrace.

Galaxies spin around us, a scorching wind rising, tugging at our clothes and hair. He groans and presses closer, lips soft but urgent against mine. With a ragged sigh, I melt against him.

Night noises, the hoots of owls, strange mewls and cries of the forest creatures all disappear, while internal sounds rage. The roar of my blood pulsing through my veins, pummeling at my ears, and words—crazy, crazy words like *need*. Want. More. Fire. Burn. Now.

Always now.

I tug the shirt over his broad shoulders, revealing marble-smooth skin, the demon tattoo on his neck and other strange glyphs glowing like rivers of fire. Behind my eyelids, images flicker—flames and burning pyres—not frightening as they should be but urging me to make the fire prince mine.

As a fae who cannot lie, he must believe the words of love he spoke to me before...but do I? He loves me, he loves me not... I don't care. I don't care. I'll have him anyway.

Tawny hair silky under my fingers. Lush lips smiling. "Isla," he says, teeth scraping my lips. "I cannot control the fire. This is...too much...I—"

"Let it rage," I whisper, and kiss him again.

His fingers dig into my waist. He cradles my jaw, angling my face, pressing deeper. His body trembles, shakes. I can feel his restraint crumbling, his control slipping. It is the most wonderful thing—my power over him. "Raff... Let it go."

Another groan, a whispered curse—and he does.

A circle of waist-high flames roar around us, the heat intense, the glow maddening. And perfect. I'm not afraid.

His kisses change, becoming wild and urgent, ragged breaths panting over me. This is everything. All there is. All I need. My skin blisteringly hot, I peel the straps of my dress down.

Raff's dark-honey gaze devours me, his fingers brushing mine aside and taking over the task. Between savage kisses, we undress each other, then lie on a cushion of wildflowers.

His weight heavy over my body, he draws his head back, his gaze searing, otherworldly. Terrifying. "By moon and stars, fire and blood, by the Elements Five and all the powers of the Seven Realms, you are mine, Isla, and I am yours."

"Yes." I nod, the longing to make it true like a dagger twisting at my heart.

"Say it."

"I'm yours. You're mine. No words are truer, Raff. Just like you've always said—I'm the girl you've been waiting for. Nothing is truer."

Then he surges forward, and we become one, the promise we've made to each other branding our souls forever.

I kiss him the way I've been dreaming about ever since he pressed his palm against my back and spun me around the Great Hall, the curve of his sneering lips a lush temptation. Our first touch. Our first dance.

And now I kiss him deeply, holding nothing back as his hands trail over my body, the sounds he makes heady and intoxicating. Setting me on fire. Ruining me and remaking me with every sigh.

Our bodies' rhythm, like old tales of faery tricks, is a dance I want to be spellbound in forever. It's everything I dreamed it would be. The pulse, the beat, the flames that consume me. The fire.

Heat coils deep in my belly, an inferno spreading to my toes, my fingertips. Movements no longer smooth, he hooks an arm in the crook of my knee, taking more. His fingers press and pull, urging me closer. Teeth scrape, sharper, harder.

"Isla. Isla," he says, and the flames swallow me, splintering my bones to ashes.

Warm lips kiss my shoulder, my neck, then my lips. "I love you," says the fire prince, his body still, his breathing a mess.

A fox shrieks in the distance, reminding me where we are—the meadow, encircled by magical flames. "I know. I love you too. I can't believe this...that I'm here, who you are, how I feel. It's crazy. Crazy but brilliant."

He smiles. "Like fresh, sweet poison, you have ruined me, and I do not wish you to stop."

I stroke from the pointed tip of his ear down to his cheek, cupping it softly. "You might regret those words when I tell you the other reason I asked to meet you here."

"What? This was not it?" His eyebrows lift. "Tell me now."

"Soon," I say, then hoping to distract him, "Kiss me again?"

His lips curve. "You are a demanding creature."

I laugh. "Eh. You can handle it."

"But can you handle me?"

Guess I'm about to find out.

# 26

## Queen of Fire

### Raff

"So, this wasn't part of your plan?" I ask, breathing slowly to settle my chaotic pulse. The poison has retreated, and I am filled with light and calm for the first time since the curse entered my blood, damning me, enslaving me. Until Isla.

"It definitely wasn't. But I really like the way events unfolded."

"I couldn't agree more." I pat the grass to find Isla's gown, then hand it to her. "Let us dress quickly. I cannot wait to return to my chambers and begin planning our wedding. You will move your personal items to my rooms tomorrow." I kiss her hand, interrupting her efforts to dress. "You'll have no need of them tonight."

She gives me a sweet smile as I stroke locks of gold from her face. "I can hardly believe my luck, Isla. Here you are, my future Queen of Fire and, finally, you are mine."

"Yeah... About that queen business."

My hand stills at her temple, a frown creasing my brow. "What do you mean? Surely, you agree we must marry as soon as possible?"

"I want to—I do, but..."

A moment of panic makes the flames around us sputter, sparks igniting the cobalt sky. "For us, there can be no doubts. After what we have just experienced together, no month-long revel, no wild hunt, no magic or mischief could ever compare. Do you not feel it too, Isla?"

"Of course I do. It's just—"

I draw her onto my lap. My thumbs pressing into her cheekbones, I try to explain how I feel, what I have taken far too long to realize she means to me. "Every being, fae or human, longs to find another who will hold the mirror that reveals our best selves, the one who will show us who we can be if only we believe in ourselves. You are my perfect mirror, Isla. In your eyes, I see reflected the man I want to be. The man I am determined to become if he will bring you happiness."

Her smile is brighter and brings more joy than a Beltane fire.

"I feel the same, but if you love me, you have to..." She takes a shuddering breath. "You have to let me go."

Fear coils around my heart, a deadly serpent squeezing and tightening until I can't breathe. I shake my head. This cannot be. The taste of her still melting on my tongue, there is no way in the seven realms I will let her leave me. Why would she want to go?

"No, Raff, it's okay. I promise. Just tell me one thing, do you trust me?"

"Yes. Of course I do."

"Then forget about weddings and curses and saving your kingdom for now. Before all that, you have to let me burn."

"What?" I flick my hand over my shoulder, extinguishing the flames completely. Darkness falls, gilded by moonlight. "No, Isla. Absolutely, not. I will not do what you ask." I move her off my lap, fasten my breeches, then my boots, the weight of her gaze tingling over my skin as I do so.

She grips my wrist as, still seated on the ground, I shrug into my shirt. "You told me before, anything I asked, you'd give it to me. Did you lie?"

Raking my hands through my hair, I groan in frustration. "You know I cannot."

"Then trust me. Please. If you want your fire queen, this is the way you'll get her."

I watch her stand, moonlight shining on her naked skin. She's beautiful. She is my chosen one. I trust her; I do.

"Alright. I do not like this, but alright," I say, staring up into her smiling face. My goddess of fire. My love.

She offers her outstretched palms. I take them and stand, my breaths labored as I scan her face, memorizing each sweet slope and curve. "This isn't goodbye. I won't let it be the end."

"No, Raff. It's the beginning. Bring the flames again."

I close my eyes and stretch my arms on either side of my body, slowly raising my palms. Heat kindles. Magic shudders through me. Flames leap from my skin, and I throw them to the ground, north, south, east, and west. Spinning on my heels I picture them joining, the four directions merging into a circle.

She claps her hands, giggling like a water sprite. "Beautiful! Now you have to move out of the circle."

"Isla—"

"Do it."

With a sigh, I do as she commands.

Standing in the middle of my circular wall of magic, she brings her palms to her chest and pushes them out, scoops the air and draws it backward. To my astonishment, the flames follow, tumbling and roaring to become a gigantic fire, a pyre with no wood, no fuel, only Isla at the center.

She closes her eyes and flames lick around her feet, climbing quickly upward to swallow her whole. She is the golden-haired girl of my tortured dreams, standing in the middle of an inferno, her soft skin charring slightly. Just like in my visions, instead of fear, ecstasy emanates from her.

Her hair is richest buttermilk, her eyes a blistering blue, and her smile—her smile is the brightest flame—fierce and taunting. For she is not the slightest bit afraid as the flames leap higher and take her over, crumble her to her knees, drag her under and consume her.

There are no screams, no cries for help. No sounds but the sizzle and crackle of magic.

I clench my fists, every muscle tight.

I am not afraid.

Isla is a Princess of Fire. When my mother abdicates—she'll become my Queen of Five.

Knuckles cracking, my feet braced wide, I stand statue-still until the sky above glows like the End of Days. It burns orange, red, then finally the deepest black, blocking out the stars.

Time passes—days, a lifetime.

When the air is thick with smoke and I can see no hint of Isla, my heart beating slowly, soul braced for the worst, I step toward the flames.

Embers fall like snow. Do I quell the fire now? Is it time? A sudden wind rages up the valley, crackling through branches and leaves, extinguishing the fire before I make a decision.

"Isla?"

She's huddled on the ground, head resting on her raised knees, her arms wrapped tightly around them. Her skin is perfect, unmarred, no burns, no scars. Golden hair tumbles over her body, as silky as it has ever been.

Slowly, her head lifts. Tears paint her face, but she is smiling. *She is smiling.* "Raff."

I drop to my knees in front of her, searching for marks, for signs of injury. "Are you alright?"

Her joy-filled smile is worth my worry, the doubt, the fear, the fall of seven kingdoms.

"Yes. Unbelievably, never better. But I must say I'm really hungry. I might have to start on those cookies if the field mice and goblins haven't run off with them."

I laugh as I help her to stand. "Here, wear my shirt. Hurry. In my chambers, I'll have the grandest snack imaginable brought to you."

She shrugs into my shirt, the hem covering her smooth thighs. "That sounds great. But I'd rather not wake the cooks. How about you and I go hang out in the kitchen instead, and I'll whip something up for us?"

"Of course, if you wish it. But first, you must tell my why you made me watch you burn? What did it prove?"

"I wanted to see if you could, if you trusted me enough. And look at this..." She steps out of my embrace, thrusting her palm out. A bright arc of flames shoots across the field setting alight a line of shrubs in the distance. A flick of her hand and the fire disappears.

"That is amazing! Your magic has increased a thousandfold."

"And that was the second point of the fire exercise." With a proud smile, she drops a curtsy. "Now I'm fully equipped to be this kickass Queen of Fire you're always bragging about."

Drawing her into my arms, I kiss her until she pushes against my chest.

"Wait... Raff, I have to tell you something, and this will be an even more difficult test of your faith in me. When I was with the Merits, I learned something, something horribly important that, in the future, will come to affect all of us. But I can't tell you everything I know. If I did, it would cost me your life, not mine, *yours*. And I'm not prepared to risk it."

"Isla, I trust you to tell me what you can. You ask nothing difficult of me because this is the way of the fae. Life is a complicated riddle. We do our best to accept what befalls us and attempt to bend the situation to our will when what arises does not please us. I trust you to bear this knowledge you speak of for both our sakes. Tell me only what allows you to keep your peace."

"Okay. Thank you, Raff." She closes her eyes, breathes slowly, then traps me in her ocean-blue gaze. "I vowed to Salamander that

I would keep the details secret, but what I can tell you, and it's the most important part, is that all will be well—for you, for Ever and Lara, all the future heirs of Talamh Cúig, before long, you will all be free."

Relief flows warm through my veins. "I believe this because I trust you with my life and my soul, from the depths of my poisoned heart. Forever."

"It won't be poisoned for much longer. When we marry, you'll be free of the curse. If you die, our oldest male child will inherit the poisoned blood. But we don't need to worry about that anymore, Raff. There is a cure for the curse. In our lifetime, your line will be free of the evil Aer inflicted on your kingdom."

"I dare not believe I will live to see its end."

"You will see it. I promise you. Riven has seen the cure. Aer gave it to the Merit druids, and after El Fannon murdered them all, Riven has been protecting their secrets. Aer always hinted that there was a cure hidden away somewhere. Guess she supposed the last place Elementals would look for it was in the land of your enemies. All you need to do is have faith that it will end and try to be happy while you wait. Can you do that?"

My chest swells with equal parts gratitude, joy, and love. "Yes, I can."

"One more thing."

"Anything."

"Kiss me again?"

"With pleasure. But I warn you, once I start, I may never stop."

"Promises. Promises."

I cannot lie. I will not lie. I dip my head, soft lips brushing, and begin the endless count—a lifetime, an eternity of magical kisses.

# *Epilogue*

## Riven

Heavy as a mountain, my crown bows my head low as I peer into the druid's well—long spikes of black crystal reflecting in the water like arrows piercing my skull.

Arrows of sorrow.

The well's mirrored surface ripples, revealing two more crowns. Golden crowns: a matched pair of twisted fire and rubies.

The dark water before my eyes displays the grandeur of a coronation, the Fire King and his Queen of Flames, their smiles as bright as sunshine and blazing only for each other. All around them bustles the luminous Court of Five. Magic and revelry, music and mayhem, love and light and joy.

A bright court, the opposite of mine, lit by all I can never have and will never deserve.

It taunts me. Terrifies me.

My gaze seeks the red-haired child with quicksilver eyes, eyes that show no mercy. Ever's daughter. The one, who when she comes of age, I must ensure I never meet. Never gaze at in person, even though I long to do so with all my being.

But I must never allow it.

*Never.*

Yet night after night I descend ancient stairs to the druid's well...again and again to view images of her as a young woman grown. To see her smile and dance.

And while I watch, I vow over and over...

*Never her,* I whisper.

*Never her.*

She is my kingdom's enemy, and if given into my hands, the cure to their cursed blood.

The girl is *their* cure. The girl is *my* curse.

The curse I long for but won't ever allow myself to surrender to. I won't.

A wave across the silver water, another ripple, then the Bright Court is gone.

Then *she* appears. Merri grown, ribbons of long red locks catching on branches as she wanders through a forest, lost and alone. She stops at a pond to drink, and as she does so, the very fabric of the spring day rends, breaking as a dark force moves closer.

Danger lurks behind the leaves, hidden deftly by the forest. A crack, a rustle, and then a tall traveler appears behind her. His cloak is dark, silver hair twisting around his shoulders despite the stillness of the air and trees. No breeze. Not a whisper. But magic moves inside him.

He bends, placing a jeweled hand upon the blue velvet covering her shoulder.

She turns.

Silver eyes skewer. Silver eyes tantalize and enslave the stranger, trapping him in the bonds of a long-ago cast fate.

The man smiles, the left side of his mouth curling with long-bridled intent.

Is this being good or evil? Does he come to help or harm?

Dark humor shivers through me. Why do I ask when I already know the answer?

For the man in the woods is *me*, Riven Èadra na Duinn.

I am the Silver King.

And Merrin Airgetlám Fionbharr is my destiny.

The destiny I must forever shun.

Red floods the surface of the water, concealing the image of the couple, shrouding them in crimson blood.

In the vision, just as it always does.

In life, as it must never do.


Thank you for reading King of Always! Keep turning for details on other books in the series and a sneak peek at King of Merits.


Sign up to my Newsletter and be the first to receive release news and sneaky sales alerts.

Hear Ever and Lara brought to life by the amazing narrators, James Fouhey and Gina Rogers in the AUDIOBOOK!

# King of Merits Excerpt

## Chapter 1 - Land of Five - Merri

With a flick of my wrist, my bedroom chamber's teal drapes fly open, and I scowl down at the Faery city of Talamh Cúig. Most mornings, the sparkling emerald and black surfaces of the buildings fill my heart with joy.

But not today.

The dream that woke me still clings to my skin like a cloying velvet gown worn on a hot summer's day. But here in the Land of Five, it's springtime. My favorite season. I should be happy. And I would be...if not for the dream.

The dream of snow and winter.

The dream that is light and bright before it turns a deep suffocating purple, the color of bitter longing.

This nightmare of the silver fae with haunted eyes has plagued me since childhood. It doesn't occur every night. And, sometimes, not every moon turn. But when it does, it lingers until the next time, following me through the brightest days and tormenting me during the darkest hours until morning light creeps across my green and gold walls, saving me.

Every day, I ask myself, why do I see this fae? What's so special about him?

He performs no remarkable deed nor utters a single word, only stares with his mournful gaze. His silence entices me into a void of white where red flows from deep gashes and wounds—whose injuries these are, I never know.

Sighing, I move away from the windows, snatch my favorite bow and quiver from the floor, and throw them on my bed. With my fingers, I rake knots from my hair, tugging hard on the long red strands.

I dress quickly in hunting leathers and a light emerald cape, hoping a ride before breakfast will erase the vision of the fae with the sorrowful, glowing blue gaze.

Halfway to the door, I skid to a stop. Cara! I'd forgotten all about her. Backtracking, I close in on the happily snoring lump and then give the bed furs a good poke.

"Wake up, lazybones," I say, "or you'll miss a ride through the mountains."

A muffled squeak resounds from under the covers. A long brown nose wriggles out, followed by shiny black eyes blinking in confusion.

"No? Not interested? Goodbye then. I hope you enjoy your day with Arellena." My elven chambermaid is famously stern and not very fond of my roommate. "I believe she plans to spend the entire day here, sorting and mending clothes. I'm sure you'll be a great helper."

A mass of brown and purple fur explodes from the bed, landing on the shiny wooden floor at my feet. I laugh and scoop up my adorable mire squirrel and tuck her warm body into the crook of my neck. Her striped tail wraps gently around my throat as she scolds me with angry chirps.

"Worry not," I say, patting her with one hand as I collect the bow and quiver with the other, and then sling them over my shoulder. "I wouldn't have left you behind. I know how Arellena terrifies you."

As I stride through beams of sunshine in the Emerald Castle's hallways, I mock salute the striking images of my father, Prince Ever, and King Raff, fighting ferociously side-by-side in their gleaming armor from the tapestries that line the walls. Thankfully, at breakfast time, they behave a little more civilized. Mostly.

When I enter the Great Hall via a back staircase, a chaotic scene greets me. I bite my cheek, trying not to laugh. It's impossible.

Father and King Raff are arm wrestling, their wild movements sending goblets and platters sliding along the rectangular table. My mother sits in Father's lap, heckling him to decrease his chances of winning.

Raff's mire fox, Spark, screeches and bounces atop Isla's shoulders, her furry little hands buried in the queen's golden hair and distracting adorable baby Aodhan from his breakfast.

Magret, Alorus, Orlinda, and Lord Gavrin play quiet games of hnefatafl, and next to them, my younger brother, Wynter, clomps the heels of his boots onto the six-pointed star in the middle of the table. Chunks of jet-black hair hide the devious twinkle in his brilliant eyes that are so similar to our mother's. My eyes are silver, like Father's, the color as changeable as the weather our magic controls.

Tumbled cups, messy food platters, and all manner of entertainments, such as wooden puzzles, instruments, paper scrolls, and arrow fletchings cover the table's surface. Yes, my family breaks their fast like an encampment of warmongering giants rather than refined, graceful fae royalty.

A small band of winged musicians, drunk and already falling over each other at this early hour, play haphazardly from the dais, and Balor chases my brother's black wolf around the table in time to the lively beat, snapping at his tail as they go.

When the king married my mom's cousin, a human like Mother, fun-loving Raff and Isla became rulers of the Elemental fae, and the strict courtly standards that my grandmother, Varenus, upheld are only adhered to on important, formal occasions. Of which breakfast isn't one.

With a deep breath, I straighten my spine and sully forth into the fray.

"Good morning, brat," says Wyn as I pad across the floor toward him.

With my sharpest nail, I flick the tip of his straight nose. *Hard.* "You'd do well to remain silent if you can't respect your elders. Heed your wolf's manners. Ivor could easily best Balor with those formidable fangs but regularly quashes his beastly nature to maintain goodwill."

Wyn rolls his eyes in reply.

"Good morning, sweetheart," says Mom. She tickles my father's side, helping Raff gain the advantage and send Dad's fist crashing into Lord Gavrin's bowl of curd porridge. The king winks at me, straightening his sunstone-encrusted crown. Next to Raff, Alorus and Orlinda smother giggles.

I greet the loud chorus of "Morning, Merri" with a grin, then blow kisses to my parents. Humans who met them would never believe that Prince Ever and Princess Lara could possibly have two grown children. They barely look a day older than me and Wyn.

Wyn throws a grape, and I catch it before it hits my nose. "I'll speak as pleases me, Sister. And if you continue to be annoying, I'll toss Cara into the mix, and we'll see how your rodent fares against my wolf."

"Don't call her a rodent." Cara's whiskers tremble against my neck. I soothe her with a gentle chin scratch, then blast Wyn with an icy wind that tears his hair toward the ceiling. Unsurprisingly, a frenzied mess is quite a good look on him.

"Stop that, you terror." He laughs, smoothing his hair in a battle against my air magic.

"Make me."

"If you insist." With a click of his fingers, the walls begin to shake, emerald-colored dust powdering my hair and face. Spluttering, I create a breeze and blow it back at him. Curse his filthy earth magic!

"Show off," I say, releasing his mop from the wind spell.

Like me, Wyn is a halfling, but in an unfair trick of fate, his powers are almost as strong as a full-blooded fae's and more powerful than mine. My air magic is unreliable, and my visions are often hard to decipher. Or completely useless if they're about a certain silver-haired fae.

"Dear Son. Sweet Daughter," says Father. "Must you act like bog trolls every mealtime?"

I aim a pointed smirk at Lord Gavrin who is busy mopping porridge from his face.

"Yes, Father, you're right," says Wyn. "I humbly beg your pardon and will attempt to follow *your* fine example at all times in the future."

"Which means he can do as he likes." King Raff laughs. "He has you there, Brother. In human years, your son is a mere youth of sixteen and already smarter than you."

"Or just more insufferable," I suggest.

"Come and join us, Merri," Isla says, bouncing Aodhan on her lap.

The little prince is a beautiful golden-haired child with eyes of brightest amber, like his father's, the king. It saddens me to think that when he comes of age, the family's vile curse will course through his veins.

"I've made chocolate croissants," continues the queen. "Your favorite."

Smiling, I pour pear juice into a goblet and swipe a delicious pastry from a plate. I take a drink, then a bite, and say around a big mouthful, "I'd love to sit awhile, but I don't have time. I'm going riding."

"Before breakfast?" Mom asks, her hair tumbling around her shoulders as she speaks, dozens of threaded emeralds glinting among the strawberry waves.

My hair is even brighter, making it hard to hide unless I don a cloak with a hood, which I always do when I venture into the forest. A Princess of Air doesn't see many interesting occurrences, but a stealthy stranger does.

"No, Mother." I take another large bite, bitter-sweet chocolate melting on my tongue. "As you can see, I'm eating it now."

"It's difficult to believe you could willingly choose to forgo my company," Wyn says in his annoying, deep voice.

One year my junior, he has the voice of a king—as arrogant and charming as our father's. He throws a purple grape at me. "Here, your rat looks hungry. No, don't thank me."

Refusing to argue, I smile serenely and offer Cara some of my croissant.

I gaze at my pouting family and shrug. "Sorry, but I need to get outside and let the wind chase a bad dream away. A hard ride toward the Dún Mountains should do the trick."

Frowning, Isla studies me. She does that a lot, examines me as though I'm a puzzle she needs to solve, and asks questions about my dreams as if they contain the answers she seeks. I don't know why she does this. She thinks she's subtle, but trust me, she's not.

Mother smiles, her fingers stroking Father's neck as she hugs him closer. According to her, my dreams are typical for a young girl and they'll go away when I meet the right fae, the one whose actions, not just their handsome face, will speak to my heart. Be patient, she says, and I just shrug. I'm not interested in love, anyway.

"You have your bow?" Father asks. "The draygonets are on the move again. Kian saw a weyr of them not far from Serpent River only two days past."

Bending at the waist, I flourish a curtsy, making my quiver full of arrows pop over my shoulder. He gives Mom a dimpled smile, confident in the knowledge he's raised a child who's not entirely reckless. Like he was. And still is.

Their happiness warms my heart, and I think again how disturbed humans would be to see their parents glowing blissfully before their eyes, as strong and beautiful as they've ever been, but it doesn't bother me. An ageless appearance is the way of the fae and the mortals who form mate bonds with them, as my mother and Isla did with Father and Raff. In one hundred years, I'll likely remain unchanged, too. In appearance, at least.

Wyn issues a sharp whistle, and his wolf pricks his ears, his alert orange eyes fixing on my brother. "Ivor and I will come with you," he says, swinging his long legs off the table, boots thudding onto the marble.

"No, you won't." I push him deeper into his high-backed chair, my fingers snagging on the chain of white daisies lying against his chest.

I fasten a button on his forest-green shirt that hangs raggedly open as if he doesn't give two hoots about his appearance, which is a ruse.

Wynter only behaves like a lazy troll so the ladies of the court can take care of his every need. But he's capable of doing anything he sets his devious mind to, including dressing himself properly.

"You broke my necklace," he shouts, feigning great offense.

"Oh, boohoo. I'm sure there are a bevy of sweet sprites hovering around the corner, ready to make you a new daisy chain. Fret not, dear one."

Secure in the knowledge he is precious to me, he flashes the dimpled smile that makes all of Faery weep, his smattering of freckles glittering in the soft morning light. And he's not wrong about his value. I'd stick a blade in anyone's eye to protect him.

Not that he needs defending—he's skilled with his sword, and his magic is strong. Wynter inherited all the advantages of a Prince of Five, while I bear the shortcomings of my halfling constitution.

Unfair, in my opinion.

Isla's words circle through my mind: *Power may follow the Elemental male line, but you, darling Merri, are destined for something far greater than to sit upon the Throne of Five and look pretty for the rest of your days.*

Whenever I ask her what this amazing destiny is, she finds an urgent matter to rush off to, looking oddly guilty. Even stranger, she never repeats these words in front of my parents. Or Wyn, for that matter.

I give a mock bow to my family. "Okay, later, guys," I say as I spin to face the exit, my eyes on the bronze star decorating the arched doors that lead to fresh air and freedom.

"Some of us here happen to be female," says Magret, who, despite living with humans and halflings for many years, still insists on taking everything we say literally. "Have fun on your ride, Merri, but please remember that if your grandmother's spies hear you speaking like that, there'll be seven hells to pay when you return."

Tell me about it. Grandma Varenus greatly disapproves when I speak in *the mortal gibberish*, as she calls it. I've picked the slang up from visits to Mom's birthplace over the years and admit I'm very fond of it.

Earth. What an extraordinary world. My favorite mortal hangout is, of course, Max's Vinyl City diner, where Mother and Isla worked when they were young. I hope we visit the human realm soon, though Father says we're needed here, and it's therefore unlikely.

Truthfully, I'm glad Varenus only dines with us during the grander feasts. She disapproves of the way we tease each other and set the dining table on the floor in front of the dais instead of on it.

When Grandmother lectures, my parents only grin secretly at each other. But her callous words hurt me, make me feel inferior, and I'm glad I don't have to suffer her disdain very often. *And certainly not today*, I think, as I hop down the last steps onto a city pathway.

Outside, it's a perfect day, a clear blue sky and a sweet-scented breeze blowing my dream a little further away. Thank the Elements.

Fae are opening up market stalls that line the silver-paved streets behind the castle, calling out greetings as I hurry past. I shout back to them and breathe deep the delicious smells of cinnamon and baking bread as I leap over a low wall and take a shortcut to the stables.

When I round the bend into the cobblestone courtyard, five moss elves appear, the sleeves of their bark-colored tunics sweeping the ground as they bow low. They don't look happy, their dark hair framing deep frowns.

It is a family I know well and love dearly, for the older members have been mine and Balor's playmates since I first arrived in Faery as a child. The tallest of them scratches one of his curling horns, and then tugs impatiently on the hem of my cloak.

"Good morning, Tanisha, Marelius, Jasper, Fern, baby Velvet. What disturbs you on this fine morning?" I say, keen to pass by and be on my way.

Pointing at the stalls, they speak in the fast Elvish of their tribe, a language I'm not fully fluent in. The only word I understand from their excited babble is *Kian* because it's repeated so often.

Oh, not again. The moss elves despise Kian and spout regular dire warnings about him for the slightest of reasons. Cara chirps loudly in my ear, and I know she agrees with them. I'm not fond of Kian either. But he's infuriating, not dangerous.

"Is Kian in there?" I ask, pointing at the stables.

"Yes," says Tanisha, the matriarch of the clan. The others nod furiously. "No good. No good."

"I'll be fine." I squat down and meet the elves' worried gazes. "Relax, everyone. I'm well aware that Kian is a pain in the neck, but I won't be with him for long. Nahla and I are going riding."

Marelius, Tanisha's mate, hugs my leg and tries to drag me toward the market district. Although tall for a moss elf, the top of his head only comes up to my knees.

"No, Merri, stay," he pleads, his eyes bright beams of gold against his mossy-green skin. "We elves have some very bad feelings today."

Don't they always? A distraction is needed.

"Hey, I have good news. Queen Isla is looking for someone to entertain Aodhan after breakfast. You should hurry along to the Great Hall, because Salamander is probably heading over right now, trying to beat you to it. You know how obsessed the fire mage is with her little fire prince."

Hugging each other, the elves squeal and move away as one bouncing mass.

They take great pride in being the favorite playmates of the royal children and maintain a fierce rivalry with any member of the court who challenges their positions as chief babysitters.

Dusting my hands off as I watch them dash toward the castle's teal spires, I try not to feel too guilty about using my halfling skill and twisting the truth into an almost-lie, something a full-blooded fae can't do without experiencing extreme pain. Wyn is skilled in the art, too, but rarely chooses to employ it. Mainly because he refuses to do anything that might make him appear less fae and more human.

Warm sun on my back, I stride into the stables and find Kian with his head practically grafted onto Seven's, the imp's rainbow-colored horns tangling with his red locks as they whisper next to Jinn's stall.

"Morning," I boom, startling them into bumping foreheads as they look up.

"Hello, sweet Merrin," says Kian, his voice sending chills over my skin as he struts forward, peacock-blue cape rippling behind him. In his richly embroidered outfit, he's dressed far too finely to be mucking out horse dung. Not that he'd ever lower himself to such a task. I wonder what mischief he's up to.

"I guessed you would be riding out early on such a fine day," he says, stopping in front of me. "I've already saddled your mount for you."

"That seems kind of you." I'm fully aware that he's never nice without an ulterior motive. He probably thinks I'll invite him to come along, but I'd rather take an amorous mountain troll on an outing than Kian Leondearg.

Jinn and his daughter, Nahla, nicker from their stalls in greeting. "Hello there," I say, drawing out a small bunch of carrots from my pocket. "Care for a treat?"

Jinn gobbles two with astonishing speed, but Nahla turns her head away, which is most unusual. Normally, she'll eat anything she's given, including my cooking, which is brave of her. Perhaps she's feeling poorly.

Stroking her warm neck, I ask, "Are you all right, dear one? We can go to the meadow and lie about in the sun if you're not up to a gallop."

My horse neighs loudly, nudging me with her nose. If it weren't for the white star on her face, she'd look exactly like her coal-black father. "Fine, then. A ride it is."

Giving Kian my back, I hook my bow onto Nahla's saddle and then climb up into it.

A barely dressed Seven scampers up beside Kian and links arms with him. She gives me a cheerful wave.

"I'm certain I heard you swear off dallying with Kian three Beltane festivals ago," I tell the imp.

Her one black eye blinks innocently at me from the middle of her brow. "Although full of himself, Kian is rather pretty, and I do like to check now and then to see if his bed skills have improved."

"Or stable skills," I suggest.

Kian's bright-blue eyes glitter darkly. Foolishly, he reaches out to pat Cara who has crawled down to my forearm, and she sinks her teeth into his fingers.

"Blasted mire trolls!" He snarls, raising a hand to slap her snout.

My anger wakes the sky, thunder shaking the walls, and Kian holds his palms open, a gesture of surrender. "Calm yourself, Princess. I won't retaliate against your creature, although she deserves it many times over."

Patting Nahla's coat, I click my tongue, and she moves out of the stall, knocking Kian sideways.

"Would you like company?" he asks, already opening Jinn's stall as though sure of my answer.

Jinn screams, kicking the walls, clearly wishing they were Kian's breeding organs or his pocket potatoes, as Isla is fond of calling them.

"I prefer the company of my animals, and even if I agreed to bear yours, you couldn't keep up with us anyway." I stab two fingers at my chest, the black and gold feather ruff around my neck stirring with the movement. "Air magic, remember? Nahla and I ride like the wind."

I bend and kiss Nahla's neck. "Let's go, girl."

And we're off, flying through the courtyard.

# Also By Juno Heart

Prince of Then: Gadriel and Holly's story, the prequel.

Prince of Never: Ever and Lara's story.

King of Always: Raff & Isla's story.
King of Merits: Riven and Merri's tale.

**Ebook & paperback covers**

## Hardcovers

I also write about damaged heroes and the girls who heal them under a steamy romance pen name. Stay tuned for steamy fae books coming soon and Wyn & Aodhan's stories!

Join my newsletter list and be the first to hear of new releases, read-first opportunities, and other sweet deals.
You can sign up at my website: junoheartfaeromance.com

And don't forget to have a listen to the Prince of Never audiobook! Available at all retailers.

# Acknowledgments

Thank you for reading Raff and Isla's story! I hope you enjoyed it. I love hearing from readers, and I'm so grateful for every kind email and thoughtful review I've received. You guys rock! Massive thanks and virtual hugs for taking the time to reach out and, also, for sharing my stories with your friends!

Huge thank yous to Amelie, Anna, Joanne, Ken, and Cissell Ink for your awesome feedback. Thank you for helping me make Raff and Isla's story a whole lot better!

And big thanks to the amazing cover designers for the beautiful covers, saintjupit3rgr4phic for the eBook and paperback covers and to Covers by Juan for the hardcovers!

# About the Author

Juno Heart writes enemies-to-lovers romances about cursed fae princes and the feisty mortal girls they fall hard for.
When she's not busy writing, she's chatting with her magical talking cat, spilling coffee on her keyboard, or searching local alleyways for a portal into Faery.
She also publishes books about damaged heroes under her spicy contemporary romance pen name.

For release news and sales alerts, join Juno's newsletter!

Website: Junoheartfaeromance.com

Email: juno@junoheartfaeromance.com

Come say hi on Tik Tok!